To Charles L. Blockson

collector
historian
bibliophile
genealogist
kindred spirit
and
Black scholar extraordinaire

whose encouragement, from the beginning, inspired us

whose belief in this project sustained us

whose wise counsel informed our work

whose intelligence and sensitivity enriched and
deepened our understanding of the erotic

we dedicate

EROTIQUE NOIRE/BLACK EROTICA

Erotique Noire

Black Erotica

EDITORS

Miriam DeCosta-Willis

Reginald Martin

Roseann P. Bell

ANCHOR BOOKS

DOUBLEDAY

New York London Toronto Sydney Auckland

AN ANCHOR BOOK
PUBLISHED BY DOUBLEDAY
a division of Bantam Doubleday Dell Publishing Group, Inc.
1540 Broadway, New York, New York 10036

ANCHOR BOOKS, DOUBLEDAY, and the portrayal of an anchor
are trademarks of Doubleday, a division of Bantam Doubleday Dell
Publishing Group, Inc.

Photograph of Josephine Baker by Hoyningen-Huene/*Vanity Fair*. Copyright 1930 (renewed 1958) by Condé Nast Publications Inc. Photograph by courtesy of the Harvard Theatre Collection, F. R. Koch Collection, Harvard College Library, Harvard University. *Nude by Fireplace, 1923* by James Van Der Zee copyright © 1969 by Donna Van Der Zee. Reprinted by permission of Donna Van Der Zee. All other art reprinted by permission of the artists.

Erotique Noire/Black Erotica is published simultaneously in a hardcover edition by Doubleday, a division of Bantam Doubleday Dell Publishing Group, Inc.

Library of Congress Cataloging-in-Publication Data

Erotique noire = black erotica/editors, Miriam DeCosta-Willis,
Reginald Martin, Roseann P. Bell.—1st Anchor Books ed.
p. cm.
1. Erotic literature, American—Afro-American authors. 2. Erotic
literature—Black authors—Translations into English. 3. Afro-
Americans—Sexual behavior—Literary collections. 4. Blacks—
Sexual behavior—Literary collections. 5. Erotic literature—Black
authors. I. DeCosta-Willis, Miriam. II. Martin, Reginald, 1956–
III. Bell, Roseann P. IV. Title: Black erotica.
[PS509.E7E7713   1992b]
810.8'03538—dc20   92-22050
CIP

CONTENTS

Dew's Song
CALVIN HERNTON
119

Fore/Play

Ntozake Shange

A collection of Black erotica at the end of the twentieth century, five hundred years into the Diaspora, one hundred and twenty-nine years since emancipation, thirty-seven years since Emmett Till's slaughter, three years from Bensonhurst, and in the time of 'sexsational' personalities from Prince and Michael Jackson to Hoes Wit Attitude (HWA) and 2 Live Crew. What do Hughes's 'Susana Jones' and Baraka's 'weepin Ruby Dee' have to do with the date-rape victim of St. John's University's lacrosse team and Shahrazad Ali's lamentable epistle? We are lost in the confusion of myths and fears of race and sex. To be a 'good' people, to be 'respectable' and 'worthy citizens,' we've had to combat absurd phantasmagoric stereotypes about our sexuality, our lusts and loves, to the extent that we disavow our own sensuality to each other. Rape and rapists are intimately connected to the culture's unconscious perception and prescriptions for people of color anywhere in this hemisphere. In Cuba, folk songs record *campesinos* who want *mi café negro,* while in the United States we chime 'the blacker the berry, the sweeter the juice.'

Yet Melvin Van Peebles's Sweetback and Bill Gunn's Ganja and Hess suggest morbid and dark fleshly delights. Filmmaker Spike Lee and writer Frank Yerby in many of their works constantly combat the cultural expectations that 'Big Black Buck' must ravage 'dusky jungle woman':

witness, *She's Gotta Have It* and *The Foxes of Harrow.* So how do we speak of our desires for each other to each other in a language where our relationships to our bodies and desires lack dignity as well as nuance? As always, we look to music and the sporting life (double entendre intended), from Hank Ballard to Bo Diddley, from Little Richard to George Clinton right on round from Jack Johnson and Sugar Ray Robinson to Sugar Ray Leonard and Miles's style on top of Mr. October. Once again the arena for our passions is communal and publicly affirmed. But we have to go home singularly and we all aren't going home with Jackie Wilson or Smokey. What are our names and the touch, taste of our bodies? Where do our tongues linger on each other and what is the nature of the language we speak? Can generations of Black girls chastened by the thoughts/realities of White men in pickup trucks loosen gingerly for one of our own? Do Black men who've battled brutally for the right to walk on sidewalks where White women walk resent women, the idea of sex, so much that the scent of a particular woman, her sighs or pleasures, escape them?

I don't think so. However we might attempt to minimize the pungency and urgency of our sensual realities, folks from Jean Toomer to Romare Bearden have documented our lyricism, falling on each other by forests or riverbeds. In Archie Shepp's urban-slick boleros and Cecil Taylor's throbbing cascades of melody, we surrender to the energy of ourselves—unselfconscious, lustful, fragile, trusting. Here, at the end of the twentieth century, with the African continent shattered by war, famine, and AIDS, with our folks dazed by the deconstruction of Reconstruction, sex and sensuality are elements of any progressive discussion. Years ago, Felipe Luciano brought a smile to my face when he incanted, "Jazz is a woman's tongue stuck dead in your throat," while Gylan Kain protested, "I am the golden flute your vulva lips refuse to play." Here in these stories and poems we are not myths or stereotypes, art forms or sex objects. We are simply folks at intimate play; our fierce rhythms of desire, the exotic unencumbered by the 'other,' close and hot.

PREFACE

In(se)duction: Out of the Closet and into the Bedroom

It was one of those liquid copper fall mornings and we were heading out of Memphis up Route 40 between catfish farms and country ham truck stops, bodies moving, fingers snapping to the oldies but gooodies. Marvin was begging and pleading for love,

> I been really tryin, baby,
> Tryin to hold back this feelin for sooo long,
> And if you feel like I feel, baby,
> Cummon, ooohhh, cummon, wooo,
> Les get it on, aaahhh, baby.

and we were feeling like he felt about getting it on, thinking about the wild moments and the erotic minutes of our individual pasts. "Chile, did I tell you about the time in Washington when . . . ?" "Yeah, but I don't mind hearing it again." The lies were getting contagious. "One time there was this Rasta man on the beach in the Virgin—ha!—Isles!" Our imaginations bloomed in the warmth of all that remembered passion. "You know Lulu? She had this party one time and got to signifyin about the sixty-five men she'd fucked. Andy: skilled technician but a dawg. Dennis: needs tutoring but I don't mind. Tyrone: can you believe from side to side? Me? I shut up behind Lulu, cause I hadn't fucked but three. Tee-hee-hee."

Going south now toward Chattanooga, we broke out the Chee-tos and chocolate kisses under the intensity of all that heat—outside *and* inside the car. Musically, we were moving back in time to the thirties, when a bunch of Wild Women Blues Singers—Memphis Minnie, Bessie Jackson, and Lucille Bogan—got down and dirty with their erotic lyrics. "Wait till you hear Lucille doin 'Shave Em Dry' from her *Copulation Blues* album," Roseann piped up from the back seat.

> I got nipples on my titties
> Big as the end of my thumb,
> I got sumpin tween my legs'll
> Make a dead man come.
> Ahuhwwweee, ohuhwwweee, Daddy

"Ohhh, that lady is bad!" "A sho nuf baaad mutha. Pass me another piece of chocolate and turn that music up." (We were bilingual: Black and Standard.) Rolling down the highway now, accelerator to the floor, feeling absolutely no pain. Meanwhile, Lucille, on tape, was getting outrageous.

> Say, I fucked all night an all the night befo,
> Baby, an feel like I wanna fuck some mo.
> Ohhh, Great God, Daddy, grind me, honey,
> Baby, won't you shave em dry.

Somewhere between the blues and the chocolate and the tall tales *Erotique Noire* was conceived. Not in a bed with clean white sheets smelling of soap suds and spray starch, mind you, but on a Tennessee highway with the planet in Venus and the rhythms, oh, so right. It suddenly hit us: "Hey, if we're having so much fun swapping lies and telling raunchy tales, why not spread the joy around!" Besides, Af-Am lit profs that we were, we didn't think *our* writers had ever published a whole collection of erotica, but we had a deep down, gnawing suspicion that Black folk could really DO IT . . . write stuff that made you feel sexy and sensual . . . so we decided to package all the good stuff under one HARD cover.

We were an unholy threesome: Roseann in her short fro and African garb, looking like she had just blown in from Ibadan or St. Croix (where she spent a lotta time); Reggie, a serious academic type by day and a burn-the-candle-at-both-ends poet and novelist by night; and Miriam, who had just entered her third life and reinvented herself as Dolores of the wayward ways. Roseann is, perhaps, the most experienced (in terms of her, uh, writing) of us erotophiles because she got her first piece . . . published, that is . . . back in the sixties when she and another colleague, both strapped for money, wrote an X-rated book and sold the rights—for just three hundred damn dollars (shades of Anaïs)—to a publisher who supplied porn shops. Ever the innovator and entrepreneur, she later teamed up with another friend and started a sexy phone service called Tantra. Trying to keep her distance with recorded messages like "I'm Tantra, here to satisfy *all* your needs, so write me about what moves you and I'll get back to you," she was deluged by hundreds of letters and calls from persistent males, like the pilot who wanted to know: "Well, Tantra, can't you make an exception in my case? I really need to talk to you, so puhleeez call me right back."

Reggie had also been dabbling around in erotica for quite a spell and even had the nerve to add "The 1st 3 Daze"—published in *Yellow Silk* (the Rolls of the erotic mags)—to his academic résumé. "Hunh, that took some balls!" commented Roseann. "Well," Miriam pointed out, "Reggie can be brave if he wants to—he's a man—but we're gonna be chicken and go under cover," so we conjured up R. Pope and Dolores da Costa (our *real* names, sorta, from other lives). "Maybe there's some money in this thing," thought Miriam . . . that is, until her first erotic prose poem, "I Wanna Be Wild and Wonderful," was accepted for publication by *Libido* and she received a check for *thirty dollars!* By that time, though, we were off and running—hard! But if you think this project was easy, listen to what Roseann has to say:

> Anyone who has attempted a single-author book knows the hell involved, sometimes called writer's block, and sometimes (especially if one has full-time academic responsibilities that include delivering papers, grading tests, and attending often ridiculous committee meetings) the BURNOUT is real. As Fannie Lou Hamer used to say, it's also called being "sick and tired of being sick and tired." But when a collaborative effort is involved such as this one, there are many considerations in this land of hype and irreality that intervene.

Like last summer when Roseann got pissed off at Miriam's bossiness. "Just listen to yourself, girl: 'We need your intros by next week.' 'We got to get this to the typist by June 30.' Makes me sick! Whaddaya think we are, workhorses? Um gonna buy you a whip!" To which Miriam replied, a devilish gleam in her eye, "Oh boy, and what about some black garters and high-heeled boots to go with the whip?"

Step One: Make it official. We rented a post office box and printed a lovely lavender letterhead and fliers adorned with a photo of La Baker, semi-nude and seductive. Miriam mailed in a subscription to an erotic magazine and landed on the naughty hit list: fliers arrived from Down There Press, video ads from the Sexuality Library, and a catalogue from Good Vibrations, touting sex toys like dildos and butt plugs, vibrators and Ben-wa Balls. Wheh! Turn the fan on!

Step Two: Get the word out. We sent in ads to various periodicals, called friends—writers and artists—all over the country, and passed out fliers at conferences. Our colleagues, comfortable in their terminal (you can say that again!) degrees and their tenured posts, went into SHOCK! "You're compiling a collection of *what?*" Raised eyebrows all over the place. "Is there any literary merit to erotica?" Pinched noses in the air. "Do Black people actually *write* that?" Disbelief everywhere. And in two months—one submission. Off to a pitiful start . . . but we kept the faith, cause we knew we were on to something. Reggie, who has a unique sense of humor, reminded us, "It may not *come* when you want it, but it always *comes* on time," while Roseann, serious for a change, wrote:

> The uninformed and unthinking may take issue with the axiom that they who create the image control the idea, indeed possibly the mind. To an astounding degree so much of the prejudice against anyone who is not young, white, male, rich, heterosexual, and physically "attractive" continues, unreined and unabashed because of the dynamic between image and idea. So it was with two purposes connected with icons and imagination—to have fun and be actively iconoclastic—that *Erotique Noire* was conceived.

> *Step Three:* Collect the data. Writers and artists started asking *pointed* questions like "How much will I be PAID for a poem or photo?" "Who is the publisher?" and even more to the point, "What the hell is e-r-o-t-i-c-a?" Pause. Miriam, tentatively: "I don't exactly know, but it's something like love: hard to define, but you know it when you see it." Uh-uh, we all agreed, that won't git it. Roseann, a little huffy: "Well it's certainly not *pornography.*" Reggie, tongue in cheek: "Somebody explain to me the difference between pornography and erotica?" Time for the academics to break out the books! Since Miriam is convinced that when she dies she'll ascend into the Library of Congress instead of heaven, she seemed like the logical one to do the research, but her first foray into the Memphis Public Library liked to have put out her lights.

> I got turned on when I saw all these titles in the card catalogue: *Erotic Art of the West, The Complete Book of Erotic Art,* and *On the Nature of Things Erotic.* But I searched up and down the stacks and couldn't find a single book. "Damn, somebody else must be researching erotica and got all the books." Finally, in desperation, I asked the librarian, a plump matronly type, to help me. She checked me out over the top of her horn-rimmed glasses, probably trying to figure out what kind of sex pervert I was, and then disappeared into the dark womb of the library's second floor. She was gone for days, but finally came back with everything I'd requested. Can you beat that—hiding erotica from the public in 1989!

The research was eye-(and everything else)opening! Writers were coming out of the closet as their books rolled off the presses: *Herotica,* an anthology of erotic fiction; *Shared Intimacies,* a collection of interviews; *Erotic Interludes,* stories with sexual turn-ons; *Pleasures,* twelve stories by women writers; *Touching Fire,* an anthology of provocative pieces; *Deep Down,* sensual writing by women; *Serious Pleasure,* a collection of lesbian writing; and the beautiful *Erotic by Nature,* a celebration of sensuality. These books provided for pants-soaking reading cause some of the stuff was HOT!! . . . *But* other than a token piece by Shange, Derricotte, Gomez, or McMillan, we couldn't find our dark-skinned selves between those particular sheets. We knew then we'd have to make our own bed.

During the research phase, Reggie, who was into radio, film, computers, and all kinds of electronic shit, came up with another bright idea: "We need to check out what's happening with X-rated movies." Guess who got drafted again? Well, Miriam wasn't about to step into one of those adult theaters like Eve's out on Airways Boulevard. (What would the neighbors think?) No way, José! Not in Memphis, Tennessee, heart of the foot-stompin Bible Belt! As luck would have it, though, she ran into Frank Lamont Phillips, who once worked in an adult bookstore and had a humongous collection of X-rated films on video. So the three of us, research nuts that we were, passed around a coupla classics like *Behind the Green Door, The Devil in Miss Jones,* and *Autobiography of a Flea,* as well as umpteen of the bump-and-grind variety: *Insatiable, Romp in the Hay,* and *Nuns on the Loose.* Eyes glazed and mouths dry after weeks of watching all that unimaginative Boom Bam, Thank You, Ma'm, we decided that we'd done enough research and needed to get on with our work because, as Roseann put it:

> We thought about how much fun it would be to turn the disgusting pornographic obsessions of the West upside down, mainly by producing a quality product that defied THE OTHERS' money/exploitation-based/aberrated penchant for using dark-skinned people to work out and expose themselves, although they (THE OTHERS) lived under rocks and at the bottom of trenches.

We were still operating on faith, though, until one day the phone rang and a man with a low, sexy voice asked, "Hello, Dolores?" Pause. "Who?" Recollection. "Oh yes, this is she." "My name is Charles Blockson. Beverly gave me your name and told me you're doing a collection of erotica. That's great!" For the first time . . . affirmation that was even better than wine after sex. Charles, a bibliophile and collector of erotica, knew writers all over the country and talked about the book everywhere he went; he sent us one of the first essays, "The Blacker the Berry," and he even wrote a promo that we included in our letters to prospective contributors:

[The editors] have taken Black erotica from its former clandestine place into a well-deserved enlightened perspective. Their standpoint is both Apollonian and Dionysian, which makes this book truly worthy of our attention.

Bless Charles . . . we were on our way! Other friends helped too: Selwyn and James and Ethelbert sent us the addresses of writers they knew. More letters went out and, slowly, the manuscripts started trickling in.

Another breakthrough came in late summer when we received a letter that began: "I have no new work to submit, but I am happy to grant permission for use of my short story 'Olive Oil.' " It was signed "Alice Walker." We knew that Alice wrote things erotic and sensual, not just because of Celie and Shug or Zede and Arveyda, but because of essays like "All the Bearded Irises of Life":

It was through erotica that I first understood that two women or two men could be sexually attracted to each other. I was staying in the borrowed rooms of a former college classmate, and she had books that graphically described methods of attaining orgasm. Some of these methods were very strange. One of them I'll never forget described the languid inventiveness of a young woman guest at a boring dinner party who masturbated herself—underneath the table and while ostensibly listening to the tiresome monologue of her host—with a fork. She was actually gazing at the woman across the table from her at the time. This seemed to me wonderfully different from the usual story of "boy meets girl."

Living by the Word (1988)

Later, other prominent writers—Gloria Naylor, Dennis Brutus, Ntozake Shange, Ann Allen Shockley, Jan Carew—sent us material or agreed to let us reprint previously published works.

Roseann sums up that phase of the project this way: Pulling in manuscripts from those promised by information brokers, those who had seen our ads in various journals and magazines, those hedging on what their pseudonyms should be if they sent in anything, posed problems. Miriam, an indefatigable reader, writer, caller, editor, and life-giver, did the bulk of the personal communicating—a job made more complicated because the first two of us had moved to visiting teaching assignments outside Tennessee, while attempting to return to our base—the Memphis connection—at least once a month. The hard work began in December 1989. By then, our most respected colleagues and supporters knew we were serious about *Erotique Noire,* and the inevitable started. We began receiving notes about fliers we had distributed at various conferences and sent to practicing imaginative writers, librarians, and personal acquaintances we suspected had sensual and sexual images that would echo through the book—obviously people without the intellect of mud, especially where sex is concerned. Telephone calls came: "Tell me more about this erotic thing."

Step Four: Select and edit. Reggie handled a lot of the editing, so why don't we let him tell his story.

Editing *Erotique Noire* has not been the most difficult editing task I've faced, but it certainly has been the most . . . interesting. I think editing, say, corporate histories, as I have, is infinitely more difficult and considerably more boring, but, clearly, editing what we as editors thought of as Black "erotica" brought with it reading and editing complications that I could not have foreseen.

For one, what the editors thought of as "erotic" clearly differed sometimes from what individual writers thought of as "erotic." This did not surprise me, but the width of this erotic gulf did take me unawares. Feeling, as I do, that I am—er—"pliable," with very elastic borders for the erotic, even I found my rubber snapping again and again as I had to vote "NO" on certain things that belonged more in a kind of Black Twilight Zone of deviations, which should be entered only by those who are devoid of funk. Let me explain.

One could certainly not accuse me of being narrow in my erotic literary tastes. I voted "YES" on pieces wherein characters have heated discussions with their sex organs, transgress against fruit in ways I am sure are against all state laws, or peeped at things that one would normally have to pay quite a bit to see on Forty-second Street or in certain hotel rooms in Las Vegas. All of these "pieces" I thought were quite erotic in different ways. However, my erotic elasticity broke at other points.

The number of writers who seem to think that internecine domestic fights (both as a precursor and an afterthought to lovemaking) are necessary catalysts for making love not only turned me off but struck me as quite sad. Exactly what is erotic about beating the hell out of someone with your fists (I am *not* talking about Madonna wanting to be "spanked," which can be quite a nice precursor to things) is beyond me. After repeatedly reading about things that most people would find embarrassing or uninteresting, I remain an advocate of individual eroticism: if it works for you or for your consenting partner, then I think you should carry on. That does not mean, however, that it should have been published in *Erotique Noire*.

The editors could often be just as individual and eclectic in their erotic tastes as the authors of the pieces submitted. This also meant that I was able to learn more about the nature of an erotic text *and* to get a good free laugh by asking the other editors *why* they thought a piece was or was not erotic. Both would pause before speaking, but one can be quite verbose about why something is hot or cold, while the other is more reluctant to explain her reasoning, stumbling as she tries to tell-without-showing or seeming to enjoy. I found the alternating verbosity and reticence immensely hilarious for different reasons, and I found myself slipping into a theretofore unknown erotic abyss of my own that . . . I decline to discuss. Suffice it to say that there are personal reasons that some things are not best (or fit) to print, and learning more about the boundaries of eroticism helps one's editorial eye to see that—clearly.

Principally, I served as a kind of catchall copy and stylistic editor for *Erotique Noire,* so that often, just before I would take accepted pieces to the typist, I would make different editorial "passes" at the text, each pass focused on one kind of accuracy or consistency. But making passes in some of the pieces selected for *Erotique Noire* made this editor invent entirely new passes. For instance, in R. Bruce Nugent's piece from *Smoke, Lilies and Jade,* does one make a pass to make sure that there are three ellipses at each pause when such pauses number in the hundreds? In "Black Borealis" by Hillery Jacque Knight III, should one pass at the sexual or excretory functions as discrete lists or joint lists? The sperm names or the ovum names? These authors' visions are completely new lasers in the spectrum of erotic light.

In an editing enterprise such as this one, the written exchange between editors can also be enlightening, providing, as it does, both editorial insight and new discourse possibilities. Working alone, my yellow-tab notes to myself would normally consist of such expressions as "misspelled" or "insert extra em space." I had no experiential preparation for the yellow notes that would be exchanged between us on this venture. As I opened a piece previously read by another editor, a yellow note might pop up erect that said, "Quite hot, but not as erotic as some of the other poems on this topic we've already selected; what do you think?" and the response: "Agreed, but goddam, this *is* NASTY!" and then there would be the appropriate initials and date at the bottom of the tab. Or consider such editorial tabs as "This is great HARDENING material" or "I wouldn't mind having some of these things done to me, but I wouldn't want this writer to describe them to me." "This is our first piece of voyeurism. Have you peeped at it?" "YES YES YES YES! Ooh, this is well written and wet!" So as our joint editing venture came to an end, I began to realize that we had invented an entirely new form of erotic discourse: tab sex for the editorial eye. To be in on the creation of such an erotic form was certainly worth the mountainous amount of work involved in this project.

MIRIAM / REGGIE / ROSEANN

INTRODUCTION

The sexual and sensual impulses stir deep in the alluvium of the soul that animates us, its currents eddying and surging like the inscrutable tides that stir the vast torrent of existence. All hail the delicious surges of lust that move our being.

DENNIS BRUTUS (April 26, 1990)

EROTICISM: The powerful life force within us from which spring desire and creativity and our deepest knowledge of the universe. The life force that flows like an inscrutable tide through all things, linking man to woman, man to man, woman to woman, bird to flower, and flesh to spirit. Our ancestors taught us this in their songs of love, their myths of creation, their celebrations of birth, and their rituals of initiation. Desire. Pleasure. Wholeness.

EROTIC: (adj.) concerning or arousing sexual desire or giving sexual pleasure; (n.) a person who is especially responsive to sexual stimulation. The opposite of pornography: "the writing of harlots" (from the Greek *porne,* "harlot," and *graphein,* "to write"); (n.) description of life and manners of prostitutes and their patrons; hence the suggestion or expression of obscene or unchaste subjects in literature or art.

. . . pornography is a direct denial of the power of the erotic, for it represents the suppression of true feeling

AUDRE LORDE, "Uses of the Erotic"

The difference between eroticism and pornography is the difference between celebratory and masturbatory sex.

HERBERT MARCUSE, *Eros and Civilization*

EROTICA: African Nights In The Realm Of The Senses Adam Behind The Green Door Erotisme Et Litératures Herotica An Erotic Memoir The Kama-Sutra Black Eros Serious Pleasures Autobiography Of A Flea My Secret Garden The Chinese Way Of Love The Keeper Of The Bed Delta Of Venus Erotismo Negro Fanny Erotic By Nature The Gate Of Happy Sparrows Black Erotic Folk Tales The Joy Of Sex Gavriliad Reminiscences Of Beautiful And Accomplished Girls Erotic Interludes African Sojourn Forbidden Flowers Touching Fire Blue Skies Oroonoko Or The Royal Slave The Pearl The Paramours Of The Creoles Little Birds The Tides of Lust Down Deep Visages De Femmes Memoirs Of A Woman Of Pleasure The Keeper Of The Bed . . .

EROTIQUE: A feast of forbidden fruit: temple oranges, licorice nights, all-day suckers, and tasty knees. Spirits coming in lunar signs and sudden ecstasies. The rhythm of conga drums, the sweet sound of the blues and Sparrow on the air. Wet warm kisses in the park with dew on the grass. Thoughts straying over poems and telegrams, dyke hands and dildos. Feeling good and hard trotting through the park or bursting from the earth. Diving deep into the sweet thing; discovering opening nights and three whole daze. Lonnie and Phil, the X-lovers, coming to terms with lust, touching the wild wonderful one. Finally, victory over madness and celibate joy in the sultan's harem beside pyramids on the Nile. EROTIQUE NOIRE.

Six essays, as well as John A. Williams's afterword, describe the historical, cultural, and philosophical context in which Black erotica has developed. In his provocative essay on collecting Black erotica, "African American Erotica and Other Curiosities: 'The Blacker the Berry, the Sweeter the Juice . . . ,' " Charles L. Blockson traces the literary history of this genre in books written by both Blacks and Whites. Erotic works by Europeans include such diverse narratives as *Oroonoko: or the Royal Slave, Black Eros* by de Rachelwitz, *African Nights, Black Erotic Folk Tales* by Leo Frobenius, and Jean De Villio's *Black Lust.* Many of us are familiar with the poetry and fiction of nineteenth-century Europeans of African descent, such as Alexander Pushkin and Alexandre Dumas, although we may not realize that these men wrote erotica; many of us, however, have probably never heard of the erotic works of other nineteenth-century people of color—works such as *The Great Free-Love Trial, A Colored Man*

Round the World, and *The New Black Mahogany Hall* (by a "quadroon lady"). Blockson's essay makes us aware that the recovery and study of early Black erotica is fertile terrain for scholars of Afro-American literature.

In her illuminating essay "Forbidden Fruits and Unholy Lusts: Illicit Sex in Black American Literature," Sandra Y. Govan examines the literary treatment by Afro-American writers of sexual practices that long were taboo, practices such as incest, rape, voyeurism, lesbianism, and sadomasochism. She decodes the sexual subtext in the slave narratives of Frederick Douglass and Linda Brent, and she analyzes the more overt treatment of these themes by twentieth-century writers like Richard Wright, James Baldwin, Octavia Butler, Ralph Ellison, and Ann Allen Shockley. In analyzing the poetry and novels of contemporary women writers such as Toni Morrison, Ntozake Shange, and Alice Walker, Govan demonstrates that "literary treatment of illicit sex is neither a recent occurrence nor a contemporary by-product of the radical feminist movement."

In her essay "Edible or Incredible: Black Erotic Collectibles," Jessie Carney Smith examines the erotic and exotic representation of Blacks in American popular culture. She explains that Black memorabilia, including books, toys, records, films, photographs, greeting cards, party items, and "fucking books" (erotic comic books), were mass-produced from the mid-1800s to the present as novelty and souvenir items. Such memorabilia often treat erotic myths about the sexual proclivities of Black men and women. As Smith points out, "Black erotic collectibles," which reflect the hidden or ribald underside of Black popular culture, "need to come out of the closet." Daryl Dance has pulled from the closet another form of Black popular culture—erotic proverbs, poems, and tales—in her collection of folk literature, *Shuckin' and Jivin'.* Several of these short, humorous works, like "Pass the Pussy, Please" and "Yo' Mama" (included in *Erotique Noire*), are raucous responses to prevailing myths. One of the editors' favorites is this one:

> Master got his slave with the longest dick and said, "I don't want no black screwing my daughter, but she wants sixteen inches."
> John said, "Naw, suh, boss. Not even for a white woman. I wouldn't cut two inches off my dick for nobody."

In "After/Play," John A. Williams notes the "importance of Black people in the fantasies of Whites," who as early as the Victorian period were titillated by exotic myths and Black stereotypes like the Hottentot Venus. In depicting an exciting and previously undertreated dimension of our diverse and complex culture, *Erotique Noire* will perhaps help to dispel many of the myths and stereotypes about Black sexual difference.

Black erotica has not been considered an art form and has not been the subject of serious study for a variety of reasons, some historical, others cultural. One of the legacies of slavery was the "genteel tradition," which shaped Black life and letters. Many nineteenth-century and early-twentieth-century Afro-American writers and artists felt compelled to prove the moral worth and intellectual integrity of Blacks by avoiding the literary representation of physical desire and sexual pleasure. Only recently, through efforts to recover and reinterpret literary texts, have we begun to understand and to appreciate the sensuality, passion, and adventurous lifestyles of early writers like Alice Dunbar-Nelson, who wrote the following entry in her diary on July 27, 1929, when she was fifty-four years old, had been married three times, and had had female and male lovers:

> Swimming, swimming out to infinity—racing in under the pulsing water to the solitary light on shore. An experience worth having—a glorious, wonderful climax. Only equalled by the velvety luxuriousness of the times when swimming far out—we slipped off our bathing suits —Emily, Tea and I and let the water caress our naked forms.
>
> <div align="right">GLORIA HULL, <i>Give Us Each Day</i></div>

Dunbar-Nelson chose the private, intimate form of the diary to reveal her sensual and erotic feelings because, in the 1920s and 1930s, American readers, generally, were not receptive to the public expression of such personal experiences. A few writers, like Zora Neale Hurston, R. Bruce Nugent, and Chester Himes, had the temerity to oppose prevailing standards of "correctness." In 1926, Nugent published "Smoke, Lilies and Jade" (included here) in *FIRE!!,* the literary journal edited by Wallace Thurman, in association with Zora Neale Hurston and Langston Hughes, who were characterized as "the more adventurous and unconventional of the younger Afro-American intellectuals" (Thomas H. Wirth). Nugent's work—a delicate, suggestive, and subtle prose piece—is one of the first treatments of two taboo themes: homosexuality and interracial sex. In the passage below, Beauty is a White male:

> Alex opened his eyes . . . into Beauty's . . . parted his lips . . . Dulce . . . Beauty's breath was hot and short . . . Alex ran his hand through Beauty's hair . . . Beauty's lips pressed hard against his teeth . . . Alex trembled . . . could feel Beauty's body . . . close against his . . . hot . . . tense white . . . and soft . . . soft . . . soft . . .

Himes's novel *Pinktoes,* published in 1965 at the height of the Civil Rights Movement, also treated interracial sex at a time when this subject was quite unpopular. While Himes, Nugent, and Dunbar-Nelson dared to be different, many Black writers were constrained by social mores and literary conventions. For example, one of Dunbar's contemporaries Angelina Weld Grimké, expressed her repressed desires and frustrated longings in a coded language with images like these:

Tell her white, gold, red my love is—
And for her,—for her.

If I might taste but once, just once
The dew
Upon her lips
GLORIA HULL. "Under the Days" from *Home Girls*

As Gloria T. Hull (a contributor to *Erotique Noire*) explains, Grimke "lived a buried life. We research and resurrect—but have to struggle to find and connect with her, for she had no spirit left to send us." The unfortunate fact of life is that so many of us still lead dispirited, buried lives in which full sexual expression is denied us. Beryl Gilroy, a psychologist and poet, whose work is included in this collection, attests to the liberating effect of erotica. She explains in a letter to the editors:

> I think erotic poetry is excellent therapy. I work mainly with ethnic minority women who have never experienced "verbalization" in love and the poems (I firmly believe) trigger all kinds of sensations.
>
> (April 3, 1990)

Aware that this anthology should allow for alternative representations of the erotic, the editors developed a set of criteria to govern the selection of submissions. Generally, each work had to

1. be well written and crafted: effective, concise, clear, organized, and unified,
2. conform to high aesthetic standards,
3. be original and imaginative rather than trite,
4. contain writing that is feeling and sensitive, sensual and moving,
5. present sex as a beautiful, joyous, and powerful experience,
6. have a celebratory, affirmative, and life-enhancing tone,
7. and *not demean or diminish people by using stereotypes and caricatures to disrespect other people or persons of different sexual orientations.*

Every piece in the collection does not conform completely to *all* of the criteria, and we have included one or two poems or narratives that were not enthusiastically endorsed by all of us. On occasion, we shared the feelings of one of our readers, who commented, "Some of these works are so moving, so well written and beautiful; others make me blush." But we followed a "two out of three votes and it's in" rule to allow for our own and our readers' differences in gender, taste, sexual preference, cultural background, and aesthetic sensibility. Sadomasochism, however, turns the three of us off. Although many sensitive and sexual people practice SM because they enjoy the heightened feelings and rush of adrenaline that come with the sexual frisson of fear, we exercised editorial license in rejecting stories of violent sex.

One of our objectives in editing this collection was to select material that offered a balance in gender, sexual preference, forms of erotic expression, and literary genre. A perfect balance, however, was not always possible. John A. Williams pointed out that "here [women] are a multitude and, like the men, released from the conventions of the past, a situation some called 'the sexual revolution.' " We were, indeed, surprised at the extent to which contemporary Black women are *willing* and *able* to reveal their most intimate thoughts, their most private practices, and their most erotic fantasies. In "Making Whoopee," for example, SDiane Bogus communicates the joy of masturbation; in "Commitment to Hardness," M. Nourbese Philip evokes the delight of a "ramrod, big big bamboo, pole, driving shaft"; and in "Piece of Time," Jewelle Gomez describes a woman pushing inside another and feeling "the dams burst."

The works included in *Erotique Noire* are diverse in form, theme, tone, and language. Represented here are traditional literary genres, including essays, poems (Cooper's "Faded Roses" and Miller's "Summer"), short stories (Martin's "The 1st 3 Daze" and McMillan's "Touching"), and excerpts from novels (Naylor's *The Women of Brewster Place*, Hunter's *Lakestown Rebellion*, and Ellis's *Platitudes*). The collection also includes other, less conventional forms of literature such as letters (Letitia and Michael's "Hot Missives"), diary excerpts (Douglas's "Dear Diary"), a prose poem (da Costa and Wade-Gayles's "I Wanna Be Wild and Wonderful"), a horoscope (Balfour's "Sexy Signs"), folk tales (Dance's "Teasing Tales"), urban tales (da Costa's "Black Male/Tales"), and a quiz (Pope's "Sexionnaire"). The themes also run the gamut from the taste of fruit to the joy of massage, from adolescent initiation to sex at sixty, and from self-pleasuring to four-person orgies. The language is also distinctive: Shange is, well, Shangean (" '& you wanna fuck' / 'i dont wanna fuck / i told you that i wanna make love' "); Price is downright sassy ("I'm starving for a taste / of you. May I fellate?"); and Hemphill is iconoclastically funky ("You stood beneath a tree / guarding moonlight . . . jerking your dick slowly"). The language is, above all, lyrical, for beautiful poetic images are cast in words of desire:

> the tip of pink tongue on soft-hard brown nipple (Cooper)
> the sweep of satin flanks and thews (Brutus)
> in the open mirrors of your demanded body (Lorde)
> riding the waves of our knowing (Palmer)
> disappearance of the bone / annihilation of the self (Hull)

The tone of other selections is provocatively hot and raunchy. R. Pope's "Three-Token Stradivarius," Calvin Hernton's "Dew's Song," and Charles Frye's "a good knight's leap" are delightfully "nasty" pieces of prose, graphically describing, as they do, various forms of "coming"-together: cunnilingus, fellatio, anal sex, and so forth.

Although our first submissions came from Afro-American writers, we actively solicited erotic material from Latin American, Caribbean, and African writers, because we wanted this book to have cultural diversity and international breadth. Françoise Pfaff, a French scholar of Martinican descent, who teaches Francophone literature and film at Howard University, has written a fascinating study of sub-Saharan African film in which she points out that filmmakers like Ousmane Sembene of Senegal, Timité Bassori of the Ivory Coast, Souleymane Cissé of Mali, and Dikongue Pipa of Cameroon often treat sex lyrically or symbolically, using erotic suggestion rather than direct visualization in their work. Two of the most erotic films, according to Pfaff, are *Touki Bouki* by Djibril Diop Mambety of Senegal, which presents an "intellectualized, ritualistic, and metaphoric depiction of intercourse," and *Visages de femmes* by Désiré Ecaré of the Ivory Coast, which "includes the most explicit act of intercourse in the history of African cinema: shots of a licentious Eden in which bronze bodies dive into a river and copulate on the banks of the river, surrounded by thick, erect trees." Such sexual explicitness, however, is rare in these films, according to Pfaff, "because of the puritanism of traditional African cultures or because filmmakers . . . want to destroy the stereotype of the sexually potent African."

Also included in *Erotique Noire* are the poems of African writers such as Lemuel Johnson (Sierra Leone) and Dennis Brutus (Zimbabwe), as well as writers from Colombia, Panama, Ecuador, Trinidad, Cuba, and Canada—all of whom were enthusiastic about a collection of erotica by Blacks. Poet and novelist Nelson Estupiñán Bass of Ecuador commented:

. . . considero [*Erotique Noire*] un libro singular, que tendrá magnífica acogida, y, por lo tanto, gran circulación. Me parece una magnífica idea esta compilación.

(I consider [*Erotique Noire*] a unique book that will be well received, and, as a result, have extensive circulation. This collection seems a wonderful idea to me.)

(February 23, 1990)

Selections such as Cuban Nancy Morejón's "To a Boy," Guyanese O. R. Dathorne's *Woman Story,* and Ecuadorian Luz Argentina Chiriboga's *Under the Skin of the Drums* attest to the varied forms and styles of Black erotic expression in other countries. Trinidadian Keith Warner, for example, examines the sexual innuendos—taking a six for a nine—of calypso lyrics. Tongue in cheek, calypsonians refer to the phallus as "iron" or "wood" in lines like these:

> The wood here in Trinidad no wood could surpass
> Ah like how it thick and hard and how it does last

while they allude to the female genitals as "saltfish." Every time, for instance, that Sparrow sings "when you out to eat / all saltfish sweet," Trinidadians know his subject is oral sex.

In this essay, Warner mentions birth control and, by implication, safe sex. Noting that sexual freedom is part and parcel of carnival, he adds: "If this were not so, why would the local Family Planning Association issue its yearly warning to 'love carefully'?" John A. Williams, who has the last word in *Erotique Noire,* observes: "Only now and again does a shadow fall across the pages, driven by mention of 'condom' or, as R. Pope puts it, 'Satan-Is-a-Bitch diseases,' the darker reality of our times." Wilamina and Geoffery, the teenagers in P. J. Gibson's "We'll Be Real Good Together," fumble around with this "darker reality" as it affects unwanted pregnancy. Wilamina says:

> "If you don't have protection, I can't let you do this. I want to go to college."
> "I'm way ahead of you, Wilamina." He reached down between the cushions of the sofa and pulled out a sealed prophylactic. Wilamina sat straight up.
> "How long has that been there?"
> "I just put it there."
> "Where'd you get it from?"
> "I got it from the pack. I got a pack of three."
> "Where do you keep them? . . . You're not using no rubber on me you had in your back pocket or wallet. . . ."

(Perhaps we should have dealt with the issue of safe sex, as did the editors of *Serious Pleasure,* who included an appendix, "Notes on AIDS and Safer Sex," and wrote: "[Although] we do not believe that all fictional writing . . . should incorporate safer sex guidelines . . . we feel it is important that the issue of safer sex is always acknowledged in some way." One thing is for certain: you'll be very safe if you limit your sexual praxis to slipping between the sheets of *Erotique Noire* from time to time and indulging in a few sexual fantasies.)

But the true issue at hand is diversity of erotic expression. We discovered that several Black writers from other countries are quite subtle and indirect in their treatment of sex, and we attributed this reservation to differences of religion, values, social customs, and literary traditions. Manuel Zapata Olivella, for example, one of Colombia's most prolific novelists and author of the celebrated *Shangó, el gran putas* (*Shango, the Holy Mother*), discovered, on reflection, that his novels are not very sexually explicit. He wrote:

Interesado en seleccionar algunas páginas de mis novelas sobre este tópico, descubro que no he sido muy dado a escribir escenas eróticas, aunque el amor siempre impregna la vida de mis protagonistas. Son muchos los romances, pero poca la exploración del momento íntimo de las caricias y la entrega.

(Interested in selecting some pages of my novels on this topic, I discover that I have not been very inclined to write erotic scenes, although love always saturates the life of my protagonists. There are many romantic works, but few that explore the intimate moment of embrace and surrender.)

(March 5, 1990)

On the other hand, "The Initiation of Belfon" by Jan Carew of Guyana and *Hadriana* by René Depestre of Martinque are very open and direct. Indeed, the excerpt from Depestre's novel is a delightfully witty collage of sexual fantasies; it is a hilarious romp in the hay that reminds one of Rabelais's celebrated wit and verve:

[Balthazar Granchiré] impregnated the atmosphere with aphrodisiacal effluvium. Within moments buttocks snapped the elastic of panties, breasts popped the buttons of nightgowns, enflamed thighs spread with desire, vaginas, fascinated, demanded to drink and above all to eat.

It is interesting that both Depestre and Carew have lived abroad for many years (as have most West African filmmakers) and have been influenced, perhaps, by European and North American modes of erotic expressivity—modes that were shaped by such "liberating" social and cultural phenomena as urbanization, modern technology, the sexual revolution, and the women's movement. On the other hand, many non-Western writers deliberately resist Western cultural hegemony, maintaining that Euro-American books, films, magazines, and television programs commercialize sex, converting it into what Audre Lorde calls "the confused, the trivial, the psychotic, the plasticized sensation."

In this regard, one of our earliest and most ardent supporters was concerned that titles like "In(se)duction" and "Ooohweee, Baby," as well as "Fore/Play" and "After/Play," were too commercial and even, perhaps, sexist. Our purpose from the beginning was to make this a *fun* book. Because, however, the erotic appeals not just to the libido but also to the mind and spirit, we wanted to engage the whole person in the reading of texts. We selected material that was funny (Derricotte's "Dildo"), serious (Lorde's "Uses of the Erotic"), futuristic (Knight's "Black Borealis"), touching (Walker's "Olive Oil"), and raunchy (West's "A Dinner Invitation"). We also reflected seriously about the implications of the writer's reservations. When one wrote: "I don't think of myself as a *Playmate,*" we changed the title of the last section, "Playmates," to the more formal "Notes on Contributors."

We are not of one mind and we do not move with a single step, for we are a multicolored people of varied emotional hues and diverse erotic shades: from the green of a "verde que te quiero verde" to the hot pink of lovers' lips. This rainbow-hued eroticism fires the imagination of ethnic Americans—Nuyorican writers like Piri Thomas and Esperanza Malavé Cintrón, who evoke the moods and rhythms of Spanish Harlem, fuse Black and Spanish linguistic forms, and treat Afro-American and Puerto Rican themes and motifs. The cultural fusion cuts both ways. Ntozake Shange is an Afro-American who captures the rhythms, styles, and languages of Spanish-, French-, and Portuguese-speaking Blacks in many of her works. She manifests this linguistic and cultural dexterity in the erotic prose piece "Tócame":

> Turn over. From then on, *negrita,* he played for his life every *canción, cada coro,* cause his *chabala* would dance and cry his *ritmo* for him and then give it all back with her tears, her tears from feelin' what she had no name for, had never felt before, and couldn't do without. Right, Liliane, isn't that how it is for you?

Another example of cultural fusion can be found in the beautifully sensuous and evocative poetry of Lemuel Johnson, whose verse illustrates the richness and diversity of Black erotica. A Sierra Leonese who has lived in Europe, Mexico, and the United States, where he studied the literatures of Francophone and Hispanophone writers, Johnson weaves the varied threads of our diverse cultures into a single golden fabric. In "sudden ecstasies in lefthanded places," his epigrams conjure up a Caribbean landscape with "ripe mango in a mash up place" (the words of a Jamaican song), and a sugarcane plantation (the words of Bartolomé de las Casas's historical text), while his first lines, "you reach west / an then the place rise," suggest the passage from Africa to the Americas. With images of blood and the "vexing sweet cavity," the poet conveys the holy mystery of union—"love's parenthesis between night and night!"—in the midst of the pain and madness of our past: *"then* is when God's own body turn to juice like a watering of disorder sour with lunacy and love." While Johnson celebrates a wholeness, that joining of body and spirit, "like sweet desolation come in a tight place," Dennis Brutus of Zimbabwe stresses the human rather than the spiritual roots of our sensuality.

> Erotic—primordial as the human race—needs no goddess or gods to legitimate it. Neither Apollo nor Dionysus (with whom I have a special affinity) nor the great goddesses and gods whose towering shadows

fall athwart the shadowy recesses of the Nile Valley, reaching into prehistory, where the imagination stands dumb, appalled.

(April 26, 1990)

Poets like Brutus and Johnson, as well as John Turpin, Opal Palmer Adisa, Kalamu Ya Salaam, and Jerry W. Ward, Jr., help us to enlarge the range of our sensual and erotic experiences. But those who do not read or write poems, who do not touch flesh or sing joy, may be "beggars at the erotic feast" (Reynolds). Beryl Gilroy, a poet, discovered, in her professional practice in London, the effects of sexual repression on her clients, and explains in a letter:

> I work with West Indian women seeking to change things in their lives and from my chair I sincerely believe that the irritability, resistance to insight, and acceptance of institutionalized oppression has much to do with frustrated sexuality—a fact so well portrayed in Morrison's *The Bluest Eye.*
>
> (May 12, 1990)

For many individuals, private, intimate, confessional writing gives them a means of articulating this pain and of resisting institutional oppression. One Caribbean writer, who, at first, submitted two selections for this anthology and then withdrew them, explained her equivocation in this way:

> My journal is filled with my journey as a woman, emotional conflicts, confusion about my sexuality, exploits and experiences that I could only face in detail in the journal. My entries have always represented closed chapters in my life. Snapshots of my hidden self which I am either afraid to or not ready to look at. I am now opening these vaults and trying to sift through the confusion, the pain and the guilt—without conflict.
>
> (March 27, 1990)

"Opening these vaults" to reveal the "hidden [erotic] self" not only frees the wo/man but also releases the creative energies of the writer. Audre Lorde calls this life force "creative energy empowered, the knowledge and use of which we are now reclaiming in our language, our history, our dancing, our loving, our work, our lives."

Given the other side of our sexual history—the myths and stereotypes, the sexual taboos and genteel tradition, the repressed desires and frustrated longings, the hidden selves and closed vaults—we find that *Erotique Noire,* which includes the poems and tales, the essays and short stories of so many Black writers from around the world, is something of a miracle in its affirmation of our sensuality and eroticism. It is a collective work of art whose time has come. It is our gift to *you.*

Introduction xxxix

One of the real joys in editing this anthology was that the work prompted several poets and novelists to write their first piece of erotica, to look at previously published work with an eye for the erotic or to increase their productivity in this area. I met Toi Derricotte almost a year after receiving no response to my letters requesting a submission, but when I gave her copies of the table of contents, an erotic prose poem, and a Good Vibrations catalogue (to stimulate her *imagination*), she wrote the delightfully funny "Dildo," her first piece of erotica. "I read it to a crowd of three hundred in New York this winter," she reported, "and they loved it."

When I first asked Marita Golden about contributing a prose piece, she answered, "Oh, I don't think my writing is erotic," but later she said, "Well, maybe you could call that scene in *Long Distance Life* erotic." Yes, ma'am, it certainly is.

He buried his face in her and she smelled of some gentle cologne and sweat and Ivory soap and longing for him and she tasted better than she used to and there was her hand inside his pants, releasing him, and he wanted to kiss her, there, forever, and there was her mouth on him, a perfect fit . . .

Meanwhile I received a wonderful letter from P. J. Gibson which began:

You have opened a Pandora's Box for me in this area of eroticism. [Now] I am in the process of completing a collection of erotic/sensuous short stories. I thank you for being a stimulant to this project.

(April 5, 1991)

So here it is—*Erotique Noire*—this collection of sexy and sensual delights, ranging from the lyrical to the lurid, from the prurient to the provocative, and from the merely risqué to the more than raunchy. Now we invite you to COME with us and, in the words of Thomas Stanley, PUT YOUR TONGUE IN IT!

—MIRIAM DeCOSTA-WILLIS

PART ONE

Love Juices and Other Squeezables

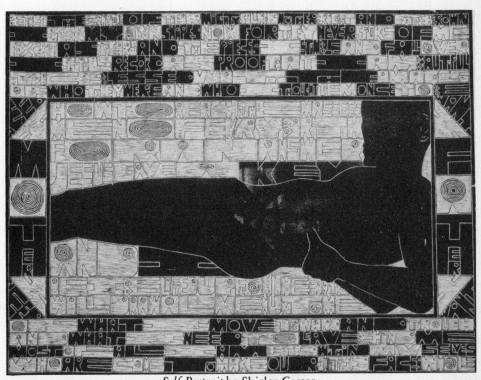

Self-Portrait by Shirley Carter

Long nights of prepubescent longing begin to make you think you're a bit odd when there's no one else like you around to bounce your uniquely erotic self off of. I'm sure the writers in this first section of *Erotique Noire* had that problem. But they couldn't help themselves, because there are only two types of people in this world, and they are not Black or White, or hetero- or homo-, or even male or female; there are only two types of people in this world, a friend of the first persuasion overwhelmingly convinced me: there are HOT people, and there are COLD people, and the twain have as much chance of meeting on any erotic plane as has Liberty University in North Carolina of running a course on Black erotica. There is absolutely no corporeal way to turn a cold person into a hot person. Buy as many see-through nightgowns and sets of leopard-print bikini underwear as you can afford, leave all the "right" books and pictures in the bathroom and on the nightstand, have long conversations that start as soon as the cold one is finished watching the news—conversations that go on until your voice cracks—and still cold people will be . . . well, cold. This is the 69th law of physics that no one talks about in college.

But there is some hope that we, the admirers of the hot-natured, have. Hot people equally cannot be turned into that which they intrinsically are not. Oh, beat the hell out of them if you will, make them be home every night at sundown, and don't allow them to read anything or touch themselves, but as soon as you leave the house or go to the bathroom, they're going to be thinking thoughts that your cold ass could never comprehend, much less constrain; it's the nature of the beast. Let them read something as neuter as a cake-box recipe and right away they start thinking about the various orifiy they can insert the finished cake into— to be licked out at their leisure, of course. Try to have a dull phone conversation with them and suddenly in the middle they shout out your name and throw the phone against the wall. Try to explain the necessity of staying serious in a deadly serious world and they just watch your lips and tongue the whole time. And they may tell you they're through with you forever and ever, but trust me, they always want some more. Hot people burn all the time, and nothing can put out their fire.

Obviously hot by birth—as are all these writers in Part I—Kalamu Ya Salaam burns and exaggerates, but my, my, my, "Tasty Knees" is a nasty, tasty piece of hot poetry that segues nicely into ReVonne L. Romney's "Beached." It's important, I think, when reading Romney's uncold piece of work to remember that waves keep returning, coming over and over again. Frank Lamont Phillips's bittersweet "Stolen" knows all about coming and licking, which guides our tongues gently over Morgan's "My All Day Sucker" and into P. G. Gibson's "Midnight Licorice Nights," the best argument for not letting a drop spill that I've ever read. In a similar frame of mind, Ted Joans's lips "hunger for that morsel of body cuntinent," while Esperanza Malavé Cintrón's tongue caresses a golden Temple orange:

> I have bitten into the juicy mass. There is pulp on my nose and juice drips from my chin. I am into a second, maybe third, bite. It is sticky and sweet, sweet, sweet.

Indeed, there is so much sweet stuff to eat in this section. In Gloria Naylor's field, Butch introduces Mattie to the pleasures of sucking on sugarcane. We know, of course, that sugar is addictive, and the more we eat, the more we want. Sooo, we sneak into Sandra Y. Govan's orchard to savor some of her forbidden fruits, and we don't give a tat if they're illicit or illegal, we've just got to have some. And then it's time, don't you think, to celebrate all our erotic blessings, and we couldn't do this better than with Yana West's "A Dinner Invitation," where we can lick, suck, and nibble . . . and bite and bite until we scream!

Finally, a word of instruction: If you are still a cold person after reading this initial section of *Erotique Noire,* someone in your family should let me know where to send the flowers.

Tasty Knees

Kalamu Ya Salaam

in the dark of touch
my face cleaved heavy
to your head i open
my eyes and see the
night hair of you dark
as the lightless black
of a warm womb's interior,
your wetness inviting touch
your earth quakes, shakes and opens
as my rod my staff
slides across your ground
though i want to scream i
resolve to remain mute
as a militant refusing to snitch
to the improper authorities, but
suddenly, a riot of joy breaches my resolve
and i disperse the moist quiet of our union
with an involuntary shout loud
as a bull elephant's triumphant ejaculation

of course i am exaggerating, but my, my, my
your knees did taste some good, yeah

Love Poem

Audre Lorde

Speak earth and bless me with what is richest
make sky flow honey out of my hips
rigid as mountains
spread over a valley
carved out by the mouth of rain.

And I knew when I entered her I was
high wind in her forests hollow
fingers whispering sound
honey flowed
from the split cup
impaled on a lance of tongues
on the tips of her breasts on her navel
and my breath
howling into her entrances
through lungs of pain.

Greedy as herring-gulls
or a child
I swing out over the earth
over and over
again.

From *The Women of Brewster Place*

Sweet Sugarcane

Gloria Naylor

They soon came to the edge of the cane field, and Butch took the machete from her and went through the tall grass, picking out the best stalks. She felt disquieting stirrings at the base of her stomach and in her fingertips as she watched his strong lean body bend and swing the wide-bladed knife against the green and brownish stalks.

Whenever he came upon one that was especially ripe, he would hold it over his head, his two muscled arms glistening with sweat, and call out, "This one's like you, Mattie—plump and sweet," or, "Lord, see how that beautiful gal is makin' me work."

She knew it was all in fun. Everything about Butch was like puffed air and cotton candy, but it thrilled her anyway whenever he straightened up to call to her through the tall grass.

When he had cut about a dozen canes, he gathered them up and brought them out to the edge of the field. He kneeled down, took some cord from his pocket, and bound the stalks into two bundles. When he got off his knees, he smelled like a mixture of clean sweat, raw syrup, and topsoil. He took a bundle of cane under each arm.

"Mattie, reach into my overall top and pull my kerchief. This sweat is blindin' me."

She was conscious of the hardness of his chest under her probing fingers as she sought the handkerchief, and when she stood on her toes to wipe his wet brow, her nipples brushed the coarse denim of his overalls and began to strain against the thin dress. These new feelings confused Mattie, and she felt that she had somehow drifted too far into strange waters and if she didn't turn around soon, she would completely forget in which direction the shore lay—or worse, not even care.

"Well, we got our cane. Let's get home," she said abruptly.

"Now, ain't that just like a woman?" Butch shifted the heavy stalks. "Bring a man clear out of his way to cut three times as much cane as he needed for hisself and then want to double-time him back home before he gets a minute's rest or them wild herbs he really came all this way fo'."

"Aw right." Mattie sucked her teeth impatiently and picked up the machete. "Where's the herb patch?"

"Just by the clearing of them woods."

The temperature dropped at least ten degrees on the edge of the thick, tangled dogwood, and the deep green basil and wild thyme formed a fragrant blanket on the mossy earth. Butch dropped the cane and sank down on the ground with a sigh.

"Jesus, this is nice," he said, looking around and inhaling the cool air. He seemed puzzled that Mattie was still standing. "Lord, gal, ain't your feet tired after all that walking?"

Mattie cautiously sat down on the ground and put her father's machete between them. The refreshing dampness of the forest air did little to relieve the prickling heat beneath her skin.

"You blaspheme too much," she said irritably. "You ain't supposed to use the Lord's name in vain."

Butch shook his head. "You folks and your ain'ts. You ain't supposed to do this and you ain't supposed to do that. That's why I never been no Christian—to me it means you can't enjoy life and since we only here once, that seems a shame."

"Nobody said nothin' about not enjoying life, but I suppose runnin' after every woman that moves is your idea of enjoyment?" Mattie was trying desperately to work up a righteous anger against Butch. She needed something to neutralize the lingering effect of his touch and smell.

"Mattie, I don't run after a lot of women, I just don't stay long enough to let the good times turn sour. Ya know, befo' the two of us get into a rut and we're cussing and fighting and just holding on because we done forgot how to let go. Ya see, all the women I've known can never remember no bad days with me. So when they stuck with them men who are ignorin' 'em or beatin' and cheatin' on 'em, they sit up on their back porches shelling peas and they thinks about old Butch, and they say, Yeah, that was one sweet, red nigger—all our days were sunlight; maybe it was a short time, but it sure felt good."

What he said made sense to Mattie, but there was something remiss in his reasoning and she couldn't quite figure out what it was.

"Now you think about it," he said, "how many women I ever went with ever had anything ornery to say about me? Maybe their mamas or papas had something to say," and he smiled slyly across the grass, "or their husbands—but never them. Think about it."

She searched her mind and, surprisingly, couldn't come up with one name.

Butch grinned triumphantly as he watched her face and could almost see the mental checklist she was running through.

"Well," Mattie threw at him, "there's probably a couple I just ain't met."

Butch laid his head back and his laughter lit up the dark trees.

"Lord, that's what I like about you Michael women—you hardly ever at a loss for words. Mattie, Mattie Michael," he chanted softly under his breath, his eyes caressing her face. "Where'd you get a sir name like Michael? Shouldn't it be Michaels?"

"Naw, Papa said that when the emancipation came, his daddy was just a little boy, and he had been hard of hearing so his master and everyone on the plantation had to call him twice to get his attention. So his name being Michael, they always called him Michael-Michael. And when the Union census taker came and was registering black folks, they asked what my granddaddy's name was, and they said Michael-Michael was all they knew. So the dumb Yankee put that down and we been Michael ever since."

Mattie's father loved telling her that story, and she in turn enjoyed repeating it to anyone who questioned her strange last name. As she talked, Butch was careful not to let his eyes wander below her neck. He knew she was sitting over there like a timid starling, poised for flight. And the slightest movement on his part would frighten her away for good.

So he listened to her with his eyes intently on her face while his mind slipped down the ebony neck that was just plump enough for a man to bury his nose into and suck up tiny bits of flesh that were almost as smooth as the skin on the top of her full round breasts that held nipples that were high, tilted, and unbelievably even darker than the breasts, so that when they touched the tongue there was the sensation of drinking rich, double cocoa. A man could spend half a lifetime there alone, but the soft mound of her belly whispered to him, and his mind reached down and kneaded it ever so gently until it was supple and waiting. And then the tip of his tongue played round and round the small cavern in the center of her stomach, while the hands tried to memorize every curve and texture of the inner thighs and lightly pressed outward to widen the legs so they could move through them and get lost in the eternity of softness on her behind. And she would wait and wait, getting fuller and fuller until finally pleading with him to do something—anything—to stop the expansion before she burst open her skin and lay in a million pieces among the roots of the trees and the leaves of the tiny basil.

When Mattie finished her story, Butch was looking down at the sugarcane and tracing the handle of his jackknife along the thick segmented ridges.

"You know how to eat sugarcane, Mattie?" he asked, still tracing the ridges. He avoided looking at her, afraid of what she would read in his eyes.

"You a crazy nigger, Butch Fuller. First you ask me 'bout my name and then come up with some out-the-way question like that. I been eating sugar cane all my life, fool!"

"Naw," Butch said, "some folks die and never learn how to eat cane the right way." He got on his knees, broke off one of the stalks, and began to peel it with his knife. He was speaking so softly Mattie had to lean closer to hear him.

"You see," he said, "eating cane is like living life. You gotta know when to stop chewing—when to stop trying to wrench every last bit of sweetness out of a wedge—or you find yourself with a jawful of coarse straw that irritates your gums and the roof of your mouth."

The thick blade of the knife slid under the heavy green covering on the stalk, and clear, beady juices sprang to the edges and glistened in the dying afternoon sun.

"The trick," he said, cutting off a slice of the stiff, yellow fiber, "is to spit it out while the wedge is still firm and that last bit of juice—the one that promises to be the sweetest of the whole mouthful—just escapes the tongue. It's hard, but you gotta spit it out right then, or you gonna find yourself chewing on nothin' but straw in that last round. Ya know what I mean, Mattie?"

He finally looked her straight in the face, and Mattie found herself floating far away in the brown sea of his irises, where the words, shoreline and anchor, became like gibberish in some foreign tongue.

"Here," he said, holding out a piece of the cane wedge to her, "try it the way I told you."

And she did.

Stolen

Frank Lamont Phillips

Finally, I taste your eyelids with my tongue
and you touch me the way and the precise number of times
it takes to cause me fever, become arrhythmical
with the music you are and put on.

While I yank out of my clothes, take my cheaters off,
sit them on the dresser so that their candy wrapper
colored lenses stare into its dark mirror,
you move backwards, slowly at first, then blur, like scenery
viewed from a train window, come chattering
out of your dress, your camisole, lie athwart
the bed, a tight bud on the bedcover,
arms reaching, legs opening, bloom in candlelight.

Nothing is so sweet, I think, as what is yours
because you've taken it not once or twice but over and
over until you can't see doing without,
and you say, I hope to shout, here we're at this again,
no matter that I keep saying no, no! in my head, but hold me honey,

again, honey me with all you say and don't mean,
and all I mean to say but can't,

and we're like that, making love until our ardor gives out
and we leave the house where your mother raised you
and lived until she died, and we both have to go home,
where you are to your husband what he needs
and thought rides you still with the train,
our noise and its sounding in my ears harsh percussives,
labials, baby breaths, blessed release.

Afro-Hispanic Triptych: Three Women

Manuel Zapata Olivella

Translated by Ian Smart

LOVE WITH THE WHITE WOMAN[1]

The protagonists are the young Black man, Manuel Saturio, and the White woman, Eustaquia Orobio, a beautiful older woman. The secret tryst takes place in a room above a stable.

His obsession with the obeah man's charm fanned the fire in his lower abdomen. A warm wave rose up from his flank through to his left collarbone, right there where he had attached the "talisman." "Tonight I'll be expecting you in my room. Come in by way of the mules' corral." The animals were not sleeping. Their eyes were big and round, their nostrils wide open to drink in his scent. He heard them stomp nervously. The Notary could come out with his lantern to see why they were so restless. The ammoniacal smell of grass steeped in urine. "A mule can never breed." Their bellies are broad, made to receive and shelter the little ones that will never be engendered in their wombs. "Could Eustaquia be still a virgin?" She liked males; she pursued them without ever catching them,

[1] From *El fusilamiento del diablo* [*The Devil's Execution by Firing Squad*] by Manuel Zapata Olivella.

or was it they who refused to impregnate her? No one had ever seen her big-bellied. "White women give birth to sickly, jellyfish children, sometimes stillborn ones with no life in them." They are frightened of the biblical condemnation to bear children in pain and suffering. Eustaquia would give him a White child, without the strength to stay alive. One day he would be creeping along, and as he tried to stand up, his legs would shake. He would have preferred a Black child who would not succumb to the Orobios' evil eye. Right after his birth he would wrap him up in pieces of cloth and take him off to his sister and aunt, who between them would raise him. They would give him donkey milk to drink to build up his strength and they would hang an ox's eye around his throat to counteract the uncle's evil spells. There was a light in Eustaquia's room. She was waiting for him. The corral fence was high. Even standing on the railing, it would be impossible for him to reach the window. "Come in!" If he went up by the stairs that led to the yard, he would have to pass in front of the Notary's bedroom. His wife, always on the watch, would hear even the brush of his shadow as it trailed along the floor. He imagined Eustaquia naked, caressing her abdomen in expectation of his arrival. The water-laden clouds electrified him. It would not be long before rain would fall and awaken everyone. The servant woman would get up to place calabashes and basins where the leaks usually occurred. "Saturio, pass through the mules' corral!" Her voice came through a hole in the wall and he could see the white sheet incandescent in the candlelight. A loose board left a narrow opening and through it she reached out with her white hand to squeeze his. He managed to climb up on one of the mules and put his head through the hole, fearful of not being able to fit through it. He had the odd sensation of having his legs cut off as they hung in the air over the animal's ears. Eustaquia helped him to wriggle through, and, once inside, they put out the candle. They didn't move a muscle. Someone was walking along the balcony and for long seconds all they could hear was their own breathing. Then the rain.

Love with the Indian Woman[2]

The protagonists are a Black man, Manuel Saturio, called the "freedman," a name used by the Indians to refer to a recently emancipated slave, and a pubescent Indian girl, a chola *in colloquial parlance. The episode takes place in a marsh in the jungle, near a* tambo *or native dwelling.*

Without loosening her grip on the arrows, the Indian girl moves toward the door. The "freedman" feels his hands filled with the whole of her vulva. He was not going to let her get away, not if she were to protect

[2] *El fusilamiento.*

herself with twenty poisoned arrows. He had tried before to follow her but the old woman raised her eyes and flashed him a deadly look. He knew then that she was no mummy and that she was keeping a close eye on his movements. She would warn the other Indians. He, nevertheless, keeps approaching. The old woman is quite still. The Indian girl slides from a tree trunk and sinks smoothly into the waters of the pond, while the other Indians stand by motionless. The moonlight molds them into a tableau in stone. The "freedman's" eyes begin to bulge, his nose is still full of the scent of the Indian girl. He moves stealthily to the edge of the hut and, standing quite still, he scours the silent waters. He catches sight of the underwater bubbles the Indian girl makes in the pond; he cautiously glides off, sinking into the crystal liquid. A cloud of vapor envelops his body: the last embers of his fever die out but the spark of desire ignites. A little distance away the Indian girl's sloe eyes glow. He senses that her bow is taut and that she would fire on him if he approaches. The warm water keeps him aroused. In his mind her wet hair and navel feel like a warm wave. In vain he seeks a shadow into which his black body could blend. The glowing eyes disappear again, slipping away fast into the water. The hut behind him seems uninhabited. The medicine man and the old man are still anesthetized by their steady chewing of coca leaves. Quite close to him, he hears the croak of a toad in the embrace of a female and straightaway his lower abdomen swells. Submerged, with only his head exposed, he hears the splashing sound of the Indian girl's undulating hips. The pace of the pursuit picks up. Suddenly, the silence stills the cries of the toad. He's still on the hunt, his breath bated. A long time, a way without end . . . then she reappears, naked, her breasts sleek. The furrow of her back dividing her buttocks in two. His instincts tell him that she will head back to the hut and with a dive he intercepts her. His clenched hand rapidly relieves her of the arrows and, straddling her body, he presses down on her genitals with both hands. Sighs and shadows disturb the calm of the marsh. The Indian girl fights back without a cry, contracting the angle of her thighs at the point where the horn spews forth life.

Love with the Black Woman[3]

This scene takes place in Lawrence, Kansas, on a riverbank. It is an important moment when the novel's protagonist, Agne Brown, and her boyfriend, Joe, participate in the work's only erotic episode.

She was waiting for you leaning against the garden fence. On another occasion you had caught her by surprise there under the maple tree, out of sight, smoking her long Virginia cigarettes. It was Thursday and her

[3] From *Shangó, el gran putas* [*Shango, the Holy Mother*].

waiting there surely had nothing to do with her son. From a distance she made you out even though night had fallen. You were returning from the university, loaded down with books, and she came out to meet you, before you could enter the big house.

" 'Aunt' Ann, what are you doing here?"

It surprised you to find her out of the kitchen.

"Joe is leaving tonight for New York."

The books fell at your feet. You knew of his decision to go off to Harlem, but felt you never believed that the time would actually come. "Aunt" Ann brought you back from your stupefaction:

"You have time to see him."

You reacted, an echo on the heels of a cry. "Aunt" Ann tried to follow you with the books she had picked up from the ground. You were running and soon your steps drowned out her words, lost in the distance:

"Let him write, let him not be voiceless like his father . . ."

Long before you reached the bus station you had seen him overwrought with anxiety.

"Joe! Joe!"

He came forward to take you in his arms and he sought out your mouth. His sighs mixed with your tears.

"I never imagined that you could leave me . . ."

He drank up your kisses, your words.

"I didn't believe I could love you so much!"

He drew you tight against his side and he carried you off with him as if you were part of his body. They walked away from the station with no hint as to where they were going. You abandoned yourself totally to that tremor shaking your very core.

"You're hurting me, Joe!"

They got to the riverbank. The levee channeled the flow of the waters. They walked along the darkness; they discovered the paths they had traversed together as children. Not even the wet sand could put out the fire in their bodies. You wanted him to go on pressing against your breasts and you wanted his mouth, that rough, thirsty mouth, to suck away your breath. Joe began to tremble. It is his first time too.

Haiku #9

Kalamu Ya Salaam

i watch your slow walk,
you stroke my beard, we soft suck
juice from this brief peace

Midnight Licorice Nights

P. J. Gibson

I want midnight licorice nights to find us
Sucking on the juice of our evening sup
Savoring the full course of the midday feast
Arms, legs, breasts, chests wet in the waves of love's spicy sauces
I want the sautéed makings of morning's rise to seduce our nostrils
And beckon us to dine again
Swallowing rounds of bursting orange on the sheets of the universe
I want to forever unfold the menu of you
Open the dish of chance
Sip the ambrosia of erotic litchi
Pithing and sweatshop juice
I want to banquet eternally in you and you in me
Marinating in the liquids of our joys
Simmering in the heat of
Cool blue flames of midnight licorice nights
Midnight licorice nights of you

Put Your Tongue in It

Thomas Stanley

1990 and the vitreous walls that surround me are more frustrating and confining than prison bars. Clear plates of limited space extending underfoot slicing through the thin air above my head—legislated ceiling bruising down even my daydreams. Goddamn. I'm running out of room. "Hey, Joe, where you going with that gun in your hand?" My memory cradles a notion of a different kind of pain. Goddamn. Who put cocaine on my dick? Dick rock hard and throbbing and I can't feel a motherfucking thing. Taken for a ride in the wounded space of collective disregard, collective ease, collective amnesia. My memory cradles a notion of a different kind of misery. Goddamn. Back that up! Let me smell it. Naw, naw. That shit's bogus. I know that smell. I've smelled that smell before.

1990. This is the longest year of my life and it's barely nine months long. Conceived in the absence of safety in a confused and dirty place. Please don't lie to me. Loving you wasn't easy, it was hard. Goddamn, who put cocaine on my dick? I mean it, y'all.

Anybody else remember what really good sex feels like? The warm aromas of a nice moist piece of ass. Pushing your dick through wet pink folds like you want it to come out the other side. Holding on for dear life while your sweats mingle with the cum and drench the sheets. The taste of your semen on her lips.

Ten more years and we crack the hymen on a new century, a new millennium. And I want to know just one small thing—is your DICK hard? Will it rise to the occasion?

I won't miss you . . . exactly. But it would be nice, just one more time, to put my tongue in it.

A Dinner Invitation

Yana West

My Dearest Reuben,

I have prepared my meal especially for you. We will begin with an appetizer of toes cleaned and covered with peppermint oil to begin your pleasure and delight. And with every suck and bite a little cream is added to the soup to come. But just before I serve you a cup of soup, I'll let you stick a finger in to see if it's been seasoned and stirred to your taste.

And when the soup is to your taste, your tongue will be allowed to finally engage. To lick and lap in the privacy of my home where juices can flow and we never have to stop to wipe our mouths. So slurp it up, for there is plenty more, but this is simply served to whet your appetite.

The entrée will include nipples toasted a deep brown and sautéed to gleam and stand erect. And while you are massaging these in your mouth, I've prepared my tongue to arouse your throat and ears. More cream is coming to cover the vegetables and, if you want, you can take your finger and stick it in and then cover those tits with more sweet juicy cream: and bite and bite until I scream.

And on the table just in front of you, you will find oils and creams that you may spread both in my twat and my ass. The vegetables are there for you to choose. Now a cock should be ready for this meal I've prepared.

And, believe me, there is enough for your insatiable appetite. Just take what you want. My pleasure will come in knowing that you've come.

Sure, I've prepared your coffee with sugar. And while you relax I'll suck you off to get the cream.

And finally dessert will be served to you, a bone to fuck both front and back to make you smile and want to come back.

I'll look for you at half past two. So that we can make each course last an hour or two.

Love,
YANA

Cuntinent

Ted Joans

To laymates

I want, I shall, I must cross your body cuntinent
I trust that my trip is mutually hip
My tongue shall be my means of travel
Your seven sensual holes will be navigated with skill
My tongue and lips shall chart your cuntinent

   I begin by letting my tongue f l o w steadily into your half opened mouth
      which has issued a visa and carte blanche my tongue gliding into your
      mouth wanders like a virgin tourist
my tongue sliding around the insides of that vast cave of meat
my tongue caresses your own tongue in friendship
it is your tongue that welcomes the approach of my tongue
in the daylight of your closed mouth they embrace
it is your mouth that is the greatest hangout for my tongue
your mouth moaning its own volcanic blues of pleasure
your mouth flowing joyous juices from all sides
your white teeth some of them blushing yellow coyly smile
your sharpest teeth cannot bare nor harm my tongue's soft touch

our tongues entangled suggest that our lips join
our lips join together in ecstatic rhythms
our joined lips throw themselves fully in this oral orgy
our lips suck our mouths insides
our tongues untangle and watch our lips in awe
my tongue touches your flowerlike tonsils
and finally in sheer madness our tongues say farewell
my tongue glides outside of your mouth waving goodbyes
your teeth gnash to hold back their farewell tears
the goodness of your mouth smells and causes my teeth to chatter my tongue
     on the edge of soft lips
leaving a soft trail of thin saliva that shines like the sun
leaving your lips tender corners and proceeding toward the cheeks
cheeks round flesh mountains that lead to small hair forest small hair forest
that runs down from the great head of hair forest
this small forest range separates the province of cheeks from ear
dragging my tongue and treading quietly on my lips I approach ear
your ear that saucer shaped well of no sound and yet the greatest authority
    and receiver of all sounds
the ear as timid as a gazelle before a clumsy deer hunter
your dear ear awaiting with all its doors, windows, and portals ajar
your ear wearing a tense grin that causes it to tingle
my tongue deserts my mouth and speeds toward the ear alone
I witness your shoulder come up toward your ticklish ear as it arrives
this tongue of mine that speeds into your ear looking for its drum
magnificent ear of harmless protective fur I salute you!
my tongue enters deep turning twisting and lapping around edges of ear abyss
my tongue maps the contours of your outer and inner ear republic
my lips arrive snorting warm air into your ear crevices
my tongue comes out and makes a pass at your ear lobe
it giggles
your saliva stained under lobe complains of negligence
my tongue like a feather gives your ear unforgettable thrills
my tongue whispers poetry that only an ear can understand
my tongue licks your ear until your entire body cuntinent shakes
romantic shivers cross your face and cheeks grow tight like a fist
my tongue in your ear causes your shoulders to hunch and asshole to tighten
    and of course your perfumed toes to curl up like thin slabs of bacon in
    a frying pan or wood shaving under a plane
my tongue causing you passionate body quakes of pleasure
my tongue causing your fluids to flood under arms, between legs and toes
my teeth nibble your ear but they dare not harm such a prize
exhausted with cannibal comforts and contentment my tongue departs
your ear sobs goodbye from a spent position

tremors can still be felt from the ear orgy that my tongue had laid
your body cuntinent shakes with gratifying gestures
my tongue slides wet from your spent ear
my tongue sets out in the direction of nape of neck
your delicious neck that my tongue will explore
my lips too hunger for that morsel of your body cuntinent
my lips speeded on by rapacious encouragement attacks your neck
teeth cannot resist sinking themselves deep into your soft neck
like a pretentious vampire they attack a soft neck curve
a bite of love leaves a mark but does not tear or bruise the neck
my mouth sucks like an oriental ocean octopus on your neck sucking fast and
       tenderly swallowing all your sweet pore juices
after what seems to be a lifetime of licking and sucking my lips release
my teeth-lip insignia sensual stamp of approval is revealed
your neck will be lonesome during the siestas without sucking
tongue waves a goodbye by stroking neck with "please forgive us-ism"
tongue lips and mouth set out southward down neck peninsula
trekking slowly south along the nape of warm neck filled with joy
even from this great distance one can perceive the peaks of Tit
Twin Tit peaks rise high above the vast fleshy plains of body cuntinent
my tongues destination is those twin mountains of elastic pleasures
the breast of mammary mountains lips hope to climb speedily
two tits bearing precious unclimbed nipple tops
my lips rave up and across the vast sweet smelling valley of Tit
a bit confused as to which peak of the twin tit to climb
I hesitate
stumbling like a clumsy ostrich trying to fly my mouth rushes up
licking right and left at that base of mount right tit is my tongue
around the base contours goes my lips lavishly sucking
I sniff the fragrant tit funk strengthening my desire to climb upward
your titties grow tense being assaulted by my mouths forces
tongue-lips supported by greedy teeth start up toward tit tip
in the shadow of tit do these carnivorous mouth members ascend
your right and left tit palpitate causing thousands of pimples
pimples from expected pleasures aid the climb up your right breast
my tongue ignores a tremendous tremor of body cuntinent
mouth-lips supported by tongue-teeth lunges upward toward tit peak
the extraordinary tit top the capitol of breast grows harder
it does nothing to conceal its real feeling about my invasion
lips make giant strides toward that perfect peak of pleasure
the tit top welcomes my tongue as the first to mount it
my lips follow and surround the nipple territory
having rushed to titties top thus capturing all of nipple my tongue stabs
      around the base of nipple whilst lips suck tit top

closing down over tit top with entire mouth forces teeth close in
gentle at first is teeths strategy daring not to scar tit top
rougher tactics are applied as tongue laps back and forth
mouth spreads wide as possible trying to enclose entire tit top
your great breast of beauty that is a target for my mouth
your marvelous mammary mountains making my mouth work
your double breasted full chested pleasure domes
magnificent motions that determine your firm carriage
your breast of sensual comprehensibilities
that first feeder of humanity made to be sucked caressed and licked
from dusk until dawn they welcome my mouths offerings
I suck your tit I lick your tit I caress your tit the both of them
Now leaving the spent and gasping for-a-marvelous-bit-more I depart
bidding a farewell to the best of breast of body cuntinent
I continue south walking on the lips of my mouth
I stop only to investigate some part that I perhaps left untouched
crossing the vast desert of upper stomach I blow and hum
toward the republic of navel passing through the douane of stomach
travelling onward south by southwest from breast I journey on
your wide soft tender and sweetbody cuntinent I kiss at every mile
traveling down the body cuntinent stopping here and there
to investigate thoroughly investigate no precious part should I miss
arriving on the grand voluptuous veldt of skin of lower stomach
lips, tongue cheered on by teeth push rapidly toward the distant woods
these woods are the beginning of that great dark forest pubic forest
upper pubic forest awaiting with all mystery and magic
this magnificent growth of hair leads downward to the tropic vagina basin
down there is where the most sought after prize in all the world lies
down there is why humanity has continued   it is place of birth
down there humidity is a great feeling and smell
down there all is marvelous and each movement is a throw of the dice
dense entangled dark hairs each having been blessed by sorcerers
coiled hairs from earthly hole cover the area
the cave of creation can be found below the great forest
this cave is where truth dwells
in the district of vagina one must be guided
tongue alone can find the entrance into the warm crevice
your body cuntinents masterpiece of treasures this canyon
your entire cuntinent is sometimes jealous of this beautiful soft crack
your cuntinent offers and opens the portal of pleasure for my tongue
my tongue journeys through the entangled forest swift as an arrow
my lips blow warm air along the basin of vagina trail
my teeth sink back deep into my mouth with hairs between them
a giant turtle, a short eskimo, and a broken bidet couldnt be more wanted

my tongue rushes toward the highly sought after prize
your vagina is steaming and hissing a code that only tongue and penis
    comprehend
your vagina smells of all the great smells that are good for the nose
your vagina tastes of all the great tastes that are good for the mouth
your vagina looks like what a god would look like if there was a god
black magic causes it to move   white science keeps it from pregnancy
my tongue bears no seed but seven thousand messages with each thrust
weak men with turtle necked sweaters cannot tongue their way there
weak minded men with erected tongues and unerected penises are unwanted
it is I who is forever welcome   my lips, tongue and penis
your vagina basin welcomes my approach by opening all for me
your vagina itself winks at my tongue whilst the hairy forest waves
your vagina giggles a group of happy phrases of laughter
my lips and tongue race wrecklessly into the delicious pit licking it with lovely
    strokes lapping its sides tenderly
your body cuntinent shakes with enthusiastic truth tremors of want of need
your vagina region's magnetic forces pull all of me toward it
your gentle pubic forest of shiny kinky hairs sprays tiny jets of water
your groovy good graciousness lays open like an awesome abyss
I hesitate to describe what this fabulous flesh-hair area offers
I hesitate to report what treasures of the senses dwell within
I hesitate because my teeth, my lips, and tongue are greedy at this point
I hesitate because they would never share this divine part
I hesitate no longer on my journey   I speed onward into the clearing
my tongue plunges into that vivacious vast slit of terrifying truth
my lips stagger downward along the slope of saintly slime
my teeth separate to gather up spare vagina basin bush hairs
my teeth sing a gnashed out chant of joy   hairs held between them
my tongue leads my head down into the warmth between your legs
my tongue is erected like my penis causing your vagina to blush
I have your huge mountain of thighs pressed against my ears
I feel those twin range of inside legs imprisoned my head
your body cuntinent encloses my bodys head
your cuntinent with all its flavors of curves
your cuntinent possessor of fantastic oceans of flesh
your cuntinent that runs north-south as well as east-west
your body cuntinent more beautiful than sunshine
your cuntinent infested with pleasures and treasures
your cuntinent saturated with hair forests and awesome openings
your cuntinent of beautiful adventures during the horizontal hours
your cuntinent of mental love/physical love/and active love
your cuntinent that eros admires and that encourages my safari
your cuntinent that you have allowed my lips tongue and teeth to cross

your cuntinent that welcomed my every desire
your cuntinent is now flying our flag of togetherness from my staff
your cuntinent is under me to bring paradise to euphoria with joy
your cuntinent surrounds my all and takes my mileage and in inches
your body cuntinent that elegant spread of solid space
your body cuntinent my world of travel in search of my findings
your cuntinent that you gave to me
your cuntinent that is now mine
your cuntinent with its every edge and end rounded
your great body cuntinent that is for me to journey on
we have this adventure together today for tomorrow is the climax
body cuntinent I have claimed you
body cuntinent I have conquered your all
body cuntinent you are mine
I place my staff into that gaping hole in the middle of your forest
Body cuntinent! Oh dear cuntinent of contentment/Body cuntinent!!

Temple Oranges

Esperanza Malavé Cintrón

Hot, sticky, sun-filled days. The good part is that the car starts up on the first try and it doesn't need long to warm up. The bad is that the vinyl seats stick to and burn the backs of my legs, turning them red and making indented lines like seams sown together. The hard hot plastic of the steering wheel stings my hands as I pull out into the street. I whip the visor down to shield my eyes from the sun's glare.

I am headed to the supermarket. It's grocery day and I've grudgingly convinced myself to leave the dim comfort of my apartment to face this cruel heat and ultimately the refrigerator frost of the supermarket air conditioner. Not to mention, it's Saturday, and the shopping carts will be bumper to bumper. But I know that the Temple oranges are in; I called ahead. Besides, I need a few staples: milk, bread, margarine, and maybe something for dinner.

I make it through the checkout, my Temples staring at me through their clear plastic sheath. I've kept them nearest me, by themselves on the children's seat in the buggy, so they wouldn't get crushed by the other things. It was all that I could do to keep my hands off of them. The only thing that kept me from tearing into one was the fact that I knew they weren't mine yet.

The bags, propped up on the back seat, lean heavily against each other.

Bright orange Temples crowd the top of one, their waxy coats and dimples tempting me. But I can wait.

With my foot on the brake, I turn on the ignition and push Paula Abdul into the cassette hole. She starts hip-hopping with "It's the Way That You Love Me," and I turn on the air, a little, just enough to simulate a breeze. She sings, "It's the Way That You Love Me," and I'm bouncing back and forth thinking about my Temples. That's enough!

I turn the ignition off, then back on, just a notch so that the air and music stay on, then I reach back and grab me a fat juicy Temple. I roll it around in the palms of my hands to get its juices to loosen up and to feel the firmness. It's wonderful. I press its cool skin to my cheek, then my forehead. With my front teeth, I tug at it, creating an opening just large enough for the tip of my forefinger, which I use to slowly pull the skin back. It comes away easily. Slender strands of white tease my lips as I press the white meat on the inside of the skin to my mouth, gnawing gently at the membrane. When I'm done with the skin, it falls exhausted into my lap and I'm left holding the naked flesh of my Temple.

What to do? Should I separate its segments? I imagine how easily they would come apart, how sweet, how juicy . . . Or should I just bite into it, allowing the juices to ooze and spray over my face? Contemplating my options, I nibble at stray strands of membrane with my lips. But before I am conscious, I have bitten into the juicy mass. There is pulp on my nose and juice drips from my chin. I am into a second, maybe third, bite. It is sticky and sweet, sweet, sweet. I take greedy bites, the bits of pulp burst in my mouth. I lick the remaining juice from my lips as I search through the glove compartment for napkins to mop up the evidence.

Beached

ReVonne L. Romney

The Key lime satin moon, heavy and full as a mule's eye, laid down a shaft of ghostly light across this simple room. An opal shining shimmered up over the narrow bed, dressed in fragrant linen, along the full length of me to rest lightly upon my cheek and lips so sweetly. He repeats in a gravel whisper, "I am going to eat your pussy."

Sleep easily overtook me. The excitement of a week of rest and pleasure on this beautiful semitropical island lured whatever failings from my every nerve and weary limbs. I rolled easily into the soft and silence, vaguely aware of some strange and bold lover whispering seductive promises from the wild garden beneath my window. This night was a quiet and dreamless one, for tomorrow my blood would sing.

In just moments, or so it seemed, I was refreshed and roused by the sweetest air in memory. No dawn had ever dressed herself in such beguiling raiment as this silver queen of the morning. Dove gray, silver and periwinkle plumes rose like the spires of some great cathedral to touch the salmon and vermeil of the dawn's mischievous eye. I quickly dressed and went down to the sea's edge.

The water was cold and forbidding to the touch, but enchanting to the eye. I stepped forth shivering to the ocean's lip, and stood my ground as the sea snatched grain after grain from beneath my anxious and grasping toes. Challenged, I stepped forward; the chilly azure slithered around my knees and playfully bounced crystal droplets into my hair and eyes, stinging me with its cold and brilliance.

A bouncing wave cupped my buttocks and cut an icy path between the orbs of my clutched and nervous rump. The sun rose quickly toward its peak and flung her golden lucre down upon the waves. With each heave and breath, my lover rocked me with horny pleasure that gained force in rhythm with his whim.

Not wanting to be cheated of the sight of my lover's eagerness, I rose upon my elbows and drew my knees up to my shoulders. Tickled by my wantonness, the naughty brine gripped my ankle and spun me 'round then heaved a salty wash all over me.

Done with his teasing and eager for a serious joust, I spread my thighs and dug my heels into the shore's shifting end. With elbows and shoulders locked, I readied myself for his next vigorous move.

He played the fickle coquette and abandoned me to frolic with plankton, sylph and sunbeams. Further my lover retreated from me. Vexed and impatient, my labia flex and twitch convulsively. "Tend to me!" I snap. "NOW!"

My dark and stony sisters, rooted in a ring around the beach, are all too familiar with his greedy lust. He rises slowly with a frightful roar to a magnificent and terrible height. With each caress and cosset he pounds mercilessly upon the beach's breast. I am consumed, breathless, impaled upon his cunning pelagic tongue. Measure upon glorious measure of his exquisite and salty foam collects in a copious crescent along the beach's mile, while I free a million happy goldfish from between my firm and sumptuous thighs. He delights in my wild wickedness, and I in his power and tenderness.

In empathy and glee, a chevron of whooping cranes wings by my head and returns me to my waning senses. Still I lie, drained and exhausted. The gentle waves lap softly around me. The daystar, now directly overhead, kicks up its blaze to warm me. I reach up to clasp the sun and draw it to my bosom, "Make me black, for I have been loved beautifully this day. Make me very, very, very black!"

In time my strength returns to me. Slowly and deliberately, I collect my limbs and turn to the now innocent and pacific waters. I bow in homage.

My All Day Sucker

M. J. Morgan

I loved my all day sucker.
He was my best fucker
He could suck, lick and fuck until day's end.

You took my all day sucker,
and I thought you were my friend.

Just because I told you
he bathed me in oils and loved
my every curve.

Didn't mean you should try it.
You know you've got some nerve.

All I ever dreamed of was a man
that could lick my luscious body
till it overflowed.

Seems like you couldn't stand it
I saw how you glowed.

I loved my all day sucker
Like a baby loves the nipple

Never thought I'd lose him,
how could I be so simple?

Know I've learned my lesson
next time I get an all day sucker
I ain't goin to tell no motherfucker.

Forbidden Fruits
and Unholy Lusts:
Illicit Sex in Black
American Literature

Sandra Y. Govan

An examination of early texts in the Black canon clearly shows that "unholy lust" is not an uncommon theme and that the idea of unsanctioned sex, frequently but not always in a master/slave or Black/White context, is part and parcel of these early texts and permeates the tradition. Not only is this a recurrent pattern apparent in literature of the 19th century, but it doesn't require a particularly erotic imagination to note this same pattern appearing both explicitly and implicitly in modern and contemporary texts. No longer veiled behind the delicate, careful, polite Victorian prose of our foremothers and forefathers, illicit sex or tabooed sexual desire is out of the closet and into the streets—or onto the printed page —in all its vivid possibilities. At any rate, that is the premise of this essay, which sprang, to be candid, from the query of a student who wanted to know whether the "weird sex" she was then reading was a theme in Black literature.

Those of us who teach the slave narrative regularly focus on the narratives of Frederick Douglass and Linda Brent as representative texts. What we seldom discuss in detail is the erotica of both texts. To be sure, we note the "birth" of the "mulatto class" and we allude to the forced sexual liaisons between master and slave woman, but I doubt that many teachers really focus on the sexual tension in these works. Recall, for instance,

Douglass's 1845 *Narrative*. Reread the early segment when he describes his initiation into slavery, an identifiable archetypal motif wherein the slave narrator shares his abrupt realization of his slave status. He was a child; he had previously lived with his grandmother on the outskirts of the plantation; he had never witnessed a beating. What he "witnessed" was Captain Anthony's punishment of his Aunt Hester for the crime of being "found in the company of Lloyd's Ned," a slave on another plantation. Had his master, Douglass expounded, "been a man of pure morals himself, he might have been thought interested in protecting the innocence of my aunt; but those who knew him will not suspect him of any such virtue." Because Douglass couched his observations in ironic understatement, many readers may not recognize that Captain Anthony was also a jealous sadist. He would take Aunt Hester, tie her semi-nude to a joist with her arms above her head, and "whip upon her naked back till she was literally covered with blood." Douglass says that Anthony "at times seem[ed] to take great pleasure" in these whippings; no tears, words, or prayers "from his gory victim" deterred him. Note that the following description is an almost textbook example of sadomasochism:

> The louder she screamed, the harder he whipped; and where the blood ran fastest, there he whipped longest. He would whip her to make her scream, and whip her to make her hush; and not until overcome by fatigue, would he cease to swing the blood-clotted cowskin.

Two quick observations. First, Anthony clearly enjoys his task. As his whip is curling about the naked flesh of Hester, ripping into her tender breasts as well as scoring her "naked back," his "fatigue" or exhaustion comes as much from sexual release as it does from physical exertion. Second, Aunt Hester either loved pain or loved Lloyd's Ned entirely too much, for Douglass claims he "often" heard her "heart-rending shrieks" at the dawn of day. It seems a clear-cut case of a White man who wants "his own" Black woman getting bested, sexually, by a Black man while the Black woman "love" object suffers because of their lust.

Turning to Brent's *Incidents in the Life of a Slave Girl* (1861), we find a stronger emphasis on "licentiousness," on the "corruption" of young slave girls by White men, on the "foul wrongs" endured by slave women "begetting," if you will, mulatto children by White fathers. Black girls are "violated" with impunity, and those who, like Brent, tried desperately to hold to the ideals of the "cult of true womanhood" (wherein women maintain their piety, purity, morality, virtue, and chastity, and yet remain "submissive and domestic") had an impossible struggle against the "licentiousness and fear" rampant in an atmosphere of "all-pervading corruption" produced by slavery. Brent approaches what she and her 19th-century audience considered the indelicate topic of perverse lust with all the delicacy she could manage. Slave women have their "purity" violated; the word "rape" is never mentioned. Occasionally, these women are bribed or tempted with presents; should these methods fail, the lash or starvation can follow. In any event, they mostly live in a "cage of obscene birds" and their "submission" is compelled.

Apart, however, from detailing the travails of the slave woman, Brent expends tremendous energy detailing how slavery—sexual profligacy in slavery—dramatically affects not only slaves but Whites as well. White wives are often embittered and crippled by jealousy, their normal humanity stripped from them by the continual effrontery of recognizing, but being unable to acknowledge, the bastard children of their husbands. White children of slaveholding families are also affected. "The slave-holder's sons are, of course, vitiated, even while boys, by the unclean influences everywhere around them. Nor do the master's daughters always escape." Brent reveals how one such daughter had "selected one of the meanest slaves" on the plantation to father her father's first grandchild. This is not love but lust (and probably hatred), illicit sexual conduct, unlicensed and unbridled sexuality deriving from pure power relationships and not from genuine human feeling.

When Brent, at age fifteen, yields to the flattering attentions of a White "lover" (the Black man who had courted her had been driven away by her master), and bears his child, she does so solely because she wants some control of her sexual identity. Mr. Sands is not her master and he is not married, significant virtues in a situation with few redeeming options. He was also an educated "gentleman" and thus even more "agreeable to the pride and feelings of a slave, if her miserable situation has left her any pride or sentiment." It seemed to Brent "less degrading to give one's self than to submit to compulsion." "There [was]," she felt, "something akin to freedom in having a lover who has no control over you, except that which he gains by kindness and attachment." Brent also recognized that she was violating moral codes sanctioned by her family and her Christian beliefs. She asks her "virtuous reader[s]" for pardon, explaining that they simply did not know "what it is to be a slave; to be entirely unprotected by law or custom." While she knew she "did wrong," and felt her loss of virtue intensely, she also felt "that the slave woman ought not to be judged by the same standard as others" because of the conditions of chattel slavery.

Early Afro-American novelists, borrowing liberally from slave narratives to construct their plots, depict scenes from slave life, and expound upon themes they thought the public needed to hear. Such novelists also made a point of indicting sexual immorality in the American South. In every version of *Clotel* (1853), whose protagonist is alleged at first to be the slave offspring of Thomas Jefferson, William Wells Brown treats not only the "tragic mulatto" as a character and the unplanned creation of a whole "new race" in America, but also levels his finger at the social and moral consequences of unrestrained lust. In the novels, "beautiful" quadroon and mulatto women are "revered" and "loved" by their White suitors/masters. They are given homes in delicate bowers, apart from the real world, where they have an almost ideal near-marital relationship. Then, by social dictate, the White lover marries a White woman, his race and caste; his cast-aside Black lover begins to suffer in earnest. Often these women are readmitted to slavery at the meanest levels because of the jealousy of a White wife or mother-in-law who discovers the unlicensed, though accepted and supported by the White patriarchy, sexual liaison. The husband/lover wants it all—his White wife and his Black/quadroon lover. Brown argues that he cannot have it all without paying a terrible price. His marriage is destroyed by an absence of trust and his Black family is sold away before his eyes. Because of his "sensitivity," this pivotal player in an American tragedy may be consumed by guilt and by failure to act on his conscience. This scenario occurs in Brown's fictitious re-creation of slavery because he strives to touch a responsive chord in a largely White audience. However, neither the Douglass nor the Brent narrative showed many White males who suffered as severely as Brown's White men; nor did Brown dwell on the feelings of these men. Rather, he emphasized what became of the women and children these men betrayed.

Contemporary historical novels that look at slavery and Reconstruction do so with all the verve available to the modern novelists. Themes and plot lines implicitly suggested or delicately alluded to in the early texts are today treated with forthright dispatch. Sherley Anne Williams's *Dessa Rose* (1986), for instance, explicitly describes in one segment the forbidden liaisons between slave men and White women. When asked what he did as a slave, Nathan says succinctly that he "loved pretty white womens like" Rufel, the lonely White reluctant benefactor who has given sanctuary to escaped slaves. Just before he confidently makes love to her, he describes vividly his initiation into various forms of sex by "Miz Lorraine"—a single, older White woman with a "wild nature" who took her "belly warmers from among the lowest of the low." "Freakish" Miz Lorraine trained her young slave lovers, teaching them about the joys of oral copulation and the terrors of making love, with death ever close at hand, to a White woman, truly forbidden fruit. If a slave sex partner ever initiated sexual activity, if she ever lost the feel of control, the slave could be sold or worse; Miz Lorraine, who swore each "lover" to silence, could scream rape.

Octavia Butler's *Kindred* (1979) is a grim fantasy wherein science fiction meditates upon Black history. It proceeds from the premise of a modern woman pulled back and forth across time and space to emerge periodically in 1830s Maryland. Dana Franklin and Alice, her great-great-forebear several times removed, are the proverbial flip sides of the same coin. Dana must help mother nurture, teach, and raise young Rufus Weylin, the White child later destined to become the male progenitor of her family tree, because of his forced attentions to Alice. (This relationship is another one of those Black man/White man/Black woman triangles; Alice has a Black lover. Jean Toomer also plays with the loaded triangle through Louisa's story in *Cane* [1923]). When Alice dies, Rufus, intellectually attracted to Dana, now expects from her not only intellectual stimulation but the same sexual intimacy he demanded and coerced from Alice. And this from a woman who had been his surrogate mother!

Morrison's *Beloved* (1987) gives us insight into what destroyed the relationship between Sethe and Halle, her slave husband. It seems that shortly before the family and some selected others made their escape attempt, Sethe is attacked and Halle must watch the sexual humiliation and desecration of his wife from a hiding place, as two young White men attack her, suckling at her breast as if she were an animal, stealing her milk, while their schoolteacher uncle merely observes. Though pregnant, Sethe is whipped with a cowhide. But another character, Paul D. also has a tale of sexual perversion to relate. While a prisoner, chained with forty-six other slaves, Paul D. and the others are forced to perform oral copulation, as "breakfast," on the White men who guard them. Those who rebelled, died. "Occasionally, a kneeling man chose gunshot in his head as the price, maybe, of taking a bit of foreskin with him to Jesus."

Black autobiography is another genre where illicit sex is illustrated. That, however, is another discussion. Suffice it to say here that Langston Hughes (*The Big Sea*, 1940), while virtually ignoring his own sexuality and sexual experiences, quickly sketches the plight of two young African prostitutes who become victims of a gang rape or "gang bang." For all their "service" or "labor," these two women are never paid, just used by the crew in the hold of the steamship. And then there's Maya Angelou's *Caged Bird* (1970). Here, you recall, Maya remains silent for four years following her rape, at eight years old, by the boyfriend of her mother. Later, as a teenager, she thinks herself some kind of abnormal sexual freak and so solicits a sexual relationship with a young man just to prove to herself that there is "nothing wrong" with her.

Returning to fiction, I could also mention James Baldwin and the sexual tension that animates his works. At fifteen, I first read *Another Country* (1962) almost solely for the titillation factor (the Chicago public school system had debated banning the book for its "sex and violence," so naturally . . .). I found the violent and sordid "love" story of Rufus and Leona—Black man and southern White woman—both compelling and vivid; soon the whole novel, complex though it was, had my undivided attention. But Baldwin hooked me first with his tale of illicit sex. In other works, few readers can ignore the rape and sexual degradation of Deborah, Gabriel's first wife, or miss the suggestion of homosexual erotica that connects young John Grimes to Elisha in *Go Tell It on the Mountain* (1953); and incest is part of the text of *Just Above My Head* (1979).

There is, of course, more than a suggestion of dangerous sexual energy in Richard Wright's *Native Son* (1940). Bigger Thomas murders Mary Dalton purely because he fears being caught with forbidden fruit in his hands. Quite literally, he has been carrying a drunken Mary in his arms, and becomes sexually stimulated by the feel of her lips against his, the scent of her hair and skin, and the feel of her breasts in his hands. What Wright calls "hysterical terror" seizes him when blind Mrs. Dalton enters the room, and we all know what happens next. Later, to protect his secret, Bigger kills Bessie, his Black girlfriend. But before he kills her, to relieve his own tension and because of "insistent and demanding" desire, he forces an "inert, unresisting" Bessie into position for intercourse. Then, despite her urgent pleas for him to stop, he proceeds to yield to the demands of his body and his needs, and riding "roughshod over her whimpering protests," he rapes her. Here again, we're told that fear drives Bigger, but there is an ironic juxtaposition between the little death of sexual copulation and the big one of Bessie's murder.

Wright's *Eight Men* (1961) contains two stories where sexual tension is the dominant element of the story. "The Man Who Killed a Shadow" focuses on two ordinarily insignificant characters—Saul, a Black male in his thirties and married, and a nameless, single, forty-year-old White librarian. In the larger scheme of things, they are not important characters in their respective worlds and both are deemed "shadows." The White woman is a stereotype personified, a sexless nonentity, a white shadow. However, she apparently sees Wright's male protagonist as a way of ending her virginity. Saul is a janitor who does his work thoroughly. The librarian, for no obvious reason, complains to his boss that he has not cleaned under her desk. Shortly thereafter, she demands that Saul come and look under her desk, as if to see what he has not cleaned. When Saul looks, he is shocked: ". . . his mind protested against what his eyes saw, and then his senses leaped in wonder. She was sitting with her knees sprawled apart and her dress was drawn halfway up her legs . . . her white legs whose thighs thickened as they went to a V clothed in tight, sheer pink panties." Her sexual overtures, coded as they are by race and caste, drive Saul to "protect himself" by preventing any further intimation of sexual energy from her. Ironically, she dies still a virgin.

The second story, "Man of All Work," is by contrast almost funny, although, as usual, it is framed by Wright's grim humor. In this tale, an unemployed Black husband, Carl, dons his sick wife's clothes to find work as a cook and housekeeper to earn money. What he encounters, apart from an observant child who notices immediately the physical differences between "Lucy" and Bertha, the former maid, is the kind of sexual harassment many Black domestic workers endured while laboring in white houses. Mrs. David Fairchild knows that her husband has a penchant for young and attractive Black maids. She calls her new maid into the bathroom to bathe her back while she discusses her husband's tendencies, warning the "maid" to "just push him away" should he "bother" her. The stifled sexual tension generated as our man-in-maid's-clothing suffers through this bath would be hilarious were it not for the implicit sexual/racial violence resonating through the scene. Later, Mr. Fairchild makes the predictable pass just as his wife returns for lunch. She gets her gun, resolves to shoot—not her husband, but the maid!—and actually winds up hitting Wright's disguised hero. At this point, neither husband nor wife is as yet aware of the gender switch.

In *Invisible Man* (1952), Ralph Ellison goes beyond the suggestion of sexual tension to consummation of perverted, unsanctioned sex. Consider the Trueblood/Norton episode. If you recall, Ellison's nameless Black protagonist takes Mr. Norton, a wealthy White philanthropist, for a ride. Norton asks him to stop at what seems to be a picturesque, old-fashioned cabin, where he meets the sharecropper, Jim Trueblood, who resides there with his family. His is the eerie case of a Black father who, during a dream, commits incest upon his daughter, raping her while his wife sleeps on the other side of the bed! Central to the tale is Norton's response to the story, which the White villagers repeatedly encourage Jim Trueblood to tell. Norton, it seems, desires his own fair yet unattainable daughter, but must settle for the vicarious sexual satisfaction of hearing how Trueblood "did it." A clear-cut case of unholy, vicarious lust.

Having recounted telling episodes from some of the earlier works that inform the canon, I realize that I still have not gotten to most of the contemporary women writers who stand accused of putting the dirty linen in the public's eye by speaking directly to issues of sexual violence, sexual abuse, and abnormal or illicit sexual behavior. I've cited one of Toni Morrison's novels, but I have not yet discussed the works of Ntozake Shange, Ann Allen Shockley, Gloria Naylor, or Alice Walker. My belief is that closer examination of early texts within the canon and other modern texts by men and women writers should exonerate the accused and make the point sufficiently clear; literary treatment of illicit sex is neither a recent occurrence nor a contemporary by-product of the radical feminist movement. Nonetheless, since works by these authors have been decried for their depictions of shocking or abhorrent sexual tensions between men and women, most often indicted for presenting "negative images of Black men," it follows that at least a cursory glance at some novels from the 1970s and 1980s is appropriate.

Anyone looking for heavily accentuated sexuality to undergird a tale—normal or abnormal, licensed or unlicensed sexuality—has only to look at Shange's *for colored girls* (1975), Shockley's *Say Jesus and Come to Me*

(1982), Walker's *The Third Life of Grange Copeland* (1970), or *The Color Purple* (1982), and some would say, Naylor's *The Women of Brewster Place* (1982). And unlike a thesis I once heard propounded at a conference, I do not think *Purple* is "as instructive as a how-to sex manual" merely because Shug Avery explains clitoral function to Celie or because she teaches her to feel genuine orgasmic response, as opposed to feeling only as if someone had simply done "his business" on her. Nor is *Purple* the first time Walker flirted with the idea of incest, sexual violence, aberrant or abhorrent sexual conduct, or child abuse in Black life. I would direct attention to the complex relationships of father and son, Grange and Brownfield Copeland, with the women in their lives—both with their martyred wives and with the mother-and-daughter pair of whores, Fat Josie and Lorene, whom both men have utilized. I would also encourage a careful rereading of Walker's "The Child Who Favored Daughter" from *In Love and Trouble: Stories of Black Women* (1967).

"Daughter" resonates with overt yet paradoxically suppressed sexual energy. Curiously, the story is seldom discussed because of a palpable pain radiating from its core, pain so horrifying it makes most readers want to bury it deeply and ignore its message, for how do we "explicate" in the face of such raw emotion? In an era when crimes of violence against women permeate the society, how do we as teachers surmount the brutality to teach this tale as mere fiction? In the story, set in the South of the sixties, issues of race and caste are mixed together with the twin taboo of brother/sister and father/daughter incestuous urges and ugly family violence. The child who favors Daughter, the father's sister, is doomed in this tale because of twisted obsessive love. The nameless father, who has seen his beloved sister give herself to too many men, including White men, attacks his only daughter as being a "replica." Not only has she taken a lover but that lover is White. A misogynist who has always anticipated "evil and deception" from women, the father has consequently mistreated all the women in his life, including his wife, fearing "imaginary overtures" from White men. He beats his child with a harness; then, having brutally beaten her clothes half off and subsequently seen her half naked, he is consumed by "unnameable desire." Motivated by both lust and jealousy ("Jealousy is being nervous about something that has never, and probably won't ever, belong to you."), he attacks his child, cuts her bare breasts from her chest, and casts "what he finds in his hands" to the dogs.

In *for colored girls,* Ntozake Shange's choreopoem, several vignettes show the vagaries of male/female relationships shrouded in sexual feeling. The Lady in Red tells two poignant tales. The most striking is the dreadful saga of Beau Willie Brown, who drops his child from a window as a twisted act of revenge against his wife; the second recounts the bittersweet story of a painted and perfumed woman who, almost immediately following intercourse with strange men she seduces, puts them out of her bed and her house, records her sexual exploits in a diary, and subsequently cries herself to sleep, alone.

Ann Shockley's *Say Jesus* breaks precedent by presenting the taboo theme of lesbianism as the principal plot. Her protagonist, a charismatic female minister named Myrtle Black, is a well-developed, emotionally complex, and rounded character whose lovers are women. Apart from the issues of Black and White feminists working together and of homophobia and strained male/female relationships, Shockley also raises ethical questions—just as male ministers occasionally stray by using the pulpit for sexual conquests, Myrtle uses her position to select sexual partners from among vulnerable members of various church congregations. Any minister caught violating the moral tenets of church and society would be subject to censure. But when the minister is lesbian, the risks in exposure are magnified because society condemns homosexuality as perversion.

Gloria Naylor currently has three major works to her credit. *Mama Day* (1988) utilizes the supernatural to frame the story of the power of love and lust to affect lives in Willow Springs. *Linden Hills* (1985) also makes some strong statements about lust and perverted love among the Black middle-class residents of the Linden Hills community. But it was *The Women of Brewster Place* (1982), those bruised blues women, that projected Naylor into the first tier of Black contemporary writers. The vivid and brutal gang rape of Lorraine in the story "The Two" is one of the most chilling descriptions in literature. That the rapists "justify" their action on the grounds that Lorraine is lesbian and has never known sex with a man adds to the horror.

Perhaps because the sexual violence in contemporary tales, especially those told by Black women novelists, is particularly graphic and powerfully fixed in the imagination, we think of these writers as being the first to probe this area. But again, what we have is not so much a new tack as it is an "unapologetic foregrounding of the madness" which has marked our past and "infected" our present. The specter of unholy lust, illicit sex, suppressed erotica, and unlicensed sexual violence, acknowledged or not, permeates both our history and, sadly, our society. That such themes recur in our literature should be recognized as necessary revelations, as psychological insight into individuals and the culture which produced and "sustains" them.

PART TWO

When the Spirits Come

Josephine Baker by George Hoyningen-Huene

In her essay "Uses of the Erotic: The Erotic as Power," Audre Lorde examines the ability of the erotic to empower us in ways that inform and illuminate our actions, to unleash creative energies that intensify and sensitize our experiences, and to heighten spirituality through the exploration of our deepest feelings. Since the Old Testament scribes first penned the erotically haunting "Song of Songs," writers have used the sexual experience as a metaphor to convey the ineffability and transcendence of wo/man's deepest spiritual feelings. Poets such as Gloria T. Hull and Barbara Chase-Riboud use spirit language—words like "holy," "saint," and "church"—to suggest the metaphysical power of the erotic, while Kalamu Ya Salaam writes

> i enter your church
> you receive my offerings
> our screaming choirs merge

Poets search for a language that expresses the transcendence of those merged choirs, of that holy "coming-together." Lemuel Johnson writes of "sudden ecstasies," while Nelson Estupiñán Bass describes "the nectar of madness unrestrained" and Opal Palmer Adisa speaks of "enrapturing / falling / falling . . ." "Ecstasy," "madness," "rapture": words that evoke strong emotion, intense bliss or beatitude, rapturous delight, a mystic or prophetic trance, and a state of being beyond reason and self-control. Writers like Beryl Gilroy, Afua Cooper, S. D. Allen, and Dennis Brutus feel for words and images to convey the ineffability of that transcendent experience.

In the excerpt from her novel *Say Jesus and Come to Me,* Ann Allen Shockley underscores the relationship between the sacred and the secular, the spiritual and the erotic, as she describes the sexual power of the charismatic female minister. The sexual dynamic undergirding religious experiences—shouting, dancing, getting happy—is evident in the historical Black church, and scholars suggest that this phenomenon has its roots in African culture, which celebrates the whole person: physical, intellectual, and spiritual. Charles Blockson, in his essay "The Blacker the Berry, the Sweeter the Juice," cites works which treat the African roots of Black erotica. While in another vein, Thelma Balfour reads astrological sun signs—an ancient African art—to predict which creative, innovative, and downright kinky folk will swing from the rafters and hang mirrors on the ceiling; the sage knows that a Leo is a tiger in bed, a Scorpion is obsessed by sex, and a Sagittarian is adventurous and free-spirited.

The spirit comes, unleashing the divine within, while the saint chants her song of songs:

> Flow with me—
> or hold us crowning under—
> chanting like the saint you are

(Gloria T. Hull, "Saint Chant")

Saint Chant

Gloria T. Hull

Against your black shoulder
body quirky as a woman's

Muffled, still
picking responsibility from apple vines
heavy as stones
I take the weight

You can't bear it
can't bear me
opening like dark-thighed marble
pouring rivers oceans seas
sucking you in
and under—

primeval nightmares
men have always had:
the disappearance of the bone
annihilation of the self

in a swirl of blood
flooding

Look
I can't help this love
can't harness my passion

Flow with me—
or hold us drowning under—
chanting like the saint you are

The Seal

Barbara Chase-Riboud

Stranger when you place your delicate hands on me write your dreams on my left side undo my hair suddenly and for no good reason stranger when you place your mouth hot as Alexandrian sand that cools my parched throat like well-water place your mouth on my mouths one and then the other until I taste myself stranger when you weight my flesh desperately burden it politely mold it and knead it and penetrate it asking and giving no quarter stranger when you take from me that sound primordial which is silence quits me with the stealth of a rain-forest beast fleeing stranger when with a finger I trace your lips that debauched mouth (voluptuary) (you) (egoist) with that cynical left side and that right side dissolved in sensibility stranger when I tongue your breast as hard and as flat as outlaw country trail your rivers and streams your banks and valleys to my final destination stranger when your nostrils narrow your cries escape cries I extract with feral tenderness you! your arrogant silences silenced stranger when I can your face beauty-ravaged-male-body the Rector rectified done in under mine/reversed when that hour strikes I think ah well well-loved stranger when will we be friends?

Sexy Signs

Thelma Balfour

For all of you skeptics who don't believe in astrology, here's a short lesson on how you can get more than your share of orgasms just by knowing what the sun signs are of people who swing from the rafters, try innovative techniques, and like to please their partners.

ARIES, THE RAM
March 21 to April 19

Thin-skinned folks, beware of this sign! If you're skeptical about soaring with the eagles, stay away, because an Arian is not squeamish about trying anything old or new, and wants a partner similarly uninhibited.

Women, don't be surprised by a male who will lick your navel, tongue your clitoris, and ram his penis into your mouth. If you want your nipples sucked, you'll get your toes, ears, fingers, and all other extremities sucked as well. Like the Scorpion, the Arian has an insatiable appetite that few can satisfy, and once involved with this dynamic sign, there's no turning back. The more you thwart his advances, the more turned on he gets. Screams of mercy from pain he inflicts during sex just turn him on; the more you protest, the better he likes it. You name it—pulling, biting, thrusting, and spanking—he does it all.

For a man involved with an Arian woman, the sexual explosion could take place anywhere, including the back seat of a car, an office desk, or even your mother's house. Completely sensual and passionate, this woman has a voracious appetite and likes to call the shots in sex, sometimes resorting to thick ropes, leather whips, and spiked heels to gain control. These women pride themselves in giving "good head," but look out for her sharp teeth and fingernails.

Arians are physically attracted to Librans, their opposite sign, but this combination won't go far outside the bedroom. Their compatible signs are Gemini, Leo, Aquarius, and Sagittarius.

TAURUS, THE BULL
April 20 to May 21

Although there won't be any group sex or whips and chains, this sign loves sex and has an insatiable appetite. With both the male and the female, we're talking a straight fuck of the up-and-down variety.

The Taurus man prides himself on being a good lover because he sets out to master the art of lovemaking at an early age. There won't be much kinkiness with this slow, methodical lover, but the end result is a satisfying encounter. What he lacks in creativity, he makes up tenfold in his ability to "hang in there" (no pun intended) when others fall short. Men are turned on by musty odors, kisses, and light touches to the neck and throat area. They also adore large asses, preferring these to tits.

The Taurus woman is titillated by hot, wet kisses in/on the mouth and neck, and lots of sucking everywhere. Her usually flawless skin should be complimented as soon as she discards her clothes, and her body should be treated like a temple. She craves oral sex and is a master (mistress?) at giving head; although she likes to satisfy her partner, don't expect any unconventional sexual behavior until she gains your trust. Taurus women have an affinity for lesbianism (*everybody* loves a Taurus!) as well as for nymphomania because they need sex and they need it often.

Scorpio is the opposite sign of Taurus. In fact, these two can barely stay out of the bedroom long enough to eat—food, that is. Compatible signs include Cancer, Pisces, Capricorn, and Virgo.

GEMINI, THE TWINS
May 22 to June 21

The sign of the twins means two distinct personalities, so the wonderful man or woman that you had sex with last week may be a different person the next. Beware, you may be taken for a ride, but then again you may enjoy the trip. You may flirtatiously stroke the hands and arms of a Gemini, only to discover that he or she is running hot and cold at the same time. Remember, you're dealing with two distinct personalities—

one who enjoys watching his/her partner's reaction, and one who's busy analyzing his/her own performance.

Although the Gemini man often courts prostitutes and leans toward bisexuality, he gets a C for performance because he's more concerned about himself than about his partner's satisfaction. He loves kinky sex with groups because of the chance to have sex with a variety of partners. Don't be surprised by mirrors on the ceilings and walls, red and blue night-lights in the room, and an assortment of toys—penis extenders, vibrators, Ben-wa Balls—because the bed is the Gemini's playground.

The female Gemini is often the aggressor, seeking more and more satisfaction from sex. Stimulated by a vivid imagination, she too likes games and toys, but revels in spontaneity and surprise. She's curious rather than kinky, and is easily aroused by body odors: semen, perspiration, soiled sheets.

Signs compatible with Gemini include Aquarius, Leo, Libra, and Aries.

CANCER, THE CRAB
June 22 to July 22

Moody, insecure Cancer likes to have nipples, breasts, and chest caressed and kissed. In fact, they are extraordinary kissers themselves. This should come as no surprise since they are the true romantics of the Zodiac and embody the idealized view of love and sex in that order. They wrote the book on romance, moonlight, and music, so you'll get no open, raw, mind-blowing sex. Proceed with caution.

The woman's sexual gratification is just as important to the male as his own, so let him run the show initially. Restless and idealistic, sensitive and insecure, complex and moody, he takes love seriously, so settle in for a long-term relationship. A fairly traditional lover, he's good at foreplay, lingering long and lovingly over the clitoris, which he will stroke to climax. About as kinky as he gets is to dress up in women's clothes.

The Cancer woman tends to be shy and inhibited, but, once aroused, she is capable of great passion. She likes to stroke her lover's penis and testicles, as well as to kiss the inside of his thighs before bringing him to climax. These women often masturbate or have sex with lesbians, young boys, or family members.

Compatible signs are Taurus, Pisces, Virgo, and Scorpio.

LEO, THE LION
July 23 to August 22

With Leos, you better come prepared for total submission or a less than equal relationship. And if you don't give pleasure readily, you're outta there!

Remember the symbolism here: the lion is the king of the jungle and must be treated with respect. Both sexes want to be in total control of lovemaking. Of course, they must be told how wonderful the encounter was because they are self-assured and work hard at what they enjoy. The trouble is, if you like lots of foreplay you may be disappointed, because Leos put their energy into the sexual act and the afterplay.

Once aroused, a Leo woman will take the lead and match an aggressive lover stroke for stroke. When you enter her plush boudoir, you'd better perform or you'll be thrown out of the queen's bee hive never to enjoy her "honey" again. She may be receptive to a little kinkiness because it alleviates sexual boredom, and may even use a dildo to enter her lover from behind.

Her male counterpart is a tiger in bed and doesn't like a tease; he expects his partner to be ready and willing whenever he wants her, which is most of the time. A Leo, like a Gemini, loves to screw with the lights on, not for analytical purposes, but so you can admire his body. A Leo man is the most unconventional when it comes to sticking to the rules of the "pajama game," so sit back, relax, and enjoy the erotic roller coaster ride.

Aquarius is Leo's opposite sign. This combination may work for a while as passion seeks new heights, but over the long haul it won't last. Compatible signs are Aries, Gemini, Sagittarius, and Libra.

VIRGO, THE VIRGIN
August 23 to September 22

With the Virgo, there won't be any hot, romantic, impromptu interludes on the beaches, in the back seat of cars, or in a swimming pool, but if you're looking for commitment, you've hit the jackpot!

The erogenous zones of Virgo include the stomach and lower chest, so gentle rubbing during a shower and sex will steam up any bathroom or bedroom. Virgos have an affinity for cleanliness, so a shower before sex is always a good idea. They are also realists and traditionalists who find unconventional sex contrary to their prudish nature. They're more responsive in marriage or a long-term relationship, and once they decide to have sex, the encounter is well worth the wait.

You can't jump right into bed with this sign, but don't misunderstand —these are not monks and nuns we're talking about. You won't have any wild, kinky, and crazy days or any late-night carousing in bars; sex play will be orderly, methodical, and scheduled, just like his/her life. She has some sexual hang-ups and prefers the missionary position, but she'll do a lot to please a lover and enjoys mutual masturbation.

He knows the female body and can really turn a woman on, but tends to be fairly conventional unless stimulated by an imaginative partner.

This man has good potential, but sometimes gets sidetracked into voyeurism, masturbation, and sexual obsessions.

A Virgo fits best with a Capricorn, Taurus, Cancer, or Scorpio.

LIBRA, THE SCALES
September 23 to October 23

Libra's decisiveness will drive you crazy!!!! This sign is one of the kinkiest of the kinky, especially the Libran woman. The symbolism is the scales, which usually means weighing the pros and cons of life and sex.

The Libra man has the art of making love down to a fine science, but he sometimes gets lost in the foreplay, forgetting about the "play." He will sip champagne from your navel or insert objects into your vagina and release them at the point of orgasm. But don't rush the man, because Librans love to play in bed all day and most of the night. He can be dramatic in his approach; he'll begin with an intimate candlelight dinner (which he's prepared!) and champagne, followed by a bath with you, massage, and "dessert."

The woman of this sign has unusual control of the vaginal muscles and can constrict them to bring her partner to orgasm. She'll take it slow and easy, while she explores your body. In bed, she's willing and ready to do what's needed, and she'll try anything once.

The opposite sign of Libra is Aries, and the Aries/Libra combination is "hot to trot" in the bedroom, but unless this pair comes up with something stimulating, a long-term commitment is not in the cards. They are most compatible with Leos, Sagittarians, Aquarians, and Gemini.

SCORPIO, THE SCORPION
October 24 to November 21

If you're looking for kinky sex, you've come to the right person, but you better understand what you're getting into, because there's no turning back once you're involved with a Scorpion. While most people are satisfied with two orgasms, a Scorpion wants twelve!

"Sex" is the key word here. The Scorpio man or woman is totally obsessed with it. By that I mean how to get it and more of it, how to keep it, and how to improve on it. Nothing is taboo to them, and, once aroused, they'll perform anytime and anyplace. When in bed, they mean business, and they must satisfy their insatiable appetite for sex. They will use electric devices, props, and whips without hesitation, and they love cunnilingus and fellatio. Soft caresses are out: he's an animal in bed and she'll scratch 'til you holler.

One male Scorpion told me that he makes preparations for sexual encounters weeks in advance, choosing just the right music and lighting.

But once intercourse begins, he enjoys six or seven encounters a night, making his companions beg for mercy. The goal of a Scorpion is to totally possess his mate, both physically and mentally, so proceed with caution. Don't tease unless you plan to deliver, because Scorpions will rape if attempts at sex are thwarted by their companions.

The Scorpio woman is daring and experimental, and she'll do anything to prolong sex, from using vibrators and dildos to popping your behind with a whip. Boring routines and methodical schedules are not her cup of tea because she brings intensity to all her sexual encounters. This woman is active in bed and likes to gain control by mounting her partner.

A Scorpion's best bet is someone born under the sign of Cancer, Pisces, Capricorn, or Virgo.

SAGITTARIUS, THE ARCHER
November 22 to December 21

Never think you can totally possess a Sagittarian. They are flirts by nature and will move from person to person without a thought. They are adventurous and free-spirited. Their erogenous zones are hips, thighs, and all areas in between.

The males of this sign are happy-go-lucky types who view sex as play. They have a liberal attitude toward life and love. I once knew a dentist who had very little sex as a teenager, so, as an adult, he saw nothing wrong with carrying on two or three affairs at the same time. Nothing embarrasses the Sagittarian; he's turned on by body odors and he loves gadgets like dildos in the bedroom. Let's get something straight now, a Sag man is his own person and will always be a bachelor even when he's married.

The Sagittarian woman loves to screw out of doors, and she prefers the man-on-top arrangement. Although she likes the appetizers, she wants to move as quickly as possible to the main course; once at the table, however, she likes to linger over the entree. She doesn't like to experiment, and frequently moves from man to man in her search for sexual gratification. Her free spirit can lead her to lesbianism and bestiality.

Compatible signs are Libra, Leo, Aquarius, and Aries.

CAPRICORN, THE GOAT
December 22 to January 19

Capricorns are self-absorbed and are more interested in the sexual act itself than in the sexual partner. They want to dominate in bed because control is important to them. Outwardly, they seem quite cold, but that's only a defense mechanism; once aroused, they are rough and sadistic—eager to use paddles, whips, or vibrators for their sexual pleasure.

A Capricorn woman doesn't like to be surprised in bed; she wants to know what to expect. And don't worry about a lot of preliminaries, because getting her aroused requires just a few nibbles of the ears and navel. A traditionalist who prefers the missionary position, she can be turned on, however, by cunnilingus, but doesn't want to perform fellatio. A screamer, scratcher, biter, and spanker, she has a strong sex drive and likes prolonged lovemaking. As her partner, you're in for a very long night!

The Capricorn man prides himself on his stamina and his ability to satisfy a woman. Don't make the mistake, however, of trying to lead the goat, because he won't tolerate it. Instead, let him take the lead. This man is easily aroused when everything is in place: slow, seductive music, soft lights turned low, and an exotic setting. He can be sadistic, though, sometimes resorting to simulated rape, and he prefers to climax by anal penetration.

S/he mates best with Virgo, Taurus, Pisces, or Scorpio.

AQUARIUS, THE WATER BEARER
January 20 to February 18

Men and women of this sign are highly experimental, and will add bisexuality, homosexuality, and lesbianism to their repertoire. They move slowly in a relationship, but don't let that fool you; once these innovators of the sex world are aroused, watch out!!!! They will do anything to please their lovers, even setting their own pleasure aside in order to please their mates. Like the Scorpion, nothing is taboo to the Aquarian.

The Aquarius male can get bogged down in foreplay because he's a slow, considerate lover, but climax with him is worth waiting for. He's a "no holds barred" kind of man, who quickly gets bored with routine sex. A real doctor of love, he likes French ticklers and tasty sprays; he'll take two or three sex partners at the same time; and likes the taste of honey on the clitoris and lemon oil on the nipples.

The woman is a slow starter, but, once aroused, she's extremely creative and imaginative because she loves variety. She is very sympathetic and giving in a relationship, so is sometimes attracted to impotent men, lonely women, and unhappy husbands. Idealistic and courageous, she is the most sexually liberated of women, and will do anything and everything for love. In a relationship, she is very tender, warm, and compassionate; consequently, she is often exploited by men who misread her romantic nature.

The Aquarian is drawn to those born under Aries, Gemini, Sagittarius, and Libra.

PISCES, THE FISH
February 19 to March 20

Pisceans enjoy sex to the fullest: they are very creative in bed and are most cooperative in trying innovative types of sex. They will do just about anything short of death to please their partners. Their apparent shyness and timidity is only a front, for, once the doors are closed, they'll take you on the adventure of a lifetime. On the darker side, Pisceans sometimes join sex cults, become prostitutes, or engage in long-term master/slave relationships.

Attractive, intelligent, and charismatic, the male is extremely passionate, self-indulgent, and sensitive to others. Although he likes to take the lead in bed, he likes an experienced, sexually demanding woman who will make all of his erotic fantasies come true. He's definitely a foot man; a mate will drive him wild by massaging his feet and sucking his toes.

The Pisces woman is sexually liberated and will do anything—wear outrageous costumes, endure bondage, give a tongue bath, lie under a "golden shower"—to please her lover. Easily turned on by exotic settings and erotic games, she is a passionate woman who enjoys sex to the fullest and will sometimes use her body to get what she wants.

Capricorn, Taurus, Cancer, and Scorpio are compatible signs.

Haiku #79

Kalamu Ya Salaam

i enter your church
you receive my offerings
our screaming choirs merge

sudden ecstasies in lefthanded places (whatever the traffic will bear)

Lemuel Johnson

"Come 'ere, boy, you sweeter than ripe mango in a mash up place."
—Matilda's Corner (Kingston)

I have already mentioned that a certain Avilón de la Vega was the first man to make sugar in Cuba.
—Padre BARTOLOMÉ DE LAS CASAS

I

Too far west you reach west
an then the place rise an come
after a fumble
like sudden ecstasy
in a lefthanded place

too much blood about the heart
an the business must finish
    bull daft with jubilation—
but if we lick an lick the fingers of two hands,

an more,
—well then the business must finish in beauty!

somethings there are will touch you an pass
like breeze only in a bone flute;
but too much meat, an wet cane
will rise an reach bone; it will come
an nest so, an lie, in a cavity vexing sweet
under the naked leg
of a man deaddrunk in his heart

then is when God's own body turn to juice,
like a watering of disorder
sour with lunacy and love

then is where
even god's radiant self have a feeling
when sugar come in cane
an tantalize heart pain an loose muscle
an make a man forget
dead people are dead meat,
that stone an star can't sing
a note
when night fall in matilda's corner

II
unnerve
vexatious
the woman's self also forget
how,
not worrying the wound
with a crotchful of tales,
how she keep vigil on daylight itself
—an how her flesh dry up so
each day
in love's parenthesis
between night and night!

but night fall as she bend
over, there where corner meet corner,
to make even cane brake taste like sugar;
an she say,
              "come 'ere, boy, come hard

you sweeter than ripe mango
in a mash up place."

she can make her body's self again
intact in all its parts
like sweet desolation come in a tight place.
an when she put her mind to it too
    I tell you
the woman conquer god deadcrazy
there where she sing us out
of canebrake an jerusalem.

From *Say Jesus and Come to Me*

Ann Allen Shockley

Travis's fingers interlocked with Myrtle's, a peach glaze over dark caramel. The touch was like a warm glove. Because she did not want Travis
to feel her tremble, Myrtle withdrew her hand. Going into her minstrel
routine, she quipped: "Why, chile, don't y'all know all us black women
'spose to be strong!"

"Strong for our men," Travis bantered back. "Only we're weak in that
strength, or else we wouldn't be taking so much dirt from them. Like I
took from Rudy." Travis ran a finger up and down the stem of her glass.
"But that's all over. No more Rudy's—no one. I guess that I'm like
Agnes now."

"You have the joy of *yourself.*"

"And you!" Travis smiled. "But look who you have—all those people
in your church who worship you. Why Heavenly Delight simply adores
the ground you walk on."

"I furnished Heavenly Delight a way to a new life."

Travis looked mischievous, face impish. "Did your father have all the
sisters in the church crazy over him? Most preachers do."

"They liked him." Her father handled the Jezebels delicately, suc-
cumbing to a mere few discreet liaisons. This she later came to understand. Men in the public view constantly had women after them, and

being men, they could only withstand so much female pressure. She knew he loved her mother. That was the most important thing.

"Knowing men, what do you do when they make passes at you? As attractive as you are, I'm sure they do."

Myrtle shrugged. "I ignore them, or if the pass is too gross, I handle it with divine diplomacy," she laughed.

Travis finished the contents of her glass, as if for courage, before posing the next question. "You welcome gay people into your church. Have any women made passes at you?"

Myrtle's face grew guarded. "Occasionally."

"This morning, when I was in your arms"—Travis hesitated, seeming flustered—"I felt something that I hadn't before for a . . . woman."

Myrtle's composure was of stone, not wanting to break the flow of words, an enlightening discourse of self-revelation.

"I was . . . well . . . sexually aroused by you." At Myrtle's silence, she asked quickly, apologetically, "Am I being offensive?"

"No, you are not," Myrtle said softly. How could Travis offend when she was saying at last exactly what Myrtle wanted to hear? But don't pounce too soon, she warned herself, because it may not yet be the time to cross the waters. Assume the role of counselor. "Sermons can sexually stimulate people, for they appeal to the emotions as well as intellect. This in turn can project to the listener a physical attraction for the minister."

"What does it do for you?" Travis turned fully to face her, eyes wide. With the movement, the loosely tied robe fell apart, exposing a mound of breasts enclosed in a web of lacy pink brassiere. "I had a feeling you—you felt like I did. The way you held me."

Looking everywhere but at Travis, Myrtle was tense. "I, too, am human, my dear. Ministers aren't icons, as I have told you. We go to the bathroom, eat, sleep, and make love like everybody else. People believing that ministers are an earthly deity is one of our major problems. Look at the priests and nuns who defect. They know they are not. For me to say I wasn't excited by you would be untrue. I was."

"Hey—" A tiny smile tagged Travis's lips as she reached for Myrtle's hand again. "I have a feeling we're wasting a lot of time, aren't we?" Moving closer, she brushed her lips across Myrtle's cheek, a touch light as wind. "Why don't we hold each other?" A weak beckoning in a tight moment.

Myrtle drew Travis into her arms, as Travis's head made a nest on her shoulder. Gently Myrtle's fingers traced caressing flights from the nape of her neck to tangle in the underbrush of her hair. Travis was warm earth against her, a miracle of perfume, softness, and woman. Tentatively she lifted Travis's face to scan the amber slanted eyes brimming with brightness. Myrtle's fingers traced the pattern of Travis's nose which broadened gracefully at the nostrils, and the gentle curve of her full lips.

"You are gorgeous," Myrtle breathed, misting kisses of flower petals over Travis's face. She hovered at the corners of her mouth before matching their lips as one and the same together.

Travis emitted a low moan, closing her eyes and tightening her arms around Myrtle's neck. The kiss was long, deep and exploring, wonderfully new and fresh to them as first lovers' kisses can be.

Myrtle contoured her face between the groove of Travis's breasts, inhaling the woman-smell of sweetness and salty dampness. "I want to take you to bed. To get closer, to cradle, to feel, and to love." She could hear Travis's heart beating unsteadily in her ear, a wee outcry of its own.

"I want you to!" Travis inhaled a hiss, hugging her in delight.

Turning on the bedlamp, Myrtle shakily pulled back the covers. When Travis started to undress, Myrtle stopped her with, "No—let me, please."

Tenderly Myrtle began to disrobe her, pausing to kiss, nibble, and lick unexpected places on bare flesh. Travis had a mole on her right shoulder blade which Myrtle now sucked gently. Hands deftly unfastened the flimsy tissue of brassiere to make the pendulous breasts fall freely in view. Myrtle bent, kissed and tongued the eye of each brown nipple. Easing down the sheer lattice of panties, she uncovered the coarse black curly bush of hair securing the Venus of loving. Lying her down on the bed, Myrtle withdrew momentarily to undress herself, keeping her eyes a rivet of flame on Travis.

Nude now too, Myrtle slid down beside Travis, rolling over to let their breasts touch. Travis's hands moved to Myrtle's hair, shaking loose the bun. "I've never seen it loose." The waves of Myrtle's hair fell like a shawl across her shoulders and around her face. "My Indian part," she teased.

Nuzzling Travis's nose in an Eskimo kiss, Myrtle laughed. "Black folks have everything in them."

Travis wrapped her arms around Myrtle. "I want your mouth again. It's so soft." Myrtle's lips made tickling brush movements painting Travis's mouth before she kissed her hard, rocking her head from side to side, hands roaming a venturesome route along Travis's copious body. She caressed the broad stomach and thick, luscious thighs. The whole of Travis was a plunging, plush cushion where she sank into a gorge of pliable curves.

"I want you to like it," Myrtle said low, voice an intimate stroke. "I have wanted to do this with you for a long time." Myrtle blew a loop of warmth into her ear. "We'll do it this way—first." Her fingers tangled below in the moist crevice of Travis, sliding into the pit of her.

"God-d-d—" Travis gasped, closing her eyes to the pulsating hotness flooding her.

Myrtle straddled the swell of her hips to couple the lower lips of Travis with her own. Here their bodies met in slow, cyclone movements, pelvis joining pelvis in love. Travis's legs clamped Myrtle as she moaned in ecstasy, face a distorted peekaboo of pleasurable sexual pain between the strands of Myrtle's hair. The ache of loving swelled through them like a heated saber, swathing wounds of flame.

"Is it good?" Myrtle rasped between clenched teeth.

"Ah-h-h, yes-s-s!"

In a few moments, a song of gratification burst from them in a paroxysm of bliss. Travis cried out first, squeezing Myrtle with a clasp of steel. Then Myrtle answered in mutual intensity, her exaltation a volcanic quake which subsided into a whimper.

They lay in a heaven of their own, the sweat between them like paste, cementing them together for a nirvana in time. Suddenly Travis strained upward, hips seeking Myrtle's once more. "I can't get enough of you!"

Myrtle responded by moving in rhythm anew with her. "Nor I you—"

Travis made small kitteny sounds in Myrtle's ear as the body movements of woman loving woman in a special way submerged them in the climax of Sapphic paradise. Drained, but happy in their discovery, they went to sleep braided in arms of love.

Before the early threads of dawn, they awakened to the wonderment and enchantment of each other. Travis's lips pressed a diamond into the hollow of Myrtle's neck, stirring her. Myrtle smiled, moving an arm slightly stiff from cradling Travis's head on her shoulder.

Travis ran a hand over the thin, flat plane of Myrtle's long body, fingers traversing the black woman's smooth regions of firm, straight back, tight buttocks, and tapered thighs. Myrtle had the lithe body of a dancer. Palming the two round cheeks, Travis wove an experimental finger between the cleft of them. "This is the first time I've made love with a woman."

Trembling, Myrtle's voice sounded trapped. "You *are* learning fast!"

"It's coming naturally to me," Travis said, moving deeper into her. "I know what *I* like. This in turn helps me to know what you want, doesn't it?"

Myrtle hid her face in the curly bush of Travis's hair, the scent of the coconut oil she used a sachet of sweetness.

"Lying here like this close to you is like being next to satin. Your body is so sleek, silky and soft. I didn't realize what making love to a woman could do to you!"

"Don't go crazy and try it with everybody," Myrtle warned facetiously.

Hugging her in elation, Travis laughed. "It's made me hungry!"

Myrtle sat up. "What would you like to eat?"

"Let's go to the kitchen and find out. Something washed down with the wine."

"Which is warm now. I didn't take time to put it back in the refrigerator." Getting up, Myrtle stepped over the clothes left in a lascivious hasty heap on the floor to get a bathrobe.

Watching her at the closet, Travis giggled. "Don't put anything on. Let's be nudists. It makes me feel sexy."

"Sex maniac." Myrtle indented a kiss on her forehead.

At three o'clock in the morning with the radio still playing, they sat at the chrome kitchen table under the fluorescent light and ate scrambled eggs with cheese, and toast dripping with honey butter, washed down with wine cooled by ice cubes.

When Myrtle stacked the dishes in the dishwasher, Travis came up behind her and encircled her waist, breasts velvet naked prongs titillating her back. Travis pushed her hips into the pliant globes of Myrtle's rear. "I'm obsessed with you!" she purred, coupling Myrtle's breasts and kneading them gently as she moved her hips back and forth into Myrtle's. Whispering softly, she murmured: "If I keep this up, I'll be coming again—right here!"

"Nothing wrong with that," Myrtle said, "unless you would rather do it in bed."

"Un-hun-n-n, bed! And let's take the wine." Travis licked Myrtle between her shoulder blades, making an exclusive brand of wetness.

Back in bed wrapped together in a fold of arms, Myrtle's words came out in the sponge of Travis's cheek: "I wish you didn't have to go tomorrow."

"I don't have to."

"Then stay longer with me."

"Why?" Travis taunted, laughing.

"We have just found each other—you and me."

Travis stretched to get her glass off the nightstand. The bedlamp gleamed a private glow on their warm corner. "I'll have to call Agnes."

"Yes, by all means, call Agnes," Myrtle murmured a groan. Raising her head from the pillow cushioning them as one, she said, "Give me a sip, please, darling."

"Darling—" Travis repeated, savoring the endearment. "I like that word coming from you." She drank the wine, held it in her mouth and leaned to kiss Myrtle, who drank the liquid from the fountain of Travis's mouth.

"Delicious! Filled with you."

Travis's face mirrored the contentment of a cat. "Who would ever guess that the cool Reverend Myrtle Black could be such a terrific lover?"

Myrtle nuzzled her tenderly. "I am glad you think so." She should be, from the experience with the others whom she would never tell Travis about. Maybe one or two, if asked, but not all. There were things that should be kept even from lovers. Compared to the past line of mostly transitory young and a few old things, Travis was vintage wine. "Call Agnes first thing when you get up."

"*If* I get up!" Travis laughed. "I like being in bed with you."

"My sex pot." Myrtle took the glass from her and placed it back on the stand. "Lie back and relax. We are going to do it another way," she commanded softly, moving above her and down.

"Yes, ma'am," Travis said obediently, closing her eyes with a smile on her lips.

Man to Man

Beryl Gilroy

Hiram enters his latrine and closes the door firmly.
Lord, forgive this unworthy pulpit, but in here I talks Man to Man to
you. I finds it easy to talk to you, it and me.

Extraordinary appendage to me, poor man. For that is what I truly is.
And I knows it well. My body may be despised but you is finely carved
out of the musculature of Africa.

You is self-maintaining, and easily show your "strongness" which is
God's gift to you.

You is all the power I have, all I shall ever have. You grows into terrifying size, when I least expects. Oh yes! Oh yes!

You is what boss calls stamina and I calls proud endurance.

Your sweetness overwhelms woman for she is but a vessel to receive and
contain what you bestows.

You responds to every shade of my touch and every turn of my thinking.

You answers all instructions and you endures all disappointments of life
without a murmur as I does.

You is a true seeker of satisfaction and in your young-days you was, I shame to say it, a timeserver.

You, my stalwart servant, rises to every occasion to show your skill and dexterity.

You dances to de drums and de flutes of desire. You is generous with your steps. You sings a sweet song.

You oppresses with subjugation and even with malediction. As ejaculator and procreator your mystique is boundless. Life is yours to create and you creates it either by intention or false speechification.

You is de Lord of Good Temptation. Through you maidens become women and women mothers either by surreptitious surrender or by what I calls see-and-take and boss call rape.

Your eye rest on where de penny drop but de final choice is always yours. You is majesty making me a Man, making me a King in de eyes of love.

You causes maleness to be known by such appellations as gigolo, cuckold, libertine, man, husband, fool, and even pa. But here I stands holding you, de panacea for all afflictions in my hands; and I is me—A MAN when I holds you. And I knows that I is. Neither beast of burden nor animal to fetch and heave from day-dawn to dark night. Neither is I a creature to be overworked, frightened, or wearied, so weary I cannot even motion my wife to come unto me. You is . . .

"Hiram, Hiram. Come outta there. I wan to pee now. My tail leakin," Harriet, his wife and helpmate calls out.

There is silence, then a series of unearthly moans and Hiram emerges, tears glistening on his face.

There

Opal Palmer Adisa

a candle burns
red

outside
the night   sleeps

on the sofa
where you are   dozing

i kiss
forehead
lick eyes   cheeks   nose   yearning

the refrigerator   whines
a cat   somewhere
cries a baby's need

your hands
reach   for me

turning on your side
you pull   me to you
mouths   open
greedily
breaths   explode   into breath
lips   lace   lips
tongues   circle   teeth
we   suck each other

clutching

kneading

playing a tune
with fingers and tongues

flesh and skin   meeting

the candle burns
quiet
but for the urgency
of our desire

blue lacy gown   slips
down ecru skin
green shorts   caught
tangled at feet
then freed   crumpled

the moon
watches us
through large living room windows

breaths explode
puff   out

tongue   sends shivers
from ears to back
an involuntary escaping
of air between teeth

skin   flames

cold   wetness

a cavern in the center of your stomach
for tongue to bathe

flesh against
bodies   pressed to gel

heaving

thighs give way
for you to find me

yes
i'm your woman
yes
i want you
yes . . .

naming

riding the waves
of our knowing
soaring
swirling
splashing
swelling bigger

starchy wetness

pungent

prickles   skin
irrigates   desire

holding on
enrapturing

falling
falling . . .
we tumble   out
satiated

sweat drenched
arid mouths
seek   liquid

to still our blaze
too wild
to be contained

murmur
thigh against thigh
palms on stomachs

again
we make waves

Faded Roses

Afua Cooper

The roses you bought me on that Saturday evening
in summer, have now turned a dull brown in the vase
yet, I refuse to throw them out
these faded roses . . .
Because every time I see them I remember
with sharp precision every second we spent together
last summer
the seduction of a glance
the touching of fingertips
the tip of pink tongue on soft-hard brown nipples
the way you move under me
the way you move on top of me
and the way you nibble at me greedily
it seemed we spent the summer rediscovering
the wonders of love and the delight
Then one evening you had to leave
and you gave me red roses
"to honor our passion" you said
the passion that surges in me now
as I see the faded roses
and remember you

A Single Rose

S. D. Allen

In my solitude on this eve, resisting capture by fatigue
I watch this vulnerable blood red thorn head
And contemplate how brutal, how naive it is
For love to conquer all.

I know the babe with weapon piercing heart,
The seduction in the dark with a gentle scent rising.
Dazed by desire to feel, I forget and stare,
And stroke, hold too close, and love.

Stroking this long stem softly, pains
Toiling to keep it, tires
For the perfect beauty of the guarded bloom briefly stays
Held inside my vase—then fairly fades.

Not to fret, it is truly a loss without regret
The warmth tonight will bring a flame
To light a new day once again
I turn in.

Uses of the Erotic:
The Erotic as Power

Audre Lorde

There are many kinds of power, used and unused, acknowledged or otherwise. The erotic is a resource within each of us that lies in a deeply female and spiritual plane, firmly rooted in the power of our unexpressed or unrecognized feeling. In order to perpetuate itself, every oppression must corrupt or distort those various sources of power within the culture of the oppressed that can provide energy for change. For women, this has meant a suppression of the erotic as a considered source of power and information within our lives.

We have been taught to suspect this resource, vilified, abused, and devalued within western society. On the one hand, the superficially erotic has been encouraged as a sign of female inferiority; on the other hand, women have been made to suffer and to feel both contemptible and suspect by virtue of its existence.

It is a short step from there to the false belief that only by the suppression of the erotic within our lives and consciousness can women be truly strong. But that strength is illusory, for it is fashioned within the context of male models of power.

As women, we have come to distrust that power which rises from our deepest and nonrational knowledge. We have been warned against it all our lives by the male world, which values this depth of feeling enough to keep women around in order to exercise it in the service of men, but which fears this same depth too much to examine the possibilities of it within themselves. So women are maintained at a distant/inferior position to be psychically milked, much the same way ants maintain colonies of aphids to provide a life-giving substance for their masters.

But the erotic offers a well of replenishing and provocative force to the woman who does not fear its revelation, nor succumb to the belief that sensation is enough.

The erotic has often been misnamed by men and used against women. It has been made into the confused, the trivial, the psychotic, the plasti-cized sensation. For this reason, we have often turned away from the exploration and consideration of the erotic as a source of power and infor-mation, confusing it with its opposite, the pornographic, but pornogra-phy is a direct denial of the power of the erotic, for it represents the suppression of true feeling. Pornography emphasizes sensation without feeling.

The erotic is a measure between the beginnings of our sense of self and the chaos of our strongest feelings. It is an internal sense of satisfaction to which, once we have experienced it, we know we can aspire. For having experienced the fullness of this depth of feeling and recognizing its power, in honor and self-respect we can require no less of ourselves.

It is never easy to demand the most from ourselves, from our lives, from our work. To encourage excellence is to go beyond the encouraged mediocrity of our society is to encourage excellence. But giving in to the fear of feeling and working to capacity is a luxury only the unintentional can afford, and the unintentional are those who do not wish to guide their own destinies.

This internal requirement toward excellence which we learn from the erotic must not be misconstrued as demanding the impossible from our-selves nor from others. Such a demand incapacitates everyone in the pro-cess, for the erotic is not a question only of what we do; it is a question of how acutely and fully we can feel in the doing. Once we know the extent to which we are capable of feeling that sense of satisfaction and comple-tion, we can then observe which of our various life endeavors bring us closest to that fullness.

The aim of each thing which we do is to make our lives and the lives of our children richer and more possible. Within the celebration of the erotic in all our endeavors, my work becomes a conscious decision—a longed-for bed which I enter gratefully and from which I rise up empow-ered.

Of course, women so empowered are dangerous. So we are taught to separate the erotic demand from most vital areas of our lives other than sex. And the lack of concern for the erotic root and satisfactions of our work is felt in our disaffection from so much of what we do. For instance, how often do we truly love our work even at its most difficult?

The principal horror of any system which defines the good in terms of profit rather than in terms of human need, or which defines human need to the exclusion of the psychic and emotional components of that need—the principal horror of such a system is that it robs our work of its erotic value, its erotic power and life appeal and fulfillment. Such a system reduces work to a travesty of necessities, a duty by which we earn bread or oblivion for ourselves and those we love. But this is tantamount to blinding a painter and then telling her to improve her work and enjoy the act of painting. It is not only next to impossible, it is also profoundly cruel. As women, we need to examine the ways in which our world can be truly different. I am speaking here of the necessity for reassessing the quality of all the aspects of our lives and of our work, and of how we move toward and through them.

The very word "erotic" comes from the Greek word *eros,* the personification of love in all its aspects—born of Chaos, and personifying creative power and harmony. When I speak of the erotic, then, I speak of it as an assertion of the lifeforce of women, of that creative energy empowered, the knowledge and use of which we are now reclaiming in our language, our history, our dancing, our loving, our work, our lives.

There are frequent attempts to equate pornography and eroticism, two diametrically opposed uses of the sexual. Because of these attempts, it has become fashionable to separate the spiritual (psychic and emotional) from the political, to see them as contradictory or antithetical. "What do you mean, a poetic revolutionary, a meditating gunrunner?" In the same way, we have attempted to separate the spiritual and the erotic, thereby reducing the spiritual to a world of flattened affect, a world of the ascetic who aspires to feel nothing. But nothing is further from the truth. For the ascetic position is one of the highest fears, the gravest immobility. The severe abstinence of the ascetic becomes the ruling obsession. And it is one not of self-discipline but of self-abnegation.

The dichotomy between the spiritual and the political is also false, resulting from an incomplete attention to our erotic knowledge. For the bridge which connects them is formed by the erotic—the sensual—those physical, emotional, and psychic expressions of what is deepest and strongest and richest within each of us, being shared: the passions of love, in its deepest meanings.

Beyond the superficial, the considered phrase "It feels right to me" acknowledges the strength of the erotic into a true knowledge, for what that means is the first and most powerful guiding light toward any understanding. And understanding is a handmaiden which can only wait upon, or clarify, that knowledge, deeply born. The erotic is the nurturer or nursemaid of all our deepest knowledge.

The erotic functions for me in several ways, and the first is in providing the power which comes from sharing deeply any pursuit with another person. The sharing of joy, whether physical, emotional, psychic, or intellectual, forms as a bridge between the sharers which can be the basis for understanding much of what is not shared between them, and lessens the threat of their difference.

Another important way in which the erotic connection functions is the open and fearless underlining of my capacity for joy. In the way my body stretches to music and opens into response, hearkening to its deepest rhythms, so every level upon which I sense also opens to the erotically satisfying experience, whether it is dancing, building a bookcase, writing a poem, examining an idea.

That self-connection shared is a measure of the joy which I know myself to be capable of feeling, a reminder of my capacity for feeling. And that deep and irreplaceable knowledge of my capacity for joy comes to demand from all of my life that it be lived within the knowledge that such satisfaction is possible, and does not have to be called *marriage*, nor *god*, nor *an afterlife*.

This is one reason why the erotic is so feared, and so often relegated to the bedroom alone, when it is recognized at all. For once we begin to feel deeply all the aspects of our lives, we begin to demand from ourselves and from our life-pursuits that they feel in accordance with that joy which we know ourselves to be capable of. Our erotic knowledge empowers us, becomes a lens through which we scrutinize all aspects of our existence, forcing meaning within our lives. And this is a grave responsibility, projected from within each of us, not to settle for the convenient, the shoddy, the conventionally expected, nor the merely safe.

During World War II, we bought sealed plastic packets of white, uncolored margarine, with a tiny, intense pellet of yellow coloring perched like a topaz just inside the clear skin of the bag. We would leave the margarine out for a while to soften, and then we would pinch the little pellet to break it inside the bag, releasing the rich yellowness into the soft pale mass of margarine. Then taking it carefully between our fingers, we would knead it gently back and forth, over and over, until the color had spread throughout the whole pound bag of margarine, thoroughly coloring it.

I find the erotic such a kernel within myself. When released from its intense and constrained pellet, it flows through and colors my life with a kind of energy that heightens and sensitizes and strengthens all my experience.

We have been raised to fear the *yes* within ourselves, our deepest cravings. But, once recognized, those which do not enhance our future lose their power and can be altered. The fear of our desires keeps them suspect and indiscriminately powerful, for to suppress any truth is to give it strength beyond endurance. The fear that we cannot grow beyond whatever distortions we may find within ourselves keeps us docile and loyal and obedient, externally defined, and leads us to accept many facets of our oppression as women.

When we live outside ourselves, and by that I mean on external directives only rather than from our internal knowledge and needs, when we move away from those erotic guides from within ourselves, then our lives are limited by external and alien forms, and we conform to the needs of a structure that is not based on human need, let alone an individual's. But when we begin to live from within *outward,* in touch with the power of the erotic within ourselves, and allowing that power to inform and illuminate our actions upon the world around us, then we begin to be responsible to ourselves in the deepest sense. For as we begin to recognize our deepest feelings, we begin to give up, of necessity, being satisfied with suffering and self-negation, and with the numbness which so often seems like their only alternative in our society. Our acts against oppression become integral with self, motivated and empowered from within.

In touch with the erotic, I become less willing to accept powerlessness, or those other supplied states of being which are not native to me, such as resignation, despair, self-effacement, depression, self-denial.

And yes, there is a hierarchy. There is a difference between painting a back fence and writing a poem, but only one of quantity. And there is, for me, no difference between writing a good poem and moving into sunlight against the body of a woman I love.

This brings me to the last consideration of the erotic. To share the power of each other's feelings is different from using another's feelings as we would use a Kleenex. When we look the other way from our experience, erotic or otherwise, we use rather than share the feelings of those others who participate in the experience with us. And use without consent of the used is abuse.

In order to be utilized, our erotic feelings must be recognized. The need for sharing deep feeling is a human need. But within the European-American tradition, this need is satisfied by certain proscribed erotic comings-together. These occasions are almost always characterized by a simultaneous looking away, a pretense of calling them something else, whether a religion, a fit, mob violence, or even playing doctor. And this misnaming of the need and the deed give rise to that distortion which results in pornography and obscenity—the abuse of feeling.

When we look away from the importance of the erotic in the development and sustenance of our power, or when we look away from ourselves as we satisfy our erotic needs in concert with others, we use each other as objects of satisfaction rather than share our joy in the satisfying, rather than make connection with our similarities and our differences. To refuse to be conscious of what we are feeling at any time, however comfortable that might seem, is to deny a large part of the experience, and to allow ourselves to be reduced to the pornographic, the absurd.

The erotic cannot be felt secondhand. As a Black lesbian feminist, I have a particular feeling, knowledge, and understanding for those sisters with whom I have danced hard, played, or even fought. This deep participation has often been the forerunner for joint concerted actions not possible before.

But this erotic charge is not easily shared by women who continue to operate under an exclusively European-American male tradition. I know it was not available to me when I was trying to adapt my consciousness to this mode of living and sensation.

Only now, I find more and more women-identified women brave enough to risk sharing the erotic's electrical charge without having to look away, and without distorting the enormously powerful and creative nature of that exchange. Recognizing the power of the erotic within our lives can give us the energy to pursue genuine change within our world, rather than merely settling for a shift of characters in the same weary drama.

For not only do we touch our most profoundly creative source, but we do that which is female and self-affirming in the face of a racist, patriarchal, and anti-erotic society.

At Sixty

Dennis Brutus

Even at sixty
as sap leaps with the spring,
lust flames in my blood.

All in Good Taste

Nelson Estupiñán Bass

Translated by Lemuel Johnson

You should, my love, let me have you all in good taste
naked: strip you piece by piece down, if you please,
to where, your beauty exposed, I would have you
laid back against the earth, tree branch and sky above

Mangos that they are, just let me suck at your breasts,
take into myself, drop by drop, the sweetness that you are
mounted, let me celebrate you with the nectar of madness
unrestrained, at the curve and the hollow of your waist

You'll see, then, and very much in good taste, too
how your body shivers and turns under tongues of fire,
how a sword cuts a softsweet path through your defenses.

Past those hidden locks, and full force, you'll feel
how my sperm surges upward, a flood that reaches
its overflow at the ramparts of your high walls

African-American Erotica and Other Curiosities: "The Blacker the Berry, the Sweeter the Juice . . ."

Charles L. Blockson

I began my erotic book collecting in earnest in 1968. I was browsing through a pile of what looked to be uninteresting books at the annual Bryn Mawr College book sale in Princeton, New Jersey, when a small pile of books tied together caught my eye. They turned out to be a first edition of *Pinktoes* by Chester Himes, Robert Gover's *One Hundred Dollar Misunderstanding,* and Chaucer's *Unabridged Dictionary.* I was very excited by my find and curious as to why the books were tied together. When I asked the saleswoman, she patiently explained that the books came from the estate of a former Princeton professor.

I soon realized that I could combine two areas of collecting. Unlike my Afro-American collection, which threatened to overflow the rooms in my house, erotica took up a small space. I didn't seek these items with the same passion that I sought my Afro-American books, yet they continued to fascinate me. Part of the excitement in assembling a Black collection is its variety. If you are a true bibliophile, collecting erotica is part and parcel of that endeavor. But for me, finding erotica by, and/or about participants in the African diaspora is like finding that perfect, extra-sweet berry at the bottom of the vine, close to the earth. I am reminded of just those sentiments every time I read Harlem Renaissance writer Wallace Thurman's sensational book, *The Blacker the Berry.* In his first novel, published by Macauley in 1927, Thurman uses the familiar folk saying to illustrate the wrongs perpetrated against dark-skinned women because of their alleged overwrought sexual abilities and proclivities.

Collecting erotica is an appreciation of the lyrical sights and sounds of the written word used to express the fullness and the beauty of the meaning of sex and its consequences. Collecting erotica remains one of the best-kept secrets among collectors, scholars, and booksellers. Those with money and those in the know have always had access to these clandestine treasures of literature. Many of these works were long hidden in private rooms of major literary institutions throughout the world, including the Vatican Library in Rome. Prominent Italian families like the Borgias and the Medicis collected erotica and had the power to impound whatever treasures they wanted.

In his *A Rare Book Saga,* bookdealer Hans P. Kraus noted that erotica has always appealed to collectors even when it was banned, sold under the counter or mailed in plain wrappers. Often writers of erotica use pseudonyms, and the real names of authors remain, in some instances, unknown. Moreover, large collections of these gems repose today on restricted shelves in major libraries throughout the world.

People who have collected erotica in the past have done so secretly, because they risked prosecution or public scorn. Today, however, collectors are, so to speak, coming out of the closet. Society has become somewhat more open with its views. Collectors can now talk about their acquisitions with a certain amount of pride.

As a collector of African-American books, prints, and pamphlets, I have become acutely aware of the difficulties involved in purchasing Black erotic literature for my collection; erotic works written by Blacks are far more scarce than are erotic works by Whites. Certainly other collectors have shared an experience similar to mine, because in some instances so few copies of a known work exist. Such is the case with Alexander Pushkin's exceedingly rare twenty-three-page *Gavriliad,* bound in half-black moroccon leather. Several years ago I had the remarkable good fortune to purchase this erotic poem in Austin, Texas, for five hundred dollars. Dealing with the impregnation of the Virgin Mary in a frivolous fashion, this book was never printed in Russia before the Revolution, and the only known copy in Russia was in Lenin's personal library.

A few words might be said about the type of Black erotica that can be found in my collection. I include anthropological, ethnographic, and scientific literature. I have the works of Jacobus Sutor as well as *Black Eros* by de Rachelwitz. I have in my collection the book *African Nights, Black Erotic Folk Tales* by the noted anthropologist Leo Frobenius. Also included are works of fiction such as *Dolly Morton or Queenie,* which involves interracial sex in the 18th century. I also collect literature pertaining to pimps and whores. For instance, I have collected all of the works of Robert Beck, better known as "Iceberg Slim." Author Susan Hall's *Gentleman of Leisure* is the true story of a professional pimp. Three of the contemporary jewels in my collection are Léopold Sédar Senghor's *African Sojourn,* Robert Mapplethorpe's *Black Book,* and Geoffrey Holder's *Adam.*

Eroticism is as old as humankind itself. Since the beginning of time, the ancients looked upon eroticism as natural and life-giving. In the ancient civilizations of Egypt, China, India, and Persia, eroticism was an integral part of the culture. Greco-Roman culture also adopted eroticism as a form of expression.* I recall my visit to Pompeii and the impact of the erotic renderings that nature had preserved.

In my collection I have many books on eroticism in Western culture. For example, Charles Baudelaire was so taken by the beauty of a Black woman, Jeanne Duval, that he immortalized her in his masterpiece *Les Fleurs du mal.* In his poem "Sed Non Satiata," Baudelaire wrote:

> Bizarre Deity, dark as infernal nights,
> Whose perfume mixes with musk Arabian
> Work of some Obi, Faustus, that learned man
> Sorceress of ebony thighs, Child of midnights.
> I prefer to all things, opium and the night.
>
> Thy mouth's elixir, strange as a Pavane:
> When towards thee my desires in a caravan
> Pass thine eyes, vent-holes of thy soul's shame.
> Oh pitiless Demon, pour on me less flame;
> I am not the Styx to embrace thee nine times, nay . . .

Napoleon Bonaparte's favorite sister, Pauline, one of the classic beauties of her time, was known for her amorous behavior. While gazing upon Antonio Canova's most popular nude sculpture of her in Rome's Villa Borghese, I recalled her fascination with Black men. Some of the writers of Napoleon's era claimed that she had affairs with several prominent men of African descent. Among those are General Alexandre Dumas, father of the novelist; Henri Christophe, king of Haiti; Alexandre Pétion; and Paul, her valet de chambre.

The Duke de Pasquier, Napoleon's chancellor, wrote: "She, like Josephine, had a lusty Negro to lift her into her bath." Pauline is reported to have bathed every morning in a tub filled with twenty liters of milk mixed with hot water. When teased by onlookers about her Paul, she is said to have replied, "But why not? A Negro is not a man." I would like to elaborate on my copy of A. E. Retana's book *Espejo de Pauline Bona-*

---

* Households in Greece and Rome contained Black African statuettes with erect penises as symbols of fertility and as protective charms against evil spirits. Early Christians depicted the Devil as a Black man with a large penis, who seduced Christian virgins.

parte, but his accounts of Pauline and her Black servant are far too lewd to be noted here.

It would enhance my collection if I had some of the bawdy writings of Alexandre Dumas, who had an insatiable appetite for literature, food, and women. Dumas led a life as eventful and thrilling as the lives of his characters. His lovers described Dumas as being like a force of nature. As he grew older, the prolific author amused himself by presenting his numerous mistresses with ribald epigrams and obscene poems that he had written. When a mistress was offended, he declared that "all that comes from Daddy Dumas will fetch a good price someday." I sometimes wonder what one of Dumas's ribald epigrams and poems would sell for in today's market.

Within my collection I have a number of books that describe how the early European explorers who went to Africa were smitten by the beauty of the Black woman. In the explorers' minds, these women represented wild, untutored, erotic savages. They were enthralled by the body structure of the celebrated Hottentot Venus. Brought from South Africa and exhibited nude in Europe, she was a sensation. Her voluptuous derriere set a fashion in Victorian times among White women, who, in attempting to recapture the interest of their men, adopted the bustle, which placed more emphasis on the buttocks.

I cannot resist the temptation to say a few words about Bryan Edwards, an English historian, whose erotic poem "Ode to the Sable Venus" immortalized the beauty of Black women who were brought from West Africa to the West Indies:

> O Sable Queen! thy wild domain
> I seek and court thy gentle reign
> So soothing, soft and sweet
> Where melting love, sincere delight
> Fond pleasure, ready joys invite
> And unpriced, rapture meet!

My subject is Erotique Noire, so I do not feel the slightest bit uncomfortable in leaping from Europe to the Middle East. Black eroticism appeared in many Arabian tales, such as the famous pieces in *The Arabian Nights,* translated by Sir Richard Burton, the notorious English explorer, linguist, and anthropologist. Burton was fascinated with tales such as "The Story of King Sharar and His Brothers," "The Story of the Eunuch Buhkayt," "The Man of Al Yemen and His Six Slave Girls," and "The Ensorcelled Prince," many of which deal with the sexual prowess of Black men in harems.

There have also been other stories and poems about harems, eunuchs, and lusty Blackamoors. Barbara Chase-Riboud related to me that while doing research in the Library of Congress, she found material on a Martinican woman who was taken to a harem. She used this material in her novel *Valide*, which contains erotic poetry and passages in a harem setting. Quite a different kind of text was offered to me a few years ago by a Lambertville, New Jersey, bookdealer. Who could refuse a book with the title *Black Lust?* Written by Jean De Villiot in 1931, the book was printed for private collectors of erotica, limited to 2,000 press-numbered copies, and included the following blurb: "The love and hate of a white woman for a black Mohammedan chief forms the overtone of this historic novel whose background paints the native people in the Valley of the Nile before the turn of the century. This diabolic novel is an encyclopedia of venery, a kaleidoscope of perversions, a jungle of horrors."

Another book of the genre is John Cameron Grant's *The Ethiopian*. While the style of *The Ethiopian* is somewhat stilted for modern tastes, the text is surprisingly risqué. Although written in English, the novel was published privately in Paris, in 1935. The book caused a worldwide stir because it contains, among other interesting matters, an account of a White woman who advertised for a Black lover.

Speaking of privately printed books, I have collected books illustrated by Charles Cullen, with gorgeous erotic renderings. Cullen also illustrated several books by Harlem Renaissance writers. His illustrations also appeared in Charles S. Johnson's masterpiece, *Ebony and Topaz,* published in 1927.

As I was browsing one day among the shelves in a New Haven, Connecticut, antiquarian store, my eyes, followed by my hand, alighted upon a book which some writers call America's delicious contribution to Victorian erotica. *The Memoirs of Dolly Morton* was published by the Society of Private Bibliophiles in Philadelphia in 1904. The 1899 edition of this book is very rare and often sells for more than a thousand dollars. *Dolly Morton* is the story of a remarkably beautiful young Quaker woman of Philadelphia whose travels and exploits on behalf of slaves on the Underground Railroad forced her to become the mistress of a wealthy young plantation owner and, ironically, virtually a slave herself. Written anonymously, this Victorian classic has been out of print for over fifty years. *Dolly Morton* was read avidly in an age which looked upon such explicit description as pornography.

Now, the city of Philadelphia itself has always had a reputation as a rather quiet, nonsexual sort of place. But according to my learned friend, the bibliophile Edwin Wolf, there is a publication which details houses of prostitution or joy during the antebellum period in the so-called City of Brotherly Love. "A Guide to the Stranger or Pocket Companion for the Fancy—A List of the Gay Houses and Ladies of Pleasure in the City of Brotherly and Sisterly Affection" was issued in 1849. According to Wolf, the addresses listed were located in the most respectable part of the city, known today as Society Hill. It is amusing to read that a certain Mrs.

Nelson at Sixth and Pine streets had "everything comfortable for the accommodation of married ladies, sly misses and their lovers."

The most notorious house of ill fame, according to the author, was located on South Street, above Eighth: "There is a brothel occupied by a swarm of yellow girls, who promenade up and down Chestnut Street every evening, with their faces well powdered, and strange to say, they meet with more custom than their fairer skinned rivals in the trade of prostitution. There is no accounting for taste, however, and we have no objection to a white man hugging a Negro wench to his bosom, providing his stomach is strong enough to relish the infliction."

Of considerably more importance to Philadelphia is the name of Benjamin Franklin, who possessed a many-sided mind. He drew lightning from the clouds with his kite string and key; his autobiography became the first American literary classic; and, later in his life, he spoke out boldly against slavery. Unknown to most scholars of American literature is Franklin's scatological erotic masterpiece on "Fart-hing." The ubiquitous Franklin was openly accused of keeping Black paramours in two pamphlets: "What Is Sauce for a Goose Is Also Sauce for a Gander," published in 1764, and "A Humbel Attempt at Scurrility," published in 1765. "What Is Sauce" is written in the popular political lampooning style of the day, in epithets in which the vices of an opponent were drawn out. The specific reference is to Franklin's Black maid, Barbara, whom some of Franklin's contemporaries called an illicit intimate or prostitute.

As anyone at all versed in history knows, Thomas Jefferson's relationship with Sally Hemings has long been a sticky scandal for historians and other writers, many of whom refuse to believe that it ever occurred. I believe it did, and Barbara Chase-Riboud believes it too, for her novel *Sally Hemings* became an international best-seller. Jefferson was also lampooned in a raunchy ballad, "Black Sal: Or seek in dark and dirty alley / A Mr. Jefferson's Miss Sally."

It is impossible to sort out every Black person who has written erotica, but a few deserve special mention to illustrate the variety. One great curiosity would be Beverley Paschal Randolph's unusually rare 96-page work *The Great Free-Love Trial . . . Address to the Jury, and Mankind,* published in Boston in 1872. Born in New York in 1825, Randolph claimed that his mother was the granddaughter of a queen of Madagascar, his father a Randolph of Virginia. Orphan, street urchin, sailor, self-proclaimed doctor, Reconstruction politician in Louisiana, and, by his own account, a friend of President Lincoln, Randolph was an author of mystical erotic works, according to *Allibone's Directory of Authors.* He was arrested for circulating obscene books in Boston in 1871, but was quickly acquitted. His book was his version of the trial. Printed on the wrapper cover is Randolph's motto: "Love well and wisely, but not too muchly." I am almost ashamed to admit I don't have a copy of this unique work.

Randolph's book is as scarce and as complicated as anything dreamed up by Chester Himes or Octavia Butler.

Still relatively unknown outside of bibliographic circles is the erotic writing of women. I would most like to have an original copy of Aphra Behn's *Oroonoko: or the Royal Slave.* An extremely rare novel, it would fit nicely in my Black history collection. A liberated and intelligent woman, Behn is reported to have been an Englishwoman who wrote for a living. Her coarsely written and erotic plays are said to have packed theaters in 17th-century London.

Slices of erotica can be found in many bibliographic corners. Today's Harlequin novels and others by the likes of Judith Krantz, Janet Dailey, and Danielle Steele fill the shelves of supermarkets and corner bookstores around the globe and titillate the sensibilities of scores of readers. Women read most of these books, and according to research, at least half of these readers are college-educated. A Chester County, Pennsylvania, used-book seller once said to me, "Charley, you would be surprised if I told you that a group of nuns from a local institution are among our best customers for these spicy novels!"

Women not only read erotica, they write it too. In the guise of Anne Rampling, Anne Rice, author of *Interview with a Vampire* and *The Vampire Lestat,* wrote the provocative *Exit to Eden.* The works of Anaïs Nin, Sappho, Jean de Berg, and Lonnie Barbach all hold places in the pantheon of true erotic literature, although theirs were the types of books you once read under the covers by flashlight so your parents couldn't see what you were reading.

Despite the growing competition to collect erotica, an extensive knowledge of a specialty can still reward the collector with an occasional "sleeper." I had such luck with David F. Dorr's anonymous, privately printed *A Colored Man Round the World,* which appeared in 1858. A slave in New Orleans, Dorr was sent or fled to Ohio, where he became a free man in 1851. He traveled through Europe, the Near East, and Africa. He provides his readers with some colorful anecdotes about his erotic interludes. For example, in France, Dorr saw a typical Parisian pornographic show "with a dozen beautiful women habilitated like Eve." This literary oddity is a very costly book. I will not hesitate to tell you that Dorr's book brightens the somber tone of most of my Black history acquisitions.

It is appropriate at this point to introduce the Blue Books. It has long been a recognized fact that New Orleans's famous Blue Books are among the most sought-after items by collectors of Americana, Afro-Americana, and erotica. These notorious books were just as important to the ladies of the evening as are the Blue Books that list the upper crust of society today. Yet, unlike its counterpart, *The Blue Book of the Old Guard,* the notorious New Orleans Blue Books were guides which included race and color classification such as octoroon, quadroon, and colored. Copiously documented, the guides described the houses and the special services offered by the ladies. The Blue Books were just the tonic for many tourists who were willing to spend their money to indulge their taste for illicit sex.

Similar to the Blue Books and among the most valuable additions to any collection, *The New Black Mahogany Hall* was written by an accomplished quadroon lady. Her book is astonishingly candid. One can almost smell the scent of flesh, linen, and bourbon and hear the laughter of beautiful, voluptuous women *de couleur* in this sporting house.

The mention of New Orleans takes us to Pierre Paul Ebeyer's book *The Paramours of the Creoles, a Story of New Orleans,* which recounts the methods of promiscuous mating between White Creole men and Black and mulatto slaves or free women. Published in 1944, the book could be found prominently displayed on the counters of all sorts of stores in the city. It was evidently intended for the gullible tourist trade.

Few would quarrel with Duke Ellington, who likened the Harlem Renaissance to the Arabian Nights. Anyone with a vivid response to life who was in search of erotic interludes found Harlem irresistible. One such person was R. Bruce Nugent, a popular self-conscious bohemian member of Harlem's "Talented Tenth" who was a forerunner in articulating Black gay themes. In 1926, his first story, "Smoke, Lilies and Jade," appeared in *FIRE!!,* a quarterly devoted to the younger Negro artists. One critic labeled "Smoke, Lilies and Jade" "a deliberately impressionistic piece . . . punctuated with ellipses, and vaguely pornographic and homosexual." Nugent called his story a "precious piece of folderol."

A later writer Samuel R. Delany usually confines himself to writing science fiction books, so I was elated when a New England bookdealer sold me a copy of Delany's first erotic paperback edition of *The Tides of Lust* for twenty dollars. The book is an explosive mixture of fantasy and sex whose unusual tale sweeps you along in a grip of erotic intensity. *The Tides of Lust* deserves a prime place in my erotic collection; I am happy to put it there. For example, that is where I keep my three issues of *Penthouse* magazine with their sophisticated and highly explicit renderings of Vanessa Williams, exposed during the time when she resigned as Miss America. To anyone who wants to seriously start collecting erotica, these illustrations will always be valuable because of the viewpoint of history. It may be added that these issues have practically disappeared. The same applies to the erotic drawings of Romare Bearden and other well-known Black artists.

Some years ago, the Erotic Art Book Society placed me on their mailing list, and I became an enthusiastic member of that organization. Although I realize that collecting erotica is no longer a furtive, back-door, undercover activity, I still hesitate to tell book sellers what I collect.

In the past few years, several reputable publishers have produced serious collections of erotica, but none, before now, has published a book on Black erotica. What makes *Erotique Noire* such an extraordinary book is not so much its sexual content, as the fact that it includes the poetry and prose of some of the finest writers of the African diaspora. These writers have reached within the intimate recesses of their minds and spirits to make this significant contribution to American literature, for reading *Erotique Noire* is a liberating experience.

PART THREE

Movin to the Beat

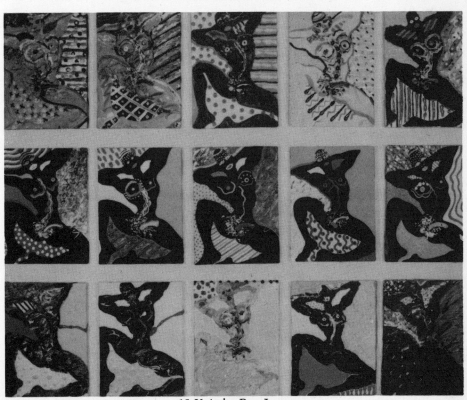

15 Units by Ben Jones

Verbs—words in motion—underscore the tempo of the moves: scatting, rocking, slipping, dancing, wiggling, kicking, spinning, singing, shaping, riding, grooving. In "Movin to the Beat," writers like Dennis Brutus, Akua Lezli Hope, and Luz Argentina Chiriboga make sounds of joy, rocking us to the edge of time, as fingers snap and bodies shake.

> On a night like tonight
> When the rhythm's just right.
> I feel the need to play . . .
> > (Lee Ben)

Can you feel the beat, the beat going on and on? Listen, and you'll feel it . . . in the air we breathe, in the songs we sing, in the way we strut: Robin swinging her hips and Prince shaking his butt in a tribal celebration of dark body moves. Aretha urges, "Rock steady, Baby, rock steady," and we do, uh-huh, we do. Ray Charles bangs out a *boop boop da doop* on the keys, and we dry-fuck, breast to breast, stomach to stomach, and thigh against thigh. Michael gyrates, lightning-quick through funky blue lights, to the syncopated vibes of drums, and we catch the rhythm of the race beneath the skin of the drums.

> My sperm bang their heads on the wall
> Of their subway like commuters
> Going mad with the current events
> > (Lorenzo Thomas)

Ann T. Greene sets the mood for this chapter, evoking the sounds and the setting of an after-hours joint—a dark, smoke-filled basement—where frenzied bodies move in the shadows:

> One note, a whole note
> > will tumble and slide
> across the lounge, catching
> > (like a bb frenzied)
> > > on the rim
> > > of my next man's ear

Onstage, a drummer plays his double congas and a stringman kicks the guitars into a two-note one-riff orbit, while Gorgeous Puddin' scats blue notes through the pillars of her teeth. We are moving now, moving to the beat of blood and the ripe fullness of "a cornucopia of tissue and muscle and juice and air and fire" (Calvin Hernton).

Hernton's Yakubu screams: "Ride me, Dew. Ride me, magnificent rider. Go on and ride me, please . . ." And she does, mounting high in the saddle, legs astride broad back, thighs clasping smooth dark flanks. Together, they jump hurdles and race over the course—*clickety, clack clickety, clack*—until they come to a stop, winded and sweating, at the end of the track. It was a fast move, Sugah!

The beat is contagious. In the corner, someone shapes kisses, his tongue moving to a familiar flicker (Dennis Brutus), his heart beating furiously in the formless, warming sound of joy that makes him holler: "Lord Lady my dungeon shakes!" Invisible drummers strum the night air, as singers blow rhymed lies into purple darkness. Lovers sway in a sensual cacophony of sound: hands clapping, feet stomping, horns wailing, pianos playing, drums beating.

Cut to Port of Spain. Midnight sky. Moonlit sea. Palm trees. Steel band. Carnival. A different kinda beat. Lord Kitchener, Scrunter, and Sparrow—calypsonians all—sing songs as innocent as Sunday-school hymns, unless you take a six for a nine:

> Sparrow, don't bite me
> Don't do that, honey
> I never had a man to ever do that to me
> Oy yo yoy yo yoy, doux doux darling
> Look me pores raise up
> You making me feel so weak
> Stop, Sparrow, stop.

Another adoring fan with a strong "musical appetite" urges Lord Shorty: "Baby, leave the needle in the groove and keep it in the center."

The music may be different. The beat is the thing!

The Sweetest Sound

Kalamu Ya Salaam

Once

You made me holler

Worse than the time
I got shot in the leg
With a thirty-eight

God, it was
Great!

Double Congas

Lee Ben, Jr.

On a night like tonight
When the rhythm's just right
I feel the need to play . . .

                              my double congas

From *Under the Skin of the Drums*

Luz Argentina Chiriboga

Translated by Stanley Cyrus

INTRODUCTION

The narrator of the novel is Rebecca Gonzalez, who lives in Sikán,* a farm on the northern coast of Ecuador. Her parents have sent her to Quito to forget Milton Cevallos, her first lover.

FIRST FRAGMENT

While Rebecca was in a girl's boarding school, Vicenta Paez, a man disguised as a woman, fell in love with her. One Sunday, when they were playing chess, he tried unsuccessfully to rape her.

I tasted the candy that Vicenta offered me and discovered that it was made of liquor: my tongue became numb and my body began to ache. Thoughts about sex and chess were intertwined. The king mounted the queen. Vicenta's hands lifted my skirt and felt between my legs. It was like the mating of the bulls and cows in Sikán. I threw the candy away. Fascinated, I watched the dogs mating. Adela, the maid, called, "Come inside. Don't look at that. It will affect you." I had a passionate urge to take off my clothes. My blood was boiling. "Let's go now, darling." We rushed to the bathroom. Seated on the toilet, Vicenta put her hands

---

* In African mythology Sikán is a voluptuous woman.

under my stockings and, with faltering strokes, pulled me down on her knees. She took out her penis. "Don't be afraid, Doll Baby. It won't hurt. You'll see that it's beautiful."

SECOND FRAGMENT

Rebecca and her school friends went out for a drive in Juan Lorenti's Mercedes-Benz. The father of one of the girls, Lorenti, tried to seduce Rebecca.

Without meaning to, I looked in the rearview mirror. His eyes met mine. I watched his gestures: he moistened his lips and smiled wickedly; he kept licking his lips. We looked at each other for a few seconds. I didn't look at him again, but I imagined that he was undressing me. First, he unbuttoned my blouse and then slipped off my skirt. As he ran his fingers down my back, I felt my blood burning. When he took off my brassiere, the nipples on my breasts stood out. Slowly, he lowered his hands, and when he reached my buttocks, he got carried away. I raised my legs and began undressing. "Rebecca," I asked myself, "when are you going back to Sikán?"

THIRD FRAGMENT

Rebecca returned to Sikán and when her mother refused to sell the farm, the girl made love to Milton out of revenge. One afternoon, when they were talking, a donkey became aroused, and then made love to Milton.

The donkey's braying, coming closer and closer, ended the conversation. Surprised, we looked at each other. We waited, motionless, in silence. The donkey poked its head through the foliage and, when it saw me, came forward, groaning pitifully and foaming at the mouth. For the first time, I faced a desperately panting animal that stuck out its phallus and stamped the ground, while spitting out a thick spermlike foam. . . When the donkey beat its breast with its penis, which got longer and harder, I mounted my horse. The only thing I could think of was to put on my mask. I trotted off on my horse, but kept thinking about the donkey. I could tell by the noise that Milton was following me. I didn't want to look; I thought he was riding the donkey. When we reached the village of El Salto, we stopped. As Milton grabbed my waist to help me alight, we could still hear the donkey braying. I didn't have the energy to fend off Milton's caress. He fumbled passionately with my breasts. Slowly, we rolled in the grass. Then I felt the mist of the earth mixed with the donkey's foam. Milton slipped off my mask, while the evening and its music waned.

FOURTH FRAGMENT

Rebecca, ashamed of having given in to Milton, broke off relations with him, but after a month she could no longer resist him and returned to El Salto.

One evening, I could no longer do without him. Desire inflamed my whole body, so I went to meet him. Without waiting for him, I threw off my clothes and ran naked into the clear waters of El Salto. Milton quickly followed me. He reached under the water and fondled my buttocks. Our pleasure intensified; we forgot our differences. From then on, the sound of the river became the background for all our amorous trysts. Aroused by the singing of the birds, we mated passionately, rolling in the grass as if bound together. When we couldn't meet in the day, we found one another at night. Milton would climb up to the flat roof, and we would make love by moonlight in my dormitory hammock; the lovemaking was different, more delightful. Milton was a wonderful lover: creative, untiring, and passionate.

FIFTH FRAGMENT
When Milton took another lover, Rebecca became involved with Father Santiago Santacruz. The priest built a secluded house near Sikán, where they made love.

When I arrived, Santiago took my arm and, so that I could go up without difficulty, led me to the window to look out at the view. He started kissing the tips of my fingers, and I did not know how or when his lips reached my breasts. He seized my shoulders roughly, as I began slowly, very slowly, to take off my blouse and slip. I threw the blouse on the floor and then lifted my leg, slipping off my skirt and everything else I had on. I picked up the skirt with the tip of my toe. I was happy now because I was repaying Milton for his mistreatment. Without realizing it, I slid my lips down to Santiago's penis. I felt him groan and tremble. Now I could forget my life with Milton. He had his lover. I had mine.

when the horn fits, blow it

Akua Lezli Hope

nipple reflex attends
your eyes eating words
rather me be spread
book flapping wings
flamingo blush, lotus flight
smoky leg trail, wax ribbon in sun
watch this ascent, swift this consumption.

Gorgeous Puddin'

Ann T. Greene

In my next life
(if I get one)
I'm coming back as
Gorgeous Puddin'.

I'm coming back
to sing
scatting blue notes
through the pillars
that are my teeth.
They'll hesitate,
blue notes will,
quavering in their need
honeyed on the vulva
that is my mouth.

One note, a whole note
will tumble and slide
across the lounge, catching
(like a bb frenzied)

on the rim
of my next man's ear
where it will tickle him
and unsettle him and
make his hands to stumble
(his fingers to splay).

They'll flutter and sigh
and long to send me
one finger.
For me, one haloed digit,
upstage, at my piano.
Here where I lay playing
with tongue heavy
and lips ready
for his love.

Taking a Six for a Nine: Sexual Imagery in the Trinidad Calypso

Keith Warner

In 1956, the calypsonian who would go on to proclaim himself Calypso King of the World, the Mighty Sparrow, won almost instant acclaim singing about Trinidadian women of easy virtue. His "Yankees Gone," popularly known as "Jean and Dinah," told of their being forced to sell their wares for almost nothing with the departure of the U.S. soldiers after the second World War. Despite the instant popularity of that calypso, it was not until several years had passed that it was played on the local radio. It was never clear whether the denial of airplay stemmed from the calypso's biting social commentary, or from the fact that Sparrow had sung, among other things, about his getting "it" all for nothing. It was widely suspected, however, that it was the risqué nature of the lyrics at that time that led to the auto-censorship practiced by the radio stations.

If the listener had to guess what the "it" was in "Yankees Gone," Sparrow left no doubt what he was singing about in his "Mae Mae," also considered too risqué for airplay in the late 50s. "Mae Mae" was also an immediate success as all lovers of this particularly Trinidadian art form bought the newly released LP record, and young and old alike sang with Sparrow:

> Making love one day
> With a girl they call Mae Mae
> I pick up Mae Mae by the railway
> And we take a taxi straight to Claxton Bay
> Before we lay down on the carpet
> She start catching fit.

But it was the chorus that caused eyebrows (if only those) to be raised:

> Sparrow, don't bite me
> Don't do that, honey
> I never had a man to ever do that to me
> Oy yo yoy yo yoy, doux doux darling
> Look me pores raise up
> You making me feel so weak
> Stop, Sparrow, stop.

What had been announced from the very first verse was thus described in somewhat graphic detail for the 50s in a colony still under British rule. Sparrow had done the unthinkable. He had actually come right out and sung about making love to a woman, describing in every detail her reaction to intercourse, telling even about the sand fly that bit him "down dey." It was unthinkable, of course, only because it was so direct. Sparrow was telling it like it was. For years calypsonians had been doing precisely the same thing, but had found every imaginable way to talk around what they were in fact describing. They had dressed up their lyrics so cleverly at times that the listening public was duped into believing it was hearing one thing when in fact it was hearing something else. It was taken in by clever double entendre. In other words, it was taking a six for a nine, as we are fond of saying in Trinidad when we have been bamboozled.

For all the directness of a calypso like "Mae Mae," Sparrow did not introduce a new era of sexuality into the art form, and, fortunately, he and other calypsonians still regaled listeners with their many imaginative ways of singing about what men and women do together. In other words, the portrayal of sexuality in the calypso continued its traditional way, and the overriding interest we have in each year's crop of calypsos comes precisely from the pleasure we derive from deciphering how cleverly we are made to take the six for the nine.

In the male-dominated world of the calypso, countless songs have dealt with women and their relationships with men, and, to be honest, the treatment of the female has not always been a pleasant one. Year after year, one hears complaints from the public that, once again, the calypsonians are denigrating their sisters by singing about their physical attributes, or lack thereof, their personal hygiene, and the like. But while some of these complaints are justified, as is evidenced by the embarrassment of many female listeners, what must also be noted is the fact that what the calypsonians are doing is celebrating sexuality and one of its offshoots.

Indeed, for all the complaining by certain sectors of the public, there can be no other conclusion but that the calypsonians have struck the right nerve when it comes to dealing with sexuality. For all the puritanical pretense that it does not like the continued emphasis on male-female interplay, the conservative sector of the public still enjoys the cleverness of a well-composed "smutty" calypso. In fact, every young calypsonian is aware of this fact, and usually has in reserve a sexually oriented number in his repertoire as a sure way of livening up an unresponsive audience.

Further, calypsonians, whose songs provide all the music played during the yearly carnival, are acutely aware of the carnival/sexuality connection. They see how carnival draws thousands of men and women into the streets; they see how scantily clad the majority of these players are as they enjoy the revelry; they see how people who normally would not give you the time of day allow themselves to be hugged by others they hardly know; in other words, they see revelers predisposed to celebrate life to the fullest, and they know that it would be futile to pretend that sex is not part of that celebration. If this were not so, why would the local Family Planning Association issue its yearly warning to "love carefully"? The simple fact, then, is that calypso and carnival are part of a climate that makes enjoyment of sexual innuendo a communal experience.

Popular calypsos quickly become part of Trinidad lore, and it is not unusual for the listener to identify with what is being sung. In fact, it is obvious that the public uses the calypso as a convenient cover, since, after all, one can always claim that one did not really say what the listener thought he or she had heard. When, a few years ago, calypsonian Crazy won the Road March—the most popular calypso sung by masqueraders during the carnival celebrations—with "Suck Me, Soucouyant,"* it was clear that as revelers sang the chorus they had something else in mind beside the vampire-like act of blood sucking by the soucouyant as mentioned in the calypso. The physical gestures that accompanied the boisterous singing of this calypso on the streets meant that those singing were able to mouth the unspoken desire for oral sex all the while remaining on the level, so to speak. And, of course, there were those who sang another word that, in the boisterousness of the moment, only sounded like "suck!"

One has, therefore, to be on the lookout for sexual imagery to crop up in the most innocent of contexts, and although, as we shall see later,

* In Trinidadian folklore, a soucouyant is a female spirit.

creativity is stretched to the limit, there are some fairly standard images that recur. Since, as we have indicated, calypso is a male-dominated arena, it is only natural that any image that could possibly allude to the phallus is used to represent the male organ doing its job. One of the most frequent is that of wood, a commonly understood term for the male organ; so that when Kitchener has his Venezuelan friend Maria comment:

> The wood here in Trinidad no wood could surpass
> Ah like how it thick and hard and how it does last

this is heard not as an observation on the country's flora, but as a comment on the virility and stamina of the local males. It naturally flatters the men's egos, but also allows the women to fantasize about sexual fulfillment.

And the alert listener can hear talk of "wood" in this sexual sense even when there is apparently no such talk, as, for example, when the woman tells her calypsonian man that she is afraid he would make good his threat to beat her if she ever deserted him. "Darling, ah fraid you would," she says. On the one hand, she means that she is afraid he would carry out the threat, but, on the other, clever distortion of phonemes allows us to hear, and to accept as quite natural: "Darling, ah fraid yuh (= your) wood." Thus, the fear of leaving the lover is not only because of the eventual battering but also because of the persistent and possibly vigorous lovemaking to which she would be subjected.

"Iron" has gained much currency for a very interesting reason. As it happens, one of the percussion "instruments" in nearly every steel band, is the discarded brake drum—the iron. Those who play this instrument are naturally called "iron men," thus allowing for a play on words between the iron man of the steel band, and the iron (the male organ, of course) a man possesses. Thus, when Lord Shorty sings of how the famous musician Corey sends women into ecstasy with his iron, we immediately hear the sexual side, and know that when a woman longs for iron, she is longing for sexual and not musical fulfillment.

Another frequent method of disguising talk of open sexuality is in the many images of water. When Lord Kitchener sang about "bathing in Miss Elsie river," it was immediately understood that he meant making love to the woman, but at times other references are not so apparent to the uninitiated. However, once one realizes that the male ejaculate is called break or break water in the islands, then a whole world of calypso interpretations opens up: Sparrow going all the way to Jamaica to "water Lucy garden," and being surprised when her husband wants his garden watered as well; Shadow suggesting that his female acquaintance's problem stems from the fact that "she garden want water"; Scrunter becoming the most popular man in the village because he is the only one with water after the water authority is forced to ration its supply, with the result that all the women beg him to "give them some water, please." Indeed, nearly any image of water being spilled or spewed forth is one of sexual activity, of ejaculation, so that the calypsonian at times stretches his imagery and creativity to the limit, as can be seen in this account of driving as intercourse:

> When I start my fast driving
> Lots of funny things start happening
> The wire cross one another
> The water hose bust loose the radiator
> Well the gearbox started a grinding
> The gear so hard I can't get it to go in
> So I pull out my gear lever
> Water fly through the muffler
> And the whole car went on fire.

To this male-oriented description is added the alleged urging of the female partner: ". . . if the radiator start to boil / don't stop till water overflow the coil." In like vein, the inability to perform sexually is often equated with a car running out of gas or not being able to start.

Clearly, any service that the male calypsonian performs for the female contains the seeds of a double entendre, whether it be cutting down a tree, digging a well, clearing a lot of land, hanging a picture. A picture? one might ask. Yes, because the female asks her male friend to hang it "in the center." Similarly, when the calypsonian performs for his female friend as a deejay, she continually exhorts him to leave the needle in the groove, to keep it in the center, obviously the place that brings the most pleasure. And when Lord Kitchener portrays himself as "the little drummer boy" and bestows thirty-two bars on his female friend, we who know what to listen for hear a much more erotic tale than one of a calypsonian satisfying the musical appetite of an adoring fan.

Yet another favorite image among the calypsonians as they describe their relationships with women is to sing about all that they do to pussycats. Of course, in this area, they are very close to their American counterparts, who use similar imagery equating the pussy with the female genitals. What is somewhat different is the extent to which the calypsonians manage to have even the women singing the decidedly derogatory lyrics in obvious enjoyment, as was the case with Kitchener's "My Pussin":

> Is my pussin, is my pussin
> I bathe her, feed her since I small
> Mister, move you' hand from dey
> Don't touch my pussin at all.

A calypso such as this catches the delicious naughtiness of the moment, and can be enjoyed by both sexes, all of which ensures the continued presence of this type of calypso in the artist's repertoire.

Variations of the sexual theme are also present. While references to homosexuality are not anathema, they are nonetheless in the distinct minority. Lord Funny sang of a certain well-known female calypsonian "bowling" with some of her friends, and this relatively innocent activity assumed graver proportions when the calypsonian deliberately stretched his pronunciation of "bowling" to sound like "bulling," it being understood that this latter term is the one used for homosexual activity in Trinidad.

The most popular variation concerns oral sex, because it is so easy to combine many of the terms used for the female genitals with terms of eating. For example, one such term for the female organ is "saltfish," once almost a staple among the poorer classes and a dish that one did not readily admit to eating because it betrayed one's poor financial status. In addition, saltfish (salted cod) usually had a pungent odor. This was a deadly combination in the hand of the calypsonians, allowing them to poke fun at both sexes: at the women for not "washing their saltfish" and at the men for "eating saltfish" anyway, for, as Sparrow says, "when you out to eat / all saltfish sweet."

In one clever mixture of sexual and racial stereotypes, Sparrow has himself envying a man from the Congo—a cannibal for all intents and purposes—because he has just caught two White women and is cooking them in a huge pot:

> I envy the Congo man
> I wish I coulda go and shake he hand
> He eat until he stomach upset
> And I . . . never eat a white meat yet.

There were the politically sensitive who criticized Sparrow for perpetrating the stereotype of the African cannibal. There could be no doubt that such prejudicial images were in the calypso. But it was also clear that the majority of those who enjoyed the song, and who in fact gave it two extremely popular lives virtually a quarter of a century apart, heard something else. They delighted in the fun being poked at the alleged prohibition of interracial sex, and interracial oral sex at that. Sparrow made it possible for many Black men in Trinidad and Tobago to sing with gusto (perhaps making the late Frantz Fanon turn in his grave) about an act they could only whisper about under normal circumstances.

Therein, I believe, lies the popularity of these calypsos. They afford the singer the opportunity not to hide, yet provide sufficient cover to allow him or her to claim that the lyrics are as innocent as Sunday school hymns. Calypsonians are fond of saying that "is the vice in their own head," and are just as quick to point out that many standard ballads on the American and British musical scene are equally suggestive. Equally suggestive I am willing to admit, but not equally imaginative. So whenever a calypso evokes peals of laughter among aficionados, and the words seem innocent at first glance, look again. Chances are the listener was led to believing only one part of what is in the song. And how does he or she come to understand and appreciate all that the artist has put in the song? By learning how not to take a six for a nine.

From *Sounds of Joy*

Lorenzo Thomas

New black music. Light. The loss
Of the Cosmos. Bending sss
Slipping their spine. Wiggle their
Heads hands up cupped to fists
For the moment to kick the guitars
Into two note one riff substantial
Orbit. Fire and water. A poor man's
Heartbreak. I see the light
Spinning around you
Through my jail windows. Ice
Hearts. I touch your black
Nipples ringed with stars
Like any cheap dancing girl
But they really are stars and
Lord Lady my dungeon shakes!
Your thigh shining like the desert dark
In the night full moon after flood
The water transmitting your name
From the black antennas of hair
Standing up for the music we make

From an astral dream
I hear the charge in the chests of invisible drummers
Telling rhymed lies in your blood
And the singer steps forth in your
Eyes wearing an aluminum dashiki
And purple bush in the cabaret light
Day creeping in your blinds
As my heart rolls down in the dirt
And my arms scream like young horny
Schoolgirls. The lump in my body
Counterfeits knots from the terrible
Priest books. Unravel. Knot again.
My sperm bang their heads on the wall
Of their subway like commuters
Going mad with the current events

Of superior worlds they cannot
Know anything more about the tortures
They have been trained up to desire.
My sister. My fingers ruffle the small
Snake coiled above your behind

As kingly mannikins might jerk their wands
The cobra wakes and strikes. My sister.
As Erzulie climbs out of her glass. Might
Moves to speak. Sout. Sout. As Isis later.
Sasa. Sasa. As the knot complains in her
Throat where the pulse lays the duppies
Our sad Christian yearning birthing our
Ancient dark African self. Sa. Sa. Sout.

As she fights me and my temple breaks
She slays me. Dancing. And I slake my heart
With the mist of her hiss in her mirror
And I rest in the dark hold of her eyes.

And the lines of my vocal extend, the hand
Moves further from the skin. The strings.
And returns less often to caress her. And
My dungeon trembles. And my body shakes.

Please. Whosoever our motions may please as we are pleased
In the ocean of our mad moment

And I am tied up in the knot of her
Escape from being an earth girl.

She becomes heaven more than stars. And stars
Of our children glisten in the dark oasis
Marked by her tangled hair. She calls me Kush.
A star our bodies' tears in her hair

This is our Mother. Her dark soft face
Shines beneath hair plaited like palm trees
Forever and ever and ever. She touches me.
She calls me by our Father's name because she

Means she loves me. She says. Shh.
Her white teeth glint in the dark sky
Of her soft heavy lips. They are like
Stars trying to learn how to dance

Untitled

Dennis Brutus

I will not agonize over you:

when my heartbeats' steady pulses
surge to an impulse to ejaculate your name
(my tongue moves to a familiar flicker)

or my muscles' tensing and thrust
mount through my body till my lips pout
shaping kisses for your imagined mouth

when all my being remembers
and exclaims my love for you—
I will be steadfast and firm,
calmly observe and quiet my mind.

I will not agonize over you.

Songs They Could Sing #789

Akua Lezli Hope

Fill me, fill me 'til i choke
felt i felt you to my throat
pressed my womb against my spine
rocked me to the edge of time

rode on to another space
lost all sense of sight and place
found a formless warming sound
wrapped and clung so tight, so round.

suddenly a starstung night
suddenly a purple sea, a dolphin dream
suddenly an azure wing
suddenly, another me.

me another and a one
being that this flight becomes
there is no earth without the sky
and no night without the sun

Dew's Song

Calvin Hernton

June 22, 1990
Lund, Sweden

Dearest Beloved, Dew:
I arrived from concert in Copenhagen and found your letter under the door of my room. I beat drum and did a dance of joy.

Copenhagen was my last performance of this very long tour. I am tired. But a great deal of money has been raised for the cause of freedom.

I wish I were with you at the Tracy Chapman concert. I have seen her only on television. I love your experience of her and your pleasure in her. I wonder why chance has not made our paths cross on these tours? Speaking of tours, you have one soon in Africa, yes? Perhaps we can meet in Ghana, however briefly. How long since we visited my grandchildren. And how is your daughter, Corianne?

I am constantly thinking of you. My body is in perpetual ferment, my belly, my bladder, my bowels, my ass, my penis, every part of me, calling out for you. I love you so much I long to play with you, for I have never played so freely with anyone before. Oh, Dew! I long to play on the fibers and sinews of your flesh, your breasts, your vagina, and every nerve ending of your magnificent ass.

Arriving Pan Am #215 from Kennedy on Monday, July 2nd, at 20 hundred hours. I love you, Dew.

YAKUBU

Helene Johnson-Jones rolled out of bed. Her bare feet landed on the cool carpet. Completely nude, she stood there momentarily dazed from having read the letter, which she still held in her right hand. She raised her left wrist and checked her watch: 4 o'clock. The odor of her vagina on her fingers excited her again, for the letter had moved her to caress herself as she read it. She licked her fingers. *Song, Song,* she sang in her mind.

Despite the air conditioning, she was moist between her legs and her body was sweaty all over. She walked across the room and stood before the mirror. She was six feet of chocolate-brown woman: a high and goodly ass, wide hips, ample breasts, long legs, and a wide crotch. Lovingly she touched herself. Then she hurried to the bathroom. She would not wait around in the house. She would bathe and dress and go to the airport, and hang out there until Yakuba arrived.

Driving out of her Philadelphia Yorktown neighborhood, heading for the highway that would take her to the airport, Helene thought about her childhood. She had lived on York Avenue in a four-room house with her mother and stepfather and three brothers and four sisters. Although she had experienced the usual poverty of a poor, working-class Black family, and the violence, and teenage pregnancy, and abortion (she was raped once and had gotten her "ass kicked" aplenty), she had somehow gotten through high school and junior college, and then through nursing school, to marry the "catch" of Metro Central Hospital, Dr. Everett Jones. They moved into a house in Germantown, where the middle-class Negroes lived. She worked alongside her husband in the hospital and in his private practice, had their daughter, Corianne; and everything went well until she expressed her desire to return to school and become a doctor herself. "Do it and we are through," Dr. Jones had said. It was not an empty threat, for as soon as she was admitted to Meharry Medical College in Nashville, Tennessee, Dr. Jones vacated their house. One house could not hold two doctors, he declared. Two years later they were officially divorced.

Helene grinned to herself. In many ways, the breakup of her marriage had been a blessing. It had not been easy, though. She had suffered wounds and scars, and she had had to single-handedly raise Corianne, who was now in graduate school. But the struggle and the loneliness had been worth it.

"Hi, Dr. H." A young Black woman waved as Helene drove past her at the intersection leading onto the airport highway.

There, amid the traffic on the highway, the physical presence of her lover invaded her senses. She felt her clitoris enlarging. She gunned the gas pedal, sending the big, air-conditioned Buick leaping toward the airport.

Heads above the crowd, Helene and Yakubu spotted each other as he came through the exit gate. Helene had trouble pushing her way through the crowd, but Yakubu snake-hipped through the crowd with great ease. Soon they were in each other's arms, kissing and pressing their bodies together with a slow imperceptible hip-grind that was spontaneous and natural. Yakubu wore one of his traditional African outfits, which looked like a labyrinth of brightly colored cloth draped over and hanging from his gangling body. Helene wore a simple knee-length, one-piece dress. That was all they wore; neither of them wore undergarments. Each had deliberately dressed in this fashion for the other. With their bodies pressed together and lips unctuously kissing, and tongues moving inside the other's mouth, they ignored the crowd at first. But to keep from becoming as wanton as the stares on the faces of the crowd, they forced themselves apart.

"So good to see you, Dew."

"You too, Song."

They embraced again. They were more controlled this time, but only so as to more deliberately experience each other. Standing eye to eye, mouth to mouth, pelvis to pelvis, Yakubu felt his penis against her pussy beneath their clothes and Helene felt that her pussy had grown big vulva lips which clasped his hardened member to her middle. "Song"—she always called him by his last name—"let's get out of here before we cause a riot," she whispered.

The walk out of the terminal took light-years; they loved every step of the way. It was so good to be the same height. They strolled with arms around each other's waist, as their high Negroid asses and hips bounced against each other. Helene saw on the faces in the crowd the lascivious stares induced by their loving manner. Why lascivious? she thought. For one thing, she and Yakubu were Black. Nobody, not even other Blacks, liked to witness such open display of sexual feelings between Black women and men, right out in public! Such shameless behavior fed into White folks' stereotypes of Blacks. Fuck white folks' stereotypes! But these two fools are old. Can't tell how old, but both of them must be at least fifty. That old dude with the receding hairline and that Amazon woman with her head half full of gray hair. How dare they carry on this way! They were not proper role models for the young.

Cupping her mouth with her hand, Helene let go with a flurry of uncontrollable giggling, "Hee, hee, hee, hee."

"What you giggling about?" Yakubu asked, kiddingly, as he un-abashedly joined her.

As they drove home, God took care of them. Yakubu twisted his body so that his head was comfortable in Helene's lap. *Song, Song,* she sighed, and wiggled, and squirmed in her seat behind the steering wheel, and slowed down, and speeded left . . . then right . . . then straight . . . then almost swiped a car in another lane. Her dress up above her hips and her naked ass braced on the cushioned seat with his head resting on her thighs, Yakubu sent his tongue licking along the inside of her secret places and deep up into her crotch, as Helene's foot kept slipping off the gas pedal. All the while, she held his penis firmly in her free hand, squeezing and stroking and milking it. Yakubu groaned and sent his tongue into her hot juicy vagina. "Song, Song," she pleaded, "we better chill out before we kill ourselves." Coming up for air, he said, "We already dead and gone to heaven."

Once home, just inside the door, they threw off their garments, and for what seemed like an eternity, they just gazed at one another, beholding the wonder that their clothes had concealed. Her body was a miracle to him. All he could do was sigh, "Dew, Dew, Dew." His body was like an athlete's, she marveled at how he kept it that way, and his penis looked like an ebony cucumber. Then Yakubu lifted Helene in his arms, feeling and caressing her flesh and her ass, as he carried her down the short stairs leading into their special room, next to Helene's clinic, where they always made love when he visited. They were cool at first, you know, ain't no big deal, playing with each other, kissing, nibbling, teasing, hugging and just holding each other, feeling their nakedness against the other's nakedness. But soon they were coupled together in gratifying heat . . . moving without motion . . . then pumping up and down and gyrating and sighing and moaning for the joy and the love and sustenance they had so direly missed.

Back in the airport terminal, at one point they had taken their arms from around one another, and Yakubu had walked a pace or two behind Helene, just so he could gaze at her. He imagined how she experienced her own body, her own breasts, her ass and hips, moving as she walked her proud walk. He felt so much a part of her that he actually felt not his penis but her pussy between his own thighs. *Dr. Helene Johnson-Jones. Mother of a grown daughter. Top-flight surgeon, health specialist and worker among Third World people. Feminist. African-American woman!* Yakubu was at once proud and humble to pronounce her name, to feel the sound of her name on his tongue. That was when he stepped back in tune with her and put his arm back around her waist, and they walked together, high asses keeping the rhythm of their motion.

In bed, Helene arched her long legs straight up toward the ceiling, and arched her ass so that her pelvis was not really touching the bed. In between the outstretched wings of her great thighs, Yakubu flew her with his member pressed down and up in her insides. He flew her and piloted her and made love to her with a powerful yet easy grind. They loved until they ran like okra and Helene's pussy overflowed. Then they almost came uncoupled, but held themselves at the very edge of one another and moved ever so gingerly like that, up and down and round and round at the tip of Yakubu's dick and the lips of her pussy, until they both could not take the sensation any longer, and they pressed forcefully against each other, sending his dick down and up into the innermost depth of her womb, where she locked him inside and they came and came and came.

Now he follows behind her . . . up the short stairs into the kitchen . . . up the tall stairs into the main bedroom . . . into the bathroom, back downstairs to the kitchen, over by the refrigerator, then at the sink . . . he trails behind her like a pup . . . naked as she . . . with his fat penis hanging down and dangling about like a thing that is alive on its own. "Damnit, Song, go away and let me fix this salad." "You are my salad," he says, bending down, biting her buttock. Then he takes off down the short stairs, and she takes off after him, chasing him down to the bed, where she tackles and sits astride him. She reaches underneath and inserts his erect penis into her vagina. Gingerly she pushes herself down. She makes a few minor adjustments, bends her legs and knees along each side of his outstretched body. Then she webs his fingers in her fingers and pins his hands and arms back against the bed. She enjoys it this way so much. Yakubu looks up into her wide-open eyes and sees stars shining in them. He loves the control she exerts, the deliberate loosening and tightening, the twitching and relaxing of her pussy muscles. Yakubu braces his heels on the bed, raises his pelvis, and hoists her up high on his forethighs, where she sits like a jockey in a saddle of pure fucking. Horse and rider, rider and horse become one and the other. *Ride me, Dew.* Yakubu's throaty voice utters the words repeatedly. *Ride me, magnificent rider. Go on and ride me, please . . .*

Simultaneously Helene closes and tightens her eyes and tightens the muscles of her ass and makes her pussy taut with suction. She experiences Yakubu's dick fully up in her to the hilt. Barely lifting her ass, which is now taut to the breaking point, she grinds him slowly and easily and roundly. Opening his eyes, Yakubu gazes up into her serenely beautiful face. The muscles around Helene's eyes and jaws are completely relaxed, though her mouth is wide open, silent . . . but for her deep, resonant breathing.

Her pussy is gripping Yakubu and grinding him up in her so finely that he feels at once pain and pleasure. He begins to squirm beneath her. As if going in for the last stretch of her ride, Helene lets go of his hands, bends further down, and gathers him in a full embrace. He feels her pussy open completely wide. Both of them feel her pussy breathe, like a cornucopia of tissue and muscle and juice and air and fire. She has given him room to respond and work with her now. He complies with so much love that they both begin to sob and weep. Yakubu screams, "Ooooooh, ooooooh!" and begins coming until Helene is coming with him. The smell of each other, the sound and feel of their breathing, exhilarate their senses. Their pleasure is enhanced and heightened by the feel and sense of his body beneath hers, and by her animalness and his animalness, and by his compliance with her passionate mastery and power over him.

He now clings to her in full embrace. They are conscious of each other's giving and receiving. They experience rivulets of orgasms. They feel the warmth of flesh and experience the knowledge of each other all through the night, touching and smiling and hugging one another in their sleep.

In the morning Yakubu is awakened by a sensation of floating. He opens his eyes with a smile. He stretches every muscle in his long body like a cat and sighs sensuously, as he feels the warmth of Helene's mouth around his penis. Resting between his legs on the inside of one of his thighs, her head is buried beneath the sheet. She is curled, long legs and all, like a loving animal. Yakubu arches his back and flexes the muscle in his penis, giving vent to the soft erection forming in Helene's mouth. *My lollipop. I could hold you this way forever. So full in my mouth.* She holds him like that and just lies there, caressing the underside of his penis with her lapping tongue and simultaneously sucking him. Suddenly she throws off the sheet, rises and straddles him, and begins to kiss his body with her pussy.

First, she places her pussy on his legs, each in turn, from ankle to hips to thighs. Then she widens and places her vagina gently down, touching his penis as it lies flat against his belly. With her pussy wide open, she caresses the length of the shaft of Yakubu's dick with the tip of her clitoris, gently rubbing her clit up and down his now twitching meat. The wet slickness of the motion is delirious to them, and they both go *Awwwww.* Helene slides her pussy up farther on Yakubu's chest, touching his right and left tits, and then back down on his belly . . . wide-open, wet, juicy pussy . . . kissing and massaging him. She is feeling how wonderful it is to make love without shame or reservation. *Ahhhhhh,* she sighs with her entire body, as she climbs astride Yakubu's face and presses her pussy ever so gently over his mouth. "Morning Dew," she hears Yakubu utter beneath her, and feels his breath, breathing hot up into her wet, slick, sensitive crotch.

That was how she had first come to have the love name. She and Yakubu had been lying in bed one morning when, quite spontaneously, she had sat on him and he had expressed delight at how her pussy felt on his skin. She had liked the feelings too. So she began climbing up on him, touching him with her pussy as she climbed, until she reached his mouth. He had sucked her clitoris and licked her pussy, mumbling that "morning dew" was what it tasted like. Thus, "Dew" became her love name.

Yakubu tumbles Helene off of him and flattens her face-down on the bed. He goes way down and licks and kisses and nibbles her toes, the hollows of her feet, her heels, her legs, then her thighs, then her buttocks, where he licks and nibbles the cheeks and the underside of her magnificent ass. At first, Helene does not feel much of anything. But Yakubu keeps on licking, nibbling and kissing her ass, left cheek, right cheek, then way underneath and around on her buns. *Awwwwww,* Helene cries out. *Awwwwww,* again she cries as Yakubu keeps on licking and kissing and nibbling the salty sweat of her ass, until every inch of her ass becomes so sensitive that Helene can barely bear the pleasure.

Unlike at first, Helene can now feel the slightest touch of Yakubu's tongue; she can feel his taste buds, so that a lick underneath one of her buns ignites a sensuous rush of nerve endings. As Yakubu kisses, licks, and nibbles, the surface of Helene's ass becomes a labyrinth of aesthetic sensitivity, an erogenous landscape of countless intertwining branches with each branch having its own distinct sensation. The combined effect was like an ocean of erotic impulses surging in every tendon and nerve in Helene's body and brain.

For an instant, Yakubu rises and rolls Helene over, facing him. Both of them pain from the momentary cessation of touch. Quickly, though, Helene extends her legs and hoists her thighs in the wings position. Quickly Yakubu sinks deeply into her. His inside flanks caress her upturned ass, and the hairy mound of his pubis sets fire to her erect clitoris. Yakubu takes her breasts into his mouth and licks her hardened nipples, each in turn, and licks her neck, and she licks his neck and digs her fingers into the undersides of his buns. Their pleasure is so immense, so thorough, that their passion becomes total empathic immersion. They are transformed into kinetic bodies of ecstatic energy. Together they levitate above the surface of the bed. They soar in the heights of their own heaven.

PART FOUR

Swimming in Your Wetness

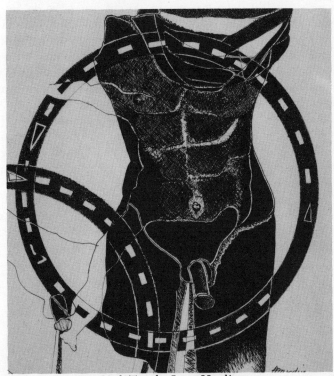

Male Torso by Lynn Hardin

Is it, as the cold sex clinicians claim, that we long for and continually remember wetness because that is our first memory: warm and safe and hot, floating in our amniotic juices? And then, later, always trying to return to that perpetual state of being wet next to someone we love? We take a bath, water and bubbles up to our chins, and we think of making love. We go to the beach, the waves beating ceaselessly against our prone torsos, and we think of making love. We go to the lake, and, as the gentle tides lap against our shins splayed over the docks, we think of love, love, love . . .

Or is it that after knowing the dryness of existence that we wantonly search for a state directly opposite? Or is it that after the realization that so few of our desires will ever be fulfilled we search for the opposites of things meant for us? Wanting to be wet, always, stays with us in ways we cannot fathom, only ask for in our own individual modes of desire.

Wetness saturates Part IV in ways that cannot be denied. We drown, though we swim like dolphins, and we do not mind, we do not mind. Dolores da Costa with her "Black Male/Tales" makes aural voyeurism and the breaking of confidentiality enticingly sweaty, as we hear one more private tale after another expose itself to us. So too, John Turpin's "All Wet in Green" and Opal Palmer Adisa's "Insatiable" overwhelm us with images of sensual inundation. With the heat generated by her "one-minute release" SDiane Bogus threatens to evaporate the wetness her "P.G." causes in us. O. R. Dathorne's "Woman Story" leaves us sweating at the sight of the initiation of his three little brown girls in well water, and we too "touch ourselves" as Kalamu Ya Salaam's haiku leaves not a dry spot on moonlit nights. Frank Lamont Phillips's "Wet Kisses" coats us with sweet saliva done room by room, and, choking, we wash ourselves in the sexually medicinal waters of E. Ethelbert Miller's "Birds."

Wet. Wet is what I said. And now why, we wonder, do we not dive, head first, into a deep, dark body of water?

All Wet in Green

John Turpin

All wet in green
I like you morning most of all
because of nothing so simple as a sentence
or so far away as a reason could not tell
and

I like you morning most of all
as you hold your secrets blushingly out of view
calming me quieting me with your summer dew
a rhyme in season
still no reason will ever tell
your morning precious secrets
mellow few
(comes noon too soon) and so
adieu

P.G.

SDiane Bogus

Pussygirl won't always come when I need her
She's no tease, she's just no machine.
"Com'on, come on!" I beg, tense and intense,
working hard for some pussy, girl.

Frustrated, I utter what I hope will be
magic-making, come-making words to entice her
"Bitch," "Slut," "Pussy . . ."
But it doesn't bring her.

I may be twenty minutes, a long time
to squirm over a one-minute release,
but I strain after my pussy, girl.

Then, quick, like a bulb blows,
the orgasm starts and ends—
it fills the walls of me with heat
as dense and sharp as an injection,
quick as the breath I exhale, it
descends like a heavy fog down,

sharp, immediate . . . It comes and
goes, a flash, an appeasement.
It is Pussygirl. Come and gone faceless,
wordless, passionless without the
sweetness of a darling woman,
without her breath or her whispered love.
That is the nature of Pussygirl
when she is summoned unwilling to my bed.

Black Male/Tales

Dolores da Costa

I don't know why my men friends tell me their darkest secrets, their most bizarre adventures, and their most engrossing sexual fantasies. Maybe it's because I was raised with men—a brother and four older cousins—and am used to listening to wild flights of fancy. Or maybe it's because I grew up a tom boy, shooting marbles, climbing chinaberry trees, and playing doctor (with me on top administering artificial respiration), so nothing easily shocks me. Then again, it may be because I "ooohh" and "aaahhh" so well, eyes aglow and ears aperk, that my friends enjoy delighting me with their verbal offerings.

At any rate, here're a few of the funniest, most improbable tales in my friends' repertoires. Any resemblance to persons living or dead is absolutely, positively coincidental (I swear on a stack of Bibles!) . . . I just hope I have some friends left after they see themselves and their tails (oops, I mean tales) in print!

CHOCOLATE DELIGHT

Neal is the creative type—a jazz musician—and he likes his women free, frisky, and forty. He has been dating an ob/gyn for several years, and likes to regale me with tales of their escapades.

"We had an encounter yesterday that blew my mind," he said over broiled trout and Caesar salad.

"Tell me about it," I encouraged, eager to hear his fantastic yarn.

"We were on our way to the Hilton for an evening of fun and games, when we passed a Safeway and she said, 'I need to stop in here a minute.' Well, she came out with a little brown paper bag, and I was curious but didn't say anything.

"After a coupla hours of expensive foreplay—pheasant under glass, two bottles of champagne, a hundred-and-fifty-dollar-a-night room on the top floor—we got down to business. Lowered the lights, turned up the radio, and pulled back the sheets."

"Uh-huh," I hummed, getting into the swing of things.

"Then she opens up the bag and pulls out a can of chocolate syrup."

"Chocolate syrup?"

"Yeah, the thick kind," he answered, smiling.

" 'Baby,' she says, real low and sexy, 'I want you to pour this chocolate all over my body and sip, lick, and suck it up with your tongue.' 'Ohhh-weee, you're so nasty,' I told her. 'And you just love it,' she countered.

"So, I started at the top, pouring a thin stream of dark chocolate over the tips of her nipples and letting it run down the sides, and then I licked her breasts, two perfectly round ice-cream cones. My tongue circled around those cones to the top, and when it reached her nipples, I sucked them into hardness. Then I poured chocolate all over her, lapping up the sweet stuff as I went. By that time, her tan skin was covered with so much dark syrup that she looked like a chocolate-covered cherry: brown and sticky on the outside, wet and pink on the inside. Uh, uh."

"That must have been a real turn-on."

"What you talking about!" he answered. "It was better than Vaseline or baby oil because I could slip and slide, as well as lick and suck at the same time."

"And then what happened?" I asked.

"Then she reached over and took the champagne out of the silver bucket and proceeded to drop and sip, pour and lick every hollow place on my body: between the nipples, in the navel, and under the arms. She was *serious* with her tongue, flicking here and there, everywhere she could find a spot. The lady doctor knew every nook and cranny of the male anatomy."

"By that time both of you musta been completely wet and sticky."

"And it was wonderful! But I didn't tell you about the pièce de résistance."

"What was it?"

"She dipped my penis into a glass of pink champagne and sucked off every single drop. The sensation was unbelievable! By the time she finished, I had melted into a pool of cum."

With friends like Neal, I don't need X-rated movies. Later that night, when I thought about what had happened, I burst out laughing again. I rang him up.

"Hey, Neal, this is Dolores. I got to thinking about something. I would love to have seen the faces on the maids when they walked in and saw those sheets! Chocolate spots and champagne stains all over the snow-whites. I can hear them now: 'Musta been some cullud folk in here last night, 'cause no decent folk woulda cut up like this!' "

"Baby, you shore are right. Who did we run into when we walked outta room 1834? The maids in their Church Lady looks. We could have gone through the floor."

TALKING DIRTY

My friend Allen—six feet, 168 pounds, good-lookin for days—called one day to tell me about this woman who had messed over him, and I, irate and all up in his corner, said, "That biiitch," in my lowest, nastiest voice. There was a pause on the other end, and then we talked and laughed some more about the strange doings of colored folk.

Later that night, after we had cleaned up from a party, Allen came up and whispered in my ear, "Ohhh, I got so excited in the shower this afternoon thinking about how you said, 'That biiitch.' I thought to myself, 'I bet Dolores can talk real dirty.' "

"Don't tell me you phone-fuck!" I laughed at my friend, all sharp in white slacks and a tan linen blazer. I had known Allen for I don't know how many years and he was always a gentleman: had season tickets to the symphony, spoke Portuguese and Italian, and traveled abroad every summer. I didn't think he could get down.

"Uh-huh. You too?" he asked.

I just smiled with a devilish look on my face.

"And it's safe," he added. "You don't have to worry about catching anything."

When Allen called the next day, he began: "You know why that word got to me? There was a movie I used to watch as a kid about a guy that fell for a beautiful movie star. He used to masturbate while looking at her picture, so he had pictures of her all over the house—over the bed, on the kitchen wall, across from the tub—just in case the spirit moved him. At the end of the movie, he just kept saying, 'Bitch. Bitch. Bitch.' Over and over. I thought that was so sexy, and every time I hear the word *bitch*, I think about that guy masturbating."

"But do you really like to talk dirty?" I asked.

"What you mean! Didn't I tell you about the time I met this woman on a flight to Rio? When we reached the hotel, I asked if I could call her room later. She looked at me kinda provocative-like and said, 'Uh-huh,' " so I asked her if she'd put on a sexy gown, turn out the lights, and stretch out on the bed. She smiled. 'So we can talk,' I explained. 'Talk dirty.' She looked me straight in the eye and asked, 'You give good phone, huh?' "

I cracked up laughing. Funniest thing I'd heard all day.

LUNCH BREAK

I ran into Lewis one day at the Library of Congress. He works in the Manuscript Division, but we hadn't seen each other in a long time, so he filled me in on the details of his love life over coffee in the employees' lunchroom.

"I've been dating a woman named Marlene, who works across the street in the Rayburn Building. She's married too, so we try to get together during lunch."

"The dangerous two-hour Washington lunch." I laughed. "That's when all the action takes place; folks lunch downstairs and then check into a room upstairs."

"Our lunches are more bizarre," Lewis announced, grinning from ear to ear. "We used to have the usual hamburger and fries at Sherrod's, but Marlene got into fitness, so she suggested we grab a low-fat yogurt and head across the Potomac to jog."

"Jog?" I asked. "What happened to the get-togethers?"

"We started meeting after work, but after a while my wife got suspicious and Marlene's husband started asking questions: 'How come you get stuck in so many traffic jams?' and 'Why don't you ever buy anything when you go shopping?' and shit like that. So we just jogged, went home after work, and got horny as hell.

"One day—I think it was Marlene's birthday—we decided to take a picnic lunch, drive over to Arlington Cemetery, and run afterwards. We were sitting in the car, me in my T-shirt and jogging shorts, Marlene in her Baryshnikov tights and body suit, drinking and eating high off the hog: mushrooms stuffed with crabmeat, marinated frog's legs, Brie, French bread, and Pinot Noir."

"Decadent!"

"A birthday celebration in the cemetery," Lewis countered.

"Some irony in that," I noted.

"It was spring! Flowers blooming. Bees buzzing. Sap rising. Between the sap and the sun and the Pinot Noir, we couldn't stand it any longer. I put my hands between Marlene's thighs; she slid her fingers under my shorts. I rubbed her pussy; she squeezed my dick. She took off her tights; I removed my shorts."

"In Arlington Cemetery? In broad daylight?"

"Uh-huh. We were gittin it, and it was good too. We just opened the car doors and fucked on the seat."

"Didn't anyone see you?"

"Yeah, there were some trucks going by and a few helicopters flying overhead, but we didn't care. In fact, the thought of all those guys looking at us was a real turn-on, so we started showing out: first, I sucked Marlene and then she went down on me; next, she stuck her ass out the door and I licked it too."

"Lewis, you didn't!"

"Yes, I did, and it was the best fuck we ever had."

"Man, you need to stick to your manuscripts!"

HOT WAX

"*Pero, chica, la mujer estaba loca.*" Tony started off. "Completely, certifiably nuts."

"*¿En qué sentido?*" I asked, egging him on.

"She was heavy into candles, like the chick in Spike's first film. Candles everywhere: dresser, bureau, tables, bookcase. *Por todas partes.* Well, okay, *me digo.* I can dig it because I really like this woman, you know. We met in my real estate finance class, and she looked so straight: dark suit, eyeglasses, briefcase—right out of *Ebony. No era exactamente guapa,* but she had a ripe sensuousness that got to me."

"*¿Y qué te pasó?*"

"*Pues, vamos a su casa,* a dark little house on the fringes of Cherokee Park, and before long we end up in bed. *Y entonces,* she reaches over, picks up a candle, blows out the flame, and slides it into her pussy. *Me mira intensamente,* all the while looking at me and working out with that candle. And I am getting aroused again *mirándola,* moistening her lips with her tongue, touching the tips of her nipples, and crying out *con placer.* I have a hard-on, but she's about to come, *la chingada!*"

"Was that it?"

"*¡Claro que no!* The worst is yet to come. She takes the same candle, wet with her *jugo,* and lights it again. Then when the wax is hot, she starts dropping candle wax, *gota a gota,* on her breasts. As each liquid drop touches her skin, she moans softly, 'Oooohhhh. Aaaahhh.' Craziest damn thing I've ever seen."

"You got that right."

A WEEKEND IN LONDON

"Hey, Dolores." It was Edward, calling from New York. "I got back last Friday, and just called to check on you."

It was after eleven, and I was in bed, half asleep, but I perked up because I could tell by the sound of his voice that Edward had gotten into something wild.

"You'll never believe what happened to me in London."

"No, tell me."

"Well, I was sitting on a bench in Trafalgar Square minding my own business, reading the *Times,* when an elderly gentleman came up and sat next to me. He was small and elegant-looking: white hair, expensive suit, well mannered. We got to talking and I told him that I was in London doing research on Egyptian art for the museum I work for in New York.

"We talked for an hour or so, and one thing led to another. We hit it off real well, so he invited me to his house later that night for dinner."

"And you went?" I asked.

"Yeah, I did. I was kinda fascinated by the old guy. He had traveled all over—Nova Scotia, Madagascar, Belize—and he'd led a fantastic life."

Edward just naturally drew people to him. He was a big teddy bear kind of man with a warm, open manner that even my momma would like.

"So what happened?"

"Well, about seven-thirty that night his chauffeur pulled up at my hotel in a big Rolls. Then he drove out into the country, turned up a circular drive, and parked in front of the biggest mansion I've ever seen: fifty-five rooms, no telling how many bathrooms, antiques all over the place, paintings on the wall, and servants for days."

"Your kinda place, huh?" I asked, thinking about Edward's Park Avenue apartment with its Oriental rugs, mahogany paneling, and Romare Bearden originals.

"Don't you know it! Anyway, we went in to dinner and a young woman glided in, Swedish-looking with light hair, blue-gray eyes, long-limbed body. Before I could ask, 'Your daughter?' Mr. Smythe (that's his name) explained, 'I'd like you to meet my wife.' "

"How old was this guy?" I wanted to know.

"Oh, seventy-one, seventy-two, but his wife looked like she might have been thirty or so. Anyway, we all sat down to dinner: six or seven courses with sorbet for the palate. After dinner, his wife (Greta was her name, I think) disappeared and Smythe and I sat around talking about Renaissance poetry. About half an hour later, the door opens, and in floats Greta in a long green chiffon gown with nothing on underneath. Beneath that diaphanous gown you could see everything: pink nipples, soft flesh, round stomach, furry mound."

"What did you say?"

"What could I say?" Edward asked. "I was trying hard not to look, and trying harder not to get hard. Then Smythe said, so softly I could barely hear him, 'I want you to fuck my wife.' 'You want what?' I asked, incredulous. 'She's never done it with a Negro, and I don't like to deny her anything. I'm flying to Paris for a few days, and I've given the servants the weekend off, so you'll have the place to yourself. Really, you'd be doing me, us, a big favor.' "

"He probably intended to watch the whole thing on closed-circuit TV," I suggested.

"You think so?"

"Yeah, the man couldn't get it up, so he got his kicks watching someone else ball his wife."

"Whatever. Honey, that was the wildest two days I've ever had. That woman could do everything but hang from the chandelier. We fucked all over the place—in the library, on the balcony, by the pool—at all times of the day and night. She never got enough. As soon as I turned over, she was rubbing up against me. Playing with my dick."

Every man's fantasy—the insatiable woman, I thought to myself. Poor Edward!

THE PET SHOP

I ran into Alexander, whom I hadn't seen in years, at a conference last spring. We were so glad to see each other that we skipped the opening session and slipped over to the bar for drinks.

"Lady, you're looking great," he started off. "If we weren't such good friends, I'd have to try you out," he added with a twinkle in his eye. (Alex could charm the pants off any woman without even half trying, but he just wasn't my type.)

"You haven't changed a bit, Alex. Still got an eye for the women. Now tell me what you've been into since last I saw you."

"I told you about Rita, didn't I?"

"Rita who?"

"The one from Cuba by way of Lenox and 142nd Street. She had my nose wide open; still does, in fact. She couldn't care less about my teaching and research; she has a one-track mind with a repertoire of tricks that won't quit. She could write the book on sexual fun and games."

"Do you love her, Alex?"

"I don't know. Probably not, but I can't get her off my mind. She gives me a hard way to go. Like the time I moved to Miami to be near her. There was this deliveryman—Afro-Cuban, good-looking, muscular —that used to bring groceries every day. After we moved to Boston, guess what? The same guy shows up on a regular basis. Coincidence? Hell, no."

"She doesn't sound like your type."

"But what can I do? I'm weak for her. Then there was the time in the pet shop."

"Pet shop?" I asked.

"Yeah, where they sell exotic animals, and Rita was the most exotic of all. One day she goes into this pet shop near the Commons and meets the owner. She doesn't even know this guy's name; still doesn't. Next thing she knows, she's in the back stretched out on top of a cage, dress pulled up to her waist."

"No!"

"Yes!"

"She told you that?" I couldn't believe it.

"Blow by blow. How she lay back across the cage and, before she knew it, the guy had his pants down and was putting his thing in her. All the while, the dogs and cats in the cage below were looking up at her fine ass, howling like mad and trying to break through the bars because her woman scent was driving them crazy. I can just hear them now: the man huffing and puffing; Rita moaning and groaning; the animals barking and meowing—a regular madhouse!"

"And she didn't even know this guy?" I asked, laughing hysterically at the scene Alex conjured up: dogs in heat, man erect, Rita horny. It was wild!

"Uh-huh, but that's Rita for you. Hikes up her skirt, pulls down her drawers, and gets her some. No matter that it's 11:30 A.M. in a downtown pet shop, and there's a balding, middle-aged stranger on top of her."

Alex had finally met his match!

A PHOTOGRAPHIC EYE

Morgan is a writer and he collects people like entomologists collect bugs —to stick on a pin and display under glass. Morgan tells some strange and convoluted tales.

We were talking on the phone one night, telling lies and swapping stories, when he started reminiscing: "In college, I had two jobs: working in an adult bookstore and taking photographs. One Saturday, a man, a professional type—gray flannel suit, paisley tie, cuff links—came into the store to talk to my buddy, Sam. Later on, Sam asked me, 'Wanna make some extra money this weekend?' 'Sure, man, doing what?'

" 'You see the dude was in here this afternoon?' 'Uh-huh.' 'He needs two men to do a job for him and one has to be a photographer,' said Sam. 'Sounds great. I'm game,' I told him. 'Okay, we're on. I'll pick you up around ten.'

"Sam pulled up at ten sharp, and we headed through Chicago to the expressway. After driving for twenty-five or thirty minutes, we came to a house that was dark except for a light in the back room."

"Weren't you curious about what was going on?" I asked.

"Yeah, but Sam was very closemouthed until we pulled up to the house. Then he told me the plan. 'We're going to break into the professor's house and rape his wife,' he explained. 'We're going to do what?' I shouted with visions of handcuffs and prison bars dancing in my head. 'Not so loud, fool! It's what they want.' "

This story was getting more and more bizarre by the minute.

" 'All you have to do is snap pictures while I'm fucking her,' he added. Sam crept up to the lighted window, broke the glass quietly, and crawled over the windowsill, with me right behind him. The professor was sitting up in bed as prim and proper as you please in a pair of new pajamas, reading *The History of the Peloponnesian Wars*. How's that for cool?"

"He didn't even look up?"

"Nope. Not once. His wife was lying next to him, asleep or pretending to be asleep, so Sam went over and turned her on her back. She put up a little resistance and Sam hit her once or twice, but not too hard, and called her all kinds of whores and bitches. I'm standing on the side of the bed snapping pictures with my Minolta 500, and I can see that the professor is getting a hard-on, but he's steady reading and turning the pages, pretending he can't hear or see anything.

"Sam is now working out real good with the wife. He has her gown up and her legs wide open, and he's feeling all over her body. She's getting wet and he's getting hard. In fact, all three of us are hard: Sam, the professor, and me. And the lady, who's seen better days, is moaning, 'Oh, please don't,' and crying, 'Stop. Stop. You're hurting me,' but looking like she's enjoying every minute of it. Well, I was afraid I would burst out laughing with the sheer comedy of it."

"A staged rape!" I exclaimed. "I never heard of such!"

"Yeah, some folk get their kicks in strange ways. By this time Sam was deep in the lady, and she was rocking and rolling all over the place, and the professor was jerking off, and I was clicking away. Honey, we shoulda been on national TV. It was a sight to see!

"The next day, Sam received an unmarked envelope with three crisp one-hundred-dollar bills for him and one for me. I thought to myself, 'Goddamn, uhm a hundred-dollar-an-hour man!' "

"And how did the pictures turn out?" I asked.

"Oh, hell, I got so excited I forgot to load the camera."

Haiku #107

Kalamu Ya Salaam

i think of you as
rain and i as dry earth cracked
beneath cloudless sky

Erotic Note #4

Cheri

WATCH OUT I'M ABOUT TO EXPLODE
ALL OVER THIS PAPER
IF YOU DON'T WATCH OUT
I MAY GET SOME ON YOU
SOME OF THAT HOT WET JUICY GOOD SMELLING STUFF
IS ABOUT TO COME TOGETHER TO COME OUT FOR A
MIGHTY BIG SPLASH

Untitled

Dennis Brutus

Gaily teetering on the bath's edge
one long bare arm outflung to balance
the sweep of satin flanks and thews
face-level the brown triangular fuzz
gray glistening with a hoar of drops,
'Kiss me!' you cried, and 'No!' morosely I.

Etched aloft against the prison-grey light
that filtered through the plastic curtaining
the smooth flesh surging tautly over
the thoracic cage to where the nipples gazed
in blandly unselfconscious innocence,
'Kiss me!' you cried, and 'No!' morosely I,

seeing within the cage the soon too-tired muscle
and all this animal spirit spent,
this emphasis on sheer carnality
re-iteration of mortality
and all immediate joys ephemeral,
angered and wounded, 'No!' and 'No!' I cried.

Wet Kisses

Frank Lamont Phillips

"What kind of girl you gonna be, baby?" her mother used to say to her. "Pretty baby. Baby pretty. Pretty, pretty baby."

She didn't think she was a pretty baby, except that maybe all babies are pretty.

"What kind of girl you gonna be, baby?" she asked her daughter, and waited a laughing moment for the infant to answer. She wondered what kind of mother she would be in her toy-filled house. She wanted to be the mother her mother had been to her, but not the daughter she feared she had been.

"Girl, don't you be out there ripping and running, running and ripping," her mother used to say with a laugh in her voice.

Sometimes she wondered if she had done the right thing by breaking it off with him. Sometimes she thought maybe he was in love with her. Then again, maybe he just wanted to fuck her for something to write about.

"What can you do for me besides fuck me? You've already fucked me. Why don't you buy me something? I don't hardly have a hard time getting fucked. Buy me something. I could use some new clothes."

She thought about him more than she should have. She wondered if he would call and, if he did, what outrageous thing he would say or try to get her to do. Sometimes it seemed to her that if he liked to do anything at all that was normal, he just liked to look at her, and he did that with an abnormal intensity exacerbated by the fact that she could never figure out just what he was thinking. She wondered if, when he called, she would continue to say no, and if so, if no would finally be an answer to him no matter how many times she said it.

One night he put passion marks all over her neck and above her breasts. She would have to go out wearing scarves, but she couldn't hide the marks from the other guy she was intimate with. The other guy. The main guy. She let her main man spend the night, making love with him in all the rooms of her house. She and her mother had lived in that house, and then she had lived in that house with her husband.

"You crazy," she said when, looking in the mirror, she noticed the cherry-red marks on her dark skin. "You're dangerous. I don't know what the fuck you might do."

He didn't say anything. He just stood looking at her standing naked in front of the bathroom mirror on her tippy-toes. They had made athletic love all over the floor of the den. He had held her by her shoulders and lifted her off the sectional sofa. She liked to fuck hard, bone to bone, until she was sopping and limp, her hair sweated out, the whole room suggestively funky.

"It's funky in here," she would say after they made love. When she looked at him, he seemed to be looking through her, the way he sometimes seemed to be fucking right through her. He was a quiet fuck except for the noise he made her make, their wet flesh coming together like handclaps, getting sticky, then pulling apart. He would talk to her sometimes in what was a normal conversational tone, using an almost professorial voice to ask her about oral or anal sex, about wearing lipstick on her nipples. He seemed to be interviewing her as he fucked her, asking her this or that, and not responding to her answers.

He was as naked as she was—more so, because he had his enormous erection pointing at her. She was really serious, really angry, but she couldn't help laughing too.

"Are you paying attention to me? Why did you put all these suck bites on me?" She reached for his erection, which was, as he liked to say, as hard as jet-age plastic, Chinese arithmetic, and recent times.

He put the covered seat down on the toilet and sat on it. Holding his erection, she moved right along with him until he pulled her arms toward him and she straddled his legs, taking his erection in her not-quite-ready vagina until it hurt the way hurting feels good.

He did like to look at her or, if he wasn't with her, to think about looking at her: the midnight-hour darkness of her skin, the lush curve of her ripe body, the luscious pout of her lips, the bedeviling, inviting whole of her. He would think about her as he sat at his desk writing about her, and he would spin involved skeins of metaphors and similes into long inconsolable, decadent poems, or stories about this or that chameleon-like bourgeois beauty.

Her eyes were almond and heavy-lidded. They looked like a child's dreamy eyes or like a doll's wide-open eyes that you have to close when it's time for sleep. Her voice sometimes had a piping, scratchy, little-girl quality to it, but usually it was as sultry as Memphis in August, so hot and sticky that even standing naked in the open door of a refrigerator or rubbing ice cubes on your flesh you couldn't cool the flicking tongue of heat. She was learning to tilt her head back and look down her nose at folk, regarding them with amusement. She practiced fluttering her eyelids, mimicking in her way the plaintive handwringing of fictive southern belles.

Her derriere was plump and heart-shaped, and he loved it and the bouncy idea of it. Since she didn't like to wear clothes around the house and liked to walk around nude in front of him, he could watch her ass when she walked away from her king-sized bed to get more wine or to go to the bathroom.

He fell for her when he heard her sing in the church choir to which they both belonged. She seemed almost slight standing in the choir stall. She couldn't have been more than five feet without heels, but she had the hauteur of those African-American princesses who were raised in the large happy-looking houses along South Parkway, whose parents—and these women always had both a mother and father—were professional people, driving shiny foreign cars that knifed through the Black community like sharks, oblivious to the envy and derision they inspired.

Quinscia was not one of the Parkway Princesses, though clearly she wanted to be. She resented little light-skinned lovelies for whom real effort was alien. The high yallers had such high times, and though in school she was friends with them, learning through such associations their manners and thoughts, they were not tolerated in her part of town. Though her mother had been a "somebody," there was a clear line of demarcation between the newly arrived bourgeoisie and those whose roots hardly seemed nappy. Whatever else she might be or become, she would always be dark-skinned. She would always be a plain Black girl, short and heavy-hipped, whose hair would never be long enough; a plain Black girl with big eyes and a shyness she tried to hide. She would always have a full set of lips and roots that reached right down into welfare, the projects, cotton chopping, gals who drank hard liquor straight, and men who either sang the blues or caused women to have them.

Armed with an M.A. degree and a desire to live not just well but large, to be somebody in the cloying confines of Memphis's Black society and make some noise, she sought to out-bourgy the bourgeoisie, to have expensive clothes and cars, to be known and renowned. Then she met him.

He called her No. Her name was Quinscia Noelle Dottry-Winston, and as much as her name was in his mouth, she was more in his eyes, pretty (to him) in an eccentric, almost exotic way, someone new ("the only thing better than good pussy is new pussy"). She snapped her shoulders when she sang, looking at the choir members, most of whom she knew well, then at her music sheet, varying her tone and demeanor, showing a smile that was megawatt.

He came to choir practice with Belinda Davis, who had been his classmate at the community college. Hardly anyone noticed him at first. He was so quiet that those few members who had seen him sitting in the back of the church, quiet but attentive, thought him shy. He introduced himself to Quinscia by lending her a copy of *The Color Purple.*

"Here, I'll write my number in the book so you can let me know what you think of it," he said.

"Well, thank you," she said. "I'm really anxious to read this. I haven't seen it anywhere. Here's my card. Wait a minute. Let me write my home number on the back of this, so that . . ." Her voice stopped suddenly, and her head turned in the direction of Chloe Edmondson, the choir director. "Here," she said, handing him her card before she went over to preen with Chloe.

It was several weeks before he called her.

"Why wouldn't I remember you?" she asked. "I liked what you said at church, and I appreciate your letting me read your book. I have to get it back to you."

He didn't say anything.

"You okay?"

"Yeah. I guess. I've been a little depressed. I feel like I'm looking into the abyss and thinking about how inviting it seems at the bottom."

"You want me to come over? I could use some company myself."

He hesitated for a moment, then finally answered, "Please."

She already knew the development in which he lived, about twenty minutes from her house on the interstate. To his surprise, she arrived in less than an hour's time. He heard her at the door, and when he went downstairs to open it, she was standing under an umbrella in a ferocious downpour.

They left her open umbrella downstairs in the living room, and went up to the bedroom. She seemed to be shivering, so he turned the heat up twice, and soon it was warm enough for her to take off everything that could be removed without seeming immodest.

As he talked about writing and about women he had dated, some of whose nude and nearly nude pictures were casually sprawled on his dresser, Quinscia began to wonder if his dick was as big as his vocabulary.

"I think I'll be celibate," he said.

"Can you do that? I mean, there is desire and obsession, and you seem to have one or both for every pretty little thing. When was the last time you slept with somebody? Are you fucking our hippie friend, Belinda?"

He just looked at her and sort of smiled. She could hear the rain coming down outside. She reached out to touch his arm. She had been talking to him about her estranged husband.

"Who is the father of your daughter? Where did you get your M.A.? You look tired and worried. Are you okay?"

Finally, he kissed her. It was a teasing first one. The next one was hungry. The next made a meal of her. He took her clothes off slowly, and she closed her eyes as he put her panties in his pants pocket. He was kissing his way down her body. He spread her legs wide, then opened her vagina with his tongue, kissing her deep, teasing her clitoris with his tongue, then coming the long way up to her mouth to give her wet kisses full of her own smell.

When they made love that first time, she was like a bird caught in his hands, struggling in the bush. She made love with her legs open welcome-wide, her ankles up around his ears, and with hard, desperate inventiveness. Moments before, he had bent her in half at the waist, his pussy finger in her anus, her knees up near her ears, her vagina open as wide as her mouth while his tongue punched in and out, tapping her clitoris like an anxious visitor poking the doorbell until she came.

Her baby was asleep when the phone rang. She knew it was he. She wanted to tell him to come over and bring his very best dick because she wanted him to nail her to the mattress. Each time they made love, he would place another wet finger in her anus, or thumb her clitoris while he ate her breasts. When he held her buttocks in his hand and licked between her legs until she came, she knew that it wouldn't be long before he came to her mouth with more wet kisses.

Meet

Audre Lorde

Woman when we met on the solstice
high over halfway between your world and mine
rimmed with full moon and no more excuses
your red hair burned my fingers as I spread you
tasting your ruff down to sweetness
and I forgot to tell you
I have heard you calling across this land
in my blood before meeting
and I greet you again
on the beaches in mines lying on platforms
in trees full of tail-tail birds flicking
and deep in your caverns of decomposed granite
even over my own laterite hills
after a long journey
licking your sons
while you wrinkle your nose at the stench

Coming to rest
in the open mirrors of your demanded body

I will be black light as you lie against me
I will be heavy as August over your hair
our rivers flow from the same sea
and I promise to leave you again
full of amazement and our illuminations
dealt through the short tongues of color
or the taste of each other's skin as it hung
from our childhood mouths.

When we meet again
will you put your hands upon me
will I ride you over our lands
will we sleep beneath trees in the rain?
You shall get young as I lick your stomach
hot and at rest before we move off again
you will be white fury in my navel
I will be sweeping night.

Mawulisa foretells our bodies
as our hands touch and learn
from each other's hurt.
Taste my milk in the ditches of Chile and Ouagadougou
in Tema's bright port while the priestess of Larteh
protects us
in the high meat stalls of Palmyra and Abomey-Calavi
now you are my child and my mother
we have always been sisters in pain.

Come in the curve of the lion's bulging stomach
lie for a season out of the judging rain
we have mated we have cubbed
we have high time for work and another meeting
women exchanging blood
in the innermost rooms of moment
we must taste of each other's fruit
at least once
before we shall both be slain.

Insatiable

Opal Palmer Adisa

(To T.F.)

this has
got to stop
not the passion
us not being
able to resist
each other
the endless craving
in my groin
the hunger of
my lips
to taste
you

         the pull
of my arms
to wrap you
to me

this has got to stop
not the unquenchable
desire
the tongue
massaging flesh
the arms
that caress
and enfold

but the interruption
of daybreak
the demands
of work
the intrusion
of friends
all those
petty things
that steal us
from each other
temper our
rhythm
wipe our
wetness

that's what has
got to stop
not you
deep in me
bodies thrashing
drinking love
from each other
not being able
to get enough
of ourselves

the moon
refusing
to surrender
her place
to the sun
us
                    interconnected
riding waves

smelting iron
us
                    resisting
drowning ourselves
in each other

this has
got to stop

but i pray
it never

From *Echo of Lions*

Barbara Chase-Riboud

The men long for their women. Often in the night the dark barn suddenly becomes warm with familiar scents and breezes, embracing me from an imaginary, distant savannah, springing like an ambuscade off the river Kalwara. I am home, I think. My eyes roam the farthest recesses and a slim figure, her naked form perfectly outlined in the moonlight, always approaches me. She glows like a firefly, her breath a haze in the smoky air. Dazed but not alarmed, I rise and follow her, stumbling amongst the mattresses of the other men. I reach an opening, an unequal circle that pierces the tangled undergrowth of a riverbank. The circle's moss is soft underfoot and spongy, and the crystal river swallows us both silently. I slide under her floating form, my arms embracing the wetness of the palm-oiled flesh, my hands groping her dark triangle and her illuminated breasts, which break the surface like tiny pyramids. Her thousand plaits fan out around her head, the multicolored cowrie shells reflecting the moonlight. Her lynx eyes open and her breath laps my face as she twists over, half swimming away. But I always catch the weightless body and carry her downstream, caressing her limbs, flanks, thorax, as she turns and turns in my arms. I dive under the surface, taking her with me, and plunge into her rotating body, carried even deeper by the tepid undertow. The current always runs counter to our movements, and we struggle down to the slimy bottom, locking and unlocking in violent spasms until, with a sigh, she releases me and all of me flees into her nest, my snake reaching her innermost parts, commanding both our cries of pleasure at the same time, while her body still swivels in my arms. I enter her again, churning the turbid waters as we grasp and ungrasp like wrestlers, her arms above her head, her body bent like a bow, her breath whistling through her, love kisses and cries that split the air as we rock, locked in an arc, still in motion, sinking onto the bed of the river shimmering with filtered moonlight. Rushing downward blindly, her body smashes against mine, I burst inside her, a roaring in my ears as my throat explodes with her name.

From *Woman Story*

O. R. Dathorne

They were three little girls bathing naked in brown well-water

She remembered the ritual. First the Old Pa came out of the shed. Usually it was about ten o'clock or thereabouts. First he sat down at the edge of the well and looked up at the sky. It was as if he were measuring time with his eye, his one seeing eye. She recalled that he always had had that one eye, when she and the other girls in the neighborhood were still very very young, and he used to see them, as if he were some kind of seer whose only task in life was to watch them, guard them, take them in through his light eye and hold them in the dark socket of the other.

When the Old Pa moved his right hand over the handle, his left caressed the pump, as one would a child, a very young child. His fingers did not seem to be knotted and bent anymore, but from where she looked out, through the glass pane, she saw the long, firm hands of a young boy caressing the stem of the handle. One, two, three. One, two, three. The Old Pa started to fill the little concrete pit near the well with water. Again his movement was steady. He didn't even seem to pay attention to what he was doing; the movements were deft and regular, one succeeded the other, as he filled the enclosure. The water was light brown, with a small splash of foam near the edge of the pit. She couldn't hear the splashing sound, but she saw the water in the pit swell first with little bubbles, then move smoothly, anonymously, to join the rest of the water in the small enclosure. There it was still, as if it had died.

We were three little girls bathing naked in brown well-water

On a day just like this she had come outside, after the well-water had settled down and the Old Pa himself was nowhere to be seen. As usual Fola and Shade were with her.

"He's gone!" Fola said. "He's gone!"

"Gone where?" she had asked.

"Back into his shadow," Shade had responded cheekily.

"He can't see us now," Fola insisted.

"He doesn't need eyes," Shade had warned. "He doesn't need eyes to see us. He can see us even when he is not looking."

"What do you mean?" she had asked.

"Nothing. I don't mean anything when I talk. It just comes out that way."

"Let's go in," Fola had said. At first they had laughed at the idea. But there was no one to see them unless you count a mango tree and a man with one eye. Then they had stripped. First, Fola loosened her wrapper and let it fall to the ground. Then she tugged at her blouse. "There," she proclaimed. "I'm ready. My chest is as flat as a board. Here, see my little nipples, and my legs straight and calfless. I'm ready!"

Next Shade undressed. Shade took off her head-scarf, saying, "Look, my plaited hair is pointing upwards and erect." Then she loosened her dress and laid it horizontally over a branch near the mango tree. She continued, "When I turn round, my eyes will be large." Shade looked at Fola and the other girl and said, "I want to consume you all."

She was last; she had lain back in the grass and watched Shade and Fola. Then slowly she wriggled out of her wrapper, legs pointing up, as Shade watched. "I'd always thought that my hands were too long and stringy." She looked at Fola, then raised her eyes to Shade, questioningly. "Now I know they can point upwards in two straight lines. I can control big things. I'm ready!"

"We have the heads and bodies of our mothers," Shade had said. The others seemed a little embarrassed.

"Come."

She had walked toward Shade, as if in a dream. She placed her hands on Shade's shoulders and felt her breasts. "They're full." Then Shade stretched out her left hand to Fola. "And you have juicy round nipples."

Shade steered them both to the edge of the little concrete pool, and the three of them looked in and saw themselves dancing with each other in the water that moved just a little, with a small rhythm: one, two, three; one, two, three; very slowly. The brown well-water lapped around their bodies, played with Fola's armpits and splashed water into her face. She could almost taste Fola. In the center, Shade held them bound tight, against the water, anchored in the image of the mango tree, and though their movement was slight, they seemed permanently locked in Shade's embrace. When they climbed in, they went toward the center, forming a ring, until Shade drew everyone in close for one, two, perhaps, three minutes. Close to them, the water bubbled and splashed, and their images, distorted, were like those of older women, but they held on, clutching tightly to each other, breathing life into the water, panting heavily, closing their eyes, and whistling through their teeth.

Then Shade screamed, a long, loud sound that ripped through the air, making that moment stand still. It was an insistent cry, almost like a serenade, and then Shade parted the water and drew them in even closer. When they looked up, the Old Pa was standing with his head against the top of the mango tree and his sandals at the rim of the little pool. He said nothing. Even when they came out, he did not speak. He looked at the dancing bubbles of the water, and the quick images that had broken up in the water, and he turned his head slightly as each girl dashed for her clothing and sprinted off. They were giggling.

Three girls bathing naked in brown well-water

Haiku #52

Kalamu Ya Salaam

a woman's long legged
wetness wrapped round my waist—dreams
truth—i touch myself

Birds

E. Ethelbert Miller

near lake washington
the afternoon turns warm
with the sun of early spring.

your face, your arms, your legs
turning in your bed
discover mine.

along the lake
birds stare at the windows of our
house. i learn to swim in the
wetness of you.

Haiku #102

Kalamu Ya Salaam

your kiss sensual
as wet moonlight licking an
ocean's naked waves

Edible or Incredible: Black Erotic Collectibles

Jessie Carney Smith

The collecting of Black memorabilia is an old practice which, in recent years, has become widespread. The range of materials is broad, both in subject matter and in the variety of items produced, and includes among other items books, advertising objects, toys, art, household objects, recordings, films, and photographs. The images that they present may be "outrageously stereotypical or exquisitely beautiful."* They also may present a mixed or confused picture. Depending on the viewer's orientation, reaction to the collectibles may range from love to hate, from amusement to anger, especially when the items are grotesque or exaggerated, and when they present images of Blacks in a demeaning manner. The practice of creating Black images dates back several centuries, but it was not until the mid-1800s to the late 1950s that they were mass-produced and more readily available to the collector. Some were imported from England, Germany, Japan, and other countries, while others were made in the northern industrial United States. Many were created as novelty and souvenir items, designed to show White America's view of Blacks and to serve as moneymaking endeavors. Since many of the items were degrading, some collectors chose to remain anonymous for fear they

* Donna C. Kaonis, "Collecting Black Memorabilia," *Collectors' Showcase* 5 (July/August 1986): 33–39.

would be judged racists or considered to have peculiar, unhealthy interests. The decade of the 1980s was one of more widespread interest in the materials for the purpose of study, research, exhibition, or as evidence of the treatment of Blacks in American popular culture.

America's appetite for Black erotic collectibles has been either unexplored or unpublished in discussions of Black cultural icons. Yet this is an area well worth research to identify examples of the art, literature, and other subject areas that give another side of Black popular culture—the underside, the hidden, and the laughable presented at parties and to some close friends. Black erotic collectibles will need to come out of the closet before we have a more complete picture of what has been produced and are able to examine the impact of the materials on American culture. At one time or another many people have been exposed to Black erotic collectibles, yet, as a result of America's attitude toward pornography, the items have yet to be made readily available. Though not designed to explore Black erotic collectibles, my recent study of Black memorabilia and their collectors, published in *Images of Blacks in American Culture,*† uncovered a few items of this nature. While these collectibles are unidentified in *Images of Blacks,* we cannot deny that Black erotica exists.

Black erotic collectibles have been seen in the form of books, art, greeting cards, circulars, posters, calendars, dolls, edibles, novelty items, party items, and films. There are erotic tales, jokes, toasts, and sayings, many versions of which folklorists have collected and published. There are Black erotic myths that characterize the typical Black man as having an enormous penis, Black women and men as being sexually overcharged, and which generally condemn the sexual behavior of Black people.

Black erotic comic books are known to have been printed as early as the 1930s, and, in the street vernacular, were called "fucking books." Once they reached the distribution point in a community, they were often circulated from friend to friend. The restrictions were that the reader had to be open-minded enough to appreciate the art and story and to keep the publication in the underground circuit. A typical book showed scenes of a Black man, usually with a super penis, who posed either as a muscleman or as a stud in bed, on the floor, or elsewhere in a love scene with a fat Black woman or one who appeared to be a whore. Characters in the books also included Uncle Remus, Sambo, and Aunt Jemima.

Among the recently published books on Black erotica is Robert Mapplethorpe's *Black Book.* This pictorial work may be used as an art textbook or it may appeal to those who have an interest in the human body as an art form. It shows naked Black men in a variety of poses, many of

† Jessie Carney Smith, ed., *Images of Blacks in American Culture* (Westport, Conn.: Greenwood Press, 1988), pp. 289–352.

which emphasize the penis. Ntozake Shange's foreword includes a powerful love poem, "irrepressibly bronze, beautiful & mine," which appeals to the lover of poetry and fits the scope of this essay. She speaks of a beach scene in which the "sun tickles lovers inviting them to make quickly some love" and later pleads: "let me be a chorus of a thousand tongues & your lips dance on a new moon / while Daddy Cool imagines syncopated niggahfied erotica on Griggs Rd."

Pornographic tales of Blacks were published in Daryl C. Dance's *Shuckin' and Jivin.'* The chapter "Are You Ready for This? Miscellaneous Risqué Tales" gives examples of tales and poems, variations of which may occur in different Black communities. Other Black erotic lore is scattered throughout the book. On this theme also is Charles H. Nichols's *Black Erotic Folk Tales.*

Among the variety of pornographic greeting cards currently available is the line with the trademark West, identified with the byline "tastefully tasteless card" and copyrighted in 1990 by West Graphics, S.F. The Chastity design presents a mixed image and message. The fat, out-of-shape Black model lifts her dress to display a brass cover and lock over her vagina; the message reads: "Don't Fuck with Me!"

Circulars are among the most common form of erotica regularly seen. Many are printed immediately after an event occurs or an incident arises, while others are created without relation to a current event. They may appear as cartoons, poems, questionnaires, or in other forms. A questionnaire entitled "Nigger Ass," which recently surfaced in the Maryland schools, asked such questions as: How do you like it? How long do you like it? How big do you like it? How often do you like it?

Dolls and other toys have been used to present a variety of erotic images. For example, a sculptured Black male doll made in Nashville, Tennessee, was well equipped with a long, hefty penis. Another common item is a Black stick doll, six to eight inches tall, painted on one side of a flat surface. When bent over, the doll becomes a penis.

Edible items are usually in the form of candy and include the penis and scrotum in dark chocolate. There are also sets of dark chocolate busts. Novelty items include mugs in the shape of a woman's bust that allow for drinking sometimes from the nipple and sometimes from the top of the bust. Another novelty item is a Black man wearing a matchbox to cover the area from his neck to his thighs; on lowering the box, his penis, depicted as a match, pops erect. A mixed message is presented in yet another novelty item—an ashtray in painted chalk—which shows a Black washerwoman whose bust is caught between the rollers of a wringer-type washing machine. The caption reads: "Oh, my aching back." While the figure depicts a cruel and inhuman act inflicted on a Black woman, it illustrates also the punch line of a game of one-upmanship known in some Black circles. Usually after an exaggerated story has been told, the next person says, "If you think that's something, you should have seen Grandma when she got her tiddy caught in the wringer; she damn near yelled to death!"

Party items show sets of plastic beverage stirrers in the shape of Black island women who are topless. Each stirrer shows the bust and its contour at various ages from twenty-five through fifty-five and over, obviously ranging from firm and well rounded to saggy, flabby, and barely identifiable. Another party or novelty item is a man's apron made in the shape and fabric of boxer shorts. The dark penis and red tip may be pulled through the fly to present a real-life appearance.

Perhaps the most widely circulated form of Black pornographic collectibles is found among film collectors and aficionados. In addition to videotapes available in pornographic shops or circulated underground, many Black films increasingly show stimulating and sexually arousing scenes. An example is the film *Superfly* with Ron O'Neal as Priest—the flamboyant drug addict and dealer who makes love with his White woman as well as his Black woman. The main sex scene, however, depicts Priest with his Black girlfriend in the bathtub. Background music plays softly in the dimly illuminated room as the two dark bodies, covered with soft white soapsuds, slither, slide, and roll gently, making just a slight splash in the water until they need to roll no more.

PART FIVE

Naughty, Nasty, and Nice

Let the Words of My Mouth . . . by Shirley Carter

Such nice and naughty delights: fingerlingus, pleasuring the self, deflowering virgins, bringing the clitoris to knot, scoring the back with scratches, and coming thirteen times in succession. Writers like René Depestre and Saundra Sharp underscore the delicious tension between contrary instincts—to *be* good, on the one hand, a "nice" boy; to be *good,* on the other hand, the "Queen of Raunch." Sandra Y. Govan intimates that some people purify their "unclean dreams in the church-house," while Bessie N. Price writes that others pray "for the chance to get into the pastor's pants." As writers mediate the distance between binary opposites—good/bad, nice/naughty, pleasure/pain—they underscore the awesome complexity of sexual feelings, encouraging readers to chart new directions in their erotic adventuring.

Exploring the boundaries of sensuality, Piri Thomas, Esperanza Malavé Cintrón, and Ntozake Shange evoke the Nuyorican landscape of Spanish Harlem. In his autobiography, *Down These Mean Streets,* New York/Puerto Rican writer Piri Thomas describes a sexual encounter on a crowded New York subway: *"Hurry, hurry,* our bodies urged, and *swoom-ooo-mmm*—girl and me and train got to the station at the same time. I felt her tremble and shiver as I boiled over." With a play on the Spanish word *tocar,* Shange suggests, in "Tócame" (touch me/play me), that the body is a fine-tuned instrument of pleasure, while Cintrón alludes to SM with images like leather curves, hot tongue, and tough bites.

In a humorous bent, Beryl Gilroy uses a different language—the folk talk of her native Guyana—to describe a mother and father's "fight":

> Dey roll out the bedroom. Dey roll out the door.
> Dey roll past the sweepy-broom laying on the floor.
> Dey roll down the bannister and drop on de grass.
> And then came a ram-goat and bite daddy ass.

Daryl Dance's collection of scatological tales, like "Not Even for a White Woman" and "Pass the Pussy, Please," also draw on folk language, that of the American South. Some of these naughty tales extol the prowess of "well-hung" Black men and the desperation of sex-starved White women.

Other writers evoke a landscape different from that of city streets, as they explore the verdant plains and lush valleys of the fe/male body. Provocative body imagery informs the poetry and fiction of Akua Lezli

Hope, who confesses to an open nose in her "Telegram from Topeka," and Yana West, whose tongue "completes the wet, hot, juicy licks and nibbles around the circles of both inner lips," In her prose piece, SDiane Bogus describes the hands as the genitalia of lesbian love, writing: "we take dyke hands finger by precious finger into our mouths . . . and perform fingerlingus." Meanwhile, under the skillful hands of Francophone novelist René Depestre, parts of the human anatomy—fecund loins and sweet gashes—acquire synecdochic significance; after Balthazar Grandchiré impregnated the atmosphere, for example, "breasts popped the buttons of nightgowns, enflamed thighs spread with desire, vaginas, fascinated, demanded to drink and above all to eat."

Nicety, in the words of the song lyrics, perhaps best describes such delicious pleasures, such nice but naughty delights.

Pin-up Poems

Bessie N. Price

For D. D. M.

JANUARY

I don't remember anything we said
that night in June when I knocked on his door
except "Hello, do you want to go to bed?"
and "I can't wait. Let's do it on the floor."
I know I gasped when he first entered me,
and that we never turned off the TV.
But I remember music: saxophones,
cool water blues, slow crooning, mellow groans.

His mouth and tongue in my mouth, on my lips,
he danced me deeper than I'd ever been
in all my love-life, leading with his hips
until fit his rhythms, sang his skin.
When he sat up for cigarettes and matches,
I saw that I had scored his back with scratches.

How beautiful your feet in boots,
your thighs in faded jeans,
your biceps in that flannel shirt,
your forearms' sweaty sheen.

I watch you from my living room
as you unload your truck:
You reach and bend, and through my window, I am passion-struck.

Your body is a dinner bell
that makes me salivate.
I'm starving for a taste
of you. May I fellate?

MARCH

The shower slicked us salty-sweet and smooth;
I tasted ocean when I kissed his neck,
and felt the subtle waves of muscles move
under my fingers as I stroked his back
and pulled his buttocks closer to my source.
I stood with one leg wound around his waist,
coughing a little when the water coursed
from his wet-plastered face into my face.
We might have been a Jane and her Tarzan,
me-youing in a jungle waterfall,
until the flooded shower overran
and brought the downstairs neighbor up to call,
"Hello? I think your bathtub's overflowed,"
as one thrust made his dam and mine explode.

APRIL

I told Mom we were going to the drive-in on our date;
instead of just the usual advice (like "don't be late"),
she sat me down and lectured me on what I should expect
the boy to try to do to me so I'd lose his respect.
She said he'd put his arm around my shoulders, clear his throat,
and sidle closer to me. Then he'd whisper (and I quote),
"Isn't it a chilly night? I'm freezing! You're so warm:
May I warm my hands on you? That won't do any harm."

"He'll paw your bra and panties, and he'll pant into your ear,"
Mom said. "Remember, Mommy's worrying about you, dear."

He parked the car. The lights went out. Inside two hundred cars,
three hundred couples started making out beneath the stars.
We sat through the refreshment stand commercials, the cartoon,
and half the movie. All the time I thought, "He'll do it soon."
At last, I put my arm around his shoulders and said, "Hurry
and move your buns on over here. Let YOUR damn mother worry!"

MAY

The pastor has a hairy chest.
On Sunday mornings, starched and pressed,
the women hearing from their pews
his preaching's passion, watch and muse
about his belly taut as bone,
and under that, his pubic zone.
His congregation's feminine
component wrestles with its sin,
and prays each Sunday for the chance
to get into the pastor's pants.

JUNE

Late phone call: It's your favorite former love,
the one whose face, for almost twenty years,
you've used to soothe yourself to sleep. Quick tears
of joy. You don't know what you're thinking of:
"Meet me tomorrow," you say. He says yes.

Awake beside your steady husband's snore,
you wonder if he'll love you anymore,
and whether you should buy a low-cut dress.

You meet: He hasn't changed so much, you think,
although his hair and beard are flecked with white.
His eyes still make you tremble with delight.
You shiver inwardly over your drink.
Promising to let your marriage be,
he takes you to his room in the hotel
and for an hour, he loves you just as well
(hell—better, even!) as in your memory.

We're long married; it's late;
we're too sleepy to wait
for a good show to come on t.v.
Well, if push comes to shove,
we could always make love . . .
Hey, how 'bout some coffee or tea?

AUGUST

The independent woman squashes spiders, unclogs drains,
and knows a good mechanic who comes cheap.
On her own at night, she neither snivels nor complains:
She entertains herself, and goes to sleep.
The independent woman is assertive, confident,
fulfilled, and happy. With no man to please,
she's free to please herself, and almost fully competent—
except when she runs out of batteries.

SEPTEMBER

Of the uncounted kisses
I calculate I've shared
and then forgotten, his is
the one that made me scared:
With soft-mouthed urgency
it said I could be free.

OCTOBER

My blues were finally diagnosed
as a clinical depression.
My shrink prescribed a drug for me
which produced a strange obsession
with yawning: I had yawning spells
so irresistibly sexy
I had orgasms when I yawned!

I'm close to apoplexy,
however, now. My shrink has just
pronounced this brilliant earful:
"You haff no furzer neet uff drucks,
Madame: You are TOO cheerful!"

NOVEMBER

I change my husband into HIM,
or more precisely, into THEM:
one man's hard chest, one's teasing laugh,
another's muscled thighs . . . In half
a minute's time I half-transform
my husband to Adonis, warm
as fantasy can make a man,
and more intensely intimate than
this numbingly familiar paunch
I straddle like the Queen of Raunch.

DECEMBER

Our two-year-old sleeps best in "Mommy's bed"
and you carry a blanket to the couch.
You wake up every morning such a grouch
I wish you'd slept in Timbuktu, instead.
My life is whelming, but not whelming-over:
My glass isn't half-empty, it's half-full.
To hell with that romantic cock-and-bull:
A mother needs a partner, not a lover.

(Though it would be a pleasure, I suppose,
  if you were still that man who sucked my toes . . .)

Tócame

Ntozake Shange

Liliane's favorite story, when she was dripping and naked, especially if she was tremblin' and holdin' me so she wouldn't leap off the bed, her favorite story was about a young girl at the Corso for the first time. This is how it goes. Once upon a time a young girl, a pretty young girl, *una morena,* bronze like you with the piquancy of a ginger flower, adorned herself in organdy and silk. She tugged at a very loud garter belt and slowly wound brand-new stockings up her long legs. She stuffed taffeta slip upon taffeta slip neath the swing of her skirts and giggled at herself in the mirror, dabbing rose lipstick from one end of her smile to the other. She put her lovely feet, toes wigglin' to dance, she put her toes in a pair of fancy cloth shoes with rhinestone butterflies twirlin' about her heels. Yes, she did. Then she tossed a velvet shawl round her shoulders and was off to the Corso.

The East Side train was not quite an appropriate carriage for such a *flaca, tan linda,* but she rode the ske-dat-tlin' bobbin' train as if it were the *QE II.* At 86th Street she ran into a mess of young brothahs who callt to her, whispered, whistled, circled her, ran up behind her, got close enough to smell her, made her change her direction once or twice, till

Tócame means touch me/play me.

they realized she was determined to walk up the steps to the Corso and they couldn't cause they had rubber-soled shoes. We all knew you can't wear rubber-soled shoes on the glorious floor of the Corso. So, *cariña,* the young girl who looked so beautiful, she looked almost as lovely as you do now, *chica.* She sashayed by the bar, through the tables crowded with every kinda Latin ever heard of, and stationed herself immediately in front of El Maraquero† in the aqua-lamé suit. *Óigame, negrita.* His skin was smooth as a star-strewn *portegría* night, see, like me, *negra.* Put your hand right there by my chin. Now, his bones jut through his face with the grace of Arawak deities. Like that, see. Now, run your fingers through my mustache *porque* his lips blessed the universe with a hallowed, taunting voice; high, high *como* a cherub. Yes, a Bronx boy on a rooftop serenading his *amante, sí.* The way I speak to you, now, *sí.* This young girl was mesmerized. She was how you say when you bein' *burguesa,* "smitten," right? No, don't move your fingers from my lips, not yet. But the most remarkable feature of El Maraquero, what did her in, as we say, had the young pussy just twitchin', ha, was *el ritmo* of the maracas in his hands. Ba-ba-ba/baba . . . Ba-ba-ba/baba. Oh, she could barely stand the tingling sounds so exact every beat, like an unremittant, *mira,* an unremittant waterfall, Ba-ba-ba/baba . . . Ba-ba-ba/baba. Oh, she started to dance all by herself. It was as if your folks said the Holy Ghost done got holdt to her. She was flyin' round them *bombas,* introducing steps the Yorubas had forgotten about. She conjured the elegance of the first *danzón* and mixed it with 21st-century Avenue D *salsa.* The girl was gone. No, *dulce,* don't move your fingers. Here, let me kiss them. One by one. Cause that's what happened to the beautiful mad dancin' girl and our *maraquero.* For she was so happy movin' to the music he was makin' and she imagined he meant for this joy to overwhelm her. She started to cry ever so slightly. Let me kiss the other one. No, not that one, the littlest one. She thought he was tossin' those maracas through the air for her with all his soul. So naturally her tears fell on the beat. No, don't laugh. Listen. Listen. The tears fell from her cheeks slowly and left aqua-lamé streaks on her cheeks. Really. Then once they hit the floor, it was like a bolt of lightning hit El Maraquero, who jumped into an improvisation whenever one of them tears let go of that girl's body. Soon it was she who was keepin' *el ritmo* and he was out there on some *marquero's sueño* of a solo. Now, you know El Maraquero has to be disciplined. He's gotta control, oh, the intricacies of Iberian and West African polyrhythms as they now exist in *salsa* music, right? Okay, let me have the other hand. No, I want to lick the palm of your other hand or I can't finish the story. You want me to finish the story, don't you? Well, good. Now I'll have kissed all your fingers and your palms and the bend in your arm and

† The Maracas Player.

then. So El Maraquero became agitated. He wanted to know where his sound had gone and, to be honest, so did the rest of the *orquesta*. Well, he hadn't noticed our beautiful young girl in her slips and organdy, her shoes with twirlin' butterflies. He wasn't like me, huh, he didn't see the surrender in her dancin' to his music. So he was astonished when he went to play and no sound came from the maracas. Our young girl, Liliane, who was so much like you, saw what he felt and she knew, as he did not know, that you do not own the beauty you create. Right, hear me. You don't own the beauty. Oh, I wanta kiss one of those rose tits of yours. No, I'm not finished with the story. Oh, she'd jump up and call me every low-down exploitative muthafuckah in the world. It was *"chinga* this" and *"chinga* that." "I'll be damned if it ain't some sick-assed voyeuristic photographer thinks his art is nurtured by a woman's tears." "Suck it, Niggah," she'd scream, or sometimes she said, "Suck it, Spic," if she was really mad. Then she'd turn around, tryin' to dress herself in this state. Something was always on backwards or she put on mismatched shoes, threw my hat on her head steada hers. She'd go stormin' out saying, "Yes, let me nearer." No don't move your fingers. El Maraquero is fuming. The young girl has been dancin' and cryin' all filled up with something she can't call by name 'cept to say that she likes it. She starts cryin' inconsolably cuz El Maraquero has lost his music and she doesn't know where it is 'cept that not owning beauty doesn't mean you lose it. Well, use that finger again. No, I want the next one. No, don't rush me. The young girl runs toward him and he's really pissed. I mean, no, I'm not pissed. I'm lickin' you, *pendeja*. He doesn't understand that he'll be playing no more music, no nothing', till he accepts that this young girl in her frilly dress and *mariposa* slippers has got holdt to his music. She's so upset about him not tink-tink-tink-/tintinkin' for her. Out of desperation she starts to sing to him and one by one the seeds that had been her tears that had been her legs and hips dancin' to his *ritmo* all returned to the maracas and El Maraquero never lost sight of her again. Turn over. From then on, *negrita*, he played for his life every *canción, cada coro,* cause his *chabala* would dance and cry his *ritmo* for him and then give it all back with her tears, her tears from feelin' what she had no name for, had never felt before, and couldn't do without. Right, Liliane, isn't that how it is for you?

"My art is not dependent on fuckin' you or lovin' you. Niggah, my art ain't gotta damn thing to do with your Puerto Rican behind. Besides, you can't take pictures, anyway. Go study with Adal Maldonado, you black muthafuckah."

That's when I would watch her go down the avenue, wet and smellin' exactly how I left her. Then I watched all the other muthafuckahs just feel how she walked, talkin' under her breath in that butchered Spanish she talks when she's mad at me. I watch them watchin' her, and I know if

I strolled down the street within the next hour I might as well be who I said I was in the beginning: Pete "El Conde" Rodríquez, *que toca la música*. Only the instrument I played is named Liliane.

Musta worked her too hard. She don't come round anymore. Well, not for a while. *Canta, mi canción, cariña, canta, canta.* Speak my tongue, *negra*, it's good for ya. Liliane, I know I was good to you. Good to you. Hasn't Victor-Jesús María always bathed you in kisses, *con besos libres?* Didn't I, *negra*, didn't I . . . ?

The Fight

Beryl Gilroy

Mother on the sofa daddy in the bed.
Daddy grab mother stand her on her head.
Mother take a tumble straight on her back.
Daddy jump on top of her all shining and black.
Mother holler "sweetheart"! Daddy holler "dear"!
Mother holler "lovey-dove"! Shove, shove, shove.
Dey roll out the bedroom. Dey roll out the door.
Dey roll past the sweepy-broom laying on the floor.
Dey roll down the bannister and drop on de grass.
And then came a ram-goat and bite daddy ass.
Daddy jump up, haul on his pants
And then he had a soiree with ten thousand red ants.

From *Hadriana dans tous mes rêves*

René Depestre

Translated by Aaron Segal

Balthazar Granchiré arrived in Jacmel for the first time in November 1936, only eight weeks after the passage of Hurricane Bathsheba, in a market town still tending its wounds. He chose to lodge with one of the cheese makers in the Place d'Armes. The night he arrived he deflowered in their sleep the Philisbourg twins and sister Natalie of the Angels, one of the sisters at the Sainte-Rose-de-Lima school. He tried out for the first time the strategy which he would perfect in coming months. He waited for darkness to sneak into their bedrooms. Then he hid under one of the beds. Once his prey was asleep he impregnated the atmosphere with aphrodisiacal effluvium. Within moments buttocks snapped the elastic of panties, breasts popped the buttons of nightgowns, enflamed thighs spread with desire, vaginas, fascinated, demanded to drink and above all to eat.

Balthazar needed only to begin his campaign. Superb adolescents went to bed virgins, awoke terrified, savagely ravished with blood everywhere. The frightened families first attributed the ravagings at home to the delayed effects of the devastating hurricane. (This trail was soon dropped.)

The next morning the accounts of the dreams that accompanied the victims' sleep frequently featured a fabulous flight. Each girl remembered flying through a season of dreams at low altitude over the Gulf of Jacmel in an uninterrupted orgasm in a machine that was neither a dirigible nor an airplane. Each one spoke of her serial journey swooning with joy. But at the moment of supreme enchantment the machine changed into a fantastically gashed mouth snatching up everything in its way.

Lolita Philisbourg felt that it was her own sweet gash, dilated to the measure of the sky above the gulf, that violently entrapped the rest of her body. Her sister Klariklé felt its tunnel of love open under her like a trap-door while her own father whispered in her ear that she should not leave the parachute at home. Sister Natalie of the Angels saw the very Catholic Grotto-of-the-Holy Father impetuously contending with the foaming waves that boiled at the sea's surface. Such was the visiting card that Balthazar Granchiré left in their sheets.

Vigilant mothers armed their daughters with steel threads attached to their bedsteads in the hope of capturing the incubus before its assault. The next morning they discovered to their stupor that they had succumbed without striking a blow to the very same sorcery as their innocent progeny.

Madame Eric Jeanjumeau confessed experiencing six orgasms a minute to Father Naélo. Madame Emil Jonassa came passionately thirteen times in succession. The widow Jastram experienced her transport as a voluptial classic: she promised to recall it beyond her dream in order to include it later in a manual of sexual education. Contrary to their dear little daughters, instead of being hurled into an abyss at the end of coitus, they saw their sexual organs gracefully placed on an ostentatious table in the midst of other sumptuously garnished dishes. They heard their own voices shouting, "My Lord: To the table! It's served hot."

Only Germaine Villaret-Joyeuse knew another adventure under the wings of Granchiré. Do you know why, Syllabaire, winking each eye, asked us in turn? Because of her loins, the others exclaimed in chorus.

Actually during my childhood the loins of Germaine Villaret-Joyeuse were an inevitable subject of coarse jokes. One spoke of them at wakes, banquets, baptisms, first communions, and marriage rejoicings. Public rumor attributed to my Godmother an excess of loins: two in her lower back, two in the forward part of her body, one to the left of the stomach, and two others, still more untimely, between her breasts. The night of her first marriage her spouse was carried out on a stretcher, finished off by a double fracture of the pelvis. "Poor Anatole was in the state of someone who had fallen from the crest of a coconut tree," Doctor Sorapal confided to my uncle Ferdinand, the local judge called in to verify the injuries.

The second husband, at this time, was admitted to Hospital Saint-Michel with several broken ribs. Only Archibald Villaret-Joyeuse, the third spouse, was able to escape these perils. The honeymoon left him safe and sound in his flourishing textile business. He succeeded in marvelously adapting to the blows from the legendary loins of campaign and fathered eight children in six years. His was a death altogether unknown to the medical faculty: a wasp's double bite to the testicles carried him off in less than 24 hours.

Lawyer Népomudène Homaire rendered a remarkable homage to his childhood friend in the *Gazette of the Southwest* on the 45th birthday of his widow. "It would be a game for his charms, helped by such a complex of loins, to cross over the year 2000. The genetic power that irrigated him had the fresh vivacity of a mountain cascade. The fecund loins of Germaine Muzac, bubbling with magic sparkles, still spurt out golden apotheoses to the male revels of the third millennium." My uncle Ferdinand remarked that with a similar pleasure center at work, our joyous one would still be capable in the year 2043 of leading our great grandsons to say hello to the angels!

Waiting that evening to listen to Scylla Syllavaire, it was Godfather General Granchiré who topped the tales! After each drossing, Germaine, illuminated within by her 36 orgasms, woke up, good buttock, good eye, to a butterfly in a full state of energy. They swore to never quit. Their liaison provided several months of respite for the families. One stopped hearing about the mystery of the deflowering, of engagements currently broken, of honeymoons robbed by break-ins, of desperate young couples, of marital bans annulled in extremis by Father Naélo.

Informed about the tragic fate that had taken Granchiré on his route to variable geometry, Germaine schemed to negotiate secretly with Okil Okilon the return of the prodigy to his human condition. In exchange for an important compensation the sorcerer was prepared to reverse the metamorphosis that exiled Balthazar *ad vitam aeternam* to the kingdom of the libertine lepidoptera. Balthazar reentered his chrysalis, reascended the larval state, followed the circuit of a caterpillar until he recovered his physique and liberty as a young actor playing lovers' parts.

I was there when a cancer of the right breast, metastasizing to the wind, balanced the flight of the other sounds of the bell in the haunted insides of my Godmother. The night arrived when she had only one loin holding out, like Leonides at Thermopalaye at the time of the attacks of a malign tumor and the "Persian Army." What was for her alone was the sensuality of her lover. Overcome by so much heroism, Balthazar decided to eternalize in heaven with Germaine the love feast begun in Jacmel. One night in a dream, between Purgatory and Eden, he saw a gulf comparable in beauty only to that carved by the Caribbean Sea in the interior of the Jacmelian coast. He places his gaudy wings over the eyes of his immortal loved one to prevent the wind from leading them astray on the maritime route to paradise.

Stray Thoughts

Esperanza Malavé Cintrón

Leather curves
Hug rock hard nipples
Cool lips
Kiss a bruised throat
Muddy blues
Tough bites
Cut into soft flesh
wavering, sharp
Red swings
Say you love me
A hot tongue surprise
creates clouded eyes

From *Down These Mean Streets*

Nasty Delightful Things

Piri Thomas

The train roared to a stop and all kinds of people pushed and shoved themselves into a sameness. The doors slid shut and the train jerked itself out of the station like it was sure of where it was going. I looked around. Everyone was in his own private world despite the close packing of bodies. I was squeezed in between a Chinaman and a soft broad. The Chinaman I ignored, but the *chica* was something else. Her ass was rocking to and fro, from side to side. The friction against my stomach caused a reaction, and the reaction kept time with the motion and the roaring insanity of the train.

I tried to think of other things, like cowboy flicks, lemonade, and "mind over matter." *Git down, stiff joint,* I commanded. *This broad's liable to think I'm some kind of weirdo instead of a nice normal Puerto Rican.* I pushed back, away from her. "Sorry," I mumbled.

Brew was reading the subway ads so he couldn't see what was happening to me hung up between the Chinaman and the soft-assed broad. The train lurched and that soft pile of rump crashed hard against my innocent joint. *Damn, she hadda feel that,* I thought ruefully. *Hope this bitch don't start yellin' up a storm.*

She didn't. She just turned and smiled expressively. It was a very damn-liberal smile. She didn't move away, and I could feel my joint playing it cool between her thighs. She pressed hard against me and let herself roll with the train. Man, I did the same. The train rooshed-sooshed to a stop at 42nd Street, and the doors slid open. Nobody got off; instead, more people piled in, and the pressure of the added closeness pushed me into the corner of the train. The softness before me went the same way. "Sorry," I said.

"It's all right," she said sweetly. "Let me see if I can get my balance."

I pushed back against the Chinaman and he, in self-defense, pushed back against the enemy. I held the weight back long enough for the girl to shift her weight and turn to face me. She looked flushed, and she smiled.

We said nothing else. The great weight came back and pushed us close together again. I felt her breasts hard against me and my joint bursting its wide vein between her thighs. Pressed together, we let ourselves roll in that hung-up closeness. I looked at her. Her eyes were closed. I made my hips dance a slow grind, and I let my hand think for itself and bite those liberal breasts. The whole motherfuckin' world was forgotten in the wingin' scene of stress and strain, grind and grain on a subway train.

We were roaring into the 14th Street station. *Hurry, hurry,* our bodies urged, and *swoom-ooo-mmm*—girl and me and train got to the station at the same time.

I felt her tremble and shiver as I boiled over. The train slowed down, and we held on tight. I dug her face, her paddy-fair face. Her eyes were still closed, and her teeth were biting into the corner of her lower lip.

The train stopped and the opened door shitted people out, releasing the pressure. We were swept out onto the platform and separated by the going-everywhere crowd. I reached out to touch her one more time, but the broken dam of people wasted the distance between us.

I tried to see which way she was cutting out, but all I caught was a pin-look see of her looking back for someone. I thought of calling out her name. But I didn't know her name, and I couldn't just start yellin', "Here I am, paddy girl." She disappeared, and I heard a voice call, "Piri! Hey, man, here Ah am. What you-all lookin' ovah that way for?" It was Brew. He chuckled and said, "Yuh lookin' for me an' here Ah am right behin' yuh."

"Yeah, Brew," I said absently, "ain't that a kick?" I felt kinda weak, like you feel when you've seen something glittering down a subway grating. You figure it's worth something, but you ain't got nothing to get ahold of it with. So you comfort yourself by saying, "Aw, it probably was a washer or something," and you never know whether or not it was for real.

Brew threw a friendly punch. I ducked and threw a couple of dummy punches, and Brew came back with a flurry. We stopped before it got serious, slapped skin, and kept walking. Brew put his arm around my shoulder, and I put my arm around his. I wondered what was the name of the girl on the train.

An hour and some thirty minutes later I was turning up the walk to the house in my world. I whistled like always and heard Momma's voice.

"Wan' to eat before you wash?" Momma said.

"Later, Moms. I want to take a shower first," I said. I undressed and got into the shower and let the water dig into me like shotgun BB's.

My shorts were stiff and starchy from the great strain on my vein, so I soaped and rinsed them and tossed them into the washbowl. The memory of that train ride stirred my joint again. I wondered if the broad was rememberin' how great it was, or if she was tellin' her friends how she made a horny Porty Rican climb the side of the wall on a subway train just by wiggling her white snatch against his black cock. I frowned. I'd thought "black cock," and that meant the broad was prob'ly sayin' "nigger" instead of "Porty Rican." I had a mental picture of all her friends hanging on her every word . . . *"You know, of course, that niggers got pricks two and three times as big as a white man . . . I tell you, girls, even through my dress I felt like I had about half of it inside me . . ."*

I shut my eyes to keep the soap out and saw her face clearly, her eyes closed and her teeth bitin' her lower lip . . . *"And when he grabbed my breast, I almost screamed, but I didn't want him to stop . . ."*

"Oh! I'd die if it were me," said one of the listening broads.

"I almost did," said my broad. *"I felt myself tremble all over and that black boy pushing all the weight of his thing into me and I felt my knees get weak and I'm pretty sure he had an orgasm, too, because he sort of sagged against me."*

"And what happened after that?"

"The train stopped and I got swept out along with him. We were separated. I'm glad 'cause I couldn't bear to have him say anything to me after my practically going to bed with him."

"Don't be foolish, that's not the same as when you're with your husband."

"I know, but regardless, it was with a colored boy. I just got away from there. I looked back once to see if he was following me and saw him looking over the heads of people as though he was looking for someone. In that one second, I was never so ashamed of myself."

"Oh, you needn't feel that way. It was just one of those nasty-delightful things one does in rare moments."

"You don't understand. I was ashamed because I wanted to fight my way back to him."

I bent down and turned off the water tap, satisfied on the ending of my mental production of "Beauty and Black's Best." But inside me, I felt hot and real stinky about this funny world and all the funny people in it.

Telegram from Topeka

Akua Lezli Hope

N O S E

O P E N

S E N D

E N D S

From *Shuckin' and Jivin'*

Teasing Tales and Tit(Bit)s

Daryl Dance

NOT EVEN FOR A WHITE WOMAN

Master's daughter was oversexed and she just demanded from her daddy to get her any man with a sixteen-inch dick. Master couldn't find such a man. She demanded again. White man or nigger—but sixteen inches.

Master got his slave with the longest dick and told him the story. He said, "I don't want no black screwing my daughter, but she wants sixteen inches."

John said, "Naw, suh, boss. Not even for a white woman. I wouldn't cut two inches off my dick for nobody!"

PRETTY LIKE A PEACOCK

White mistresses wanted some of those big black dicks, but they were afraid to death of their husbands, and could never let on that they felt so —even though they knew that their husbands slept with any nigger wench anytime they felt like it. Had a special room and bed for it.

This particular mistress would flirt with John whenever she got a chance. She would squeeze his dick and always say, "I want to be pretty like a peacock. Lord, make me pretty like a peacock. John, you are a wise nigger. Can't you make me pretty like a peacock?"

One day John got bold and told her to go down into the barn and get down on her hands and knees. John went down to the barn and thrust his rod up her. He went to town. She was panting and gasping, "Pretty like a peacock."

John bust his nuts a couple of times and then he started feeling and fondling her head and her hair.

She said, "Pretty like a peacock. John, don't bother about them head feathers. Just keep sticking them tail feathers in!"

JUST IN CASE

This man was playin' with the girl. She says, "I can't. I can't do anything like that. I'm on my period. I just can't do it."

So he went on 'round the back, you know. She says, "No! Don't touch me back there. I got hemorrhoids," you know.

"Ah-ha-a-a!"

So he gets out of his car, goes back in the trunk of his car. She's wondering what he's doing. Here he comes back—with a *crowbar*. She says, "What the crowbar for?"

He say, "Well, just in case, damnit, you got lockjaw too!"

PASS THE PUSSY, PLEASE

This woman was getting so disgusted with her husband about the way he made love to her. He was a truck driver, and he would come in after being out on the road for days, all dirty and smelly! And without taking a bath and without one caress or romantic statement, he would just jump in the bed on her. So finally she told him she just wasn't going to put up with that any longer. She said, "You're just going to have to have a little tact and finesse about the way you approach me. Why, you aren't even courteous! Clean yourself up and make yourself appealing and be more romantic. Don't just come in here jumping on me all dirty and smelly and expect me to respond."

So when he came home next time, he took a bath, shampooed his hair, shaved, put on some sweet-smelling after-shave lotion, slipped into some silk pajamas, and got in the bed. He caressed her gently and whispered sweet words in her ear. He said, "How am I doing? Is this tactful enough for you?"

She said, "Oh, yes, this is lovely."

"Am I being tactful enough?"

"Oh, yes!"

"Am I using enough finesse? Am I being courteous enough?"

"Oh, yes!"

"Well, would you pass the pussy, please!"

LET ME BE FRANK

These two secretaries had their vacation at the same time, and they both wanted to go to the beach for the summer. And to save money, they decided to share the same room. So they got off and went to the hotel. They got ready to go to bed that night. One of them said to the other, "Listen, you know, it's something about me that I . . . didn't . . . tell . . . you. Now I'm going to be frank!"

The other one said, "Oh! NO! Oh, NO! I'll be Frank!"

PETER REVERE

Listen my children and you will hear
Of the midnight fuck of Peter Revere.
Now Pete was born rugged and strong;
He had dick on 'im seven feet long.
'Twas a sad day for poor Pete
When he met an awful whore in the middle o' the street.
She challenged old Pete to a fuckin' duel
Up the hills and around the pools.
And people came from all around
To see old Pete put his fuckin' down.
There was old Big Ass Bess with her beaver hat;
She was wiggling her ass, so we can't miss that.
There was old Fart-box Sam,
Who didn't give a damn;
He just let out a fart
To give the signal, "Start!"
There was old stinking-cock Sally from Tennessee;
She acted as judge and referee.
They fucked all night and when they was still,
They had worn all the grass all over the hill.
She fucked old Pete to death, the dirty bitch,
And then she died with the seven-year itch.
And while they was carryin' old Pete's body to the graveyard,
Ass still wiggling and dick still hard . . .
And on old Pete's tombstone these words could be seen:
"Here lies a fucked-up fucking machine."

YO' MAMA

Your mother is like a doorknob. Everybody gets a turn.
Your mother is like a piece of pie. Everybody gets a piece.
Your mother is like a dresser. Everyone gets into her drawers.
Your mother thinks she's sharp 'cause her head comes to a point.

Your mother thinks she's a big wheel because her face looks like a hubcap.

[When one boy told another to go to hell, the latter responded:]
I went to hell,
The door was lock.
I found the key
In your mother's cock.

[Yo' mama's] a sweet old soul.
She got a ten-pound pussy
And a rubber asshole.
She got knobs on her tiddy
That can open a door.
She got hair on her pussy
That can sweep the floor.

Sit on a rock,
    Ooh ah!
Let the boys feel your cock,
    Ooh ah!
Don't be ashame',
    Ooh ah!
'Cause yo' mama do the same.

Warning

Saundra Sharp

WARNING!
  some blue/black
        brown   determined-minded
                      soft touchin'
                          strong thinkin'
            loud lovin'
          pretty smilin'
  big eatin'
      gentle teasin'
          honey kissin'
                eyes twinklin'
                    sweet brown
                    love man
betta come get me!
        quick!

Channeling

Sandra Y. Govan

Any time I want
I can you know
twist
my thoughts away from you.
I can, you know,
drive
without your unasked presence
cluttering space on an empty seat.

Any time I want
I can change channels
like I change bad dreams,
dialing past nightmares
of drowning in Montego Bay
or sinking in some lone stone quarry
while soft enigmatic eyes simply
smile.

Any time I want
I can box my needs

I can top the flood
I can dam the stream
I can keep within its banks the current connecting me to you;
I can cleanse my unclean dreams in the church-house
I can rinse the lust away,
be baptized in the blood of the lamb,
not awash in the love of a man.

At any time
I can turn
my attention,
I can set
my mind on a new path,
I can focus
on work, on home, on other needs,
I could even court another love . . .

Any time I want
I can, you know,
change.
I can find a clear channel
I can dial a strong station
I can
tune you out.

It's just, right now, at this moment,
I have misplaced my remote control
and the tuner in my set seems stuck.

A New Year's Eve Celebration

Yana West

At midnight Eastern Time, as the countdown begins in Times Square, you can open me up wide and take your tongue around my clock, bite my clit and make the juices come. As you salivate, the "count" is going down and by the time your tongue completes the wet, hot, juicy licks and nibbles around the circles of both inner lips, I'll be ready for your hard, sticky dick to drop into my twelve o'clock.

Our celebration has just begun. At midnight Central Standard Time, you'll begin to explore my back to massage and kiss it from the hairline down. And then you'll wet your fingers with the cream from my dripping pussy, draw a clock on my back, and place your twelve o'clock at the spot you most desire. And because this is the place I know you've longed to call home, I'll turn my ass up to meet your thrust.

For Mountain Time we can go back around the clock. But let us begin with a bath for two. A tub filled with oils and soaps to wash and scrub our bodies in preparation for our next celebration of love. To spend this hour in the water is just what I want, to spend each second touching and rubbing every inch of you. As we stand and turn the shower on to let the water hit my back, as I kiss and caress every inch of your golden brown body smelling like the peppermint oil and glistening from the rubbing and scrubbing of the oils which have penetrated your skin, as I taste and nibble at your breast, I'll take your long, thick, golden rod in my hand to knead and push your foreskin back and forth until it's seconds before midnight. As I travel down your erect torso with kisses and bites to your sweet, sweet sides, across your stomach and down to your valley of black and kinky hair, I'll prepare to take you deep into my mouth at twelve midnight, Mountain Time.

And as we go around the clock to reach Pacific Time, I'll continue to suck and suck until you run along the sides of my mouth and my own pussy is oozing with juice so wet, so ready for that last few minutes when you'll take that hard, strong, and ever so powerful rod and enter me slowly, going around and around, then touching each side with deep hard thrusts, finally penetrating so deep that it hurts, but I'll tell you to ride me, ride me because I can't get enough. As our celebration comes to an end, you decide that your last hurrah will occur with you fucking me from the back. And as the clock strikes 3 A.M., your long, hard dick is exploring the inner reaches of my tunnel of love, seemingly carving out new paths and going across oceans I never knew you could cross, but the more you traverse these places that I thought no man was meant to go, I'll relax and eagerly await each moment of the new year.

Dyke Hands

SDiane Bogus

Because dyke hands are the sexual organs of lesbian love, they can be as shocking to view as the penis through an open fly, or as bold (delicious) to behold as the breast of a woman suddenly uncovered.

Those hands you see folding laundry at the local laundromat, reaching, grasping, holding canned goods at the supermarket, may very well be the genitalia of some woman's lover, exposed. They often belong to our lovers, and those very hands come to our beds outstretched to touch, to rub, to tickle, to smooth, to run ripples of pleasure over our bodies, and often we take those very hands, finger by precious finger, into our mouths, assuming their cleanliness, their sanctity, and perform fingerlingus. We suck with reverence the hands that bring us to knotted heat, the very hands that hours before were signing some asinine form or holding a steering wheel. How can we possibly go on day after day, year after year, letting our lovers show their stuff to the world? How can we in good moral consciousness let our lovers take their naked dyke hands into a bar, reach for a beer and clutch it in front of lusting lesbian eyes? We all know that we look at the hands. We look at their size; we look for strength; we look for experience; we look for dexterity; evidence of ability, technique. But maybe I'm assuming something. Maybe I am assuming that lesbians revere the hands of their lovers, choose lovers by their hands. Maybe they don't. Never even thought of it. I mean, some go by the face, or legs, or ass. Me? I'm a hand womon. If she's got dyke hands, she's got my attention.

Recently, my lover and I went for a manicure, my first professional one. The beauty across the table grasped my lover's hand, placed it face-down on her own upturned palm. She spread the fingers wide, and proceeded to lotion the hand, up to the arm. Massaging and drawing with a near-pornographic stroke, the manicurist pulled her own encircled hand down my lover's arm, smoothly, pressing with sensual surety every molecule of lotion into the pores of her arm and hand. She did this to both hands, and I sat there allowing her the privilege to have her way with my womon, wondering what she'd think if she knew she was performing a six-dollar jack-off for the lesbian community. I was tickled by my vulgarity. But when she repeated the process, I realized she was getting into it, and I became jealous, hating her flirtatious rape of my womon. I sat seething, and giving my lover the eye. She knew. She knew, and she was tickled to death at being loved so well. A picture of ol' Madge on the Palmolive commercial flashed before me, and it all became so clear why those straight womyn flock to Madge's for soap-dish manicures. It was her dyke hand loving that they craved. Poor misguided Palmolive! At any rate, there was my lover's ten virile fingers stretched out like a naked man before a geisha, and something in me was proud and pissed at the same time. How good these hands were to my flesh when their touch wrought magic fires in my feet, raised the hair on my arms, brought my clitoris to knot and explosion! How dare this brazen money changer masturbate my beloved before my eyes! How dare she be so oblivious to the genitalia of lesbian love here naked before her. There she sat safe in her (I assumed) heterosexuality, unknowingly a whore to my womon's pleasure. If only she knew!

When it was my time, as tight-jawed as I had become, I literally squealed with pleasure. This intimate fondling, paid for or not, was delightful, one of the few good pleasures in life that is not yet overinflated. I sat back, with the joke on me, and let the manicurist, who became a human being, a womon making love to me, without the slightest notion, and I enjoyed.

The hands that stroke my hair, caress my flesh, that grip my thighs, press my love button, that slide between the satin readiness of my labia, ought not be seen by the daily populace. They belong in gloves, or mittens, and perhaps as a nation of womyn identified lesbians, white, black, or brown leather gloves can be made the symbol of our private sexuality, and between us at least the idea that we are lovers of womyn can be acknowledged by us all.

My holiest orgasms come from the probing phalanges of my lover's dyke hands. I'd not like to have them generally touching every Tom, Dick and Harriet, not my dyke's hands.

Dyke Hands 19 c

Dildo

Toi Derricotte

She had bought herself a very good-size rubber one, molded from an actual erect penis, with all the raised veins and details of the texture of the skin. It was ten inches long, and her thumb and index finger could barely fit around the circumference. It had balls, reddish dark, kind of pimply thick, with no backs, like a mask.

She had quickly brought in the box, which was waiting on the front steps. Thank God she had beat her husband and children home! She noticed with relief the return address said something innocuous, like Halcyon or Life Streams . . . Whatever it was, no way did it call up the open flood of female jism. She tore into it. Never in her Catholic life had she allowed herself to imagine! True, she had owned a wand once, a long, hard battery-operated thing that she had been afraid to put inside her for fear it would electrocute her. She had tried it a few times, but it soon r⸺ ⸺d where the battery went in, probably from washing it!! That had ⸺⸺ ⸺ years ago. Lately, however, as her sexual encounters with her ⸺⸺ ⸺ad become less frequent, less exciting, and after she had given ⸺⸺ ⸺ir—scared off by AIDS and Catholic guilt—she had sent for

⸺⸺ there was another box, with a large-as-life astounding ⸺⸺ dildo out and handling its rubber, not too stiff stiffness made her smile—as if she were a goddess looking down on herself from a distance, shaking her head. Of course she rushed upstairs to try it, and she was not disappointed! She was shocked by how quickly she responded, not even needing to be aroused first. She added a lubricant, stuck it in, and reached orgasm—a very deep orgasm—in about a minute, even though she hadn't touched her clitoris!

After, she worried. First, the box it came in was so big she couldn't get it hidden in the trash can. Her husband took out the garbage. The picture of the dildo loomed. The box was too thick to tear. Finally she turned it inside out, strapping it together with a rubber band, then folded it down tightly in the garbage and opened the step-on can several times to make sure the picture wouldn't pop out in his face.

Second, when she left the house shortly after, she noticed that the kitchen blinds were partway open. She had been so excited opening the box she had forgotten to close the blinds! Her neighbor had been out shoveling snow. She went out to check and found that one could see—if one were walking quickly—only a flash of the kitchen. Surely he wouldn't have stopped and stared! Well, maybe if he had, he would have thought it was something she and her husband had sent away for. It seemed less embarrassing if it was for conjugal purposes.

And there were other worries. Would she stretch so that her husband would notice? Would she enjoy sex with him less as a result? Would she go crazy for it, doing it several times a day? What if someone came home? What if the cleaning lady found it, the pet-sitter? What if her mother found it? She hid it in her sweater drawer in the second bedroom. But what if she died? Who would go through her drawers separating out the sweaters to give to friends, the sweaters to Goodwill?

If her husband found it, would he feel hurt, betrayed? If her son found it, would he feel repulsed, horrified? And if it was her mother, would she have a heart attack? Her mother hadn't slept with her father since she was born. She could see her mother's face—as if the dildo would jump out of the drawer and eat her alive!

She would just *tell* her husband. How would she put it? "I really enjoy sex with you, but I need a little something extra. It's in the second dresser drawer in the guest bedroom. If I die, please get it before my mother." Would she show it to him? Would he need a demonstration? That could be very bad for their sex life, which, though not perfect, was at least, let's face it, human.

Maybe, before she died, she'd outgrow the need, confess and throw it out—like Kafka burned his notebooks. But probably she'd have to stand up with it on the last day, before the complete heavenly host—John the Baptist, Peter and Paul, and all the saints, Bartholomew, Linus, and Cletus, the prophets, and even the pure angels, who are no doubt still pissed off after realizing what they *didn't* get in order to be smarter than us and immortal.

PART SIX

Ooohwee, Baby, You Feel So Good

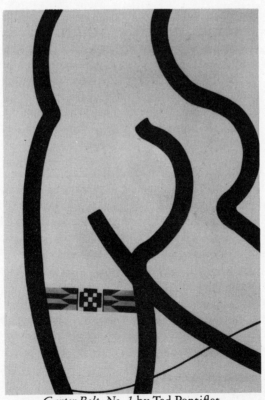

Garter Belt, No. 1 by Ted Pontiflet

Feeling good, orgasmically and otherwise, sneaks up without warning. Some people work at it—jogging, sweating, meditating, fasting. They are walking advertisements for doing the right things and reaping the rewards. But there is *nothing* like the satisfaction of good loving. *Nothing!* That, when coupled with love or simple sincere affection, makes love lyrics sell, and turns plaster of paris gazes into electric smiles. And there is the ah-h-h, when it's over, the gush of breath from the diaphragm. Without laughing, there is no more fun in the world than having good sex.

The selections in "Ooohwee, Baby, You Feel So Good" are not just about tactile expression. They are what makes Siedah zip in Reginald Martin's prose piece; Siedah explains, "My immediate game plan right now is simple: find you, fuck you, and feel you forever." Feelings like that open the link from a mouth, a taste, a melody, a smell, to God's ear. Or a woman's ear, especially when a man calls her "Baby."

> LOW & GUTTURAL
> MAKING IT SOUND
> NASTY
> & PORNOGRAPHIC
> AND
> MAKING ME LOVE
> THE WAY
> HE CALLS ME
> BABY

Yeah, Ahmasi! And it's the *thing* that joins a lonely woman and a young gigolo ex-offender on a rainy Sunday afternoon in R. Pope's "The Three-Token Stradivarius"; the *thing* that makes him holler, "begging like a coked-up blues singer, Ooo, Ooo, Mama, Mama, Baby, PLEASE DON'T STOP!" Uh-huh! And when you don't have anyone to love, you can order one of the sex toys in Constance García-Barrio's "Plain Wrappers." Feeling good makes you realize that "fun ain't sitting on an active volcano." Hell no. "You got to let that lava flow to cool it down."

Cool. Warm. Hot. Burning fire and cool mountain stream. Summer sun and night moon. John Turpin's park, wet and green; Saundra Sharp's purple blueberries, sunny rain. Nelson Estupiñán Bass of Ecuador captures the mood in his verse:

I will lay about in your heaving body:
you will feel the very air you breathe burn so
when your body rages, lit, in the fires of pleasure.

Everything hot and hard. E. Ethelbert Miller writes about hot summer days when women lift their legs, and M. Nourbese Philip describes the joy of taking a man, hard and firm. There is so much joy in coupling: two young lovers in P. J. Gibson's "We'll Be Real Good Together" (and they were!), and a pair of middle-aged lovers in Marita Golden's novel. But Kalamu Ya Salaam, perhaps, best captures the feeling in his tight, taut, Japanese-like verses of joy that make you wanna holler and shout—

the joy of riding
your round nakedness, our skins
tingling with laughter

Fresh

Saundra Sharp

Hey, Fresh

I call you Fresh
like a stolen nipple kiss
like a good cry
like a wailing note

Fresh.
like purple blueberries
an old Ashford & Simpson song
a newborn's foot.

Fresh like tomorrow
     like a sunny rain
     a low down tingle
     a moving hand

like a neck hug,
like a stroked thigh
Fresh like fast
like fast
like swifting
    on my body/heart

Hey, Fresh!

Trotting Through the Park

John Turpin

Trotting through the park
we discovered
Maggie laying Bill
what a thrill
you said
And so
you watched Bill
And I watched Maggie
twitch and twill behind the little hill

Secret thoughts yours
more secret mine
as we smiled and watched
Maggie & Bill
from behind

From *EveryBody Knows What Time It Is*

What Makes Siedah Zip

Reginald Martin

A LONG LETTER FROM SIEDAH NEVER SENT

Confused by her sudden inability to be happy with the affairs she has or to finish her engineering projects, Siedah Jackson decides to look back into her emotional and erotic past via a series of letters to herself. She hopes to find from herself the "whys" of her new impotency—especially why her psyche has suddenly—and stultifyingly—connected sex to love. She will find out or go completely insane. It is May of 2018, and New Orleans is stiflingly humid—and hot.

SUNDAY
For You

It's difficult to describe what happened to me to turn me into the person I am now. I used to not need anything from anyone and then I hit 35 and BOOM: all of a sudden I needed to love and be loved in the dumbest cinematic sense of the phrase cause in a dream he came to me and the feeling was so good that I knew that for a girl like me who ain't never had enough of nothin that the new feelings in that dream were better than the old feelings outside the dream and I knew I wanted to keep the new.

What are we doing here with the little bitty time we have? What *do* we do here? Are we doing anything of any importance at all, even the ones who are rich and powerful? Or are we just here for a minute like moths, and we go and that's the end of us? Now, that's Absurd. All our memorizing geometric theorems, groaning, and plucking our eyebrows for nothing . . . nothing of lasting significance . . . nothing done to give any significance to the moths that follow us. Then, right then, I felt all my living—all my life—to be completely Absurd, without a trace of reason.

It's so goddamn pointless to live for money at my age. First of all, you can never get enough of the stuff, and when you're done compiling it, nobody sees your emptiness clearer than you do cause you know that nobody in this world ever made a pile of money honestly, and honesty was that thing you left on the shelf with your Easy Bake Oven. Yet, that's what I've come to, living for more and more money.

So I figured there's gotta be something permanent that you can throw your temporary self into, and one morning I woke up and this time my eyes weren't still shut; I knew what the something was: "Love is like a walk down Main Street," Al Green sang, and he made me want to lay on that lyric all day.

I realize now I have so much I want to say and so many ways I want to say things that I know I won't complete this letter tonight. I'm going to have to give me some time. Right now, um gonna take this sweating, naked body into a very cold shower, stick my head under the spray, and rethink my dream 3 or 4 hundred times. Then again, maybe I'll just stay in bed with this dream for a while, since I'm already naked and all.

MONDAY

They say some things are better left unsaid, and, well, I guess that's right cause Lord knows I've said some things that I wish I could grab back and stuff down my throat. But since I don't know you yet, don't know if I ever will know you, I figure I can just say what's on my mind, and if you wanna later use my openness against me to close me, I'll just have to take that chance cause I gotta tell.

Love is a smile. And it's one of those smiles that comes when you don't expect it and you can't make it stop. In the emptiest and easiest part of my life, at a time when to be a success all I had to do was stay out of the rock house and not go to bed with white women's husbands, when cool breezes blew in from the Gulf in the heart and heat of July and my condo doubled in its FHA estimate, during the point when my most stressful days consisted primarily of choosing the taupe or the black high heels, and every design and blueprint I put together was a hit, and my co-workers weren't jealous enough to even *say* anything bad about me, when the ugliest part on my body was my 24K diamond ring, and when the

Saints had finally gotten into and won the Super Bowl, in a dream you came to me and I could not resist you.

Did my need and longing conjure you? Did I make you come just to make me come? Or were you already entitled out there and came to me cause you felt me and flew straight into my flame? Baby, you know my aloof attitude is just a chain-link fence I hide behind, and while you can't break it down, you don't have to. You can just get me through the cracks.

So if you wanna hurt me, you know it's not very hard to do, but what I really, really want from you is to see me through and stop lettin me be this halfa person.

TUESDAY

One time when I was 12, I went walking to the store. I had on my blue sailor's dress with the big, white, floppy collar and the naval insignia on it. Behind my back was a big, blue, cotton bow that was tied around my waist and bounced around on my already round behind. I was already a 32-D cup and my legs were better than my mama's. I had two strong desires in life: to go to Disney World and spend the night in Michael Jackson's suite, eating up all his jelly beans and coffee ice cream, and the other desire my parents didn't even allow me to think about.

So I'm walking down St. Charles Street and whistling some old LUTHER and I see some BOYS. BOYS I wasn't supposed to talk to; BOYS I wasn't to receive phone calls from; BOYS and BOOKS didn't mix; BOYS only wanted one thing and it was a bad thing and I wasn't supposed to want it either; BOYS started with the same letter as Bad-news, Backasswards, and Bad Breath; and I was supposed to only think of *C* words like church, chaste, children, cute, college, careers, and . . . chain-link fences.

These BOYS always teased me cause I never said a word to them and I was so cute and cuddly. None of us woulda known what to do with ourselves if I had given them some, but I sure woulda been tryin to figure out what to do. Plus, it was so easy just to flip my nose up at BOYS cause they always gave themselves away. BOYS are so transparent. If they want you, they tell you so, and then they're at a complete disadvantage. And since all of em are alike, I was perpetually like a girl in a toy store with all the money and time in the world. But you have to play with a toy before you can know if you like it or not, and Daddy had told me I better not ever get ready to play with these toy-BOYS or he'd put me on punishment.

So they started out as usual, saying stuff like "Uh uh uh, why don't you let me buy you something at the store, pretty girl," and "Hey, baby, can I walk with you?" and "Hey, Siedah, just tell me what it would take!"

"More than you have," I'd think to myself on the first-level response, but always thinking something opposite on a deeper level. But I'd never say a word.

And I just kept walkin and threw my little button up in the air. But I musta really looked like myself that day cause this day when I threw my head back I saw all of em come runnin toward me, and before I knew it they were in a circle around me—not really threatening me in any way, but just lettin their testosterone and my navy dress get the best of them, taunting me.

They said things like "Why you won't never talk to us?" and "You ain't better than us, little girl, you just a lot prettier," and "Why you never sit next to us in class or at lunch? You too fine to even eat with us?" and "Why you so stuck-up?"

And then I started to cry and one a the BOYS said "Uh oh," and they all ran away in one direction and I ran away in the opposite direction.

But what I couldn't do, what I couldn't tell them was that I was crying cause I wanted to run in their direction, with them. But then everybody in the world woulda dumped on me, including them and including me. I felt so unstuck cause I just wasn't like what I was spozed to be like.

Shoot, I had been having all this sexual energy since I was 9, and I just didn't have no place to put it. But I got a feeling Mama musta been just like me when she was little cause I was just out playing in the yard one day when I was 13 and I saw her staring at me through the window, and all of a sudden she came out and snatched me and took me to her gynecologist and she attached to my lower left side onea them then-new time-released birth-control patches, and I didn't even know what it was until I was 15; I just thought I had sprung a leak somewhere or something. But the whole episode set me on some deep thinking about what Mama was really like and what she had always pretended to be like cause she was only 13 years older than me.

And I would see BOYS walking in front of my yard or at school that I really, really liked, and I knew I wanted to make love to em and I knew I'd be clumsy at it but that I'd make up for that in enthusiasm.

But always over my shoulder was my society tellin me that good girls didn't even think that way, much less actually did it; and at the same time tellin me that black girls were all whores anyway, pressuring me to sit on my pussy to disprove a point that was a lie in the first place. Contrary to made-for-the-movies and what you think you see on the street corners, Afro-Americans are the most puritanical people in the U.S. cause they're always trying to live up to or live down stereotypes insteada being themselves.

What Makes Siedah Zip 213

And if I looked to the left, there were Mama and Daddy tellin me that I couldn't even feel nothin like that until I was 21 and that when I did feel that way it had better be for one man with a good job forever-and-ever-Amen; and on my right were my girlfriends all still wanting to play jacks and watch the Disney Channel, and all the BOYS sticking out their obnoxious little prepube tongues and makin it too easy for me; and straight ahead in the mirror was me, looking all confused and gettin down on myself because by society's definitions I was an 18-year-old BOY trapped in a 13-year-old girl's body. I thought I would blow up.

So when I finally found out what that patch was for at 15, I got as secretive as Amon, and nobody never knew that I had finally been allowed to find myself, and I was happier than I had ever been. I finally had some place to put what I was feeling, and, child, I put it every place I could.

I confided in Granny about the whole funny ordeal just before she died last year, and she burst out laughing and spit her snuff into a Maxwell House coffee can and held me by my hand and said:

"Look, *I* don't understand all this new waiting around to do it anyway. Why do you think all of us from back in the country in my generation got married at 11 and 12? Honey child, my idea of fun ain't sittin on an active volcano. You got to let that lava flow to cool it down. Don't tell your crazy-ass mama though. That po child! She's only 13 years younger than I am and she done got so un-black that I think she wants to think the Smurfs brought her here in a mushroom."

And now look at me, Nighttime Lover. All that good stuff that made me so happy for so long just ain't enough by itself no more. I want you.

WEDNESDAY

I couldn't get you off my mind today. As I pulled the Porsche into the parking garage, I just left the radio on and lay back and thought of you.

Fantasies are almost always better than the real thing. And even when the real thing is there and lives up to your desires, it can be pretty scary sometimes. Hard to pull back from the real thing, hard to control it. But in my fantasy in my car, you loved me the way I wanted to be loved.

It's a pretty simple equation, but it's so hard for most people to work out. Here it is—uh—

Step 1:   you loved me as much as you loved yourself—uh—
Step-uh—2:   you wanted me to do well in life, and none of your own insecurities would make you want to undo me—uh—

Step 3:	you always remembered what we were in the game for in the first place: TO GIVE EACH OTHER FUN, not to turn each other into our own parents and grow old and die.
—uh—Step 4:	you were always around when I needed you
and Step 5:	you always gave it to me like we wouldn't be gettin a chance to do it again—uhhh

THURSDAY

My immediate game plan right now is simple: find you, fuck you, and feel for you forever. I can really appreciate those kinda life-enhancing feelings on a day like today that was filled with those feelings' opposites.

I know lots of four-letter words, but the dirtiest and most dehumanizing one I know is W-O-R-K. *W* is for wasting my human potential slaving for superiors who don't do a quarter of my work load and whom I never see; *O* is for only making more money for people who need more money like I need more tits; *R* is for running like a rabbit on a treadmill that never ends if you have one honest microbe in your psyche; and *K* is for co-workers who hate me cause um blacker, cuter, smarter, and make more money cause I work harder.

Anyway, I know you don't want to hear all this, but um afraid that's gonna be a part of loving me too. You know how it is. Sometimes you just need somebody to tell it to.

FRIDAY

I can't decide if this would be the best night to be with you or if it would be Saturday night. I think maybe Friday cause we could dance off the workweek and later retire and do some . . . reading. I wrote a poem for you at work today, but I won't read it to you unless you give me some.

SATURDAY

Y'know, I was on this project recently. Somebody wanted to keep the basic structure of this old club that had been closed down and build a pizza joint on top of all of it. Since the club was on the 2nd floor of this building, I went over there in Storyville to see if the basic structure was strong enough to support counters, ovens, refrigerators, jukeboxes, things like that. And it was strong enough, but I really hated to do the work on the project. I got choked up in that old place.

The veneer on the wood of the dance floor, well, the floorboards really, were all scuffed and worn down. Those urban dance-floor guerrillas had left just one big rough groove in the middle of the club. And I thought, "We're gonna undo every trace of that groove, every trace of all that joy." And I just got all choked up and I started to dance even though there was no music.

I never had an "urban revitalization" project affect anything on me except the size of my Money Market account. I don't know. It's hard to explain.

SUNDAY

Missing you. Show up . . . or leave me alone.

Baby

Ahmasi

HE CALLS ME
BABY
IN THE PRIVACY
OF OUR ALONENESS
WHEN WE
SHUT THE DOOR
ON THE WORLD
LOCKING US IN
AND AWAY FROM
PRYING TONGUES
AND UN/UNDERSTANDING EYES

HE CALLS ME
BABY
IN A MANNER
THAT
DRAWS ME TO HIM
& LOCKS ME IN
THE WARMTH OF HIS

MIGHTY FOREARMS
& GRANITE BICEPS

AND
HE CALLS ME
BABY
WHEN
HE'S IN
THAT MOOD
WHEN NOTHING MORE
NEEDS
TO BE SAID

HE CALLS ME
BABY
LOW & GUTTURAL
MAKING IT SOUND
NASTY
& PORNOGRAPHIC
AND
MAKING ME LOVE
THE WAY
HE CALLS ME
BABY

We'll Be Real Good Together

P. J. Gibson

Wilamina and Geoffery stopped for sour pickles from Mr. Bob's Corner Store, being quite choosy as to which was the longest, fattest, hardest and sourest. Then they crossed the street and sat under one of the old branchy trees and ate pickles and discussed the world. Wilamina ate pickles and discussed the world. Geoffery watched Wilamina's lips and the way she sucked the juice and center of the pickle up through the small opening she had made at the top with a quick sharp little bite. He watched her as she sucked harder and harder until the top third of the pickle was drained into a sunken withered state. It was then that she bit it and crunched on it until it was gone. Then she'd talk a little more before she sucked again, long and hard on the pickle. She noticed that he had begun to say less and less and spent more and more time looking at her as she ate on her pickle.

"What? . . ." she asked.

"What? What?" was his response.

"What are you looking at me like that for?"

"We're gonna be good together." He smiled and chomped into his pickle.

"Good together . . . how?"

"You know what I'm talkin' about." He stared deep into her eyes.

"If I knew what you were talkin' about, I wouldn't have to ask you."
She knew, but she wanted him to say it out loud.

"You don't need a boy for a lover."

"How you know I need a lover?" She sucked the juice out of the pickle.

"You need a good lover. Your lips tell on you."

"And what makes you so all-knowing, Geoffery Tanner? And what you know about lovin' anyway? And how come you talking like you know so much about lovin'? You ain't but sixteen yourself. That ain't what I would call a man, you know."

"We're gonna be real good together."

"Will you stop that."

"You don't want me to stop that . . . You want me to start something we're both gonna enjoy."

"How you know I'm gonna enjoy it? And don't tell me about how I eat my pickle."

"You're gonna enjoy it because I'm going to be better than anything you ever read about or dreamed about."

"You're all mouth, Geoffery Tanner." With that she stood up. "If you didn't have a head full of brains, I wouldn't spend the time of day with you, but you got a head on your shoulders and that's why I listen to you. But you don't know nothing about what's gonna be good between you and me." He rose and pinned Wilamina softly up against the tree and gently kissed her lips.

"You've got nice lips, Wilamina."

She was speechless. He had soft lips and his breath was sweet. His breath was sweet and he'd been eating a sour pickle. It didn't make sense. She stood motionless against the tree.

"We're gonna be real good together." He moved in closer; this time planting a succulent kiss into her mouth. His tongue meeting hers, teaching hers. Hers responding. He smiled and pulled back from her body. She said nothing, but looked at him as though she were seeing him now for the first time.

Geoffery took Wilamina by the hand and crossed through the park, down the alley between Tilmer and Javitts streets until they came up on Riverside Lane and the narrow alleyway which ran parallel to Riverside Lane and Otis Drive. There, tucked in the corner between two large oak trees, was a small fading redwood shed. It was nestled back about forty or so feet away from his Uncle James's house, the "Writing Shed." Geoffery crossed between the cluster of dark green hedges to the door. He unlocked the door to the "Writing Shed." Wilamina stepped in. "You always bring your girls here?" Wilamina asked as she crossed over the bookcase.

"I don't always do nothing. And I've never brought anyone here before." He pulled down the shade.

"I'm special."

"You got a problem with that?" He liked the verbal games they played with one another.

"Whose place is this?"

"My uncles'."

"You can just walk in here like this?"

"They're out of town. I sort of babysit the place. You know, turn the lights on and off and stuff."

"What kind of stuff?" She liked the verbal games they played.

"The kind of stuff that makes me feel good."

"What makes you feel good?"

"Loving you is gonna make us both feel good." He was confident she would lie on the plaid sofa with him.

"How you know I'm going to let you do what you want to do to make us both feel good?"

"Because you want me as much as I want you."

"You get that line out of a book, Geoffery Tanner?" She smiled. She had a pretty smile.

"We're gonna be real good together, Wilamina. Why you want to drag this thing out? You're gonna be sorry when you find out what we could have been . . ." She stopped him. She didn't know if she was hurt by this, the insensitivity of his rush, or by the fact that he had negated the romanticism of the moment.

"Wait a minute. You think because you kiss good, you have a key to a hideaway for a secret rendezvous and an uncle and aunt out of town that I'm supposed to be happy, drop my panties, and let you ride me like a horse? It's not going to happen like that. And if you had half the sense I thought you had an hour ago you wouldn't have made a stupid statement like 'Why you want to drag this thing out? You're gonna be sorry when you find out . . .' " She was right. He'd fucked up. He'd forgotten the difference between being a boy and a man, patience. He apologized.

"I'm sorry. I was wrong. You're right. Would you like a RC Cola?" He crossed to the little old refrigerator which had once sat in his Aunt Candy's kitchen.

"You have any lemon to go with it?"

"No, but I have some ice."

"Thank you. Lots of ice. I'm hot." She smiled. She toyed with him on the word "hot." She sat on the sofa and crossed her legs, revealing strong tight thighs beneath her pedal pushers. He crossed to her with a glass of ice and a sixteen-ounce RC Cola.

"Sometimes I act like I'm sixteen." He sat down next to her.

"You *are* sixteen."

"Yeah, but I know more than most sixteens. I know better."

"I just don't want to be rushed like in some assembly line. I don't want my first time to be no 'wham bam, thank you, mam.' Know what I mean?"

"I'm gonna love you like a man, Wilamina. We're gonna be so good together that it ain't never gonna be no 'wham bam, thank you's' ever." He kissed her. His tongue moved into her mouth. She placed her arms up around his neck and gently pulled him in close to her. He placed his arm behind her back and tenderly guided her down onto the sofa. She could feel the hard growth of his manness pressing down onto the throbbing beats of her vagina lips. His mouth was still sweet. His tongue was still teaching hers. He moved his lips down her neck, kissing her softly.

"You won't put no hickeys on me, will you?"

"Only boys advertise," he answered, and continued his kisses down to the top button of her sleeveless madras plaid shirt. His soft warm hands made their way down her back to the button and zipper in the back of her pants.

"If you don't have protection, I can't let you do this. I want to go to college."

"I'm way ahead of you, Wilamina." He reached down between the cushions of the sofa and pulled out a sealed prophylactic. Wilamina sat straight up.

"How long has that been there?"

"I just put it there."

"Where'd you get it from?"

"I got it from the pack. I got a pack of three."

"Where do you keep them? In your back pocket? In your wallet? You're not using no rubber on me you had in your back pocket or wallet. I know what happens to rubbers in back pockets and wallets."

"What?" He couldn't believe what was happening. Just a moment ago things were going just fine and now . . . "What happens to rubbers in back pockets and wallets?"

"They get hot and old and they dry out, and then they're no good and they don't work, and the woman gets pregnant, and I don't want to get pregnant because I don't want to end up like Alison . . . I want to go to . . ."

"College. You told me."

"So . . ."

"So . . . what?"

"Where was that prophylactic before you put it between the cushions?"

"In the drugstore. I bought them last week. I brought them over here and hid them up here . . ." He crossed to a shelf at the bookcase. "And put them here behind my books. These two shelves are my shelves. Want to see? I have my name in my books."

"You planned on getting me in here? This wasn't spontaneous?"

"Yeah, it was spontaneous. But a man's got to be prepared. I can't keep these at my house; my mother goes through my things. Okay? You satisfied? They ain't old. They ain't gonna bust, and you ain't gonna get pregnant. And this whole thing is probably what the books call an exercise in . . ."

She stopped him, thrusting her tongue deep into his mouth. They took one another on the coolness of the floor, atop the old loop rug Geoffrey's Aunt Candy's mother had made. It was the beginning of many stolen moments the two would share in the discovery of their loving. They had been, as Geoffery had predicted, good together. Miss Dorothy had taught him well. He had taught Wilamina well, and that which they had together was . . . good.

Commitment to Hardness

M. Nourbese Philip

Diah lay on her back staring out into the darkness of the room; she had come awake suddenly with the feeling that something had awakened her, but all was still. There was no difference between the blackness in the room and that which she saw out the open window. It was the stars that helped her to recognize where the room ended and the window began. Ben breathed softly next to her. The physical longing for him was as sudden as it was strong: she felt her stomach muscles contract and tighten—the desire for him seemed to begin there and spread down through her cunt, where she felt the familiar sensation of waves moving through her as those muscles contracted and relaxed with him. She touched her clitoris—it was firm while the lips of her cunt vibrated ever so gently. She was wet for him—along her thighs, down her legs and up her body to her nipples, which were now tingling—the feeling for him spread, sometimes it ran slow like molasses creeping down her legs, at other times it would leap from one part of her body to another—clitoris to breast, to mouth—even her tongue felt desire, and she felt that each area of her body was feeling its own unique type of desire. The wanting of her cunt was different from the wanting of her lips, but altogether the different desires meshed until she felt herself one concentrated point of desire and want. She reached out to touch Ben where he lay on his back.

She placed her hand on his cock and she began stroking it gently as it lay curled to one side; as she stroked she felt it first shudder and then harden ever so gently. She continued to stroke, keeping up a slow rhythm, and soon what she held in her hand was the hardness—of his cock. It was a hardness that was like no other hardness—all other expressions used in calypsos, and blues songs, and what people call dirty jokes came to mind —ramrod, big big bamboo, pole, driving shaft—all these were accurate and yet not accurate—those things were all lifeless in their hardness. This hardness she now held, running her fingers up and down its surface, was a living hardness with a commitment to be hard, to be nothing but hard, and that commitment had to do with something else—something larger than her or Ben. That commitment to hardness belonged to the race— making Ben's cock a part of him and yet not a part of him. It was like a woman's stomach when it was enlarged with child—she had seen people pat a woman's pregnant stomach with a familiarity that they would never presume in ordinary circumstances. She herself had done this when her friends had been pregnant, rubbing the stomach and predicting the sex of the baby. Pregnant stomachs belonged to the race, the tribe, not in the sense that right-to-lifers and anti-abortionists said, giving them the right to dictate to a woman—it was more a sense of the stomach allowing others to share in a moment of time common to them all—that they all needed to remind themselves of. So this lance she now held in her hand belonged to the race in its commitment to hardness, but no lance was ever so soft-tipped, crowned by such a velvet head. Diah's hand continued its gentle but firm stroking; she imagined going up to a man and patting his dick and suggesting it belonged to the race. She had to stop herself from laughing out loud, as she saw the obvious limits to her analogy between women's pregnant stomachs and men's dicks. Diah's hand moved more swiftly over Ben's cock, which now trembled and shuddered with every touch as he lay there breathing softly letting her keep him hard while she grew wetter still with the wanting of him. She stopped stroking now, pushed herself up, and throwing a leg over Ben, she rolled over so that she now lay on him. She sat up and felt his cock rubbing against her buttocks, and then she raised her hips, shifted her weight back, and slowly began lowering herself on him—he groaned softly—a small sound from the base of his throat. She wanted to feel every inch of him as she lowered herself and so at times she would raise herself again so that she covered the same distance twice—three times—over and over again. She wanted him to do nothing, just lie there offering himself to her—the commitment of himself and the race present in the unbearable hardness she felt between her legs. He seemed to sense what she wanted, because unlike their usual lovemaking he made no attempt to be more active. She moved herself on him, first in circular movements making small tight sounds, then up and down, and still Ben lay there, a willing partner offering his cock and its goodness. Diah didn't know why but it was important that Ben not respond for the moment; maybe it equalized relations between them. Diah reached out to the bedside table for her tobacco and cigarette papers—Ben remained hard within her as she rolled and lit up. Every so often she moved her hips, feeling Ben pulse in response inside her. She took long slow drags on her cigarette—she had never thought that sameness could be erotic, but the first time she and a female friend had made love, the shock of the absence of power—the sameness between them—was what turned her on; no matter how gentle, loving, and non-sexist a man her lover happened to be, there was still this marker of difference—that was now inside her—so attractive yet to be feared. As if to emphasize that difference and so maybe go past it, Diah now ground herself into Ben's crotch, feeling the soft tip of his penis stroking deep inside her; she heard herself make soft moaning sounds. Quickly she butted out her cigarette, now she was jealous, she wanted to taste herself—to taste her goodness; she rolled off him and told him she wanted to suck him, to suck her juices off his cock, and she closed her mouth over his commitment to hardness. His sounds joined the rhythm of hers, she was tasting herself salt and tangy along the length of him, and when she had sucked him clean of her, he entered her again. This time they began to laugh and laugh as they rode home together, she gripping his buttocks and every so often stroking the back of his balls to make him groan with pleasure, he bracing himself on his arms as he slammed himself into her, each urging the other on and on, their mutual laughter and shouts becoming like some boisterous call and response until Diah saw herself as if separate from her body, observing Diah and Ben light up the darkness with a robust joy. As they lay together afterwards, she was grateful for the cool breeze that came through the window drying the sweat on their bodies. Thank god for commitment to hardness, she thought, and chuckled to herself; her fingers were intertwined with his and she lifted them to her lips and kissed them. He returned the gesture. She reached across him for her cigarettes.

"Stay with me, Diah—don't go back to Canada. It's not fair that you're leaving when we have this together—how can you leave?"

"I don't know—let's talk about it tomorrow."

"Yes, tomorrow."

Haiku #29

Kalamu Ya Salaam

the joy of riding
your round nakedness, our skins
tingling with laughter

Summer

E. Ethelbert Miller

on hot days
young women
dangle their legs
off stoops
cross ankles
& rock themselves
in tune to music
coming from open windows

passing men
laugh & joke
if they could
they would
lift those legs
like a warm
summer breeze
and dance

The Three-Token Stradivarius

R. Pope

It had been three years, two months, seventeen days, and one hour since I'd had a real good fuck. Who am I kidding, and what am I saying? It had been that long since I'd shared *any* tactile experience of note with anyone. And that last fuck, thousands of hours ago, wasn't even a good fuck, as I remembered. Both of us were overweight, the teasing of several months leading up to the occasion wasn't particularly unique, and there was no spiritual light, especially in me, to excuse the inexcusable—like he had one foot in the grave of impotency, or perhaps the women by whom he'd fathered eleven children didn't require sterling performance, just having a product was enough. It wasn't all his fault, though, that the fuck wasn't good. I was in the pre-dry-out stage of marathon oral excesses. I drank daring concoctions of bourbon, vodka, gin, scotch, brandy, and cheap wine with passion fruit and lemonade, or hibiscus tea, lime, and rum. I ate everything associated with decadence—lots of starch, grease, salt, hot peppers, and sugar, added to that in the drinks. I smoked. God, how I smoked. I had an herb garden. Yes, there was some of the regular stuff like Spanish thyme, basil, and bay, but the glory of my garden was HERB, which bloomed joyfully and lovingly in my garden. Even HERB, however, couldn't make me sympathetic to a limp dick trying to poke its way along a dry coarse tunnel.

And I *did* have something to compare good fucking with. I'd *known* sixty-two men in the three years, two months, seventeen days, and one hour before THE THING started to happen to me, the intrusion and revelation of a dangerous part of me I suspected existed. I think about THE THING often. Now, it visits me when I have cause to pleasure myself because there's no one else there to do what I need to be done. If you want it done right, I was taught, do it yourself.

In my small apartment, I peeled off my sweat-lined clothes as I looked for pineapple, banana, and strawberry chunks to blend with some vodka, lime juice, and a drop of pear flavoring. Finding everything, I made three generous portions for the freezer in my best goblets: I'd have company, possibly an orgy in my hallucinations. Clothes off, I had to decide how best and quickest to get to nirvana, and possibly to sleep for a while before the business of living the next day began. If I had cable, I thought, I could look at something less banal than white people writhing all over satin sheets, having trysts with forbidden fruit. Or if I had a VCR, I could probably look at something decent of my own lascivious choice: *Deep Throat, Behind the Green Door, Choklit Chile's Night Out, The Young Man Who Was an Old Whore,* or *A Good Dick Is Hard to Find.* But there was nothing but absurdia on the tube, and I felt like seeing and feeling something intimate, something that hung over me like a nameless thing from the Twilight Zone.

It sounded like the beginning of thunder, but I quickly recognized a furtive knock. Who could that be? I wasn't expecting anyone. I didn't bother to use the peephole; all I would have seen was the top of a jheri curl. On a pleasant Sunday afternoon, after good conversation and before me, myself, and I indulged in the 323 ways my mind knew how to fuck, the last thing I needed was place and time with a scary curl.

"Can I get a light?" It was Bobby, Pops's nephew who was the fine quiet one, with only one major perceivable imperfection. I thought, after I gave him a book of matches, that he'd be on his way, but he just leaned against the air, scoping my efficiency, and exuded, "Can I stay awhile?"

"Why don't you sit down and chill for a minute. It's sticky and hot outside, and if my right eye is reliable, it's gonna rain. In fact, I see a *storm* coming. Nothing to play with."

He sat on the long sofa, sucking on a Salem unhurriedly, inhaling deeply and making smoke circles. I offered him some of the fruity delight I retrieved from the freezer. He looked at it, said it was a woman's drink, and asked for a beer.

"You're gonna get fat like me if you keep swilling that beer. I'd hate to see that nice-looking body get in bad shape before you're forty. I think you're gonna look kinda good at forty, and maybe even fifty."

"What makes you think that?"

"Your shoulders, your torso, and you've got a really good-lookin' ass."

If he could have blushed, he would have, as we both smiled and recognized a sudden quiet that usually comes when people don't know what to say, or do, because they've said what they meant and meant what they've said. I felt the back of my neck begin to crawl, and my breathing became irregular. There, I was doing it, and didn't even know I was. Books had taught me to flirt very well, and I'd come like new money in fantasy when I looked in the mirror and imagined what I'd say to this or that guy I wanted to taste. And even if I was not interested in the act, the game was fun, and all women should have as much fun as possible.

"What do you do for fun?"

"Depends on the type and the time," I said as my eyes became a few centimeters narrower. "I travel, read, write, and talk with people a lot. I enjoy a lot, when I don't have to do battle with liaisons of unclear definitions."

I was beginning to feel the importance of making nothing but smooth moves. If this episode was going anywhere, and I *still* had no mollifying urge to let it, the least I wanted to achieve was some happy grinning by the time I did drop off to sleep, if I slept at all. Sometimes a superior mind fuck is better than the real thing. I wanted to fuck his mind and make him wish that he knew more, much more about me. Without some vanity, damn, what's left?

"How old are you?" I asked with my best radio voice.

Composure left and my mouth flew open as I heard "twenty-nine."

That did it! Twenty-nine *and* a scary curl! All he goddamned needed was two or three gold teeth stuck in the front of his mouth. I had been in bed with married men of the cloth, pilots, professors, policemen, short-order cooks, a few misguided minions who felt they were big fish in small ponds, and a smattering of intelligent, well-heeled thugs. Practically all of them had memorable idiosyncrasies that attracted me in the first place, but none of them did weird shit with their hair and teeth. In public.

The heat, humidity, drinks, energy, and tension imposed on new gatherings and newer relationships all descended on me simultaneously. I wanted to be alone, not just away from Bobby, but alone with the thoughts I was getting ready to have about this boy whose clean sandaled feet nestled in my shag carpet, as if they were at home. I am NOT into young boys, and am wary of most men my own age. I thought about being forty-two and knowing the shit I knew about men, me, life in general, and the vastness of nothingness in particular. I was determined that each day I would try to decomplicate my life, and that included running as far and as fast as possible from liabilities, even if they had *tarrifying* love machines, Stradivarian dicks. I didn't mind having the dog, but I couldn't deal with the fleas. I did a lot of self-destructive things, but getting tied up with young boys was not one of them.

"What kind of fun can we have together?" he asked as his mouth became one impish curl. And for the first time, I looked—really looked —at his face. His eyes were bright and clear where white is supposed to be; his skin was smooth and didn't look like it knew razors; those lips smiling at me looked handmade by a deft, experienced ceramicist who then threw the clay again for near-perfect teeth, with no open-faced gold crowns and diamond chips up front. I looked at him *hard* as I sank back onto my knees and put my hands on my hips. That is a stance all *real* Black people know. It is usually a huge brick wall that can only be transcended by absolute respect, understanding, and love, or it signals "I'll play whoshit bullshit if you want, but I think you ought to know that I don't usually play games well." I knew the next move was mine.

"Why don't we play something like poker. After we decide on the rules, we'll decide what the stakes are, what we can give up and still call fun. A problem, though, is I don't have any cards." We decided to guess personal things about each other, and the loser was at the mercy of the winner.

"You've been in jail, haven't you?" I said flippantly. He stopped draggin on his cigarette, and his head snapped back, eyes electric. Had I said the wrong thing? Something behind his eyebright was familiar. I had seen that look in many Black men's eyes of all ages, the ones who live by their wits and go for the jugular in every situation.

"Yeah, I was in for armed robbery about ten years ago, away from here, when I was sly, slick, and wicked." I saw the muscles in his jaws relax, and then he continued: "You really jump out there with a full deck, not to have no cards. Now, what you want me to do for you before it's my time to win?"

"I want you to tell me why a good-looking twenty-nine-year-old fine specimen like you is wearing that greasy shit in your head."

"Monkey was givin herself a curl and she wanted to try it out on me first."

"I believe that, and I believe that she really doesn't like you. Who is she, anyway?"

Why, in the name of all that is revered in the name of fucking and fuckery, was I sitting up in MY space with this young, corkscrew-haired gigolo ex-offender? Had my fat absorbed the gray matter that controlled discretion and common sense?

His turn.

"It's been a long time since you had someone to sex you down real good, hasn't it?" There was a hole where I thought my face had been. Did it show that I'd gone dickless for over three years; that for three years I had doubts about whether I could do magical sexerobics that I'd read about and probably tried with some of the more liberated of the sixty-three men I'd loved, tolerated, feared, or been seduced by before the present drought?

"You got me on that one, yes indeed. It *has* been a long, *long* time, but my head hasn't been where it should be to consider an involvement."

"What about now?" he almost whispered. Three pregnant words.

"I'm lookin, but not too hard."

"So you have fun with yourself. A lot?"

"Not a whole lot, but I'm glad I know how to, when I want to."

"Since you're the loser with this hand, I want you to show me how you do it."

I shivered and stood as if rooted to the thick carpet with my no-nonsense-powerful-Black-woman attitude. I didn't necessarily want to repeat certain aspects of my peripatetic behavior that were characteristic of the time between my eighteenth and fortieth year: I didn't have a bunch of problems, until that period, with finding good fucking. But intense living has a way of sucking you out or up if you don't do something like take care of your mind and your body, but especially your spirit. I've got some dawg in me, something that nags danger like a bone, something that feels comfort with the role of pioneer, voyeur, and several personalities all at once. That's how I got involved with those sixty-three men. Mostly I was just curious and found something about them irresistible. Then too, I waited eighteen years to FUCK. I even got married because I wanted to fuck all the time, and I didn't want to have to go out in the sad and affected young professionals' hunting parties, subjecting myself to all kinds of ridiculous glass-top table vapidness, all in the name of fuckling, and being fuckled. But after the marriage ran its sorry course, I became obsessed with fucking. I sent off to Eve's Garden for new joy toys —I'd burned out my other three vibrators, so I needed a new set of gear, plus I wanted some custom-made condoms. I didn't have any that Sunday afternoon.

During my time in heat, which lasted over twenty years, I went everywhere I thought I might meet good conversationalists and prospective companions (fuckers): balmy gardens where African subchiefs partied; economy flights to places where steel pans played profusely while limbo dancers undulated and reggae bands poured liquid sex over needed dreams. I looked for the most intelligent men—they make the best lovers. Forget about fucking dumb people. It's not really worth the effort, unless you're into soap operas, and melodrama gives you erotic buzzes. Twice I found my raw needs erupting with dumb people. There were probably more, but I have a very selective memory when it comes to fucking: I just "disremember" the unsavory, as if it didn't happen.

The first dumb person kept his cap and socks on in the bed, and his staying power was pitiful. Once, my daughter knocked on the door unexpectedly (she was supposed to be at the movies) when the fool was about to shoot to the stars—the full moon was out. I was so unimpressed I didn't even provide the stroke called FAKE. When I returned to the bed after answering the door, he had disappeared. I found him crouched on the floor in the closet with his little cap on, his little socks lookin alien and forlorn. As soon as my daughter left the house, I put him out and asked him to crawl away and just die, or perhaps crawl back up into his mama's womb, because that's where he belonged: maybe he would finish growing. I said I wouldn't tell anybody he was crazy. I lied.

And the other dumb person was a believer in voodoo hoodoo. He used to receive his mail, hold it up to the light, put it behind his back, and turn around three times before opening it, being sure that evil spirits had been dismissed. Sometimes, we talked late into the night and he revealed why his many male gossiping partners called him "Doctor Love." He was supposed to have powerful potions to do the nefarious as well as the precious. I found out the murky, nasty-looking stuff in the half-gallon decanters lined up importantly in a corner of his sitting room was rum, boiled peanuts, and toad balls. How I got involved with a *houngan* like that just shows how sometimes I've been unable to resist risk and the unlikely.

One night, voodoo man and I were moving toward fuckling. I like to lick and suck and blow on men, whether they're clothed or not. But this turkey, nude, kept clutching the sheets around his chest, though he was rubbing my natural hair, a deadly zone for me. I love it. I slipped my head beneath the covers and began coursing my way down the center of his body with my tongue, stopping now and then to lick with the movement of a painter, and I felt him tensing up as I neared his navel. There, I started blowing, ever so gently, until I could feel the hairs around his dick tickling my cheek. I adjusted my elbow and hips to ease down further, and he suddenly jumped out of the bed and began to scream: "Ah-h-h no! Don't do that to me! That's bad! That's so nasty! Where did you learn about doing things like that? Oh God, how could you?!" Doctor Love was out of my life that night, and I believe, since he was the last person I'd had sex with more than once (I still don't understand why), I had ample time to think about the need and the methods to avoid dumb people.

From snatches of his past that he told me about, and the easy way he volleyed with our talk, Bobby didn't strike me as being dumb. "If you're forty-three and been working over twenty-five years, you're about ready to retire, aren't you? What'll you do with all that money?"

I laughed, but a bell went off and a warning light switched on. I was glad I hadn't anesthetized myself so I could still trust my first mind and third eye. Ah-ha! Here was a person who'd be on my payroll if I ever had the nerve to become a *madam*. But all my clients would be women, and during an upscale interview, I'd find out the age, hobbies, and specialties they wanted. Some might even want a twenty-nine-year-old with a scary curl who talks low and soft and slow. And progressively sweeter. I'd call my business Rent A Dick.

"Let you see me please myself?"

It didn't take more than five seconds before I whispered a weak "No," but before then the insides of my lush thighs became warm and tingly. I felt my honey-pot muscles tightening, the way I made them function when I was doing the sexercises I'd read about. The difference was this "winking" was almost involuntary.

"If I don't let you see me get myself off, what else do you want, what else can I do?"

"You can say we can have fun together, enjoy the rest of the evening pleasing each other. You can say you want that."

"I'm old enough to know I can't have everything I want, especially in these days of Satan-Is-a-Bitch diseases." And without thinking, I quickly followed with "Do you have any rubbers?" "No." And silence came again.

Was I going to let this fuckling chance get away? Risk not just a titillating discovery in a bubble-topped glass elevator or a hotel stairwell, but risk losing my life for an afternoon of possibly some ultimates in hedonism? *Possibly.* And what if he wasn't even GOOD! He looked beneath my clothes and under my need to be a whole, private person, in control at all times. He cut into my wonder.

"I'm good. You don't have to worry 'bout a thing. Just talk to me. Tell me what you want. You can have it all."

Well damn! There are hazards to living long enough to think you've heard everything in lame and tacky from "Hey, baby, what's your sign?" to "I'm a GS-16, what are you and where do you work? And uh, by the way, my name is Michael. After we fuck, I'd like to get to know you, if we can work out some time. I've got my calendar with me." It's easy to get cynical and jaded behind shit like that. So I thought Bobby's under-the-lamplight-singing-doo-wop-songs posture was a result of his youth and limitations. I took nothing he said literally. I just thought about the pressure drops of the moment. For only a few moments.

"I need to take a shower."

"Can I come too?" he asked with his cheeks shifting positions to reveal yet another pleasantry, a statement of dimples. I said no, I needed some time to think. "Nobody should have to think about feelin good," he said.

I squeezed my eyes so tightly in the shower, my lids stung and stuck together. I was pressing for a vision, some direction from within. But even if my first mind was speaking to me, inveighing me not to be a candidate for the evening news a few months or years down the line, I ignored the warning. I needed to be warmed, held, and fucked more than I needed to be rational on that Sunday. I needed some THING to happen to me.

I turned off the water, dried hurriedly, and tidied up the bathroom, which I turned over to him with a flourish. While he bathed, I emptied two lavender sachets onto my bed and put on some classic sexy blues. Louise Bogan was already on the disc playing, so I let her stay. I felt edgy, like I always did when I was being mischievous or dangerous, like the time I went up in a plane with one of my photography instructors, supposedly trying to decide on flying lessons and then being arrested with the fabulous reality of fucking in the cockpit. It was turbulent and good.

He came out of the bathroom, dripping wet, curl and all. I drank in the lean, precise symmetry of him. He rubbed the towel through his hair, down and around all the harvest that had taken twenty-nine years to grow. I could tell he enjoyed bathing—he took his time and there was rapture lurking beneath his coquettish dimples as he pulled back the foreskin on one of the longest *pudendas* I had ever seen! For a moment he looked like the amateur baseball player he said he was, straddling his legs and squatting slightly to better grasp and fondle his member, still lethargic and giving no argument to the man with the hand. He threw his head back and shook it the way I love to see Rastafarians do in the heat of throbbing reggae music, or when they, long-dreaded, emerge from a sea bath. I was enthralled with this warm-up performance, and delight filled my warm, round face and body with almost unbearable anticipation.

Simultaneously, there was a crack and lightning before thunder, and the glow of his dick, that seemed struck before it became neon mahogany. What a feast, watching this physiological miracle, this gift that hugely separates the living from the dead.

Thunder rolled deeply and the building trembled. From beneath thick delicately arched eyebrows, he winked and directed me, "Why don't you come."

"Why should I? I like what I'm seeing."

"Forget it. Come."

There was to be no more chatter—talk about hair, jail terms, baseball, my work, or the weather. The reason for this wonder, these seconds, this THING about to happen, was upon us. He said it all in the command that rang: "Come."

I stood up to meet the body my eyes had partially liquefied and devoured. I was a full foot shorter than this magnificent Shaka, King of the Zulus, and I turned my lips immediately and naturally and easily to his chest. He took my shoulders, kissed one, and gently turned me around, backing me up to the closet door, nudging me near the knob. From one hand, long fingers cupped my chin, lifting. From the other, my neck and shoulders received soothing caresses to combat the heated sparks jabbing me just below the skin.

He didn't kiss me then, as anyone would expect, and I was so involved with his choreography I was unable to stop the shock that came next. I felt a silky sucking just at the hollow of my left knee; he had perched me over the jutting doorknob of the closet. When he bent there, effortlessly and gracefully, I thought only of the courage it takes to grow older and into enjoying what snatches of pleasure there are in times too absorbed in negative capability.

He picked all of me up, except for the few pounds that was my upper body and head. Gently, he settled me into the center of my bed, gingerly and decidedly. He said, barely audibly and without a pause or a heartbeat or a wisp of air, "I gotta be all over you. I wanna be. Gotta be."

It snaked its way down my moist throat, *movering, movering.* And before I could say "More, more," he stopped abruptly. He released both hands from my hair that he'd been rubbing, and guided his Stradivarius between my legs, never going completely in, but teasing, a centimeter here, an old-fashioned two inches there. He liked the friction of crinkly hair against mahogany dick as much as I, and the liquid beginning to flow copiously from my cave gave him added assurance to all that had directed him all afternoon.

Like an Olympic swimmer, he dived into me, seeking his lane only a split second. Then, after the flow was his own, he functioned like he had made my tunnel and knew each ridge and the limits of my depth. Occasionally, he stretched on his back, only to roll over into me again to be sure I had not regained too much breath and clarity from the confusion and delusion he thought to be my mind.

Not the rolling thunder or the lightning or the azaleas now enjoying a shower or the earlier, pleasant afternoon with neighbors matched our engagement. There was no mediocrity going on. There was so little time and no reason to think.

We searched for keys to unlock a primal hunger, and, finding them, we fed each other greedily. I bit him; he pinched me; he sucked me; I squeezed him. We made a new language of gutturals fit for two on a rainy Sunday afternoon growing toward evening.

Four hours from the time I opened the door and gave him a light, he arched his back like a big cat and rose on his knees. I'd seen many dancers and athletes achieve that graceful roll out of something intense.

"I gotta go. Monkey gets back in town tonight."

"Hmmmm. You're probably late. You don't want to get her jaws tight. She might put you out, and we wouldn't want that to happen, would we?" He didn't smile.

Without a glance at me he glided into the bathroom and was back in seconds, pulling his briefs over his muscular thighs and chiseled buttocks. I tucked an African wrap around me and stood by the door to see him out into the steamy, drizzling night. He leaned down and kissed me on the forehead and lips before he left.

I pulled open the wrap and stretched my nakedness on the floor and smelled my arms where his scent lingered deliciously. I ran my fingers around my delta, into my crotch, and savored our wetness that was now sticky sweet all in my hairs and on my thighs. The music I heard was pine needle pings slamming against the windows with the aggression of a summer storm. I chanted a mantra, breathed down to my matrix, and knew nothing until the phone jolted me awake.

It was 1:30 A.M. Late-night calls unnerve me; they usually mean bad news. I didn't want any, but I'd had a year's quota of something good a scant few hours ago.

"Hello?"

"Are you feeling all right?" It was Bobby.

"Yes. I was doing some serious thinking down here on the floor, enjoying the rain, but I guess I dropped off."

"Can I come back?"

"Well . . . maybe. When do you want to . . ."

"Now."

My back, knees, thighs, neck, breasts, lips, and pussy ached. I said yes.

I heard him running to escape the pellets of rain a few minutes later. As soon as I opened the door, he began tearing off his clothes. He saw the wide cloth on the floor and drew me on top of him with fierce passion, gyrating and guiding himself into me expertly. He poured the fruity delight that sat on the coffee table over my body, dripping larger droplets on my nipples and on the mound above my pyramid, licking me and occasionally looking up to see my face skewed in ecstasy.

He kneaded my stomach and breasts with a special urgency, and then his whole formidable weight replaced his hands and he was a giant mixer making me malleable and light as French pastry. Inside me, he was as hot as cobaltean blue. His behemoth was disarming, but he showed consummate skill, restraint, and care. Ever so softly, maybe once or twice per half hour, he'd ask, "Are you enjoying yourself? Anything special you want me to do?"

My moans and thrashes and the viselike pressure around his butt, waist, and ears with my thighs and hips so he could come and stay in deep were my answers. I squeezed his neon tree and my muscles until he cried out, begging like a coked-up blues singer, "Ooooo, Ooooo, Mama, Mama, Baby, PLEASE DON'T STOP!"

Monkey, it seems, was late coming home, so he left again at 3:30 A.M. I collapsed into my bed.

At seven, he was back, asking for a subway token to get to work. I gave it. At eight that night, he asked if he could come by. We fucked.

The next morning at six-thirty, he stopped by to ask for another transit token. Said Monkey was ticked off because he'd been acting tired since she came back from visiting her sister over the weekend. Said she took his money to cut out whatever else he was doing besides abusing his dick where it didn't belong. Could I spare a dollar, too, for a hamburger at lunch? And another token to come back to me that night?

How many life chapters in summer, temporary living will it take to see, to reach a New Day, a new grasp of the inevitable—that nothing lasts forever, and that includes THE THING that happened for three days. Including tokens that run out.

Sunburst from the Earth

Nelson Estupiñán Bass

Translated by Lemuel Johnson

When you walk by, my precious, radiant in beauty,
indifferent to the torment in your wake,
my hungry stare, even if in sacrilege, cuts through
like a honed dagger to reach for you naked

when night falls and sleep takes you down
the banked fire of the earth must burn inside you
and your two breasts rise, white, above the plain
sleepless with desire for the coming of a master.

One of these days my arms will crush you
shatter through to what you so insist upon
guarding: with your own blood I'll teach you desire

I will lay about in your heaving body:
you will feel the very air you breathe burn so
when your body rages, lit, in the fire of pleasure.

Untitled 2

Afua Cooper

when flesh and flesh
    meet
nothing can stop
    their union
when heart and heart
    meet
nothing can stop the
    passion
when soul and soul
    kiss
who can stop the
    love?

From *Long Distance Life*

Marita Golden

The Eden Bar and Grill and the stores immediately surrounding it stood intact, unscathed. From the inside of the Eden Bar and Grill, Esther heard the sound of Aretha's ecstatic, mournful, confession "Since You've Been Gone." As she opened the door, Aretha's voice pleaded, "Take me back . . ." The restaurant was empty and Aretha's voice echoed, cavernous and lonely. The shock of sunlight entered the room with Esther. She heard the whir of overhead fans. Somehow she'd expected to see Forty Carats and even Geraldine, but she saw first, in the afternoon darkness, posters along the walls, advertising the Temptations, Gladys Knight and the Pips, photos of James Brown, Jimi Hendrix, Marvin Gaye.

But what surprised Esther most was the emptiness of the place. The decor had been changed to a color that was a harsh fluorescent mix of brilliant shades. Overhead, a ball twirled and threw a shimmering cascade of stars onto the floor. A wall-high drawing of a go-go dancer claimed an entire wall. And the area that once had mostly been for dining had been turned into a dance floor. At the bar a young man in a sweatshirt that read NATION TIME stood before the wall-length mirror and picked out his hair with a plastic Afro comb. Esther walked up to the bar and when the young man had finished with his hair she asked, "Is Randolph Spenser here?"

"Yeah, he's in the back. You want to see him, sister?"

"I'm a friend of his. Just tell me where he is."

"In his office."

A side exit by the kitchen led to a narrow hallway. Esther knocked on the door.

"Who is it?"

She didn't know what to say so she merely opened the door and walked inside.

"Well I'll be damned!" Randolph shouted, throwing down the pen he'd been using to go over his books and covering his face in surprise. "Come on in. Come on in," he told her, standing up and pulling Esther from the doorway into the office. Randolph gazed at Esther uncertainly, eagerness competing with control. "Sit down. Sit down," he said finally, straightening up the small sofa cluttered with papers and books and a jacket. "When did you get back?" he asked.

"Just the other day," Esther lied. She did not want him to know that she had waited a week to see him.

"You look . . ." he said, assessing her, his eyes roaming from her face to her legs.

"I put on some weight."

"Didn't do you no harm."

"The place looks different."

"Times changed. I had to keep up with them."

"How'd this place escape the riots?"

"I was sitting at home, watching it on TV. I was seeing stores owned by friends go up in flames. I got in my car and came over here with my shotgun. Stood out front and dared anybody to even think about throwing a rock or a Molotov cocktail at the place. They got the message and ran past me up the street."

"How's business?"

"How do you think? Slow, real slow. The riots killed business. Just killed it. Who wants to spend Saturday night in an area that looks like Hiroshima? Folks trickle in on Friday and Saturday nights. I got a go-go dancer comes in and shakes her stuff around. But it'll never again be like it was. Those days are gone. I'm even thinking about getting the place off my hands. I just don't know who'd buy it now. Overnight, the location cut the value in half."

The sound of his voice—its rhythm, intensity—set Esther at ease and she sat back against the sofa.

"You finished up down there?" he asked slowly, looking at Esther as though there was no way he'd ever get enough of what he saw.

"I'm finished. Mama told me all you did for Logan."

"You forget? I'm his daddy. I did no more than when you were here."

"What made you get a divorce?"

"After the boys left home, it just seemed there was no more reason to stay. We both knew that. I let her have the house. I'm still paying the last of the mortgage."

"Blood money?"

"She deserved it."

Esther saw Randolph's slight paunch, the receding hairline, the patient eyes and knew she still loved him. Randolph stubbed out a cigarette in an ashtray and said simply, "Girl, I ain't done nothing since you left but wait for you to come back." Esther reached for his hand and gave herself up to him with a glance. Randolph said in a husky, low whisper, "Come on, let's go."

Quiet, agitated with desire, they drove to Randolph's house—a small home on a quiet tree-lined street in Northeast, not far from where he had lived with Mary. When he parked before the house he told Esther, "I thought about moving into an apartment but then I kept thinking about you coming back one day and I wanted a place big enough for all of us. I swore to myself we'd be a real family before it was over and that's what I aim for us to be."

Inside the house filled with nondescript furniture that felt as though it was yet to be fully possessed, a house that was as lonely as the man who called it home, Randolph led Esther upstairs to his bedroom. He quickly closed the door behind him, as if to prevent her escape. Esther sat on the bed in a pink blouse, under which she wore no bra, and a blue skirt, beneath which her thighs awaited Randolph's touch. Randolph knelt on the floor beside the bed and kissed Esther, his tongue unearthing her mouth, his hands roughly massaging her hair, her neck and shoulders. He unbuttoned her blouse, his hands so eager they fumbled like a careless child's. Randolph let his hands rest on her breasts, which, like the rest of her, were fuller, more radiant than before. He held her breasts in his palms and leaned forward with a groan to suckle them hard, his hands breaking the button at the back of her skirt, palms sliding into the thin sliver of cloth of her panties. Esther fell back on the bed and raised her hips, guiding Randolph's hands as he pulled off her skirt and panties. And now he saw all of her, the parts he had missed and yearned for, and he looked at her so full of desire he wondered why he did not explode. There was her dark brown skin and her ass—a full, high-riding Black woman's ass—that he leaned over to kiss, so grateful was he for the sight of it. Randolph gazed in wonder at her vagina, covered by tufts of hair as unruly and stubborn as she. He buried his face in her and she smelled of some gentle cologne and sweat and Ivory soap and longing for him and she tasted better than she used to and there was her hand inside his pants, releasing him, and he wanted to kiss her, there, forever, and there was her mouth on him, a perfect fit, loving him as he loved her, had always loved her, had never stopped loving her and he cried, "Never stop. Never stop," releasing so fast, so full she could not take all of him, let him go, yet let her fingertips discover him again as he shriveled, satisfied and happy, against her neck.

Randolph knew that Esther would not believe that he had dreamed of this moment while she was away, dreamed of it even as some other woman, some woman he was just marking time with, lay beside him. He was almost fifty and the years had taught him the meaning of dreams. He knew she would not believe him if he told her how he could hardly remember the names or faces of the other women, so little had they meant to him. But nobody believed men had hearts, not even the women who loved them. So they lay in bed the rest of the day and that night, sleeping in each other's arms, stirred periodically by a precise, perfect passion. And for the first time since he'd moved into it, that night Randolph's house sheltered him like home.

Plain Wrappers

Constance García-Barrio

The cover of the book was writhing with color. Waves of orifice orange and pumping purple swam in the background, and in the foreground lay a most attractive young woman, nude, positioned so that you could see the parting of her ways. The man's eyes were popping with anticipation as he opened the book.

"Brighten your breakfast," said the advertisement on page one, "with our erotic egg cup." Just above the words was the picture of a holder for a poached egg. It looked like a shapely bare-bottomed woman doing an open-legged handstand. The egg nestled nicely in her hollow. The blurb went on: "By popular demand we will soon be marketing a double-barreled model. Somewhat more expensive but holds twice the nourishment."

The opposite page said, "Turn the daily drudgery of tooth-brushing into an exhilarating experience. Try our delicious toothpaste, now available in two great flavors: 'Woman Before' and 'Woman After.' Please check the appropriate box on your order form."

Orville Q. Mother sat at his desk gloating, fondling the pages of the book. What he held was the catalogue, fresh from the printer's, of his own mail-order house, Mother's Index Finger. The Index Finger, after years of financial uncertainty, was finally pointing the way to wealth for

Orville. Building the business to the point where he could afford a slick professional catalogue had been a titanic task. Orville savored his triumph as one does a good wine—with much appreciation and little complacency. But fate, long ago, had determined he would never get bogged down in self-satisfaction. This was due, in part, to Orville's disposition, but there was another reason. Orville Mother had a froglike face and physique.

As a very young man when he approached a girl to ask her, "Will you . . . ?" before he could finish the sentence, she would be pointing the way to the nearest lily pad. The few girls who did get to know Orville thought him sensational. With a flick of the wrist and a twirl of the thumb he could as easily make them a clever bit of machinery as a bowel-twitching orgasm. Very entertaining once you made his acquaintance. "Orville the Finger," they used to call him. Few girls, however, came close enough to discover his talents. So Orville's adolescence was literally a hard one—bulging eyes and bulging pants from start to finish. During those years, Orville learned about the need for substitutes for female companionship first hand, or rather, both hands, for Orville was ambidextrous and found the left hand or the right equally satisfying for certain purposes.

Early on, Orville realized that to make Mother's Index Finger a success he would need not only those knowledgeable hands but money savvy too. He would have to calculate, spend, gamble. He had no choice with huge competitors. He had clever hands, razor-edged wit, and threadbare finances. The big established companies had run-of-the-mill products, mass-production mentality, and a profit of millions. Mother's was a pygmy among the giant men's mail-order firms but, Orville reasoned, he could stand on the stilts of ingenuity and come up head to head with them. Mother's would survive by being special. The company would handle the ordinary items made with extraordinary care, plus many unusual things, so that the name Mother's would be synonymous with quality, satisfaction, and distinctiveness.

Orville rented a spacious basement on one of the quieter streets in the city's business district and there set up shop. His strategy was to begin with small items—small but catchy and expensive. He invested everything in that first batch of merchandise—his poor savings and a wealth of imagination. First, he offered for sale a stamp moistener in the form of a woman's head and torso. You lifted the top on the head and poured in two tablespoons of water. This trickled down to the deep-pink sponge in the opening in the business end, then the little lady could do a couple hundred stamps. Orville also devised a titillating pencil sharpener. The sharpeners were fashioned like a buxom girl, one of whose chubby arms was the handle. They were so sexually suggestive when the pen was being inserted and while it was being sharpened that they put a head not only on the lead but on the user of the sharpener.

Not even in his most optimistic moments could Orville have imagined the wildly enthusiastic response to his products. Mother's Index Finger, in a matter of days, became a hotbed of checks, money orders, boxes, string, and plain wrappers. There was an orgy of stamp pasting from morning to night to get the products to the customers. Orville had to hire an assistant, a young man who was efficient and closemouthed with plenty of street smarts. Prompt and accurate filling of orders, Orville explained to him, was crucial to customer satisfaction. No satisfaction, no sales. The young man was not a fool. Yes, he knew that in this sort of business there could be some unpleasantness—crank calls, nasty letters, and perhaps an occasional picket. He fully realized, he said, that you had to be ready to do unorthodox things. Sure. He wasn't born yesterday and didn't plan to die tomorrow. He, personally, would be willing to wear a neon sign in his navel if it would help Mother's Index Finger and fatten his paycheck.

Orville's eyes bulged more than ever with the excitement of success. He was soon spending lots of time ogling plans for his pet project. He wanted to make a decent plastic doll for men. Most of the large mail-order houses had them, but every model Orville had ever tried—and that was an extensive sampling—was deficient in some way. Orville began by experimenting with different types of plastic. Sales from the other items were zooming, and he was grateful for the margin of error. Still, it took most of his patience and all of his profit to find the right kind of plastic, a truly convincing skin substitute. Once he succeeded in this, Orville went on to the most delicate phase of his work, the construction of the doll's organ. Here, men were very exacting. This was, after all, the hard of the matter. Orville performed experiment after experiment. His assistant got used to seeing him hop around their headquarters in rage. Painstaking work in pursuit of pleasure. After many months, Orville perfected the moistening mechanism and claimed victory. For extra assurance Orville had his assistant try the doll. When he was done yelling and squirming, he predicted that sales would be fabulous and hit Orville for a raise.

Orville was beginning to worry about how to promote his doll on a pea-sized budget. His assistant, very anxious that things should go well, suggested filling a few dolls with helium, attaching an ad, and letting them loose in strategic places. But creating the doll had drained Orville's finances. He just didn't have the money for that kind of gimmick. It was at this point that help came to him in a surprising form. He found a truckload of horse manure heaped on the pavement in front of the Index Finger one morning. It was the work of the Committee for Civic Decency. Members of the CCD felt that Mother's Index Finger was a blight on the city. They decided to give Orville a material expression of their disapproval.

More impressive than the manure was the curiosity it aroused. Orville and his assistant spent the day handing out ads to the men who came to gaze at the stuff. The Civic Decency people were furious when they saw that their efforts had backfired. "A fart in the face of morality," some said. Others suggested heaping on much more.

Thanks to Civic Decency's manure, Mother's Index Finger became notoriously prosperous in the local area. The wife of a man who had purchased a doll—an irritable elephantine woman—let out all her venom in a poison-pen letter to Orville. It began: "You little bubble-eyed cunt-maker," and ended by declaring that she had cut out the offending part of the doll and Orville would find it enclosed. The letter served to assure Orville of the effectiveness of his product.

Orville got more unexpected help. A rumor sprang up and spread that the plastic used in the dolls had a medicinal quality. The dolls were good for impotence and infections, the men were saying. Orville was quick to capitalize on this discovery. One ad about the dolls began: "Don't cry over spilled penicillin, buy yourself a Mother's doll."

Orville decided to introduce some unique features in his doll before making an all-or-nothing sales pitch. He compared the juice-producing capacity of his doll with that of the others on the market. He was satisfied that his doll made the most in the least amount of time. It was a logical step from the juice advantage to the idea of flavoring. Mother's dolls would not only boast the best holes but would have the added attraction of flavor. Flavor offerings would allow for customer individuality: natural, cherry, orange, grape, pastrami, ham hock, chicken liver, and bourbon. Moreover, a client might order a doll with as many organs as he wanted, in the place that he wanted, and in the flavor that he wanted. He could, for example, request a natural-flavored opening in the usual place, but also ask for a grape organ in the navel, a bourbon ear, a pastrami nostril, a ham-hock hole in the head, and so on to suit himself. The possibility of multiple organs was a Mother's exclusive. There was a set price per hole.

In promoting the new doll, Orville Mother made up his mind to walk the tightrope of risk again. "Operation Tantalus," he called it. Orville's assistant, through certain connections, procured a mailing list of prospective customers. For Orville, the vital information was address, income, and flavor preference. Trusting in his knowledge of men and casting his fate to the postal service, Orville sent out hundreds of dolls, unsolicited, to men on the list. Each doll had been fitted with a temporary organ, flavored to please the customer. The organ would disintegrate after one use. If pleased, the customer was to send a check for the full purchase price, and in return he would be mailed an insertable permanent organ. If not pleased, the customer could throw the doll in the trash. If too many people threw their dolls away, Orville would be ruined.

Once the dolls were mailed out, Orville sat and sweated it out. A week went by and Orville grew irritable with waiting. Another week and he was sick with it. At the beginning of the third week, when Orville's assistant planned to announce that he was going to look for another job, the checks began to arrive. After that, it was a daily deluge.

Now that Mother's Index Finger stood shoulder to shoulder with the large companies, the vicious elbowing started. The other mail-order houses grimly set out to destroy the intruder. Orville, for his part, was finding that money really did talk. It made women say that he was "handsome in an extremely rugged way," whereas before he had been "that frog-faced character." It was this newfound status, more than the money, that Orville was unwilling to give up. So he prepared to fight in the marketplace with the rest. He would crush the opposition by the superiority of his product.

He built a gyroscope into his dolls so that a man could enjoy them in any position at all. To this he added Mother's exclusive buttocks bounce. It was when Orville developed orgasmogenic suction that his competitors made their move. Hundreds of the suction models had been mailed out before the devilment came to light. Suddenly, there were reports across the country of men showing up in hospital emergency wards. They came in attached to suction dolls that simply couldn't be turned off. It was national news and international laughs.

Orville's assistant had been bribed with a fortune by his competitors. Lock a switch here, cross a wire there. It was child's play. When the truth came out, Orville had nothing to do but thank his assistant for the free headlines, the television time, and a wave of publicity that washed away the competition, all but one of the huge companies. The victims of orgasmogenic suction had, on the whole, enjoyed themselves, and were satisfied with the replacement doll.

Orville now had his catalogue and a worldwide reputation. He may have been tempted to sit on his laurels, or better yet, have the lady of his choice sit on them. On the other hand, if he had hordes of new customers he had a host of enemies too. There was bound to be a struggle with that other mammoth mail-order house, not to mention the bankrupt companies that would cheerfully see him done in. Ditto the Committee for Civic Decency. They had never forgiven him for the manure affair. They were probably responsible for having the editor of the daily local headline a story about a mock paternity suit claiming that Orville had fathered some tadpoles and wasn't supporting them properly.

The masked men who raided Mother's Index Finger one night got the shock of their lives. They had come to destroy mailing lists, computers, merchandise. But the electric eye fixed on them, the electric nose sniffed them out. When they were all inside, down came iron bars over the doors and windows, trapping them inside. Then the lights went out. They stood gaping in the darkness for a second, but instantly dozens of mechanical hands grabbed and stripped them. Soft pads saturated with wildly scented massaging oil dropped from the ceiling and began rubbing them teasingly. When the pads retracted, feathers shot out from the walls and tickled them in the most provocative manner. All the men recalled how the recording of heavy breathing and lovely moaning started playing. Some of them remembered how, simultaneously, films of the most erotic sort were projected everywhere—walls, floor, and ceiling. However, none of them could remember how they became hooked up to defective suction dolls.

The following morning, Orville returned with an army of reporters and television crews, a couple of cops, and one eager lawyer. The unfortunate raiders, who were quickly identified as members of the city council, lay blue and blinking with exhaustion. They begged to be unplugged from the dolls. Yes, Orville would gladly do that after they answered all the reporters' questions. The councilmen eagerly spoke up. They were paid a fortune in advance and were to receive another when the work was done, not to mention the political plums that would be made to fall into their laps. Well yes, they might have helped themselves to a bit of the merchandise too.

Shutters clicked, pens flew, cassettes whirled, and the upshot was a headline carried by all the big metropolitan papers: "City Fathers Screwed at Mother's." No matter which way you understood the phrase, that was putting it mildly.

PART SEVEN

Taking the Plunge

Nude by Fireplace, 1923 by James Van Der Zee

And what shall we write of initial experiences? Not all are as bad as commonly reported, not even most. What shall we write of that time when all is *new* and nothing can go wrong; that time when if everything went wrong, still we would not know it because everything is *new?* What shall we write of a time when sensual hope makes us ever young and fresh, when all the romantic things we have always wished for are possible? What shall we write when we are too busy contemplating the acts to write?

Initial experiences, initial places, initial states of mind spurred by an initial meeting, intrigue us in multi-threaded ways. These facts Reginald Martin leaves no doubt of in "The 1st 3 Daze," as the initial touch, the initial exchange, the initial sexual coupling of those desires we hold most dear, never come to us again as they come those first few hours of symbiosis. Frank Lamont Phillips's "Café Noir," R. Pope and Frank Lamont Phillips's "Sexionnaire," and Nelson Estupiñán Bass's "You Knew . . ." let us touch the initial before deflowering it forever—such exquisite joy never to be captured again. Lois Griffith's piece from *First Person Singular* shows that even in the leaving of the initial there is a quiet, sensual rightness that must be experienced to be believed. Now, as experienced voyeurs, we nod knowingly as Jan Carew's selection from *The Initiation of Belfon* takes us back to our own training grounds—real or imagined. And Jerry W. Ward's "Opening Night" makes us novices once more as we want to touch again and again the fearful symmetry of that first sensual exchange, while Kalamu Ya Salaam makes his bearded kisses the first things we taste in "Haiku #25."

What shall we write, then, when we first take the plunge?

Haiku #25

Kalamu Ya Salaam

i visit in the
morning and wash your surprised
face with bearded, black kisses

Café Noir

Frank Lamont Phillips

I opened *Homespun Images* and touched you,
naked, wearing only sweat,
the bittersweet taste and sticky touch of your thought
opened memories
wide as ransacked drawers, or
safes opened by gloved burglars.

In my mind I put my hand in your drawers,
anxious for the touch and further taste of you
on my tongue, my mouth, my face wet with you.

You're like a fast car on a sharply declining road.
I want to ride you with the top down
taking each curve without using any brake,

and the slower snaking path of my tongue on your spine
from nape to the haunting café of your derriere
is a trip I take several times before I turn you over

and open you to the middle like a book,
your spine in my hands, the dark juice of your words
overflowing, rivulets easing out of a corner of your mouth.

You've spoken only to me.
Summoned, I bid you to be the bad girl. Real baad!

Sexionnaire

R. Pope and Frank Lamont Phillips

1. How long has it been since you had sex?
2. If there has been a hiatus, was it self-imposed?
3. Do you feel less worthy when you don't have sex?
4. Do you do cosmetic things with your eyes, ears, nose, and lips to be sexy? If so, what kinds of things?
5. What smells are sexy to you?
6. What sounds are sexy to you?
7. Are there any foods that specifically remind you of sex?
8. What are the areas of your body that titillate your sensibilities? How do you know?
9. When you see others' bodies, what arouses you?
10. Have you ever had anal sex? If so, did you like it? Do you like it?
11. Do you engage in fillangia? If so, do you enjoy it?
12. Have you had cunnilingus? If so, do or did you enjoy it? Why?
13. Do you watch erotic movies?
14. Do you watch pornographic movies?
15. Are orgies appealing to you?
16. Would you like to have sex with two or more men or women at the same time?

17. Do you like hairy men or women? If so, where do you like the hair?
18. Have you thought about having sex in unconventional places: the last four rows of an airplane, the lavatory of a train or bus, the back seat of a car, an elevator, etc.?
19. Have you ever had sex on any floor? Did you enjoy it? Why?
20. How do you feel about men using your douche or enema bag during sex?
21. Do you use sexual accoutrements (dildos, vibrators, harnesses, lubricants, Ben-wa Balls, etc.)?
22. Do you use food in your lovemaking: whipped cream, strawberries or other fruits and vegetables, oils, honey, etc.?
23. Do you need a specific mood from without to have sex?
24. Do you always create an environment for sex?
25. Do you enjoy force with penetration?
26. How many of at least 369½ positions have you tried?
27. Do you masturbate (yes or no)? Why?
28. Do you enjoy sex in the water (sea, tub, rain)?
29. What is the most unusual place where you've had sex?
30. Identify the body parts that appeal in your most frequent sexual fantasies: penises, buttocks, chests, hair, legs, etc.
31. Identify the places which appear in your sexual fantasies.

To a Boy

Nancy Morejón

Translated by Miriam DeCosta-Willis

Amid the foam and the tide
he raises his back
when the solitary evening
was already falling.

I held his thin lips
like salt boiling in the sand.

I held, at last, his incense chin
beneath the sun.

A boy of the world above me
and songs of the Bible
shaped his legs, his ankles
and the grapes of his sex
and the pluvial hymns that spring from his mouth
enveloping us like two seamen
caught in love's inconstant sails.

In his arms, I live.
In his strong arms, I wished to die
like a soaked bird.

From *First Person Singular*

Lois Griffith

In Trinidad, Nigel was known as a great calypsonian, although I'd never seen demonstrations of his talents until the dawn of one Ash Wednesday. Mummy never let my sister Miriam and me go to carnival celebrations.

"I don't want my darlings on exhibition for tourists, parading around with the riffraff in primitive rites like savages. This Mas thing is almost obscene," she said. While the whole island was going about fêting, she drilled us in Lenten catechism, but I would steal from my bed before daybreak and catch the dregs of revelry. Tired parties still drunk on rum and dancing staggered along the road past the house singing songs they had learned at the marches of the battling steel bands that come down from the hills. Trinidad people drill all year for Mas. Calypso schools carefully choose their themes and design costumes and compose songs for the competitions at the Grand March.

This dawn I dressed and came out and stood at the front hedge of snake plants near the flamboyant to see what I could. Gauze weighted down with the red earth trailed over the asphalt, over muddy puddles. A bridal party like none I had ever seen paraded along the road. There was a bride in white and a shroud in black. The lacy edges of their garments were caked with mud and caught at everything in their wake. There was a gypsy masquerader in bright ballooning clothes. He had a steel drum harnessed against his body and as he played the pan, a man in a skeleton suit sang.

> . . . jumbi dancin'
> they hear the fire, fire
> in the drum
> come a-run-run-runnin'
> to the fire, fire
> of the drum . . .

And the beat was like a steady pulse. It was Nigel in the skeleton suit. His smudged makeup was painted to suggest that the flesh was not there, that the white bones of the skull lay over the surface of the face. He saw me gawking at him from behind the hedge and grinned his toothless grin.

> Jump in the line, boy!

He had maracas in his hands, and even though the pan man stopped playing when the party halted before me, Nigel kept up the same steady pulsing beat with those gourds.

> Jump in the line
> catch the fire, fire . . .

He added this to his song and I couldn't resist. My intention was to follow along for a bit, just down the way to the crossroads, but the shroud took my hand and I danced in her steps and she wouldn't let go. We came at last to a shack behind a cane field, and by then the sun had risen fully, but clouds chased each other across the sky and threatened to open in a shower.

I remember that sky, the rustling sound of the cane stalks, the heavy musk scent of sweat mixed with earth, the voice of the old man who came out of the shack to greet us.

"A good rain to wash yuh clean," he said. I learned this was Nigel's brother.

We all crowded into the house and there was Molly, Nigel's granddaughter. Her short wiry hair stood up on end giving her face a surprised look. Actually, Molly was a pretty girl, voluptuous and fleshy now that I think of her. She set food on the table for us: a strong mauby punch, pieces of cold ham and some johnny cakes still in the hot skillet.

Molly was quite taken with me. She sat me down beside her and kept stroking my cheek, patting my head.

"Him too pretty for a boy."

When she giggled, I saw her teeth were very white and even. Big sharp teeth. She picked up the meat from her plate and tore it like some voracious animal. She frightened me.

I had to relieve myself and she showed me to the outhouse behind the shack. I must have acted bewildered, being unaccustomed to the crudeness of such facilities, which were nothing more than a hole in the ground surrounded by walls, a roof and a door. She held the door open and stood there watching me, but because of the urgency of the situation there was not time to protest about the lack of privacy. As it was, I missed my mark and my sandled feet got the worst of it and she laughed.

"You need help, boy?" she said, flashing those teeth.

I wanted to run away from the place, from her. I was humiliated. I tidied myself as best I could as she pushed me aside and came into the tiny hovel.

"See how it's done, boy."

She straddled the hole and raised her skirts. I watched as she let out a stream from between her legs then wadded a sheet of newspaper that hung from a hook on the wall and wiped herself.

"You never seen a girl, boy?" she asked, still holding up her skirt.

I tried not to stare at the dark mound that she exhibited with such pride.

"Of course I have," I lied.

"You can touch it, boy," she said.

The hair was coarse and damp, a contrast to the smoothness of her inner thigh.

"You never touch a girl?"

I nodded in the affirmative, but she was not fooled and she laughingly caught my hand and pressed it against her forcefully.

"Put a finger inside," she said. "Marry me."

I tried to pull away. The thought of intruding my finger into the dark moist recess of her body filled me with dread and repulsion, yet I felt excitement and curiosity.

"You afraid, boy?"

Tentatively my finger probed between the folds of skin before it found the opening and was held and sucked as by thick wet lips.

"You like me?" she asked and before I could answer she covered my mouth with her own and let her tongue play over my clenched teeth. I pulled away, breathlessly, feeling an unaccustomed tightness in the crotch of my pants. I stood outside the lean-to just beyond her grasp and looked at her big eyes.

"You a silly boy," she laughed.

It had started to rain and huge drops splattered on my head. I just stood there. Then I turned and ran for the shelter of the house and she followed at my heels.

It was ridiculous for me to even think about returning home in the downpour, so I sat with them in the house and Nigel and the pan man kept up the music and Molly got up and danced with the bride and the

First Person Singular 263

shroud without giving me a look, although I didn't take my eyes off her rolling hips.

Mummy was furious when I finally got home, which was not until midafternoon. She had alerted the police, thinking I'd been kidnapped by the same thugs who had put an end to my father's career.

I had never seen her so distraught. She had rung up my Aunt Rani and the two of them greeted me on the veranda in tears.

"Cruel! Senseless boy!" Rani cried. She cut a switch from the garden and was ready to cane me.

"Don't hurt him! He's safe! He's safe!" Mummy wailed hugging me to her.

"Someone has to train this foolish unthinking boy or he'll grow like the father!"

How could Rani have said that, compared me with Father and revived the worst memories?

"I'm not like my father!"

I shouted at her and she took the switch to my legs. As fat and waddling as she was, she chased me up to my room.

I cried myself to sleep and the next morning Mummy gathered Miriam and me to her and told us she couldn't bear living on the island any longer. Mummy was no longer of an age then to be excited by the adventure of living the vagabond life, yet she sold the house and uprooted us. I didn't want to go.

I didn't see Nigel, but I saw Molly one last time before I left. I saw her at the market one day. She was holding hands with some dark stringbean of a fellow in a common seaman's uniform. I watched her flirting with him and he bought her a bag of sugar cakes. I know she saw me, but she gave no sign of recognition. I wondered if she would make him marry her.

You Knew . . .

Nelson Estupiñán Bass

Translated by Lemuel Johnson

You knew
and knew all along
that day and night
my passion kept watch, driven sleepless.
That my arms, empty and craving
and unrelenting reached out after you everywhere;
that this blood of mine
which had profaned temples—
yes, I always mocked the front and façade of churches!—
had risen up in tumult
against the wretched locks of this or that "thou shalt not."

You knew, too,
this inchoate anguish that drives my blood,
welling up from the dark origins of my first days.
Become articulate in the language of my hands,
it sought out a block of wild stone
from which to carve two black fists
that one day will raise
the graveyard cloth of our colors

here, in these places
forever green, invincible

Perhaps the fault lay
in the compelling power of your body,
black like degrees of night
in the tangled interiors of forests
where dream-driven rites
fill the air with vapor and alkaloid
and wild beasts close their fangs
down in the somnolent borders of sleep.

In your body, supple as the bamboo,
quick-moving like a child's kite
forever poised to be rocked by desire.
In that body, firm like the ivory nut,
resonant as is the music of the guasa,
and so much in everyday like streams
whose currents wake up the woods
to the delight of sound made music.

In the fragrance of your body
which, asleep or awake,
insistently calls
out to the vegetable summons
in the primal sap of wood.

In your body and its buoyant litheness,
alive in the sounds with which you writhed
into a clamorous vortex: the whirlwind
we danced to in that banana grove
where your body quickened, a mantuvio rudder
that slips and slides, yet is pitched
in control of the raging banks
and the rivers of Esmeraldas.

In your body, that avalanche
which was going to have
to break up against some wall
or else vanish, weightless,
drawn out in the immense time of the mountains.

In the rose apple taste that marks you,
in the siren pliancy there at your waist,

in the crystal geometry of your breasts
that aroused me to the seven deadly sins;
in your skin, firm
and resonant, a cununo drum
that sends tremors down
the stone quiet architecture of hills.

Perhaps, my black lovely, the fault lay
in the bent and that temptation of your body
which, at last, my trembling hands got into—
and tossing into a bonfire the icons of the temple—
they took you and shook you
down to the marrow
there in that banana grove.

Erector Set

Ahmasi

I REMEMBER
A PERIOD
IN MY YOUTH
AND
MY FIRST
ERECTOR SET

IT CAME
WITH
MY BODY

Teaching the Sweet Thing

P. J. Gibson

Miss Dorothy, officially known as Miss Dorothy Ganges, had employed young boys over the years to do little errands for her. She'd have them fix this thing here and that thing there and give them a dollar or two for their services. She was particular about whom she would bring into her home. The loud rowdy boys were never asked to step over the threshold of her door. Some said she had not let them in because many of them stole, and she had valuable things she'd acquired over the years. What most did know was that she always chose quiet, smart, well-spoken young boys to help with this and that. Some ran errands to the stores. Some raked leaves or cut the lawn. Some painted the banisters and porch. Some got to do work inside the house. To do a little work here and there for Miss Dorothy was an honor. She was a pretty Black woman with clear smooth deep caramel skin, the kind with a hue or two of red peeping through, and she had the body of life. Even the old men and women on the block would speak of her beautiful build. She had one man, Mr. Ray Locklear. He was a merchant marine and spent a good deal of time away at sea. That was why so many young boys had gotten an opportunity to do a thing or two for her.

Dorothy was discreet in her choice of the young men she would taunt to the sweet-smelling splendor of her bed. Not all who had painted the banisters, raked the leaves, or had gone to the supermarket had touched the tight rounds of her breasts or smelled the sweet fragrance of her woman's bush. The young men who had would grow into men who would never forget the sweet smell of woman they learned in the bed of Miss Dorothy.

Geoffery's young mind had been readied for Miss Dorothy. The years he had spent locked in the pages of seductive literature, the hours he had stolen from visions of men and women drinking and dining on one another's bodies in forbidden films, these things had prepared Geoffery for Miss Dorothy. And when she brought him to her bed and prepared herself to teach the "young sweet thing" a thing or two about "women and loving," Geoffery made her cry out: "Ooohh sweetness . . . Such sweet, sweet, sweetness . . ." She enhanced his knowledge and they were both satisfied.

From *Teach Me*

Michelle Renée Pichon

i want you
to teach me
i'm ready to learn

i want you to teach me
the warmth of your breath
the weight of your body
i want to experience
the trembles   heat
sweatfireiceconvulsionsgaspsthrusts
spasmscaressescriesscreamsuntil . . .
      i
          can   barely
                          breathe
educate me with your
mouth tongue shoulders arms fingers
chest hips thighs legs feet toes

i want you
to teach me

i'm ready
to learn

class begins

          right

              now

From *The Initiation of Belfon*

Jan Carew

Heavy raindrops began tapping on the galvanized-iron roof like desperate strangers seeking shelter. The night wind, coming from across the cane fields and blowing through the open window, brought the smell of rain and distant forests into the room. Couvade hurried outside to rescue her laundry from the clothesline in the backyard.

There was a great murmuring and sighing of wind in the trees, and a thunderclap made the pots and pans rattle in the kitchen.

Couvade stood in the doorway with her arms full of clean clothes. Her gaze, resting on me for a while, was alternately vague and sharp.

"You look tired, Belfon. The rain will help you to catch a good sleep."

The yellow glare of the naked electric bulb made her squint and her glittering anthracite eyes peering through slits had an expression that was at once mysterious and threatening. Rain was drumming on the roof like a host of washerwomen beating clothes with paddles by the riverside. Every now and then a gust of wind changed the monotonous tempo to an angry hissing.

"Yes, I'd better turn in," I said.

Couvade attached two chairs to the end of the couch, tying them together with rope so that my six-foot-six frame could stretch itself out in comfort.

I was deep in the throes of a dreamless sleep when Couvade woke me up.

"Belfon, wake up," she whispered. "The chickens keeping plenty noise, must be a thief."

She gave me a cutlass and a flashlight, and with only my underpants on, I slipped through the front door and circled the chicken coop. Switching on the flashlight, I saw an eight-foot-long yellow-tailed snake trying to crawl through a hole at the side of the coop. I cut off the snake's head, dragged the still-writhing body out of the coop and threw it over the back fence, knowing that between day-clean and midmorning carrion crows would pick it to the bone. The rain had stopped falling and it was as if the wind and the deluge had polished the stars, because they shone like low-hanging celestial lanterns with glittering crystal shades.

It was so quiet when I reentered the cottage that I was sure Couvade was asleep, but when I started tiptoeing toward the couch she said:

"Come and lie down in my warm bed. That early-morning dew can give you a chill."

I crept into her bed and she entwined her naked body around mine. I heard the songless singing of shango drums echoing from distant forests, and the beating heart of the drums and my own became one. The relentless rhythm of heart and blood and drums became an irresistible flux nourishing our beings as we performed our slow sinuous dance like serpents in the mating season.

The chickens were neglected for two days and they foraged around the backyard restlessly, cackling and scratching, and grubbing for worms and insects. Couvade, sitting up in bed, ran her fingers lightly across the surface of my chest, my abdominal ridges, and my thighs, and she said wistfully:

"What a Rod of Correction the good Lord present you with, Belfon! It's an instrument of redemption. It's not just that it's a perfect size, it's the shape of it and the feel of it, and you so tender, boy, tender like a woman. Boy, you born under a woman's sign, and woman going to feature in your life all your livelong days. Belfon darling, don't ever be 'fraid of gentleness, and to be a man with your mighty body and the brains you got in your head is to have a magnet for womankind, and that's more important than the lightning rod between your legs; though I can tell you that rod sweeter than honey, and feeling it inside me, it touches places that were sleeping for a long time; and the youngness of you and the freshness make me feel young again, and when it fill up my mouth I feel that I sucking nectar-juice at a fountainhead in Paradise." I saw her eyes fill slowly with tears and the corners of her mouth began to tremble.

I shut the guilty clamor out of my mind and asked:

"Why are you crying, Couvade?"

"Crying for the joy of living, darling, for the feel of the hot rush of blood, and for the thought that someday the flow will stop, and all that will be left will be memories that soak into the men and women you share the joy with, just as how water does soak into a tacouba. Every time I spread joy like this I always get to thinking that some little bit of me died; escaped to where I can't reach it; it's just like how you can never swim in the same water of a river twice . . . You're different, Belfon, you make every woman feel that she's special . . . Still and all," she said reflectively, and I was amazed at the ease with which she could flit from one mood to the other without a pause. She made me forget that she was naked, that her dark brown flesh was as soft as silk, that her breasts were as succulent as ripe muskmelons; that we'd been making love for two days like dancers hypnotized by rhythms that had taken them far beyond the normal limits of fatigue. "Still and all," she repeated, "I hope I was something special to you." She cut off the reassurances I was so eager to proffer and declared dryly, "Sex is like ice in sun, it can blind you with beauty, flash, and glitter and make you feel you found the biggest jewel that ever come out of the earth, but after a while, and a short while at that, all that's left is memories and a puddle."

I got out of bed and paced up and down. I had been deluding myself that I was falling in love with Couvade, that I was willing to give up my studies and marry her, but she had shattered these romantic dreams like a wrecker dynamiting a façade to reveal the dust and emptiness behind it. The cottage suddenly seemed to me to have become as constricted as a tiger trap, and I wanted to escape to open spaces again.

"Do you know something, I haven't stayed indoors this long since I was ten and had measles."

"We must go out then," Couvade said, "I don't want you to feel that I'm locking you up in a love-cage."

I searched her face to see if any vestige of annoyance was reflected on it. But it was as inscrutable as a Carib devil mask. She got up and stretched like an ocelot. I wrapped my arms around her and lifted her off her feet. "Let go of me!" she said fiercely, but she had given me a confidence that I had never known before with women. I saw passion igniting in her dark eyes and burning like acetylene flames. Her body yielded reluctantly at first, and then with a wild abandonment. When darkness surprised us once again, we opened the living-room windows to let the starlight in.

Discoveries

Gloria Wade-Gayles

I was always afraid
to tell you
with movements or even words
about the passion
I was born with,
but feared.

I kept it covered with
ginghams
plaids
long sleeves
high neckspearled

hidden in
locked diaries
secret poems
day fantasies
darknight dreams

and when I dared
share it
I camouflaged it with dry-lip lectures
on purity so stern
the Calvinists would have
etched them into the Rock
for all women to read.

Last night
I conquered my fears
put out waving flags
smoking flares
road signs
and flashing arrows
pointing you to the secret places
where my passion waited
feverishly
only for you.

With closed eyes
you discovered
secret places
I never knew existed.

Opening Night

Jerry W. Ward, Jr.

schooled in this
theatre of cruelty
you can weather
i believe, i want to believe,
anything falling from the sky,
and i believe i want you to believe
i never left the ground

i believe i want you to believe
this is really real love
not a fable
into which we happened
a romance ago

i believe
(and i know now how you know it)
the chore of love
is hardly tender
but better yet
rough rolling and rocking

the way of square circles
and waiting inside
yourself for a scene,
an implosion of fire
on fire in fire

i believe i want you to believe
you believe when you go
i'll come into wells of satisfaction,
sloshing and grunting
from your throat
and my tongue
tastes passion and electricity
cell by naked cell

i believe i want you to believe
i give your body
a standing ovation
when you stun me
with your opening tight
like lightning
on the ridges of my rod

Dear Diary

R. H. Douglas

Monday, November 15, 1976

Dear Diary,

After much deliberation, I finally gave in to my passion last night. Took a warm bath and entertained the feeling of sensuousness. My therapist said that I should feel completely relaxed and able to feel my pores open to the warmth of the water. I enjoyed the process and wanted to relieve the craving for sex. The music was playing, softly, seductively, and I turned off the lights in the bathroom, so there was only a dim reflective glow from the hallway light outside the bathroom and the light of the stars and moon filtering through my window. I scented my bath water with amber and its perfume filled the air, creating the mood for me to masturbate for the first time in my life.

I could now settle back and enjoy me, gently stroking between my thighs and slowly inserting my finger into my vagina. I stopped, sat up in the tub, wondered if I should continue, because now I began to feel the sweet sensation of ecstasy. I decided that if I was ever going to try, I might as well try now. So I lay back in the warm scented water and caressed my thighs, felt the roughness of the tender hairs on my mound as my hands slowly ran through my valley of forbidden fruits. I sighed and noted that I was enjoying what I was doing. Then shame and embarrassment overcame me. I told myself that I am the only one who knows about this and that there is no ghost spy in my apartment waiting to see me do the "forbidden" act. I wondered if by masturbating and arousing pleasure in myself I would be attracted to lesbianism.

By masturbating I am learning to love my body. I touched the softness of my flesh and licked the creases of my hands. When I did this I felt me and tasted me. I was playing both roles as giver and receiver of pleasure. I was in total control. I tried to reach a climax but was frustrated. I could not summon the fiery passion and quickened sensation I needed. I could increase the pleasure, but I needed the right rhythm to release the knot within me. I gave up after rocking to the rhythm of my finger and four other fingers to get more out of them.

Then I stopped and started douching. The insertion of the instrument caused me great pleasure and drew out a long sigh. I slowly moved the nozzle in a rotating motion, rubbing it gently on the parts which caused greatest sensations. The hardness of the instrument added to my increased pleasure. I inserted my finger again with the object to get deeper into myself. Although the depth in inches could not be increased, the depth in pleasure was. I felt the softness of my vagina walls and thought, "Oh, so this is what the man loves to feel, this softness, this sensual flesh caressing his penis, his fingers." I loved the feeling, but did not get the climax, which I was trying desperately to reach. But the pleasure was so great that I quickly forgot the climax and absorbed myself totally in the immediate pleasure which filled every inch of my body. I continued for a few minutes, while the entire side of the record played, and then I slowly withdrew my fingers and rested. I was surprised at the relaxed state of my mind and body. I thought, "It really works!" I've read accounts of people indulging for the first time, their satisfaction at the first attempt. The feeling is true. At least it was for me. I really felt more relaxed and satisfied, but not completely satisfied, for I still did not explode into a zillion tiny fireworks, but I was relaxed.

As I dried myself, I thought that I would continue relaxing with a joint, but I needed more than my fingers. I looked around the apartment and saw the candles in the candle holder. Earlier, my brother-in-law said that I needed a man, but I told him that I needed a strong dick, and he replied . . . "There's a good sturdy candle right there." So when I reached for the candle in the dark, having turned all the lights off, I smiled and said, "If only he knew." Moonlight filtered into the room and created a dreamy atmosphere. The softly playing music added to the vibrations, and I lay back and started giving myself pleasure all over again. I touched the crevices of my vagina. I rubbed the tender lips. I did not hurry. I wanted to see in my mind's eye what I was doing with my fingers. I closed my eyes and concentrated on the sensation. I was carried away on a pleasant flowing current which gently rocked me back and forth in rhythm to my sexual sounds. I stretched open the lips of my vagina and inserted the candle. The penetration was the highlight of the act. I moved the candle slowly in and out and around and thought that the candle has an advantage over the man's penis: his penis cannot go around, only in and out. I rubbed it hard against my clitoris and felt the excitement my man aroused in me. The only problem was that I could not obtain a climax pulling and sucking it out the way he did. I wished at that moment that I could, by some miracle, reach my head between my legs. I changed position. Instead of lying on the pillows, I switched to the floor with my feet up on the chair. I moaned and whispered to myself that I had the power within me to come. I said, "Get that one, girl." I was so wrapped up in the pleasure that I felt no shame, no embarrassment as I rolled and moaned on the floor. When I stopped, I was completely relaxed.

After a few minutes I wanted to start again. I still had not climaxed and the throbbing sensation between my thighs was overpowering. I had to do it again. I used the candle and one finger, which I rubbed along with the candle. I let this feeling flow for a few minutes, and then I quickly inserted the candle in and out creating a feeling of total elation. I finally reached a semi-climax and stopped. I dozed off in the same position with the candle between my thighs. Then I got up, turned the music off, fell on the pillows, and went to sleep with the candle in position. When I awoke this morning, the candle had slipped out and I was so relaxed.

I enjoyed my first attempt at masturbating and look forward to many more. I am going to relax for a few minutes now before I go out to work. My fingers will comfort me and my candle will satisfy me.

From *A Carnival of the Old Coast*

bangarang mestiçagem

Lemuel Johnson

A black slave approaching an indian prostitute with silver stolen from
his master

                         —Figure 4 (South America)

      mansoaked and bound for glory
      the thing deliverable like delirium.

      that the sea invade the land,
      that shadow and fruit are not
      hanging firm, nor underfoot,
      all that now hardly to the point

      at all, you know, crab-meat
      and bone, rice root and fish
      are not now to the point
      for the man soaking and bound for glory

      sooner or later
      the possessed will eat broken glass

and god's formidable mouth crack
human bone an make juice

but bangarang mestiçagem
it's jurema* when nightfall come
and ghost broth† in the morning
an the race improving so to a moonglow
(an jubilation long as a prick long
an longer
when you think now how they joyful together

the woman full of plan an keep her own self's milk
(though the man's good penis blindeat so inside)
So when the man move an move
   so with backward pointed feet
   an come
                  mansoaked
in a torment of coin and thrust
she arrange herself and she put it so:
"in a ditch the water hopeless and dead"

but she pull the business out:
"an why not, when the thing
so deliverable, it's a hard hard wonder
getting born take effort."

---

* **Jurema** (Pg.), a toxic substance used by Afro-Brazilian sorcerers to induce a state of trance.

† **Ghost Broth.** See ALMAS PENADAS.

Almas Penadas (Pg.), in Afro-Brazilian folklore, wandering souls in torment who, having left this world without atoning for their sins, are condemned to come back to expiate them. When they come back, they smear children's faces with "ghost broth"; for this reason, it is said that no child should neglect to wash his or her face or to take a bath first thing in the morning.

The 1st 3 Daze

Reginald Martin

FRIDAY

. . . that kind of boredom that comes from seeing the world too clearly—you know what I mean. One of those days when your job means nothing to you and you realize that you've got to squeeze some respectable actions and some fun into your little narrative time frame before the only things left of you are the memories your friends and relatives hold of you.

The leaves turn in Mobile in November, but they don't fall. And when a breeze tumbles in from the south they rustle and tinkle right through February. One of those mornings that you want to leave the coffee shop and pull some of those leaves down to the grass and roll around in them and forget all about the bad stuff that you have no control over and just roll and roll around in the leaves and forget all about going to work at the post office and your co-workers spying on you and blowing their noses. On a day like that it was, at 7:30 in the morning, she walked into the station and came to my window.

Any action that involved a male stopped in the post office for the ten minutes she was there—much to the irritation of the other females needing assistance. And the funny thing about that few minutes is that everyone knew why all action had stopped—us, the other women in line, the woman herself—but nobody said a word. The men didn't say anything to each other, but she had undone us all and we were all enjoying our little personal fantasies to the exclusion, we wanted to think, of everyone else.

It's always on those days when you think you look your worst and when you're feeling your worst, when your mind is on all the things that have recently gone wrong, that some cute guy takes an interest in you. When you're set, all the clothes on right, the makeup on right, your head on right, all you run into are these Mooks looking for you to be their mommy. But when you're worried that your hair looks as dirty as it is, it never fails. Some piece of candy who looks like he just walked out of a suit ad in *Ebony* walks up to you and says all the things you want to believe are true.

Yeah, I saw him standing behind the counter when I came in and I thought, "Uh, that's a good-looking guy." But I wasn't gon say anything to him cause I just wasn't feeling very attractive, and besides, my feelings get hurt too easily if the guy turns out to be married or gay or something. So I just thought I'd go about my business. But I could feel those brown eyes burning me and I didn't want him to stop.

So when she finally got up to be next in line I made sure I was the first one to yell out "Next!" I mean, all those other guys standing around nervous and paralyzed. Umma man, I been told "NO!" so many times that the pain just kinda stings and then it's gone, like a mosquito bite. So when she got to the counter I took her order and when I came back with the postage I said, "You sure do look good this fall morning."

"I look good every morning."

"I know that's right. Could I call you sometimes?"

"We-l-l-l . . . you might better let me call you cause um in and out. What's your number?"

The numbers came out so fast that she had to ask me to repeat them. I was blubbering all over the stamps, the veins in my neck bulging, blood rushing to my head, um dropping stuff all over the place. I told her anytime after six was a good time to call. I knew that would give me time to get my twenty-minute run in at the park and do my chest, shoulders, and triceps on the bench, clean up, and then I could put on my socializing head and be reasonably entertaining. Man, I mean everything just stopped in the post office. The woman was magnetic body from way back. After she swayed out, the whole building exhaled.

But you had to be there that morning to feel all the vibes and goodness I'm talking about that were happening between me and him. Oh my, it was just . . . I think I would have just died if he hadn't given me his number. And I felt him comin. Do you know what I mean? I mean, see, I'm a Buddhist, and I had been keeping up on my chanting pretty good, and lately I had been feeling something very . . . something big and positive was pushing in on my Karmic force field, I didn't know what or from where, but I knew something was about to go down and it wasn't going to be negative.

But, gosh, this guy was just emitting—no, he was *shooting* all these warm and sexual thoughts all over me, all around my neck, shoulders, torso, legs. And outside it was so bright and everybody seemed to be moving in slow motion. One of these semi-cool breezes was gently coming in from the direction of the beach, pushing paper cups over the asphalt outside. And we were in sync.

I didn't know what to do. He sure couldn't call me cause the kids and I were staying with a girlfriend at the time and I really hadn't worked out at that point how we were going to arrange phone courtesy and stuff, and work was kind of up in the air at the time—I do promotions, y'know—and I really didn't know when I would be in or out.

I kind of just floated around all day. Even the most tiring and degrading aspects of job hunting kind of just got done without me thinking too much about them. I was thinking about that man, honey. And the cool, wet things he said on the phone that night!

When she called that night, man I was in the mix. I wasn't able to run the conversation in the direction I wanted to, but it turned out even better than I could ever have planned. See, she was a talker. She started takin over the direction of the things we were going to talk about, steering the conversation in the directions she wanted it to go.

Oh, I don't know. I guess I've just about had enough sex for 100 people. And I'm talkin about state-of-the-art sexo-technics. I mean, people always talkin about "You'll have something to tell your grandkids." Man, I couldn't *generate* enough kids to have the number of grandkids it would take for me to give each one of em a piece of my complete tale.

So, I was just thinking for once I'd like to keep my piece in my pocket and have what dull people call "a friend." And she was makin that easy: after about five minutes you could tell that she was somebody that you really wanted to know, to keep around as a friend, because she was not only sexy and smart in every direction, she was a good person way deep inside of her. And even better, I decided that this goodness didn't just happen to be. She had made herself worth knowing, worked on herself and remade herself brand new through enough hard times to drive even Bill Cosby to the Crack House.

Anyway, we talked and talked about her, her life, things she had done, been through. From cheerleader to Black Muslim to Buddhist will take your head in a few different directions, I'll tell you that. I told her all about myself: stumbling out of college with the highest grade average of anyone majoring in sociology, only to find that the best job I could get would be at the post office as a letter handler; loving to work out with the weights, basketball; learning to read for pleasure again and to really understand what I was reading; hanging out at the museums. I mean, I was as dull as Sunday, and then she said something that—well—

Ooo, that man was fun to talk to on the phone. I was taking over the conversation as usual, but it was like he wanted me to. He was interested in the things I had to say, and he knew things about what my life had been through. I talked about my kids. He told me he didn't have any and why. He liked basketball, anything athletic really. Monster movies. And the man could make you bust out laughing in the middle of a funeral.

He told me this joke—wait, I wanna make sure I get it right. O.K., we were talking about writing and I was telling him that I had kept a very detailed diary for the past fifteen years and he told me that he wrote long letters to his grandmother, poetry, fiction, all the time, cause he just enjoyed doing it. And I asked why he thought there weren't more Black writers on the market, and he said that the best Black writers wrote in the market that paid the most and was the least hostile, which is pop music. Said he knew why, too, but it wasn't the right time or place to get into that. And then he said—oh, it was a riot! He said, "Then again, though, you know how the public perceives some things. Maybe some writers just aren't interested in giving the market what it seems to want. The miracle ain't that the mule spoke; the miracle was that the mule had even had an inclination to speak in the first place."

Oh, I fell over on the floor laughing! And he was laughing, and the next thing I knew, the words just came out. I really didn't give a damn at that point.

Man, this woman said to me she "really would be interested in finding out what it would be like to make love to me one day soon." You see what I mean? It's just like I was telling you last week, every time I try to be cool, what dull people call a "nice guy," they practically violate me. It's in the raw. So I said, "Are you sure that's what you want? I'm a wild man sometimes." And then you know what she said? She said, "I'll tame you." Just like that, with that Sade voice. "I'll tame you." Knocked me to my knees. I couldn't say a word. Then she said, "What do you want to do about disease? There's a lot of it going around." So I told her I'd cover that, and then she started going right down the list of the things she wanted us to do, but it was all in these kind of coded, erotic, mystical euphemisms. When she got through, you coulda hung your clothes out on me to dry. I mean, I was a Harley kickstand, you know what I mean? So I asked her if she kind of just wanted to let this "naturally happen," as the dull people say, or did she have some kind of agenda in mind, and there was this silence on her end of the phone for a minute. And then she said:

—I hear tomorrow is going to be a beautiful day. Hot, a little humidity—

The next thing I knew I was popping *Choose Me* into the video machine and trying harder than I ever had in my life to go to sleep so it could be the next day.

SATURDAY

I was so nervous all morning. You know how it is when it's your first time out with somebody, and plus I had made everything real black and white by being so bold, but the man's conversation just undid me. I couldn't help myself. And in a way this made things a little easier. I didn't have to be stumbling around after the movie or dinner or Trivial Pursuit or whatever waiting for some knucklehead to make the first move. I have a theory about that. Are you listening to me? Well, quit looking at those videos when I'm talking to you. This is important.

See, I think we're going about this all wrong, trying to get the type of men we want, I mean. We sit around, we wait to be asked to do this, we wait to be talked into that; and you know what you get when you wait for guys? You get the Mooks and the losers, you get what's left. And why do we wait around? For decorum, cause that's the way its spozed to be? Cause we're afraid of getting our feelings hurt?

I talked to my brother about this, and Lord knows New Breed knows a little about getting dates. And you know what he told me? He said, "Nobody knows what you want in a lover better than you do. So doesn't it make sense that you should go out and shop for what you want? You gotta look at a guy, talk to him, that way you got more of a chance of getting what you want and not getting whoever happens to be left without a date one night in the mall or something. Getting your feelings hurt? Look, let me tell you something. The first time I got rejected by a girl I just wanted to crawl up under my bunk bed and die. Overdose by eating a bunch of G.I. Joe heads. But you can't do that—not if you really want a lover. After a while being assertive, not only does the pain of being rejected vanish, but you get better at knowing what you want—and getting what you want. Say there are five guys who pass your visual test in the lobby of the theater before the play starts. Just before the lights blink, you talk to all five. Three turn out to be Mooks, one is from the dark side of the moon, and the last one is a ten and he smiles when you whisper a certain suggestion in his ear. Did you lose? Did you suffer? Naw, you got what you wanted!" Honey, he's got it down to a science that he's turned into an art. And I agree, so I just had to say what I did cause this fool was talking about being like "brother and sister" or some such nonsense, and I already got three brothers. I don't need no more.

I finally got the kids off to their father's about two. He was gonna takem to the zoo and they were gonna sleep over at his place. I got to my friend's house about three and we were on our way. Oh! We had so much fun. First we went to this museum and walked around for a couple of hours, and this guy working in the post office knows all about art and everything, right? Can you imagine? And then we went down to _____ and we had fresh shrimp and scrod and oysters with lemon sauce. Honey, that Zinfandel had me reeling. And then we drove down to the Gulf and walked around for a long time talking about Karma and special postal delivery rates, talking about my ex-husband and his latest ex-girlfriend, about the curves life throws you even when you're concentrating on the pitch. And then when it got pretty dark and the moon was pretty high, he picked me up and piggybacked me to his Toyota.

Yeah, we got into my car and we went to the museum. Man, it was a gas. I finally got a chance to use all that Western art knowledge, which is a part of all that other unmarketable knowledge I so faithfully committed to memory. But the only reason I got into it was she said she was into whatever I was into.

I told her all about Egyptian art, all about the German, French, British "scholars" running around scraping the dark paint off the figures in the tombs and chipping the Leon Sphinks noses off the statues, saying the pyramids were built by little green peoploids from Mars and all that ridiculous bullshit. Told her about Hogarth and how he drew London for what it was: the downside of Jackson, MS in 18th-century clothes. Showed her how much Voodoo is in the average Blake painting or engraving, told her how Blake's friend stayed up for several nights after Blake's death burning Blake's greatest works cause he thought Blake was crazy, demon-possessed. Showed her the African curves in all of the antebellum South's furniture. Kept a lookout while she did like I told her and rubbed her fingers over the oils in *Three Musicians,* and told her Picasso had said over and over that he didn't know what the critics were talking about, "cubism mirroring modern, disjointed life and architecture" and all that shit; Pablo said, "Hey, when you get through with all that, my art is African art." Told her how Jacob Lawrence could paint better with his toes than most "great artists" could with their hands. And she was eating this stuff up. And she just made me feel so comfortable talking about it that I just went on until my stomach started growling.

Well, I'm always fighting a losing battle with myself. I mean, um just weak. The left side of my brain says keep her as the perfect friend and all the time the right side of my brain is the one who told me not to wear underwear in the first place. Like, I *had* to take her to a seafood restaurant, y'know what I mean? It was the only kind of food my psyche would let me eat. And we had a great time.

I ordered these big boiled shrimp with juice and butter just running off them. And I ordered two liters of wine, even though I don't normally drink, but I figured I was drunk on her anyway by the time we left the museum. And then I ordered two dozen oysters, and we shot lemon juice and hot sauce on them and we fed them to each other. More wine, Burgundy, I think, and then we had halibut and long lobster tails and more wine. Man, I gotta tell you, I had to get out and get some air.

So I drove us down to the shore and let that cool air blow on me for a while. Mercy! The woman just gushes all that stuff that makes you glad you're a man. I got pretty dazed by my hormones and the wine, and I think I just started mumbling about things at the post office and Dr. J. retiring—but you got to understand. Um real high-natured, and when a connection is in my mind, it's real, real hard for me to think about anything else. And she was talking about some heavy stuff, religion, taxes, morticians, something, but I didn't mean to be rude. I just wasn't linear.

And, I don't know. That warm wind blew her scent up to me, and the moon was shining on the ripples. The next thing I knew, she was on my back and I was a stallion.

Sweat, shoulders, knees, toes, eyebrows, lips, navels, sides, mouths, eyes, hair, tongues, fuzz, saliva, backs, hands, noses, nails, butts, eighteen fingers, ears, muscles, eyelids, flesh, stomachs, thighs, collarbones, heads, ankles, necks, teeth, skin, calves, lashes, thumbs, points and conclaves.

Mirrors, *Antaeus,* angels, bracelets, headboards, pillows, untucked sheets, carpet, knocked-down pictures, sinks, rooms, doorknobs, shower curtains, linoleum, baby oil, "Love Zone" by Billy Ocean, entertainment centers, candles, honey, *Ysatis,* ice cubes, three burning logs, purple garters, cocoa butter, black bikini briefs, "You Bring Me Joy" by Anita Baker, crumpled drapes, desks, scissors, body paint, a razor, "ENTRY

May 4" by Walter Benton, windowsills, bathtubs, shaving cream, sheet burns, *Emmanuele in Bangkok* (uncut version), stuffed animals, dressers, Queen Anne chairs, white stockings. "Anyone Who Had a Heart" as sung by Luther Vandross, *real* cold Asti Spumante, and a jar of peanut butter.

A reaffirmation of the innate and absurd yet vitally necessary notion that the world is an O.K. place to live, the willingness to disbelieve all the badness your intelligence and experience have already confirmed are true, "Uh, uh, uh, will you look at that," time slows down, an atomic bomb blast couldn't move the two of you from underneath the quilt by the fireplace, views of the human body that you ain't supposed to see, "I didn't know the loving was gonna be this long," the springtime view at dusk from Philip Michael Thomas's Central Park West condo, Chinese food at midnight with *The Wolfman* in the 8 mm, "Whatever it is you want me to do, just tell me," "The Beautiful Ones" by Prince, the inability to stop telling about your past and the inability to stop telling the truth, the feeling of not being alone, a $3,500 sound system in the back seat of a chauffeur-driven 560 Mercedes at midnight on the Golden Gate Bridge, Kenya in April, your mother's ham (with pineapples and yams) on Christmas, May rain dripping from the house into a puddle by your open bedroom window, "Ooo, that's a good-looking guy," Aretha singing "Call Me" on a portable CD as you're jogging around Cape Cod, the moon rising over beachfront Miami as seen from a cruise ship, "This is my favorite," Rio at Carnival, and a partridge in a pear tree.

SUNDAY

Rewind. More of the same—only better.

Your first breakfast after the first time you've made love to somebody new is always the best breakfast in the world. It's The First Breakfast, you know, and you're like Adam and Eve and the whole garden is ripe and fresh and sweet. And it doesn't matter what time of day you eat this breakfast—well, you know damn well it's not gon be early cause your morning is filled with NEWNESS and you're gonna hold onto this NEWNESS—this thing that is so right and can't go wrong cause it's NEW—you're gonna hold onto this thing as long as you can and bear-hug every sweat drop out of it until it runs down her legs and you have to lick it off; like pineapple it tastes, a million calories of sheer joy in every micro-ounce to clog your heart, and you lick and lick and lick til it's all gone.

So I got her to breakfast about one that afternoon, and we ordered coffee and started looking over the menu, but she started rubbing up under my knee under the table, and it started me to doing what I was gonna do anyway: replay. Man, you just don't know. I get to the point sometimes where I just don't know what's more fun, the stuff we do, or the way I get to listen to myself talking to her about it, inch by inch, after we're done. It's like, one is the exquisite pleasure of doing, seeing, feeling, but the other is the never-ending pleasure of hearing myself remember, and I never get tired of remembering. And I have such a good memory. And I have so many memories.

Girl, I miss him to this day. He was just . . . I remember we were sitting at the table the third day, and I couldn't keep my hands to myself. I like to touch for a day or so after the fact; makes me believe that what just happened did happen, and it opens up the door for it to happen again. Makes me believe I could live forever.

And then he blew my mind right there in the restaurant. He put me into a world where all the brats screaming for more pastries and the Baptist crowd coming in with their orange and lime dresses and gray and blue suits ordering mountains of pancakes couldn't touch me. He went back over the night before and the morning a few hours before like a tape machine. I mean, he didn't leave *nothing* out. He even added stuff that I knew didn't happen, but I knew must have happened cause they sounded too good not to have happened. He never touched me, but he did stuff to me at that table that must be illegal after five bottles of champagne in the Honeymoon Suite on New Year's Eve in the Las Vegas Hyatt.

When the waitress brought the coffee, he was crying; she asked if he wanted to be moved to a non-smoking section. He burst out laughing so loud it almost drowned out my screaming laughter. Then he wiped his eyes and he said, "There's nowhere you can run from this smoke. Everything's on fire." We ate two big bowls of fruit salad and drank some more coffee and then he took me home and we burned down another forest. I don't think I've ever had a better time with anybody in my life than what I had with him for that little minute . . . it was real strange how it ended. But it ended.

Well, I don't think I'll be bumping into anybody like her too soon. She was . . . different . . . refreshing—yeah, that's a good word for her, refreshing. She'd refresh your ass to death if you didn't throw in the towel. Of all the memories that I rewind and push play on, hers is the one that's always in slow motion with all of Jimi Hendrix's slow songs in the background for the sound track.

We tore up the house until about seven, and then I took her back down to the Gulf to watch the moon make the waves worth watching. Man, when that night was black and the moon was so high you had to crank your neck all the way back to look at it, and the light had turned the water and the sand and the rocks all gray, it was an Andrew Wyeth painting. Far as I was concerned, you could have freeze-framed it, blown it up, and hung it on the wall. I never wanted to change that scene. I wanted to keep it just like that.

I could see her silhouetted and her sweat reflecting, and I didn't even feel the sand on my back. It was . . . real odd how we knew when it was over. I never have recovered from that. I really have not.

Just before I got out to open her car door, I told her—I told her right then; you have to tell people those kinda things when you're thinking them cause the worms are gonna eat you when you're dead—I told her, "You're a perfect diamond set in platinum. Don't ever change a thing." And she said,

"I love you."

Well, all I can tell you is that I go back inside my heart sometimes and rub that spot real gentle where he still is—in there still screaming and squirming and sweating away, child—cause that's the kinda horse he was. What I got now and who I'll have later, well, that'll be them. But this dude . . . this dude. I'll haveta keep him in some secret spot for what we were when we were alive, pull him out when I need him, then put him back again, you know what I mean?

Anyway, the fact that she made me love her before she ever touched me, that's . . . that's like winning the California lottery after you already won the Irish sweepstakes, y'know? All wet, hot gravy that you gotta gobble down even after the main course cause it won't be hot later. I mean, sex with her wasn't stipulative of nothing else: it was what it was, goddamnit. I mean, it wasn't for the future, it wasn't for the babies, it wasn't for the house, or because the right phase of the moon was up over that black water. She was on toppa me cause that's what she wanted and that's where she wanted to be for her and for me. So when you get love on toppa all that other important stuff, well . . . the way I see it is, if nothing else ever goes right, if the killer bees get here tomorrow, if they put those reruns of *The Honeymooners* on every fuckin channel 24-hours a day, if I never see this blue flame in silk again, she gave me a joy for a time that I'll always remember, and that I won't tell you all about cause it's mine. What else do you want outta life except to know that *one* time when you were in it you were alive?

PART EIGHT

Flipping to the Wild Side

Three Hands on the Towel, No. 1 by Ted Pontiflet

The unique and the unusual, the illegal and the illicit, the fantastic and the forbidden are highly arousing, for they stimulate the imagination, intensify the appetite, and heighten sexual pleasure. The characters in Charles Frye's "a good knight's leap" joyfully engage in a variety of sexual acts. Standing up, they copulate against the kitchen sink: Elvira puts her tongue in Phil's ear; Phil takes her from behind; she licks and sucks every part of him; and they note that even Phil's father (now dead) "swam against the tide," as the bloodstains on his mattress suggest. In SDiane Bogus's "Making Whoopee," the persona describes, hands between her legs, the pleasures of self-induced orgasm: "I hurry to watch her coming, coming, crying— / Whooooopeeee!" The cry becomes a moan at a woman's touch in Frank Lamont Phillips's "Love Poem."

> Your thrilling touch is a sieve
> that separates my willing body from impeding thought,
> that handles me like a moan.

In their short poems, Saundra Sharp, Kimmika Williams, John Turpin, and Kalamu Ya Salaam use verbal images—cats screeching and trees falling—to conjure up the wild and savage nature of sex. With Terry L. McMillan's female character, it's a case of déjà vu when she "reaches out to touch someone."

> I could still hear your faint cries echoing in my head right there on the concrete. Saw my tongue moistening your chest and your hands rubbing all across and around my back like I was made of silk.

Wanda Coleman's "Lonnie's Cousin" is another piece of imaginative replay, in which a husband—a latent voyeur—becomes aroused by his wife's tale of sexual indiscretion, while the couple in Ntozake Shange's "Comin to Terms" cool off because the woman wants to negotiate the terms of their coupling. Serious stuff! But, in a humorous vein, Hillery Jacque Knight's imaginative piece of science fiction describes the hilarious union of a Blessed Sacrosanct Phallus and a Glorious Ovum—"a globular twat all over popping, pouting, teasing, and spreading its brilliant dark berry lips in an enticing slow dance and funky fertility squirm." Dolores da Costa uses two voices—hers and Gloria Wade-Gayles's—in counterpoint, as she juxtaposes two female archetypes: nice girls, "prim proper demure and dainty," and "once-pure girls sprawled on semen-covered sheets waiting for kingdom come."

The characters in these poems and prose pieces exhibit a wild, spirited, and uninhibited wantonness as they sample the sixty-nine flavors of erotic delight.

From *Making Whoopee*

SDiane Bogus

In black slip, posed
One arm crossed just under the other,
A hand clasps the bare right shoulder
Between the fingers of the other dangles a cigarette

Her dreadlocks drip over browless eyes
like Black African waterfalls over rocks worn smooth
Her eyes beneath (daring, disdainful, desirable)
Bathe me in jungles of dew and rain

I lie back on the sofa—
Hands between my legs, dyke hands crouched over my vulva
I stare at her smooth Black face
as daringly as she stares out at me

She leaves the cover of the magazine
Materializing at the end of the sofa
Black slip full of her, arms at her sides, sleek and naked, dark as
walnuts
Her hair dripping, insinuating penetrations untold

I spread my legs, knees bent
I want her to see my entry, slightly parted, guarded by long finger-
like lips,
crinkled as raisins
I pull them apart by their tips, and they become butterfly wings:
pink, rimmed in black
What I reveal pleases her, invites her to show or tell

She rocks forward, then back, forward, then back
I match her motion, swiveling my hips deep into the red-flowered sofa
My eyes follow her—forward, then back, forward, then back
Her locks dip and sway, stirring the air as I am stirred
Forward again, back again, forward again, back again
I ache for her weight and entry
The walls of my vagina grow wet as color like sunset over a glistening
river

She rocks; I roll; she retreats; I heave;
I am up and down; she is in and out.
Forward, then back, forward again, then back
Touching herself as she comes and goes . . .
She rocks, and I rock, and we stay in that motion—complete

Heat squeezes against the walls of me
Building like pee withheld
It presses, and I press my clitoris like she is pressing hers
I rub it up and down, round and round like she is rubbing hers

I suck in a vibrating breath
My belly, my thighs, quaver
I am consumed with the heat and her
I am the chair, I am the motion, I am imminent
and I smile, stroking toward the release
forward, then back, forward, then back
But she grins and starts to fade

She's going, she's going
The rocker's going, her face going, her hair, the slip, her naked arms
I hurry to watch her coming, coming, crying—
Whooooopeeee!

Touching

Terry L. McMillan

I suspected someone was there in that *very* same spot before me, but I didn't let the thought grow in my mind or rot there, till I saw her swinging on your side like a shoulder-strap purse early this morning. And this was after I had already let you touch me all over with your long brown hands and break down my resistance, so that you left me feeling like the earth had been pulled from under my feet.

First, I see your lean long legs coming toward me on that crooked gray sidewalk, the silver specks glaring in my eyes like dancing stars. But I was not blinded, even when you dragged them in that elegant, yet pompous kinda way of yours. And you watched me coming from at least a half a block away and those size 13s didn't seem to lift up off the cement as high as they did the other night when we walked down this *very* same street together.

I know it was me who called you up the other night to say hello, but it was *you* who invited me to come down and walk your dog with you. Sounded innocent enough to me, but all along I'm sure you knew that I wanted to finally find out how warm it was under your shirt, behind your zipper, and if your hands were as gentle and strong as they looked. I was really hoping we could skip the walk altogether 'cause I just wanted to fall down on you slowly and get to your insides. Walk the dog another time. But since you could've misconstrued my motives as being un-ladylike, I bounced on down the street to your apartment in my white jogging outfit, trying to look as alluring as I possibly could, but without looking too eager.

I even dabbed gold oil behind my ears, under each breast and on the tips of my elbows so as to lure you closer to me in case you couldn't make up your mind. The truth of the matter is that I was nervous because I knew that we weren't gonna just chitchat tonight like we'd done before. I went out of my way in five minutes flat to brush my teeth twice, put on fresh coats of red lipstick, wash under my arms, Q-tip my ears and navel ('cause I didn't know just how far you might go), and wash my most intimate areas and sprinkle a little jasmine oil there too.

Even though it was almost ninety degrees, we walked fifteen blocks and the dog didn't let go of anything. You didn't seem to mind or notice. You handed me the leash, and even though I can't stand to see a grown man with a little cutesy-wutesy dog, I wasn't hostile as I tugged at it as we continued to walk through the thick night air. For the most part, I like dogs.

When our feet dropped from the curb, and I jumped and screamed because a fallen leaf looked like a dead mouse, I let go of the leash and grabbed your hand. You squeezed it back, though you had to drag me to chase after your dog, who had taken off down the sidewalk, running up to the tree's bark and just panting. When we finally caught him, we were both out of breath. I regretted wearing that sweaty jogging suit.

"You scared of a little mouse?" you asked.

"Yes, they give me the heebie-jeebies. My stomach turns over and I want to jump on top of chairs and stuff just to get away from them."

Then you told me about the time you busted one on your kitchen counter eating your ravioli right out of the can and how you wounded it with a broomstick and then tried to flush it down the toilet, but it wouldn't flush. I laughed loud and hard, but I wanted to make you laugh, too.

So, I told you about the time I was on my way out of my house to take a sauna when I accidentally saw a giant roach cavorting on my kitchen counter. I whacked it with my right hand just hard enough to cripple it. (I am scared of mice but I hate roaches.) I didn't want it to die immedi-ately because I had just spent $9.95 on some Roach-Pruf which I had ordered through the newspaper and wanted to see if it *really* worked. So, I sprinkled about a quarter teaspoon on his head as he was about to strug-gle to find a crack or crevice somewhere. He kept on trying so I kept on sprinkling more Pruf on his antennae. After five minutes of this, he was getting on my nerves 'cause I still had my coat on, my purse and gym bag thrown over my shoulders, and since my kitchen was designed strictly with dwarfs and children in mind, I was burning up. It was then that I decided to burn him up too. First I lit myself a cigarette, and with the same match, burned off his antennae but the sucker still kept trying to get to one corner of the counter. I got real mad because my Pruf was obviously not working and I just went ahead and burnt him up quickly and totally for not dying the way he was supposed to.

You thought this was terribly funny and cracked up. I liked hearing you laugh, but I didn't know if you thought this was indicative of my personality: torture and murder and everything.

We continued to walk a few more blocks, making small talk and the dog continued running up to tree trunks, kicking up his little white legs and finally squirting out wetness, but that was about it.

By this time, I was sweating and picturing your head nestled between my breasts. I like feeling a man's head there, and it had been so long since any man even made me feel like dreaming out loud that I didn't even hear you when you asked me if I liked the Temptations and had I ever been to a puppet show. I didn't understand the connection until we walked inside your apartment.

Today though, you watched me come toward you like this was a tug-of-war, but the rope was invisible. The gravity was so dense that it pulled us face to face and when I finally reached you I could smell your breath at the end of the rope. You were uneasy, and sorta turned in a half-turn toward me as I brushed past both of you. You loosely smiled back at me, squinting behind those tinted glasses, and I smiled back at both of you 'cause I don't have a grudge with this girl; wasn't *her* who I spent the night with.

"What are *you* doing up so early?" you asked. I didn't really think it was any of your business since you didn't call last night to see how late I was up. Besides, it was almost ten o'clock in the morning.

"I've already had my coffee, done my laundry, and now I'm trying to get to the plant store to buy some dirt so I can transplant my fern and rubber tree before the block party this afternoon."

"Oh, I'm sorry, Marie, this is Carolyn," you said, waving your hands between us like a magician.

We both nodded like ladies, fully understanding your uneasiness.

"Why don't you have the Chinese people do your laundry?" you asked.

"Because I like to know that my clothes are clean; I like to fold them up nice and neat like I want them. And besides, I like to put things together that belong together."

You just nodded your head like a fool. For a moment you looked puzzled, like someone had dropped you off in the middle of nowhere. You didn't seem to mind either that the girl was standing there watching your poise alter and sway. Me neither. But I had to move away from you 'cause I could really smell your body scent now and it was starting to stick to my skin, gravitating around me, until it got all up into my nostrils and then hit my brain, swelled up my whole head right there on the spot. This was embarrassing, so I tried to play it off by pulling my scarlet scarf down closer toward my eyebrows. But you already knew what had happened.

I make my feet move away from you as if I am trying to catch a bus I see approaching. I take my hands and wipe away the burnt-red lipstick from my mouth and cheeks at the mere thought of letting you press yours against them. Was trying to forget how handsome you were altogether. Fine. Too fine. Didn't listen to my mama. "Never look at a man that's prettier than you, 'cause he's gonna act that way." I was trying to think about dirt. The leaves of my plants. But I never have been attracted to pretty men, I thought, trying to miss the cracks in the sidewalk after stubbing my toe. You were different. Spoke correct English. Made puppets move and talk. Wrote your own grant proposals. Drank herbal tea and didn't smoke cigarettes. You crossed your legs and arms when you talked, and leaned your wide shoulders back in your chair so your behind slid to the edge. Made me think you thought about the words before letting them roll off your tongue. I admired you for contemplating things before you made them happen.

You yelled at me after I was almost halfway down the block. "Are you selling anything at the block party?"

I had already told you the other day I was making zucchini cake, but I repeated it again. "Zucchini cake!" and waved good-bye, trying to keep that stupid grin on my face though I knew you wouldn't have been able to see my expression from a distance.

I liked the attention you were giving me in spite of the girl. I thought it meant something. I was even hoping as I trucked into the plant store and got stuck by a cactus that you would call me later on to explain that she was just a friend of your cousin or your sister. I was hoping that you would tell me that your back hurt or something so I could come down with my almond oil and rub it for you. Beat it, dig my fingertips into your shoulder blades and the canals along your spine until you gave in. Or maybe you would tell me you broke your glasses and couldn't see. I would come down and read out loud to you: comic books or the Bible.

Now, I'm out here on this sidewalk with a bag of black dirt in my hands in the heat walking past your house, forcing myself not to stare up at those dingy white shutters of yours so I twist my neck in the opposite direction, looking ridiculous and completely conspicuous. I thought for sure I was gonna be your one-and-only-down-the-street sweetheart, 'cause I carried myself like a lady, not like some dog in heat.

I really had no intention of transplanting anything today. I just told you that because it sounded clean. I was more concerned about whether this girl touched you last night the way I had. Probably not, because only I can touch you the way I touch you. But as you were standing there on that sidewalk, I kept seeing still shots of us flashing across my eyes: twisting inside each other's arms like worms and caterpillars; you kissing me like you'd been getting paid for it all these years and this was your last paycheck; and my head getting lost all over your body. I could still hear your faint cries echoing in my head right there on the concrete. Saw my tongue moistening your chest and your hands rubbing all across and around my back like I was made of silk. I was silk and you knew it. You smelled so damn good. And you never stopped me when my head fell off the bed. You came after it. You never said anything when I screamed and called out your name, just took your time with me and kept pulling me inside your arms, inside the cave of your chest and would not let me go. And when I woke up, you were the dream I thought I had.

And yet, there you were out on that sidewalk in the heat with another girl chained to your arm, walking past my house without a care in the world. This shit burns me up.

I mean, look. You didn't have to make me laugh out loud, tickle me, and change the Band-Aid on my cut thumb, or sniff my hair and tell me it smelled like a cool forest. You didn't have to tell me it didn't matter that my breasts were small, and I was relieved to hear that, cause my mama always told me that a man should be more interested in how you fill his life and not how you fill your bra.

I mean, who told you to show me the puppets you'd made of James Brown and Diana Ross and the Jackson Five? Who told you to burn jasmine candles and make me listen to twelve old Temptations albums after telling me your favorite one of all was "Ain't Too Proud to Beg"? You didn't have to climb up on a barstool and drag out your scrapbook and give me the privilege of seeing four generations of your family. Showing me your picture as a little nappy-headed boy. What made you think I wanted to see you as a child when I'd really only known you as a man for three weeks? But no, you watched me turn my key in my front door for two whole months while you walked that little mutt before you allowed yourself to say more than "hello" and "good morning."

I never did get around to explaining myself, did I? I mean, I think I told you I was a special education teacher. I think I told you that once in a while I write poems. Even wrote one for you but I'm glad I didn't give it to you. Your ego probably would've popped out of your chest. But maybe I should've told you about the nights when my head pumps blood, and about the dreams I have of being loved just so. How I have always wanted to give a man more than symphony inside and outside the bedroom. But it is so hard. Look at this.

You just should not have wrapped your arms and shoulders around me like I was your firstborn child. You should not have shown me tenderness and passion. Was this just lust? I mean, I wasn't asleep when you kept on touching and rubbing my face like I was crystal and you were afraid I would break. I pretended because I didn't want you to rupture this co-coon I was inside of. So I just let you touch; never wanted you to stop touching me.

Three hours ago I transplanted my plant anyway. I baked three zuc-chini cakes that cost me almost thirty dollars, but after this morning I cannot picture myself sitting out on those cement steps in the heat trying to sell a piece of cake to total strangers. My roommate said she didn't mind. And I'm not going to sit in this hot house all day and be misera-ble.

"Wanna meet me for brunch?" I ask a girlfriend. She has no money. "I'll pay, just meet me, girl, okay?" She understands that I'm not really hungry but will eat anything just to take up inside space and get me away from this street.

The block was starting to fill up with makeshift vendors displaying junk they'd pulled out of attics and closets and basements so that they wouldn't have to drag them to the Salvation Army. I could already smell barbecue and popcorn and hear the d.j. testing his speakers for the high-est quality of sound that he could expect to get from outside. It was very hot and the sun was beating down on the pavement, making the heat penetrate through your shoes.

I'm wearing my tightest bluejeans and think I look especially good this afternoon on my way to the train station. I work hard to look good. Not for you or the general public, but for me. Here you come again, strutting toward me with that sissy little dog tagging alongside your big feet, but this time there's nothing on your arm but soft black hair and a rolled-up red plaid shirt sleeve. I can see orchards of black hair peeking out at me from your chest and though my knees want to buckle, I dig my heels deeply into the leather so as to make myself stand up straight like a dancer. You smile at me before we meet face to face and then do one of your about-face turns. Start walking beside me without even being in-vited.

"Hello," I say, as I make sure I don't lose the pace of my stride I've worked so hard on establishing when I first noticed you.

"My goodness, you *do* look pretty today. Pink and purple are definitely your colors."

I smile because I know I look good and even though I can hardly breathe from holding my stomach in to look its absolute flattest, I don't want you staring at anything on my body too tough because you've seen far too much of it already. I take that back. I want you to be mesmerized by this sight so that you remember what everything looked and felt like underneath this denim because you won't be anywhere near that close again: daytime or nighttime. I move closer to the curb.

"Where you going today?" you ask, showing some real interest. And since I want you to think I'm a very busy woman and that this little episode has not fazed me in the least, I say, "I'm having brunch with a friend." I really wanted to tell you it wasn't any of your damn business, but no, I'm not only polite, but honest.

We walked six hard hot blocks and when we finally reached the subway steps, you bent down like you were about to kiss me, and I stared at your smooth brown lips puckering up as if you had a cold sore on them, and turned my head. You kissed that girl this morning.

"Can I call you later, then?" you asked.

"If the spirit moves you," I said and disappeared underground.

By the time I got home it was almost ten o'clock and the street was still full of teenagers roller-skating, skateboarding, and dancing to the loud disco music blasting from both ends of the block. Kids were running around and through a full-spraying fire hydrant in high shrills of excitement, while grownups sat on the stoops sipping beers and drinks from Styrofoam cups. My roommate was sitting on our stoop and I joined her. Though it was hard to see, I found myself looking for your tall body over all the smaller ones. When I didn't see you immediately, this disturbed me because I could see your lights on and I knew you couldn't be sitting up in that muggy apartment with all this noise and activity going on down here.

When I saw you leaning against a wrought-iron fence across the street, there was a different girl stuck deep into your side. You spotted me through the thick crowd of teenagers and I heard you call out my name, but I ignored you. I was too proud to let myself feel sad or jealous or anything stupid like that.

My roommate told me she sold exactly three pieces of my zucchini cake because folks were afraid to buy it. Thought it might be green inside. I didn't care about the loss.

I felt spry and spunky, so I kicked off my pink pumps and marched down the steps and walked straight into the fanning water of the fire hydrant along with the kids. The hard mist felt cool and soothing as it fell against my skin. My entire body was tingling as if I had just had a massage. And even though I could feel your eyes following me, I didn't turn to acknowledge them. I sat back down on the steps, wiped the water from my forehead, the hot pink lipstick from my lips, ate a piece of my delicious zucchini cake, and popped the lid on an ice-cold beer. The foam flowed over the top of the bottle and down my fingers. I shook off the excess, and leaned back against the cement steps so it would scratch my back when I rocked from side to side and popped my fingers to the beat.

Lust

Kimmika Williams

I can't get you off of my mind
and those cats
screeching on the back
stoop
don't help.
Why does loving
have to hurt so much?
And, "fucking"—
Well, fucking just feels good
like peanut butter
getting stuck
on the roof of your mouth
forcing your tongue
to take an active role.
And role playing
brings me back to you
on my mind—
like peanut butter
and those God-damned cats—
I'm stuck

Fuck

John Turpin

Fuck
(rather than fight)
for peace.

Lonnie's Cousin

Wanda Coleman

I'm so glad you're home. I was so alone. No one here but me and the baby.

It's okay. I'm back now.

I tried so hard to keep it together. But the neighbor—that Lonnie and his people. They smile and they act nice to you but they ain't your friends and they ain't mine.

What do you mean?

While you were gone they tried to fix me up with their cousin.

What?

I was so stupid. I thought they wanted to be friends—thought they were looking out for me because you were gone.

Uh-huh.

They tried to get me into trouble—to do something I didn't want to do.

What happened?

You know what they think of us, don't you?

What do you mean by that?

They see you got a Black wife. And you livin' down here in the ghetto. You got to be pretty stupid for a White man. That's what they think of you. The only reason they pay any attention to me is because I'm with you.

We're friends—Lonnie and me.

You're the manager and they're the tenants. They've been in this building longer than we have. The owner—the only reason he made you manager is because you're the only White face in here. You're cheaper than hiring outside help. And he don't trust nobody Black.

What you're saying is really ugly. I don't believe it.

Listen to me. Listen good. They wanted their cousin in my panties. To bring us down. You hear that?

I'm not sure what I'm hearing.

Fool.

Don't cry. Look, honey. I'm willing to listen. Tell me what they did to you.

Okay.

Sunday I was planning to make you some fudge for when you got back. I was getting the cocoa and stuff ready in the kitchen—about eleven o'clock. And the baby woke up and started crying. I had his crib in there in the living room near the stereo, and I'm in the middle of finding out he's wet when the doorbell rings.

So I run to the door. And Lonnie is there grinning all in my face— acting friendly. He sure fools me, talking about why don't I bring the baby and come downstairs and visit with him and his wife. I figure it's safe because he's married. Even though I don't know them, I've seen his wife and she looks like someone I'd like to befriend. But I hesitates because I'm making fudge. But he says to come just a little while because he knows I must be lonely, you being away. Well I was. So I changed the baby, bundled him up, put a bottle and a couple of diapers in the bag and went downstairs.

See. He was just being neighborly. I knew it.

Hush up and let me tell it.

So when I get down there there's this other couple and they's dancing, smoking and drinking beer and all—having a good time. And then they introduce me to this ugly old man—he's their cousin.

What's his name?

I don't know. I forgets it. But I'll remember him as long as I live.

What did he do to you—if anything?

He put a spell on me. He hexed me.

Come on. Bullshit.

Listen.

He put a spell on you?

Those things happen. Whether you believes or not.

This is the twentieth century.

You gonna hear me out?

Go ahead.

Lonnie's wife, she come up to me cooing about the baby, asking me the usual stuff like she's really interested. She takes the baby and lays him on the loveseat near the door where I can watch him. So that means I got to sit opposite him on the couch next to Lonnie's cousin. I don't think about that. I'm just sitting there. They offer me a beer. I tell 'em I don't drink, 'specially beer because I think it tastes like cow piss. And they laugh. So Lonnie's wife she gets some cherries and she fixes me a drink with lots of cherry juice in it real cold over ice. And it don't taste too bad —like punch with a twang. Lonnie's friend—the other guy—he come over and ask me to dance.

What about the cousin?

I'm getting to that. The friend he asks me to dance. We all up dancing and the friend's lady, she's dancing too, by herself off on the side so she can change the 45s on the stereo.

Then what?

Then I notice his cousin is looking at me. He don't seem to be but I can feel his eyes got feet and they walking all over me. And they strange heavy eyes—got them thick lids. Look like he damn near half asleep or something.

How old a man is he?

I don't know. Forty maybe fifty. Way older than us. One of these country-looking men but he's not. He had on this stingy brim panama and belted slacks *and* suspenders both, like he about to lose his pants. And they was khaki. And he had on a pink shirt.

Did he have an accent?

No. He talked regular like us. And he was *real* dark. Twice—three times my color. Dark as that there fudge I made.

And all he did was look at you?

At first. But after a couple of records Lonnie pushed him up from the couch to dance and I was his partner. But he didn't touch me. We just fast-danced. He just made like he was dancing enough to make us laugh then sit down again. By that time I was having a good time. And I just naturally was relaxed and started talking to him.

Talking about what?

About stuff. Whatever he asked me or came up. You and me. The weather. Television and movies. Like that. But I felt his eyes pulling at me, drawing me into them. My heart started beating real fast. I felt hot and all sticky under my arms. And I started falling into his eyes. And then I pulled my eyes away but they got stuck on his lips. He had real thick lips. Big, dark and smooth. And he moved closer to me. I scooted back. And he eased still closer to me. And I'm on the couch with no place to go, backed against the arm of it, even leaning backwards. But I'm deeply drawn to him at the same time. I'm not talking anymore. I'm listening. He's telling me I'm beautiful. I don't know how beautiful I am, he says. And he reaches his hand up and brushes my hair back. And a feeling goes through me I've never felt before. He put his spell on me right then.

What kind of feeling was it?

I don't know. Like if I'd've been standing my feet woulda gone out from under me. He took his other hand and stroked my thighs and I almost passed out.

Describe it.

Like electricity near about. I don't know what. But I knew that if he kept touching me like that he was gonna have his way with me. And I wouldn't be able to say no to nothing.

Then what?

He put his arm around my head and kissed me, pulling me in against his chest.

Then what? Come on, tell me what it felt like. Quit crying woman. I'm not angry at you—honey, tell me.

I'm so ashamed.

Don't be. Not at all. I'm here and I'm listening.

He kissed me to my soul. I couldn't break free. I kissed him back. I couldn't help it. I was under his spell. When he let go everybody was looking at me. Lonnie and his wife and the other couple—dead in their tracks—like they were all kissing me. Like voodoo or something. It felt real strange. The strangest feeling I ever felt. I could hear what they was thinking. I came half way to myself. I said how it was getting late and I had to go finish making that fudge I'd promised you. So I scooped up the baby and hurried out of there so fast I forgot his little diapers and stuff. I ran back upstairs here.

And that's all?

He followed me up here after a few minutes. He was carrying the baby's bag.

And you let him in.

I tried not to. But he put that spell on me again—I was still under it. He just reached through the screen door when I grabbed for the bag and caught my hand. And it was his touch—he got a touch like satin and a voice like satin. Black satin. Standing right there in the doorway. Then he pulled me to him and started feeling me all over. Hands and eyes. He lifted me right into him, and I could feel him hard through his trousers. I was lost to him.

You did that?

I didn't know I was so weak. I swear I could not help myself. He had greater powers than I did. Will power don't work against no spell.

Then what?

The baby woke up and started crying. I ran over and got him and put him between us. Then I made him hold the baby while I started making the fudge. He got uneasy and said he was going downstairs and get something to drink so would I please take the baby back. Soon as he left I pulled all the curtains and locked the door. I took the baby into the bedroom here and turned up the television so loud I couldn't hear the doorbell ring when he got back. Later I fixed us dinner. Me and the baby fell asleep in here on the bed. Then you woke us up coming in this morning.

314   *Flipping to the Wild Side*

And that's all? That's it?

Ain't that enough?

You're positive you didn't let him fuck you?

I couldn't. I love you, honey. I couldn't do that and live with myself. I know that now. Spell or no spell.

You didn't let him fuck you?

Because of you. You and the baby. Plus I couldn't give Lonnie and his bunch the satisfaction of knowing their cousin got me. The thought of them laughing at us behind our backs really makes me mad. They'd love the chance to run us out of here. That's the kind of lowlife they are.

Why should I believe you didn't let him fuck you? You wanted it.

I didn't want the ugly old man. He made me want him. That's how a spell works. He was so ugly he was beautiful. He the kinda man Mama Creole used to warn me about. The kind that know women better than women know themselves.

And he touched you—your breasts.

He reached up under the blouse I had on—my little white top with the angel sleeves.

Did he kiss you at the same time?

Yes.

What else did he do?

I don't want to talk about it no more.

But I want to talk about it. I want to hear it again. All of it.

That was all of it.

I have a right to know what he did to you. I'm not sure you're telling everything.

But I said.

That was too general. I want specifics. You said he was darker than you are.

Yes. Almost purple-black. Much darker than Lonnie and his wife. It's hard to believe they're blood kin.

His hands. How big were his hands? Bigger than mine?

Why? You seen him around before?

No. I just want to know.

In case you see him again?

Quit stalling and tell me.

I'm not stalling. I'm just concerned. Yeah—his hands was twice—three times bigger than yours.

And his lips?

Thick. Very.

Did he smell?

Yeah, come to think of it.

Like what?

I hadn't thought till you asked—but he had a real strong funk to him. Like a wino. Only not so bad. Kind of pleasant. But strong and musty.

And his eyes. What were they like? What color?

Black-brown. Like big old olives swimmin' round in a yellow dish. You could see the veins in them. They was eyes that's done lots of living.

What was he built like? Was he as tall as me?

By about half a head. And he was lanky. But real strong. Like a man that works the earth.

And he kissed you?

Yes. It made me weak all over when he kissed me. Don't make me keep telling it.

Don't I ever make you feel the way he did?

It's not the same thing. You're my husband. He had me under a spell. I love you and you love me naturally. What he was about was no good.

Tell it to me again. From the beginning. Word-for-word.

No.

Come on. Tell it.

Please don't make me.

Look, honey—relax. I've forgiven you. I believe you. Really, I do understand. Things like that happen.

Do you? Oh, thank you—*thank you.*

Now, you said you felt a weakness all over when he touched you.

I was so scared. I was afraid you'd be angry and want to leave me. I was so afraid to tell you. But I had to. You needed to be warned about Lonnie and them in case they try another trick.

No, honey, I'm not going to leave you. Not because of something like that. So don't worry. And don't worry about Lonnie. I'll deal with him. Now tell me again, and start at that part about how he made you feel when he first touched you.

I don't want to talk about it no more. I want to forget it ever happened.

That's all right. I want to hear it. From the start. When you first saw him—Lonnie's cousin.

You mean, when he was telling me how beautiful I was, and stroking my hair?

Yeah. Start with that part.

Are you serious?

And then he touched your thigh. Like this?

Near about. But it felt different because I was under the spell, remember.

But what exactly did he do that caused the spell? What did he say?

It wasn't what he said as much as what he didn't say. Why you looking at me so funny like?

It's all right honey. It's really all right. Tell it to me slowly, like it's in slow motion. Close your eyes and tell it to me again. From the start. From feeling so alone—me gone—just you here and the baby—and then Lonnie comes up to the door. And when you get to the part where he touches you, tell it extremely slow. Moment to moment so I can imagine what it felt like.

What?

Come on, honey. Do it for me.

Am I hearing what you're saying?

Don't be hurt. Believe me, baby—believe in me. You believe in spells. Give me your hand. There, now. Feel that. See how hard and good that feels. And it's all yours. And after you finish telling me that story again, I'm gonna give it all to you. But before I do, I want to hear it all one more time. And don't cry when you tell it. Tell it like you enjoyed it.

Tell it just like it happened.

The X-Lovers

Reginald Lockett

she calls.
he picks up the receiver.
he ask her how she been
doin and she says fine
and ask him how he
been doin.
he says fine and mentions
that it's been over a year.
she agrees and says she
misses him at times.
he asks her what she's been into and she says she's
been goin to school, workin,
takin guitar lessons and
chantin.
then she asks him what he been
doin and he talks about
work, exercisin and hangin
out.

he asks her to come over.
she says yeah!
she's there in 30 minutes.
they sit in his room,
drink some wine, smoke a
joint, listen to some sides and
talk.
then they embrace, hug, caress
and kiss and kiss and kiss.
bust some slob like
there ain't gonna be no tomorrow.
he strokes her back and she strokes
his.
he runs his fingers through
her hair.
he kisses her eyes.
he kisses her cheeks
he bites her ears.
he moves his hands towards
them big old luscious
breasts and he's almost
there, ready for the down-stroke
when she brushes his hand
away gently and
says,
"umh!umh! i just wanted
to see if the feelin was
still there, honey, and
it ain't."

I Wanna Be Wild and Wonderful!

(Dialogue with a Friend)

Dolores da Costa
with Gloria Wade-Gayles

She wrote:

> *We are taught to be ladies*
> *prim proper demure and dainty**

No more. I want to stretch out lush and lovely on pale satin sheets beneath "where your head's at" (portrait of a lady-in-blue sitting over my bed, a dismembered head between her legs). I want to be conjured up in the dreams and visions of mysterious lovers who get hard-ons when they will themselves into my bedroom and smell my lovescent and taste the honeylemon of my body.

> *to keep our heads up and our dresses down*
> *until we are "given away"*
> *in a ceremony of funereal organ music*
> *and vows that lack poetry.*

* Gloria Wade-Gayles, "a woman's beatitudes," in *Homespun Images: An Anthology of Black Memphis Writers and Artists* (Memphis: LeMoyne-Owen College, 1989).

"Is there a difference," he asked me, disappointment in his voice, this friend of ten years, "between fucking and making love?" Yes, but I don't want to make love. I wanna fuck. There, I said it . . . the four-letter word that split my pedestal in two and sent me crashing to the ground, clay feet and all. They make us into two types, these men we love: married goddesses or fucked mistresses. To hell with pedestals. Let's get on the floor . . . throw caution to the wind . . . get down and under and over. Fuck against the window like my friend Rochelle. Fuck on the kitchen table like women in erotic tales. "Where was the most unusual place you did it?" asked one man. (Why do men always want to give you these sexual quizzes, find out if you've done this or that, and if you haven't done that, why not?) "The most unusual place I did it was on a tombstone," he volunteered. Well, I can't top that!

> Blessed are the nice girls
> for they shall be adored.

Quiero . . .

> do a mad fandango rumba samba
> red rose tucked under long dark hair
> toreador hat tilted to the wind
> eyes molten behind an Andalusian fan
> ¡Olé! ¡Andale! ¡Más rápido, por favor!
> black shawl tossed recklessly over shoulders
> red tiered skirt lifting falling twisting
> stiletto heels sharp against a concrete floor
> castanets clicking hot and Latin
> ¡Qué chica más quapa! ¡Qué niña más bella!
> Sheila E and the Miami Sound Machine
> Light my fire!

> Blessed are the sweet girls
> for they shall inherit approval

black lace under moonlight veiled against the morning come milk white on blades of green

leaping from limb to limb stripping the bark as I rise and fall in the night wind iridescent before the moon floating free as whispers caught on the tongue gliding soft and silk over midnight blue down down down into darkness

diving deep into hidden recesses beneath the surface where pleasures lie fellatioed in fantasies of lust *soixante-neuf* varieties of pleasure given taken in the lush wet undergrowth of jellyfish and eels slipping and sliding into and out of my delta

Blessed are the pure girls
for theirs is the kingdom of respectability

I ride into the Maryland night, into the fantasies of this writer who summons up visions of Black American princesses, of Manassas pretties, once-pure girls sprawled on semen-covered sheets waiting for kingdom come. I walk boldly into his dreams, teasing and tantalizing with a seductive laugh, warm-low-resonant, a wild imagination, and words spun into images of desire: legs thrust overhead, thighs in the air, heels around the neck. "I think I'm falling in love with you," he said, mistaking erotic imaginings for the real thing. Cars light up the night, pinpoints of white flicker over asphalt. Faces: a club on Georgia Avenue, blues singer at the piano, middle-aged couples eating fried chicken and tasting stale memories. A surrealistic night heavy with sexual tension and the taste of brandy. "You'd better go," I whisper.

Such is the catechism of our youth
and I was a devout convert.

running my hands along the curves of my body feeling the wet silk under my fingers smooth and supple loving the touch and taste and smell and sight of me under the glow of fourteen white candles lying in the tub the odor of Germaine Monteil's milk bath in the air sipping a glass of champagne cool warm Anita's voice husky in the damp mist jets of water rushing over thighs and hips toes tingling with delight pinpricks of desire touching my core.

But at 40 I am curious about the life
I did not live and just once
I want to defy the beatitudes.

Your pulse quickening to the aphrodisia of resistance
you were distracted by the lures at the periphery
    the deep brown eyes
    the well-turned calf
    the wide-slung hips
so that you missed the dark place within
    the pools of quiet after the storm

I want to be a siren who walks
past streetcorner men
with over-sized buttocks in painted-on pants
and shake sordid desires to all who have eyes to see.

Outrageous! Irreverent! Indiscreet! Nontraditional! Strange! Unconventional! Iconoclastic! Daring! Unprincipled! Wanton!
HE: "Voulez-vous coucher avec moi?" You don't know me that well.

SHE: "Mais non. Mais oui" She who hesitates is lost.

HE: "C'est si bon." For you or me?

SHE: "Est-ce vrai?" Men are such liars!

HE: "Voulez-vous toucher le membre?" Ooooohhhh, it feels good.

SHE: "Mais c'est très grand." Women lie too.

HE: "Voulez-vous le baiser?" An intriguing idea.

SHE: "Ohhh, la, la"

For one thousand and one nights sixty-nine ways to come tongue to tongue lips to nipples mouth to cock breasts to dick hand to cunt toes to mouth lips to labia finger to ass penis to cheeks breasts to butt fingers to vulva hands to scrotum tongue to clitoris.

> *I want to spit my anger like a tongue of fire longer than those prehistoric animals used to and roar fear into the heart of anyone who walks however gently on my life.*

I wanna be wicked: take other women's men, love 'em and leave 'em; like Frankie, throw water on a dying man. I wanna be evil. A Sapphire. A Delilah. A Jezebel. A hard-hearted Hannah, the Vamp of Savannah. Yeah, that's it. I wanna be a Vamp: roll my eyes, toss my head, put my hands on my hips and shake my thing. Be outrageous! Just once in life, I wanna be like Sula, cool, calculating, and contained, down on all fours naked, nibbling, not touching, not even looking. I wanna cast spells and draw him to me, desperately longing for the touch of my hair on his face, for the taste of my honey on his tongue, for the smell of my wetness on his finger.

> *beatitudes for my daughter*
> *I will fantasize about being a bad woman*
> *and enjoy life in my kingdom of respectability.*

"You did what!" she cried, outraged at my cowardice. "You told him goodbye! I can't believe you did that! It's that Victorian upbringing . . . all those inhibitions."

And she was right.

Images: delicate ladies steeled against life, sheltered from pleasure, guarded by the men whose names they bore.

Memories: the vows, the tears, the babies, the jobs, the meals, the laundry, the quiet evenings, the dark couplings, the sunrise, the sunset, and so on and so forth.

And always, or almost always, pleasure denied. The straight and the narrow rather than the primrose.

And so I took her advice and walked shamelessly, recklessly into the surf, the feel of sunlight on my face, the taste of salt spray on my tongue.

Love Poem

Frank Lamont Phillips

You are what sculptors search for in stone,
the summer and sun I have been struggling toward,
surrender that comes hard,
gaiety I had thought gone, more.
The restless touch of your hand,
like relentless waves reaching for blond sand,
and delivering small dead fish to shore.
I remember the need I created you with,
the dream I summoned you from,
that desire placed a trench in the floor of my mind
worrying you wouldn't come.
Your thrilling touch is a sieve
that separates my willing body from impeding thought,
that handles me like a moan.
Woman, I loved you before you were grown,
and reached for you when you were foam
left in a beer mug, settling into lonely beach sand, an ache.
Dear, I will surprise you with devotion as strong
as the hurt in your eyes,
as deep as the scars in Jesus' palms.

A Good Knight's Leap

Charles Frye

Home? The old family homestead, row house, "town house," they called them now, as though everyone had a country house as well. When he got back from Chicago, Phil moved in. He spent the first month or so pacing upstairs and down through all the rooms. And at night, as he lay in his old bed in his old room, thought he could hear his dead parents doing the same.

In the spring of that first year back home, he started weekly yard sales; room by room he'd cart things out. Sometimes he'd have to lug them back, when he found he couldn't bear to part with them. He was able to relieve the clutter of his parents' generation. "Breathing room," he kept telling Uncle Connie. The money from the sales came in handy too. Connie could appreciate that.

At night, Phil did his Brother Billy a memorial temple tour. Again, it wasn't quite the same without Brother B.

One Saturday morning in May, about 10 A.M., as Phil sat on the porch watching a few potential customers pick through the family treasures, he saw Elvira for the first time. She was examining the duck-shaped salt and pepper shakers. When she lifted one of them, two orange webbed feet swung down. The sight of those little feet amused her no end. She laughed out loud, attracting a few of the other shoppers.

Phil was hoping for a bidding war over those shakers, so he bounded down the stairs to officiate. The shoppers all greeted him with smiles and pleasantries. A few of them were regulars who showed up every week to seek what new items were on display, which old ones had been reduced. But only Elvira asked, "How much?"

"How much do you offer?" Phil asked with a turn of his chin.

"Everything," she replied.

Everything is energy, fields of energy. When certain special connections—responses—are made, the world, shocked, stops to draw a breath. And into that momentary vacuum anything can come. Anything.

What Phil hated most about some women was their willingness to throw themselves away.

Magic, he understood. It was either there or it wasn't. He wasn't much on courtship or developing a relationship or boat making of any kind.

The magic was there with Elvira. Phil usually let the bidding wars come to him. For her, he'd come down from his porch. The magic was there even before she'd said, "Everything."

"Oh, they aren't worth that much," he'd said, never missing a beat, "and I'm sure my parents would have wanted *you* to have them."

"They're dead?" She dropped the duck off a few steps. Luckily, Phil had fast hands, because the poor little duck's legs might not have survived the fall. He sat the quacker gently down near its partner.

"Yeah, they died last winter." Phil was confused by her shift in mood. ". . . It was an accident."

"I'm sorry," she said, turning to leave. But Phil grabbed her arm.

"Don't go. There are other nice things here . . ."

"I'm sorry. I have to. I . . . I thought these objects were yours. I thought you might be moving away or something."

"Nope. Just making some room." Phil was all smiles.

"I have to go," she said, pulling away.

"But why?"

She turned slowly and stared into Phil's eyes. "Dead people's things should be broken and buried or burned with their owners," she said vacantly.

Damn, she *had* intended to break a (duck's) leg, thought Phil.

"It's not good for you to live in that house, *their* house, unless you've had it exorcised." She was completely sincere. "Houses are no good," she continued. "They're full of potentially evil beings, former occupants, there to cling to their old possessions."

Phil was dumbfounded. He had to consciously close his mouth.

"At best they cause mischief and nightmares—at worst they can make you sick."

"Physically?" Phil was groping for a point of entry.

"Or mentally. Houses are no good." She placed a soft hand on Phil's chest. "Better to sleep in a grass hut, which your relatives can destroy when you die. Better still to sleep under the stars."

A future bag lady, thought Phil. She's got all the markings—but so beautiful. Her hand seemed to burn his chest right through his shirt.

"Can I see you again?" he heard himself ask.

She removed her hand from Phil's chest and gave a deep sigh, as though collecting herself.

"I'll come and do your house," she said finally. "But it will take some time for me to prepare myself."

"How long?"

"At least a week." She turned again to leave.

"So, in the meantime, can I come and visit *you*—or do you *have* a place?" Phil smiled.

"I do," she said over her shoulder, with something bordering on sadness, "but I told you, I must prepare myself." She walked swiftly away as though knowing she could deny him nothing, except the opportunity to ask for more.

She appeared at his door, unannounced, the following Saturday night. Well, not exactly unannounced. Phil had expected her that morning. Dressed all in white, her hair pulled back and wrapped in a white rag, and with an armload of candles, incense, and other items in a shopping bag. She explained that such things could only be done after dark.

Phil had considered putting up a tent in his backyard during Elvira's week of preparation, but it had rained for several days, so he abandoned that plan. He hadn't slept very much.

Phil followed her through each room while Elvira lit candles, burned incense, and murmured prayers to Buddha/Krishna, Adam/Jesus, Eve/Mary, Olorun and Oshun, the Great Spirit, and Phil's grandmother. It was dawn by the time she finished, basement to attic.

Phil had already succumbed to sleep in his own bedroom—now that it was safe. He awoke to the sun streaming through the window. Stumbling into the hallway on his way to the john, Phil bumped into the attic ladder. After his leak, Phil made his ascent.

She lay there on the floor, in the middle of the apex of the roof, in the midst of a burnt-out ring of seven candles. She lay with her back to him. She must have perspired in her sleep. It was already hot in the attic now that the sun was up. Or perhaps her "ordeal" had made her sweat.

Probably the heat of those candles, thought Phil. At any rate, the perspiration made the dress cling and revealed colors that bled through the white fabric. Colorful circular patterns were painted along her spine: red, orange, yellow, green, blue. They were beginning to run together.

"Chakras," she would later explain. Her girlfriend, the artist, had done the figures. And immediately Phil was jealous that someone had known her in a way that he had not.

It had been his intention to remove the white dress, roll her on her back, and make love to her there on the attic floor—or at the very least, he was going to kiss her. But as he approached her on his hands and knees, Phil sensed that he could never penetrate that circle. He descended the ladder again and went back to bed.

He arose about 8 A.M. and climbed the ladder again. Elvira had not moved. For an instant Phil thought she might be dead. Then he noticed her rib cage rise and fall. Now he could really see the contours of her ass glisten through the dress. And the colors were now an oblong mass running from the base of her skull to her tailbone.

No underwear, he thought. Brother Billy would have spotted that right away.

When Phil took his shower he noticed that Elvira had left her shopping bag behind the bathroom door. He summoned all his courage and investigated the contents: a few extra candles and incense sticks and a change of clothing, a black halter top, short skirt, and sandals. No underwear.

Phil puttered around the house, went out for a *Post,* and checked on Elvira at least a couple of times before noon. About 12:15, as he prepared lunch for two, Phil was distracted by Uncle Connie's arrival.

"What's that funny smell—and why are all the windows open?" Connie removed his plaid sport coat. "Turn on some air, kid, it's murder outside!"

Phil hadn't even noticed that he himself was sweating profusely. But then he realized what it must be like in the attic. "Turn it on yourself." Phil was halfway up the stairs when he heard the water running. She was taking a shower.

Connie had already closed all the windows and flicked on the air conditioner by the time Phil returned to the kitchen, where he found Connie devouring one of the two sandwiches he'd just prepared.

"You been smoking those funny cigarettes in here, kid?" Connie had brought another job opportunity: "Computer consultant in New York, at least six months' work." The consultant fee was much better than wages and more than enough for a premium payment on a great policy.

Phil's replies were "No," "No, thanks," and "No."

He hadn't heard her come downstairs. But if Connie had left the windows open, Phil would surely have smelled the smoke. He did happen to glance out the kitchen pane, though. There in the backyard was Elvira, dressed in black, burning the white dress among a pile of old leaves.

"Attics are a great combination," she would later reveal. "Egyptian pyramid and Amerindian sweat lodge in one!"

Before she left, Elvira jotted down her phone number and address. When Phil called, she invited him over. That's when he witnessed her house.

Phil, who never thought of himself as particularly sensitive, immediately *felt* that house. And he didn't like what he felt. The walls were sucking him in, the floor swallowing him up. Perhaps it was just the architecture. The walls didn't meet; the floor sagged.

Elvira offered fruit juices. Phil opened the Burgundy he'd brought. When their lips finally met, Phil watched as her eyes rolled back in her head. As he groped for her, he was impressed by the firmness of her hips and thighs. The turn of her back fit his hand exactly.

They drove back to his house in her car. Luckily it was an automatic. Phil drove left-handed, his right lingering here and there over her torso. Elvira nestled against his chest.

During the week that followed, Phil wished he had a job to report to. He was good with a woman for a weekend. But after that, he usually ran out of conversation. And after polite conversation was gone, Phil sometimes got impolite.

He asked Elvira, point-blank, didn't she have a job? "What about plants to water, phone calls to receive?"

She assured him that plants and jobs could be replaced.

"The only thing that endures is love," she said as she sucked Phil's big toe.

She licked and sucked every part of him. And Phil, to the extent he could, returned lick for lick. But after the first twenty-four hours, as they lay slightly dehydrated in Phil's single bed, it occurred to him that Elvira didn't sleep very much. Every time he dozed off, Phil awoke with his dick hard in her mouth. Or if he slept on his stomach he'd awake with her straddling him, massaging his neck and shoulders, or, turned the other way, working his buttocks and thighs.

She wasn't going to her job, if she had one, and she wasn't going to sleep—ever. So Phil suggested a larger bed, the one in his parents' old room. Besides, he was going to move in there eventually, once he redecorated it.

Elvira would have no part of that bed—not until the mattress and box springs were replaced.

"But what about all that prayer and incense burning?" Phil protested.

"*That* can only go so far; then you need a trip to the Dumpster." She looked about Phil's room for what seemed like the first time in three days.

"I think I'll bring my plants here," she finally remarked. "This room could certainly use some."

Phil heard her, but he didn't. He was busy remembering that each time he'd gone to the bathroom, she had accompanied him and insisted that he, on his knees, pee with her, while she sat on the toilet. He was remembering the refrigerator raids that had ended with stand-up copulation against the sink. He was remembering the feel and the sound of her

330   *Flipping to the Wild Side*

tongue in his ear and in his asshole. But now he was remembering that it was Monday afternoon and how wonderful his parents' bed felt.

Elvira was still talking plants when Phil rose and went to his parents' room. As usual, she followed. She stood in the doorway, for a moment, as Phil collapsed on the queen-size bed. She then stood by the bed and watched him sleep.

Phil awoke with wet fingers. Elvira had been standing on one foot, playing with herself, using Phil's hand. He snatched his hand away.

"Enough!" was all he had to say. Elvira wheeled and left the room. She gathered her clothing, dressed on the way down the stairs, and eased the front door shut behind her without a word.

Phil slept again. He awoke in the dark. He slept again. The next morning when he stumbled into his own bedroom, looking for Elvira, the sex-scent greeted him at the door. His sheets could probably have taken themselves to the washing machine—and faster than Phil would have wanted to accompany them. To slow them, he bundled them and stuffed them into a pillowcase.

Every woman has her own scent. Brother Billy had taught Phil that. Elvira's was primal, like the sap from the aloe plant, healing, soothing like that too.

Phil thought he'd hear from her. She didn't call. After two days, Phil called *her* and got her answering machine.

"Hello," it began. "This disembodied voice is mine. I leave it as a link to you. Leave yours as a link to me."

Phil recradled the phone, shook his head, and slowly dialed again. Same recorded message. He took a deep breath and, after the beep, said he wanted to see her again.

She arrived at his door that evening with her plants and stories about her new job. She was teaching at the university. Which department?

"English," she thought. "Yes, it was English." She'd used her doctorate-in-English résumé during the interview.

"You lied?" Phil was only slightly amazed.

"I told them what they wanted to hear. I pronounced the right words, mentioned the right journals, it was quite easy."

"But a doctorate?"

"They're only union cards, you know. It's more a matter of endurance than intelligence to get one. Were it merely a matter of intelligence . . ." Her voice trailed off.

What would she teach? Some novels, most of which she'd read on her own, and composition, which, of course, could not be taught.

"I mean, you can give the students the forms, but the content? Forget it!"

"Then why are you doing this?"

"For the money, of course." She directed Phil's attention to his front porch, where two deliverymen were struggling with a top-of-the-line set of queen-size mattress and box springs.

"I asked them to meet me here," she said blankly. "You can pay me later—when you get a job." She looked about the near-empty living room for plant space. "If you like, I can lend you one of my résumés."

"No, thanks." Phil opened the front door for the deliverymen.

He could hardly believe it. They actually had a conversation that wasn't punctuated by heavy breathing. The deliverymen certainly did their share, though, straining up the stairs with the new and back down again with the old. Phil looked wistfully as his last refuge was unceremoniously loaded on the back of the truck. The box springs looked to be in excellent shape.

"They're probably going to sell it again, you know?" Phil was annoyed that Elvira had tipped the men twenty bucks to haul the stuff away. He didn't mention the mattress, however; and secretly he wished she hadn't noticed the telltale love stains in the center on both sides. Phil had checked. Some were bloodstains, the kind that show up when the man swims against the tide. The others were the results of plain old passion puddles. Phil had seen enough of them to know for sure. He had even seen them on mattresses in the cloisters.

How had he missed those stains? He had changed the sheets a few times since his parents' death. The mattress cover! It was spotless so he'd never removed it. But under that cover . . . And the mattress wasn't *that* old. Had his father discovered pussy in his old age? Had his mother taken on a lover? Had Uncle Connie been creeping?

"Damn, they were in their sixties! Don't they ever stop?" The words escaped like criminals from his mouth, before he could bring his hand up to stop them.

Elvira, who, of course, had seen the stains, put down the watering can she'd been using and consoled Phil.

"The mattress *was* very old," she said softly. "But age is no factor."

Phil looked down on her, his eyes narrowing. The love-bout that followed was a rough one. Phil took her in the ass for the first time—without enough lubricant. She cried out in pain. He spanked her buttocks until his right hand stung. And she wailed. He pulled her to him by her hair and bit down on her lower lip as she dug her nails into his back. And they both moaned. When he finally spilled his seed, he did it with great deliberation on the new mattress.

Later, as Elvira sat soaking her bottom in a shallow tub of water and Epsom salts, Phil felt compelled to tell her the wedding story and everything else. Well, she'd seen that old mattress. What else could he possibly hide from her?

When he finished, he sat sideways on the closed toilet, his feet propped on the edge of the tub, as he stared at the shower head. A long, dreadful silence ensued.

Finally, Elvira asked: "Did you enjoy my ass?"

"Yeah." Phil answered without shifting his gaze.

"The idea or the act?"

He looked at her, was caught in her for a moment, and then, as he always did, he looked away. Every culture has a prohibition against looking a person *dead* in the eye. It's a power move. Provocative. *Always* dangerous: to have at the soul; to make a claim on it.

Elvira didn't have windows on her face. She had chasms, into which one stared only at the risk of falling.

"The idea or the act?" she asked again.

"Both, I guess." Suddenly Phil suspected that there were other equally dangerous chasms about.

"Your Grandpa Philip probably did the same thing to your grandmother before your father was conceived." She was still looking at Phil.

"What do you know about my father besides what I've told you?" Phil felt defensive enough to chance a brief look into her eyes.

"I know that that's how men like him are made," she said with a tinge of sadness in her voice. "Made. Not born."

Haiku #28

Kalamu Ya Salaam

i quiver inside
you like the ground shaking when
a mighty tree falls

Comin to Terms

Ntozake Shange

they hadnt slept together for months/ the nite she pulled the two thinnest blankets from on top of him & gathered one pillow under her arm to
march to the extra room/ now 'her' room/ had been jammed with minor
but telling incidents/ at dinner she had asked him to make sure the
asparagus didnt burn so he kept adding water & they, of course/ water-
logged/ a friend of hers stopped over & he got jealous of her having so
many friends/ so he sulked cuz no one came to visit him/ then she gotta
call that she made the second round of interviews for the venceremos
brigade/ he said he didnt see why that waz so important/ & with that she
went to bed/ moments later this very masculine leg threw itself over her
thighs/ she moved over/ then a long muscled arm wrapped round
her chest/ she sat up/ he was smiling/ the smile that said 'i wanna do it
now.'

mandy's shoulders dropped/ her mouth wanted to pout or frown/ her
fist waz lodged between her legs as a barrier or an alternative/ a cooling
brown hand settled on her backside/ 'listen, mandy, i just wanna little'/
mandy looked down on the other side of the bed/ maybe the floor cd talk
to him/ the hand roamed her back & bosom/ she started to make faces &
blink a lot/ ezra waznt talkin anymore/ a wet mouth waz sittin on
mandy's neck/ & teeth beginnin to nibble the curly hairs near her hand

sayin/ 'i waz dreamin bout cuba & you wanna fuck'/ 'no, mandy i dont wanna fuck/ i wanna make love to . . . love to you'/ & the hand became quite aggressive with mandy's titties/ 'i'm dreamin abt goin to cuba/ which isnt important/ i'm hungry cuz you ruined dinner/ i'm lonely cuz you embarrassed my friend: & you wanna fuck'/ 'i dont wanna fuck/ i told you that i wanna make love'/ 'well you got it/ you hear/ you got it to yr self/ cuz i'm goin to dream abt goin to cuba'/ & with that she climbed offa the hand pummelin her ass/ & pulled the two thinnest blankets & one pillow to the extra room.

the extra room waz really mandy's anyway/ that's where she read & crocheted & thot/ she cd watch the neighbors' children & hear miz nancy singin gospel/ & hear miz nancy give her sometimey lover who owned the steppin tavern/ a piece of her mind/ so the extra room/ felt full/ not as she had feared/ empty & knowin absence. in a corner under the window/ mandy settled every nite after the cuba dreams/ & watched the street-lights play thru the lace curtains to the wall/ she slept soundly the first few nites/ ezra didnt mention that she didnt sleep with him/ & they ate the breakfast she fixed & he went off to the studio/ while she went off to school he came home to find his dinner on the table & mandy in her room/ doing something that pleased her. mandy was very polite and gracious/ asked how his day waz/ did anything exciting happen/ but she never asked him to do anything for her/ like lift things or watch the stove/ or listen to her dreams/ she also never went in the room where they usedta sleep together/ tho she cleaned everywhere else as thoroughly as one of her mother's great-aunts cleaned the old house on rose tree lane in charleston/ but she never did any of this while ezra waz in the house/ if ezra waz home/ you cd be sure mandy waz out/ or in her room.

one nite just fore it's time to get up & the sky was lightening up for sunrise/ mandy felt a chill & these wet things on her neck/ she started slappin the air/ & without openin her eyes/ cuz she cd/ feel now what waz goin on/ ezra pushed his hard dick up on her thigh/ his breath covered her face/ he waz movin her covers off/ mandy kept slappin him & he kept movin. mandy screamed/ 'ezra what in hell are you doin.' & pushed him off her. he fell on the floor/ cuz mandy's little bed waz right on the floor/ & she slept usually near the edge of her mattress/ ezra stood & his dick waz aimed at mandy's face/ at her right eye/ she looked away/ & ezra/ jumped/ up & down/ in the air this time/ 'what are you talkin abt what am i doin/ i'm doin what we always do/ i'm gettin ready to fuck/ awright so you were mad/ but this cant go on forever/ i'm goin crazy/ i cant live in a house with you & not fu . . . / not make love. i mean.' mandy still lookin at the pulsing penis/ jumpin around as ezra jumped/ around/ mandy sighed 'ezra let's not let this get ugly/ please, just go to sleep/ in yr bed & we'll talk abt this tomorrow.' 'what do you mean tomorrow i'm goin crazy' . . . mandy looked into ezra's scrotum/ & spoke softly 'you'll haveta be crazy then' & turned over to go back to sleep. ezra waz still for a moment/ then he pulled the covers off mandy & jerked her around some/ talkin bout 'we live together & we're gonna fuck now'/ mandy treated him as cruelly as she wd any stranger/ kicked & bit & slugged & finally ran to the kitchen/ leavin ezra holdin her torn nitegown in his hands.

'how cd you want me/ if i dont want you/ i dont want you niggah/ i dont want you' & she worked herself into a sobbin frigidaire-beatin frenzy . . . ezra looked thru the doorway mumblin. 'i didnt wanna upset you, mandy. but you gotta understand. i'm a man & i just cant stay here like this with you . . . not bein able to touch or feel you'/ mandy screamed back 'or fuck me/ go on, say it niggah/ fuck.' ezra threw her gown on the floor & stamped off to his bed. we dont know what he did in there.

mandy put her gown in the sink & scrubbed & scrubbed til she cd get his hands off her. she changed the sheets & took a long bath & a douche. she went back to bed & didnt go to school all day. she lay in her bed thinkin of what ezra had done. i cd tell him to leave/ she thot/ but that's half the rent/ i cd leave/ but i like it here/ i cd getta dog to guard me at nite/ but ezra wd make friends with it/ i cd let him fuck me & not move/ that wd make him mad & i like to fuck ezra/ he's good/ but that's not the point/ that's not the point/ & she came up with the idea that if they were really friends like they always said/ they shd be able to enjoy each other without fucking without having to sleep in the same room/ mandy had grown to cherish waking up a solitary figure in her world/ she liked the quiet of her own noises in the night & the sound of her own voice soothin herself/ she liked to wake up in the middle of the nite & turn the lights on & read or write letters/ she even liked the grain advisory show on tv at 5:30 in the mornin/ she hadda lotta secret nurturin she had created for herself/ that ezra & his heavy gait/ ezra & his snorin/ ezra & his goin-crazy hard-on wd/ do violence to . . . so she suggested to ezra that they continue to live together as friends/ & see other people if they wanted to have a more sexual relationship than the one she waz offering . . . ezra laughed. he thot she waz a little off/ til she shouted 'you cant imagine me without a wet pussy/ you cant imagine me without yr goddamned dick stickin up in yr pants/ well yr gonna learn/ i dont start comin to life cuz you feel like fuckin/ yr gonna learn i'm alive/ ya hear' . . . ezra was usually a gentle sorta man/ but he slapped mandy this time & walked off . . . he came home two days later covered with hickeys & quite satisfied with himself. mandy fixed his dinner/ nothin special/ & left the door of her room open so he cd see her givin herself pleasure/ from then on/ ezra always asked if he cd come visit her/ waz she in need of some company/ did she want a lil lovin/ or wd she like to come visit him in his room/ there are no more assumptions in the house.

(*hug*)

Saundra Sharp

i found it
of all places
under the bed . . . .

that hug
you left

i thought by mistake
until it
curled itself
around my toes

then i knew
you
left it there
on purpose.

From *Black Borealis*

Hillery Jacque Knight, III

Last night in our hillside Moroccan villa, I lay in bed with My Love embraced, staring up at the darkened, multicolored canopy with its tassels gently fluttering in the night air off the Mediterranean and touched with slight odors from the seaside village below. The African moon anciently glowing now through the mahogany shutters and softly on the large brass arabesque Persian water pipe sitting under the window. Our two Nubian swallows sat perched in their bamboo cage cuddled and lightly asleep after singing joyously earlier to our lovemaking, and curiously eavesdropping on our deep late-night talks. I could hear the occasional sorcerous-like sound of two camels passing on the back road as their riders cropped them, probably in a hurry to get in out of the crisp night air. Lying, staring at the wind, out at the night—I tried but I absolutely could not go to sleep!

For some odd reason after loving and easing out of her I felt like I hadn't come at all. I still felt full, though I do remember, I thought, the ecstasy and the flush. Uneasily and slowly I climbed out of bed and dressed. I wasn't sure if she was asleep, so I softly whispered to My Love that I was going for a walk. Feeling compelled to go to the Temple, I arrived in the night after a short walk through the Village. As I approached the large carved teakwood doors, the huge burnished brass knobs shone softly in the moon's light. Leaving my sandals in the vestibule, I walked up to the sacred altar and lighted some incense. I slowly began to feel I was no longer alone; another presence was there, so I stopped still. I hadn't worn any underclothing and suddenly, stoutly, I was hardening so. I throbbed so wildly that I snatched open my robe to see, right there standing under the Temple's dome before the altar. And a powerful spurt of come fell right in my hand. A low shimmering hum like an ancient harp vibrated from my hand while purple and orange iridescent rays of light began to radiate from the come, something began to materialize. A shiny black speck in the ivory liquid was swelling longer and bigger as I stood there frozen to the carpet. The shimmering ancient sounds grew louder, spangling those iridescent rays of purple and orange. It kept expanding stretching undulating longer and thicker, finally falling, floating down onto about its head, but it was as large as an Anaconda. It slithered up on the altar and the pulpit and crawled up onto the top of the podium, its lower half coiled, supporting itself and its upper half stretched straight up with its magnificent Ebony head arched forward, slowing weaving as to some Eastern flute. Its eyes were blindingly bright like gold fire stars! There was no mouth. I fell weak to my knees in stark blown awe, gazing up in rapt attention—it was a SPERM!

I was flooded with a Zenith awareness. Expanded before me lay Eternity!

I heard gates opening and the roar of a flood Noah must have witnessed. The mighty roar of a river as old as the Blue Nile, but thick like ivory if it could be melted. In it were countless sperm-serpent fish gleaming with a sleek ebony brightness as if molded from flexible slabs of Onyx. Like healthy rainbow trout leaping and spawning up some mountain stream, they leaped and swam along aided by the powerful hydraulic force of the ivory water up the long phallic, night-shadowed red aqueduct. They swam the swirling heaving forces of the waters with such decided intent, determination and abandon, taking, riding the crests of the waves they could, deflecting off at an angle the ones they almost aligned with but didn't quite manage, and those waves they could only meet head-on they heaved to overtake, but if necessary smashed and crushed straight through. They passed the blood of their fallen brothers or sisters and swam on, even right past their own blood spilled on the waters along the way. After they all had passed, the blood floating on the water was invisibly quickly absorbed by the shimmering ocean. I watched for what seemed, expanded into our time, an hour of slow hot wind. The stronger ones leaping ahead and leading the school. Then suddenly they all seemed to burst forth with new extra electric energy as they broke out over the open end and mouth of the long red aqueduct. I was blinded and deafened by what seemed forever and as I came to grip and balance my senses, I saw I had been blinded by the glare of an atmosphere filled not with clear air as we know it but the constant flux of all spectral colors in the rainbow swirling through the huge sky-high dome-like place. I was momentarily overwhelmed by the heat, a sweet suffusing tropical heat at once richly warm like a slow damp wind off the lushest tropical jungle, a just crisp fast dry wind, a ghibli, off a sun-kissed desert, a cold bracing still wind out of the snowy Himalayas. The warmth or cool was whatever your body needed at anytime on any part of it flowing separately over you, different moistures, and breeze levels as so desired.

I then watched the Onyx sperms plunging down all around into the edge of the galactic liquid sea, around the outer circumference of an extraordinary wide circle like Saturn's rings all the way around the bottom of the vast circular wall of the place. Thousands of other sperms struck a radius-like path from where they were for that faraway center point. I wondered in awe what possibly could be there? — I looked out in the distance in the middle of the sacred "waters" and saw the lighted grandeur of an island or structure—a Divine Dome like a Majestic Warm Corona Borealis or sacred naked nebula of Andromeda, poised, so elegantly! There, way out in the middle of the crystal vapor sea hovering on the surface was a divinely magnanimous Ovum! Reeking, Reeking, just Reeking with Lust! As if Allah himself had taken gallons of juices from the pussies of the Blackest of a special bloodline of Earthy Funky African Women and distilled the love juice, pouring this sacrament around this heavenly isle-like fog droplets of pussy-vapor, suspended ripe rain fertile in the air around the soft violet yellow Opal Ovum.

A Globular Twat all over popping, pouting, teasing, and spreading its brilliant dark berry lips in an enticing slow dance and funky fertility squirm. I heard thrilling cries out of a passion hot seraglio lined with sable palmettos. My eyes flashed back and its "otherness," its divinity appeared, her beautiful beautiful spiritual womb. My vision touched the gentle tender subtlety of a flesh flute, a Black Lotus, a Sable Plume, a Silken Soul, the Soft Chatoyant Essence of a Deva Moor subtlely outlined with a warm cosmic aura, sacred umbra. Then it became her breast full and voluptuous as if about to explode with milk. Again, I looked and it was the Head of My Love! My Woman! My Baby's face flashing spangling on all surfaces of the dazzling sphere at once, though the sphere was smoothly globular, not faceted. It rephased seemingly becoming simply a New Moon an opal Blue Orb—revolving lazily around like Venus in mist, like a round sphere of solidified Cream Clouds during a summer night. I saw nude spirits and naked bodies of contemporary and ancient dark women of grace and power materialize and de-materialize on its surface like an extended Quad-centennial sound track, mesmerizing as the band played on! Man I tell you the Ladies! They played their loving instruments!

The lunar Isle poised itself centered in the waters of the fleshy galaxy and waited like a woman. The male and female warrior sperm were humping their way in for the great thrust that only one would make. There were several more bodies now strewn between where they began their crucial trek and about the halfway point where most of them were now. It was indeed a natural and glorious battle to watch, so masculinely heroic as the stronger sperm would ram the slower or weaker ones out of their way. There were as many strong female sperm as males; they would use guile first rather than force to overcome others in their way. The females would try and turn the attention momentarily of a male or female when it dived dolphin-like surging under the surface of the liquid momentarily removing its eyes from the overwhelming gut magnetism of that ultimate Isle of Moon poised gaseously globular out in the middle of the place. As they passed the halfway point several miles to go, only the few hearty ones left out of a multitude, the others—their Onyx bodies turned on their sides or bellies up floating shining in the vapor water. I wondered what would happen to them now, there marring the pure beauty of the divine ocean. He spoke! The Regal Black Sperm "spoke" passionately, the resounding power and masculine resonance in his "voice" was priceless.

All the multitude of resurrected sperm flew in a single-file sacrificial procession to the Royal Ovum and entered trance-like through the entry opening and it closed, not leaving a mark. The Glorious Ovum was now completely sealed. Within its shining translucence, I could see all the sperm sink in a benevolent sleep in the bottom of the Ovum, pooled in what looked like pearly egg crystal white, stored, waiting to become food for the victor. Lo! The High, the Mighty!

Infinitely the Master Head kept reelin and a-reelin, reeled on, on and on, overwhelming! Swept by a Mighty Love stressed in a Holy Masculine Hallelujah, I floated in powerful rapture for these and this new creation, limitless love and euphoria I showered forth poured out to it to Her to Him to the Infinite Creator boundless love and pride for this Son, our Son.

The Green Corona Black Borealis Ovum now Blooming Fertile, slowly, in the Galactic Celestial Spiritual Womb. Yes! it appeared to me. I did SEE. And so it was. And so it was. I saw. Sanctus.

The Great Regal Black Sperm smiled down at me and said, "So, my Zamiil,* now you know of the grand pleasure we, your fertile subject seeds, experience in your love's Womb Body on the astral level as you experience her on the physical and spiritual. It is profoundly a privilege for me to be your reigning sperm and the propagator of your son in the divine womb of such an earthly creature. So, Zamiil, now I must return, I will go now. If you will cup your hand again I will return to the sacred

* Zamiil: Arabic for a close companion or compatriot.

pools in your suede sac and wait in the ivory waters for tomorrow night. I will not return; this time I will stay in your lovely Queen and do battle for it is destined—I shall celestially spark forth your son. Zamiil, may the Infinite bless, protect, care and watch over the three of you. I go now, you have my devotion and love."

I just sat there, sat there peacefully, in the Temple, meditating the balance of the night. Occasionally opening my eyes, to gaze up at the altar and light the incense, sitting, meditating on it all in the quiet warmth.

PART NINE

Kool N Kinky/Hot N Heavy

Male Series, No. 16 by Ben Jones

The mind is of its own place and usually of its own volition. As such, we have a self-censoring opportunity to discover or lay claim to what we think is Kool and what is Kinky. Some find the daring of their youth umbilically connected to their inability to say goodbye to less hectic yesterdays, when Kool is/was an ATTITUDE as well as physical and verbal dexterity. As a definition, this explanation has substance in any dictionary of Africana, especially with appropriate illustrations:

> There he was, cruising, toe barely touching the gas pedal. It didn't matter that cars were backed up behind him. He had to be SEEN, and so did his chariot, his ride, his short. He slunk down low in the bucket seat and leaned ferociously to the left at just the right angle, with shoulders padded impressively. He pressed buttons to do decibel duty or manipulate a light show in and outside the hawg, deuce (and a quarter) or BMW (Black Man's Wheels). He was, as Haki mused, "refrigerator cool."

Kool is a signature that announces "I am in control" (even if only temporarily) and "I have arrived." Note the confidence in Chester Himes's classic, *Pinktoes:*

> "You're naked," she said, carefully examining his black body, especially his private parts which were not at all private now.
> "I sure am," he said.
> "For what"
> "For to go to bed."
> "You can't go to bed and leave me here."
> "I ain't. You're coming with me."

On the Kinky side, interracial sexual liaisons were Himes's fodder, as well as Trey Ellis's, on occasion, in *Platitudes.*

Until recently, women's Kool seemed to emulate MALEdom, especially on the docket of sexual suggestions: lots of cleavage, tight, tight, tight buttocks-clinging clothes, or none. SDiane Bogus's Kool, however, is wonderfully liberating, having been manumitted from the bartering that makes auction-block gamesmanship "work." Bogus counsels that learning the joys and power in female celibacy—for example, how Kool and comforting and empowering it is to go "mistress-bathing," and to gaze at "your own nakedness in the mirror"—is indeed Kool.

Since Kool is in the mind, which takes temporary vacations, sexual fantasy is an appreciated substitute for the earthly considerations of what is erotically Kool and penetrating on many levels. Nan Saville says, "you have vanished / and with you my sense of reason / I can think / of nothing else." It is a territorial plateau of Koolness, where one stands and can then walk and not look back. But there is a smaller emotional disc called DENIAL. It is unKool to be there, but tremendously Kool to admit you *were.*

"If fucking were graceful, desire an alibi," says and means the heartfelt one in Rita Dove's "For Kazuko," while Dennis Brutus blows cool breezes across the mind in these meaningful requests:

> Speak to me of mushrooms
> and mean aphrodisiacs
>
>   . . .
>
> only speak to me
> while I make music between your thighs

The Kinky short stories in this section are also distinctly Kool in an old-fashioned tender-loving-care way. There are no whips, chains, or Ben-wa Balls to effect mind-dissolving orgasms. Not in Alice Walker's delicate and loving "Olive Oil," which begins as a natural emollient for dry, ashy skin, but soon becomes an olfactory and tactile aphrodisiac. A man being massaged between a woman's legs is a ritual that rejuvenates—an oily urgency and union that lubricates love so well.

The delightfully tension-filled contest of wills in Kristin Hunter's "Cabin Fever" addresses a choking kind of so-called love when the "[possessions] . . . make little possessions," but the contest is a lesson in survival. Hunter raises the question: Is there anything called "almost incest" that is not really Kinky? Is it Kinky or Kool for a self-inventing person to inquire/demand: "You're more than a cock to me . . . How come I can't be more than a cunt to you?"

Some of the most intriguing Kink emanates from the minds of those who, let loose or having broken out of constricting emotional, social, and psychic confines, breathe new, unpolluted creative air and are able to say to others and themselves, "You'll only happen to me once, so . . . let's be Kool and Kinky together."

For Kazuko

Rita Dove

The bolero, silk-tasseled, the fuchsia
scarf come off: all that black hair

for the asking! You are unbraiding
small braids, your face full

behind a curtain of dark breath. Why
am I surprised when your lids emerge

from the fragrant paint? Now the couch
is baring its red throat, and now

you must understand me: your breasts,
so tiny, wound—or more precisely, echo

all the breasts which cannot swell, which
we prefer. I would like to lose myself

in those hushing things; but
sadness is not enough. A phallus

walks your dreams, Kazuko, lovely and
unidentified. Here is an anthology of wishes:

if fucking were graceful, desire an alibi.

From *The Lakestown Rebellion*

Cabin Fever

Kristin Hunter

The stereo was playing softly, those lonely, despairing moans called progressive jazz. Bella, restless, smoking, switched stations several times until she found some music that wanted her response; warm, soulful sounds instead of cool ones. There was no room for pacing or dancing, so she sat on the edge of Ikie's narrow bed, her skirt wrapped tightly around her legs, feet tapping in time to the beat.

Ikie sat on his only chair, a straight one borrowed from the Blue Moon's dining room. "Gonna jack off all by yourself?" he inquired coarsely.

"God, but you're gross tonight. I just might. Will you give me a drink?"

"Why?"

" 'Cause I want one, fool!"

"Oh, the drink. Sure," he said in his mild, courteous voice, and poured warm rye into his two enameled cups. "I meant, why do you want to fly solo when I'm right here with you?"

She tossed the liquor down, suppressing her nausea by sheer willpower. It tasted terrible. "Because," she said when she felt no more risk of retching or coughing, "you don't respect me."

Ikie's brow resembled a newly plowed field. "Baby," he said, "I can't deal with that. It's too heavy. I figured it would come up sometime. After all, you're my brother's wife. But we've been lovers for so long—five months, six—I thought I could relax and forget about it. Why'd you pick this time to throw your shit on me?"

"God, men are dumb," Bella said, banging her knees with her fist as if to lock them together permanently. "I wasn't talking about whose wife I am. Being married to Abe is my problem, not yours. I meant, you don't respect my *mind*. You laugh at my ideas."

Ikie shrugged. "Sometimes I laugh to keep from crying, you know? Like all us happy darkies."

Her voice softened. "You have no hope."

"How can I? It's a hopeless situation."

"Which one?"

"You name it. This town and that road. You and me. Both."

"You might be wrong about one of them."

"Which one?"

"Oh, I don't know, I don't know," she said, her head tossing in the beginning of passion, for she had stopped resisting—at least part of her had stopped, the part below her waist that had a life of its own, a life she had tried to cage forcibly between locked knees and failed. One touch from him, and they had sprung open. But her head was full of conflicts that did not leave enough room for her to concentrate on passion, only enough to notice little things—a rancid odor from his hair, a lack of freshness about his general person—that were distasteful. He was spent all too soon, and she was still unsatisfied.

"No good, huh, baby?" he gasped. "You didn't moan or cry out or nothin'."

"You're more than a cock to me," she said, fondling it absently, as if she were stroking a soft pet. "How come I can't be more than a cunt to you?"

"Because the rest of you belongs to someone else. And that someone happens to be my brother." He groaned. "That makes it worse. Almost incest."

"That should make it more interesting," she said with a bawdy laugh.

"You're crazy. No, you're actin' crazy, like you always do when somethin' really bothers you. You know bein' my brother's wife only makes things more worrisome. I don't need hassles."

"Does anybody?" she asked, stroking the hair that had repelled her a moment ago. "But sometimes they just come up and stare you in the face, and you have to deal with them."

"I can deal," he said pridefully, "with anything." Looking at his broad shoulders, thick arms, and wide, hairless chest, she could believe it. "Anything but you. With you I'm nothing but a big, helpless hunk of butter. I'm a fool to admit this; any man would be. But all you have to do is walk in a room, shaking all that beautiful stuff you got, and I just melt. Do it now," he pleaded. "I'm not ordering you, I'm begging you. Please, do it now."

"Do what?" she asked in puzzlement.

"Get up and walk around the room."

Ikie's cabin, an eight-by-ten cell, contained, in addition to its furniture (a single bunk, dresser and chair), numerous heaps of clothing, books, wood and carving implements, as well as crocks of clay and plaster. She had been unable to push the door open because of all the junk piled behind it, and it had taken all of his strength to open it for her. She looked at his earnest, pleading eyes and began to laugh.

"That's right. Laugh at me. I deserve it for being fool enough to get in your power."

"I wasn't laughing at you. Only at your idea."

It was his turn to be baffled. "Huh? What idea?"

"That there could possibly be enough space in here for me to walk around. There's no room for a *cockroach* to turn around in here."

Ikie looked around ruefully at his heaped-up possessions and began to laugh too.

"Clean it out and put the junk in your van," she said, "and I promise you my most spectacular walk ever."

"The van's full too." Ikie raked despairing fingers through his hair, disarranging it even more. "God, how I hate possessions. I try not to have any, but they keep accumulating anyhow. Sometimes I think they get together late at night and make little possessions. They must. They multiply like rabbits."

Bella's laugh went all the way up and down three octaves that time.

"You don't have to talk," he said. "You can sit there all night like Miss Prim if you want, with your knees stuck together. I still won't be able to keep my hands offa you."

"Your hands were too busy to touch me out there in the dining room, I suppose," she said, referring archly to the Blue Moon's hookers-in-residence, who both adored Ikie.

"You're faking again. I know you're not jealous of those pitiful bitches."

She nodded. "You're right. I was faking just then. For fun. I don't mind Lily and Booty hanging all over you. It sounds strange, I know, but I think they're good girls."

"Sure they are. The only trouble with them is, they have to *act* sexy. It's their trade. Sex is just a job to them, so they're bored with it, and they have to pretend. Now, you—you don't have to act sexy, you just *are*. You can't help being sexy any more than you can help breathing. All you have to do is be yourself. Promise me you won't ever try to be anybody else."

"I promise. What is it you like best about me? My legs, or what?"

"All of it. It's *you* I like. That womanly nature deep down inside you. Course the outside is fine too, and that's cool, but it ain't the main thing. You say men are dumb. Well, maybe so, but most women are dumb too. They think men are just interested in their outsides—in their shapes, or their legs, or in some makeup they bought in the dime store. Women like that are just empty dolls. What makes a woman is what's inside."

He had said the right things, the things she wanted to hear, but she had to test him a little more. "You say you like everything about me. Does that include my mind?"

"Even that. Sure. It's all you. Except sometimes your mind gets in the way of more important things."

"Damn you," she said, but he was not listening. He was seeing a picture from the past.

"The sexiest I ever saw you look," he said dreamily, "was before we got together. You was wearing an old raggedy sweater-shirt and some sneakers, walking in the woods around here. You had scratches on your legs, and you had a bucket in one hand for picking berries . . ."

His mouth had curved into the tender smile she saw so seldom and loved for its gentleness. "What *I* like most about *you*," she said, and bent to kiss him, "is your mouth. Sometimes. When it isn't talking."

"Mmmm," he said, his hands walking up her legs.

He knelt on the floor, removed her sandals, and began to kiss her toes. With his irresistible mouth working its way up her ankles and her legs to the inside of her thighs, Bella managed not to think for a while. But later, after her release and his, as they lay cramped together in the bunk, her mind became active again.

"For once and for all, I am not guilty about us. I don't need cheap excuses for what I do. I belong to *myself,* not to Abe or to you either, mister. If he wanted me in bed, I might feel differently; but as it is, I don't think I have a thing to be guilty about."

"What I can't understand," he said, "is how Abe can keep his hands off you. He can only screw somebody he thinks is beneath him. But he's ashamed of it too, because he thinks all screwing's sinful."

"Whew," Bella half said, half whistled at this glimpse of the torture chamber that was her husband's mind. "Where do I fit into all this?"

"You're supposed to be a high-class White lady. Pure. On a pedestal. Above sex, and all those other dirty things."

"Maybe," she said with a dim glint of dawning awareness, "that's why he gets mad when I don't shut the bathroom door."

"You leave it open?" he asked with astonishment.

"Sure. Why not? I'm his wife, aren't I? What do I have to hide?"

Ikie began to laugh. "Baby, how long you been married to my brother? You sure don't understand him. You may be his wife, but you're not his woman. As his wife, you're supposed to be like a high-class White lady. You ain't even supposed to have to go to the bathroom. Hell, you ain't even supposed to *perspire.*"

"Well, I do. I sweat a lot. Especially in this little hot box of yours. I offend him, so he avoids me."

"He avoids me too. It must be my body odor."

"Your sweat, love. And your dirty old funky poolroom."

"Please. My perspiration. And my *billiard parlor.*"

"And your sexy statues. Pornography, he calls them."

"Yes. My pornographic statues. My truck. You know I only drive a truck so I can afford to be a sculptor. I've got about as much interest in trucking as your husband has in fucking."

"Copulating," she corrected. "Fornicating."

"That may be what white people do," he said, "but it ain't what we do. Is it? Is it?"

"No," she said, barely able to speak under the crushing weight of him.

"Say it. What are we doing? Say it."

She did and he did and they did, frantically purging themselves of the evening's sadness.

As she stirred and began dressing to leave, he murmured sleepily, "Stay with me, baby."

"I can't," she said, tying her skirt securely, poking around for a misplaced shoe.

"Why not? He don't need you."

"Maybe not now. But he will."

He opened sleep-thickened eyes and said, "Aaah, forget what I said, will you? I must've been drunk. Go home."

She found the shoe and threw it at him, hard.

From *GAR*

Dennis Brutus

Speak to me of mushrooms
and mean aphrodisiacs
or nuclear clouds.
Speak to me of oysters
and mean pearls
or aphrodisiacs,
of dying
in the Elizabethan orgasmic sense
and the great relieving shuffle
of the burdensome flesh:
only speak to me
while I make music between your thighs
and let dear sorrowing tortured Yeats
rack himself in the shadows
beating upon a wall.
It is tenderness I need—
a great longing crying at the ends
of the tactile nerves
in glands and nipples,
queasily sliding in the groin:

Oh we are born to be aesthetes
to yield reluctant homage to a tree profile
poised and outlined against the lilac dusk
and all this tidal surge of lust
is surrogate for loneliness.
Where is my consolation? Where?
Sorrow with me in the bomb-drizzled skies of Vietnam
and twist with bruised hips on concrete
as my friends in prison:
Speak to me of mushrooms,
oysters,
while I make music
between your thighs.

The Joys and Power in Celibacy

SDiane Bogus

Doing nothing sexy with nobody is torture
It makes for workaholism, unreliable stress, and invites substance abuse
Do something with yourself, at least, and find out what I found out

You can have the bed to yourself
You can sprawl or you can curl up into a knot
You won't get no complaints about taking up all the space nor about
   having your knees in somebody's back

You can sleep naked or with your clothes on
It won't have to be a signal that you're ready
Or that you don't care to

Three more things:
You don't have to cut your toenails, unless you sleep with your legs
   crossed at the ankles
You can slobber in your sleep and be your own witness
And you don't have to apologize for every random pass of gas because
   someone's lying next to you

Now here's the good part:
You can experiment:
You can see how long you can hold out before true horniness sets in
You can look and see what exactly makes you horny
You can wait and see exactly what you do and how you act when you
   are horny
You can notice your cycles of horniness
Like do you feel the urge to hug/be hugged, kiss/be kissed, do it/have
   it done—once a month, once a week?

After that, you can find or let yourself be found by a lover
Or, surprisingly, you can become your own—
Providing you have a sex drive.
If you have no sex drive, celibacy is like indifference, hardly worth
   mentioning.

Now, about being your own lover.
It takes courage and practice.
You have to start slow then go for the hidden
Simple masturbation can become mistress-bathing
An innocent bath can become the delicious wet inside an imaginary
   woman's sweet stuff
Your own nakedness in the mirror invites you to call yourself some-
   thing sexy, like "Sweetmeat," or "Honeymama."

In bed alone,
you have (1) your head, (2) your closed eyes, (3) your desire, (4) your
   hands, and (5) if desired, any props you wish
Give yourself the pleasure that expectation with another denies
Forget that there is such a thing as lovemaking with any but yourself

I guess, it's fair to tell you about me in the interest of the promotion
   of celibacy.

I have a baby bottle, a feather, a candlestick, and a tube of KY
I have Prince, Whoopi, Tina and Aretha
I have naked gay boys
I have motorcycle dykes and sweet young things
I have Prynne and Dimmesdale in the forest
I have rough fantasies of submission and the love of ex-lovers
I have the safety of my room and great orgasms.

In celibacy
I learn my body, my rhythms, my wants, my expectations, my fanta-
  sies, my need.
In celibacy I seek myself and find myself
What joy, what power—what endless discovery.

From Running Come Touch

Gloria T. Hull

For M.

You told me about
your fear of penetration—
men's maleness, people pushing
all thrusts you warded off
with weapons
your mother handed you
through pain

But, then, you touched me—
amazing move—
your shy sure fingers
unbalancing my reasons,
teeth biting off my breath

It was darkness come
daylight come morning
instinct and body love
coming through hands

and breakfast and questions leading nowhere
more clothes and passion
cocaine frost
the cat licking salmon
back darkness back rubbing
lessons hanging out pleasure
from running coming touching
deep
      into

Olive Oil

Alice Walker

She was busy cooking dinner, a nice ratatouille, chopping and slicing eggplant, zucchini, and garlic. George Winston was on the box and the fire crackled in the stove. As she dripped olive oil into a pan a bit of it stuck to her thumb and she absentmindedly used her rather rough fore-finger to rub it into the cuticle which she noticed was also cracked. In fact, she had worked a lot over the last month putting in a winter garden; the weather most days had been mild, but it was also dry and occasionally there had been wind. Hence the extreme dryness of the skin on her hands.

Thinking of this, puttering about, putting a log on the fire and a pot of water for noodles on the stove, she touched her face, which along her cheekbones seemed to rustle it was so dry. Massaging the painfully dry cuticle, she swooped up the bottle of olive oil, sniffed it for freshness, and poured a tablespoonful into her hand. Rubbing her hands together she rubbed the oil all over her neck and face. Then she rubbed it into wrists, arms, and legs as well.

When John came in from splitting wood he sniffed the air hopefully, wanting to enjoy the smell of the ratatouille, one of his favorite dishes. Putting the wood down and kissing Orelia on the cheek, he noticed how bright, almost burnished her skin looked. He was sorry he had a cold and could not smell her, since her sweet fresh smell always delighted him.

"Still can't smell anything, eh?" she asked.

"Nope."

To which she replied, emphatically, "Good."

One of the sad things about their relationship was that even though she loved John she was unable to expect the best from him. John sometimes thought this was solely his fault, but it wasn't. Orelia had been brought up in a family and a society in which men did not frequently *do* their best in relation to women, but rather a kind of exaggerated approximation of what their male peers told them was correct. Then, too, at a very young age, when she was no more than seven, her older brother, Raymond, gentle and loving, whom she had adored, betrayed her. Her other brothers, insensitive and wild, had designated an ugly, derisive nickname for her, "Rhino" (because even as a little girl dryness caused the skin on elbows and knees to appear gray and thick), which she had borne as well as she could until one day he called her by it. She was shattered and never really trusted a man not to unexpectantly and obliviously hurt her feelings again no matter how much she loved him.

So John was not trusted, no matter what he did, and sometimes he pointed this out to her, but mostly he kept quiet. No matter how many times he proved himself different from other men, in her eyes he always seemed to measure up just the same, and this was depressing. However, he loved Orelia and understood many of the ways she had been hurt by society and her family and empathized with her.

While they were eating he mentioned how glowing she looked and she simply smiled and forked up bowls of salad. He was surprised she didn't tell him immediately what she had done to herself—that was her usual way.

That night before she went to bed she washed herself from face to feet in the tin washbasin he had bought, a feat that regularly amazed him because she did, indeed, manage to get clean in less than a half gallon of water, whereas John felt the need each night to fire up the wood-burning hot-water heater and luxuriate under a hot shower that used gallons. While he bathed in the bathhouse outside, she went wild in the kitchen with the olive oil, massaging it into her scalp, between her braids, into her face and body, into her feet. Glowing like a lamp, she preceded a bewitched John up the narrow ladder to the sleeping loft.

Alas, the day must soon come when John got back his sense of smell; his colds rarely lasted longer than a week. Orelia thought about this every day as she slathered on the olive oil. She had grown to love the stuff. Unlike her various sweet-smelling oils and creams, it really combated and won the battle over her skin's excessive dryness, and its purity brought the glow of honest health to her skin.

Orelia and John had been intimate for so long that any little secret kept from him ·was like a sharp piece of straw in his sock. One night when the worst of his cold seemed over, he took his shower early so that he could be in the room with her when she bathed. Over the pages of his *Natural History* he watched her peel the mauve-colored thermal underwear from her dark, glowing body and fill the tin washbasin with hot water from the copper kettle, which was almost the exact color of her face. He watched her soap her cloth and begin industriously if somewhat bemusedly washing her face, neck, and ears. He watched her soap and palpate her breasts, and he longed to be where the soap was, covering her deep brown nipples with his tongue. She looked over at him as she moved down her body with the soapy cloth and finally squatted over the pan. John riveted his eyes, which he felt were practically steaming, on a story in his magazine about the upside-down eating habits of flamingos. By the time he looked up she was sitting decorously in a kitchen chair, her feet soaking in the pan. And while she sat, she was busily rubbing something into her skin.

"What's that?" asked John.

The sad truth is that Orelia considered lying to him. And a lot of memories and unpleasant possibilities went through her mind in a flash. She remembered being a little black girl with little skinny, knock-kneed ashy legs, and how every morning her mother had reminded her to rub them with Vaseline. Vaseline was cheap and very effective. Unfortunately Orelia almost always put on too much or forgot to wipe off the excess and so everything she wore and everything on which she sat retained a slight film of grease. This greasiness about herself and her playmates (most as ashy as she) eventually sickened her, especially when television and movies made it clear that oiliness of any sort automatically put one beyond the social pale. The best white people were never oily, for instance, and she knew they put down readily any poor whites and black people who were. So Orelia graduated to Pond's and Jergens, which did the job against her ashiness, but not nearly as well or as inexpensively as simple Vaseline.

She thought about men's need to have sweet-smelling women, too, while she waited to answer John. Of John's enjoyment of her body when it was perfumed, especially. Actually, as she thought about it, either of them was likely to come to bed in a cloud of Chanel.

Then she gazed into his eyes, veritable pools of trust. Whatever else John expected of her, he never expected her to lie. He expected the best. Fuck it, she thought.

"You got your smell back?" she asked, as she dried her feet.

"Yeah," said John.

"Well, come here, then."

John came toward her, appreciating her glistening body with its full breasts that had nursed children and now gently sloped, and then stood in front of her. She raised herself against him.

"Smell," she said. If he fails me it will be just as I expect, she said to herself, waiting for Raymond's betrayal to be duplicated by John.

John sniffed her cheek and neck and rubbed his nose longingly against her shoulder. *"Um,"* he said, somewhat fervently.

She held up the bottle. "It's olive oil."

"Olive oil, eh?" he said, peering at the bottle and scanning its fine print. "From Italy. It sure looks great on you."

"What do you think of the smell?" she pressed.

"Earthy. Like sandalwood without the sweetness. I like it."

"You do?" She was suddenly radiant. Her love of John flooding her heart.

He looked at her, puzzled. He never knew what was going to make her happy. Sometimes he felt he just blundered along by the grace of God and hit the jackpot.

"I can cure your dandruff problem," she said briskly, picking up a comb. "Sit here between my knees."

"Which a way you wants me to turn my face?" said John slyly, sticking out his lips and grazing her belly button as he kneeled to put a pillow on the floor in front of her chair.

Orelia carefully covered John's shoulders with a towel and soon she was scratching huge flakes (embarrassingly many and large, to John) off his scalp and explaining how dandruff, especially among black people, was caused not only by a lack of moisture but by a lack of oil. "We're drier than most people," she said, "at least in America we are. Maybe in Africa our diet takes care of the problem." She advised that he throw his Tegrin and Head & Shoulders away.

As careful as a surgeon she divided his hair into dozens of segments and poured small amounts of oil between them. Then, using her fingers and especially her thumbs, she massaged his scalp vigorously, humming a little tune as she did so.

After she'd thoroughly oiled and massaged his scalp (which for the first time in months did not itch), she amused herself by making tiny corkscrew curls, "baby dreads," she called them, all over his head. She explained that tomorrow he could wash out any excess (though surprisingly the oil seemed to have soaked in instantly and there didn't seem to be any), leaving his scalp comfortable and his hair shiny but without any resemblance to the currently fashionable "jerri curl," which relied solely on harsh straightening chemicals and grease and which they both thought made black people look degraded. "Hyena-like," as Orelia described it.

It was all wonderful to John, sitting between Orelia's knees, feeling her hands on his head, listening to her hum and softly talk to him, an intimacy he'd longed for all his life. But one he had assumed would never be for him. His sisters, with their unruly locks, had enjoyed the haven between his mother's knees and between each other's knees, and between his aunts' cushiony knees, as they fiddled with each other's hair, but he, a boy, had been excluded. He imagined himself as a small child and how much he must have wanted to get between somebody's knees; he imagined the first few times being cajoled and then being pushed away. He knew that if he went far enough back in his memories he would come upon his childhood self weeping and uncomprehending over this.

But now. Look.

John knew there was a full moon, he could feel it in the extra sensitivity of his body, and the fire made a gentle droning sound in the stove; the leaping of the flames threw heat shadows across his face. He felt warm and cozy and accepted into an ancient women's ritual that seemed to work just fine for him too. It turned him on and gave him an idea.

"Let's continue this on yet another plane," he said.

"Say which?" said Orelia, smiling.

While Orelia sat with hair comb dangling, John went and got the futon off the guest-room bed and flung it on the floor before the fire; he threw down pillows and covered everything with large towels. Throwing off his robe, he entreated her to stretch out on the futon, where he immediately joined her, olive oil bottle in hand.

Soon they were oiling each other like children forgotten among the finger paints. Orelia oiled John's knees and elbows especially well, and as he did so she felt the hurt from Raymond's betrayal disappear from her heart. John, who had long ago learned that we massage the spot on other people that most hurts in us, went to work on Orelia's knees, rubbing a lot but then nibbling and kissing a lot too. Soon they were entwined, the olive oil easing the way to many kinds of smooth and effortless joinings. They laughed to think how like ratatouille and sautéed mushrooms they both tasted, and giggled to be slipping and sliding against each other's bodies like children in mud. And much, much later they fell happily asleep in each other's arms, as oily and contented as any lowlife anywhere. And she was healed of at least one small hurt in her life, and so was he.

Victory

Jo Smith

He counterattacked my every thrust
with the coolness of a three-flavored snow cone on a 30 degree day.

In retaliation I nibbled with patience
at the tasteless ice that cloaked his seedy strawberry, juicy grape and
refreshing lemon lime.

Soon I reached the bottom of his cone,
but there were no flavors to greet me, only a hole through which I
peered and found the juices at
my feet.

From *Pinktoes*

Wrestling and Pole Vaulting

Chester B. Himes

For one thing Panama Paul invited Cleo Daniels up to his room at the Lewis Hotel, which is situated on University Place a few blocks north of Washington Square. He invited her up to his room for the purpose of having a drink. She accepted on those grounds.

They had a drink on those grounds and then another drink on those grounds and he attempted to get chummy.

"Take off your shoes, baby."

"I will not."

So he took off his own shoes. And they had another drink.

"Take off your clothes, baby."

"I will not."

So he began taking off his own clothes.

"What are you doing?" she asked.

"I'm undressing," he replied and continued to undress until he had finished undressing.

"You're naked," she said, carefully examining his buck-naked black body, especially his private parts which were not at all private now.

"I sure am," he said.

"For what?"

"For to go to bed."

"You can't go to bed and leave me here."

"I ain't. You're coming with me."

"I am not coming with you."

"You mean you came up here and drank my whiskey and now think you're going to go? What's the matter? You scared?"

"You invited me to have a drink. You didn't say anything about going to bed."

"What else would I invite you up here to drink my whiskey for, pray tell, without going to bed with you?"

"Use your imagination."

"Oh. You thought I was going to do that?"

"Well, what else did you keep showing me your tongue for? What was that supposed to mean from an accomplished thespian like you?"

"Well, get ready, girl, I can't through your clothes."

So she took off her shoes and stockings and garter belt and panties and pulled up her skirt and sat in the armchair with her naked white legs hooked over the arms and it was ready.

And was he astonished. "It's red-headed!" he exclaimed.

"It is not," she said. "It's just red hot."

Naturally this was his cue to demonstrate his virtuosity.

And before he knew what was happening she jumped up, snatched up her shoes and stockings and garter belt, and ran out into the corridor, slamming the door behind her.

He was so mad he finished the bottle of whiskey all by himself and fell into a drunken sleep and dreamed he was in a heaven filled with naked white angels, but when he tried to fly in their direction he found that his testicles were weighted down with anvils.

And for another thing, Milt and Bessie Shirley and their guest, Arthur Tucker, went gaily into their suite of rooms in the Thomas Hotel and gaily closed the door behind. And what with all the people moving about in the corridor, it was some time before one had a chance to peek through the keyhole. And, well kiss my foot, all three of them were stark-naked.

Bessie Shirley was hanging head down from a walking stick stuck through the chandelier with her long hair hanging to the floor, and embracing Mr. Tucker, who stood confronting her. And were they having a ball! Where was Milt Shirley? He was standing to one side looking on, having his own private ball. The last thing one saw before some people came down the hall, interrupting one's enjoyment, was the chandelier gradually pulling loose from the ceiling.

. . . .

And what did Julius find out about that fashionable East Side divorcee, Fay Corson? He found out that she lived in a seven-room apartment on the eighth floor of a very swank building in the East Seventies, and that she was an animal lover. For no sooner had they disrobed than she suggested they play dogs. So they scampered about the carpeted floor in the manner of mating dogs. Then she decided to play shaggy dog and pulled down the telephone from the bed table and dialed a number. It so happened that Will Robbins answered and she said to him:

"You sneak."

"Fay!" he exclaimed. "Where are you?"

"I'm at home, you rat."

"Doing what?"

"I'm playing bitch, if you just must know."

"Is that new?"

"With a big black dog," she said.

"Lucky black dog, you lucky white bitch," he said.

"And what are you doing, you louse?"

"If you just must know, I am sitting at the kitchen table eating oysters on the half shell."

"And what is that black slut doing you took home with you? Eating oysters too, I suppose."

"That fine brown woman is not eating oysters whatsoever."

"Then why don't you give her some oysters?"

"Her turn will come when I'm finished."

"And when will that be?"

"Soon."

"Wait for me."

"Better hurry."

"Now!" she cried.

"Now!" he replied.

"Oh, now and now again and again now," she said, quoting Hemingway.

"Not any more now," he said, sighing.

"You dirty freak," she said, and banged down the receiver.

Then she pulled away from Julius and ran into the bathroom. Julius listened to the water running. And what had he found out for real? Well, he had found out where sea urchins come from.

As for Reverend Riddick and Professor Samuels, they both wound up in the Bellevue psychiatric ward for observation.

But it is not at all like you're probably thinking. What happened was that Isaiah and Kit Samuels, leaving Mamie Mason's party at the same time as Reverend Mike Riddick, could do no less than help him get the helpless Miss Lucy Pitt downtown to her abode. Then what happened after that was when they had got the young lady home and got her undressed and safely resting atop the sheet with all her sweet brown femininity exposed, Reverend Riddick was struck by such compelling compassion that he wished to say a Christian prayer for the poor helpless girl before tucking her beneath the covers. And that is the only reason he asked Professor Samuels to leave the room, which in turn precipitated the wrestling match.

. . . .

"I'll wrestle you buck-naked with the greatest of pleasure," Professor Samuels accepted his challenge.

So that is how they came about wrestling buck-naked.

But one look at Reverend Riddick's fine black body with its big impressive limbs inspired Kit Samuels to rip off her own clothes and begin wrestling buck-naked also. She wrestled about the room in circles, as though she were wrestling two buck-naked electric wires.

"Oh, oh, big black Riddick," she cried in spontaneous rapture and began throwing her white body about as though to demonstrate its potentialities, in case anyone might be interested.

"Put on your clothes, you bitch!" Professor Samuels shouted. "You're exposing yourself."

But she must have misunderstood him because she began doing the splits and the bumps and exposing herself from all directions, shouting in reply, "Oh, big black Riddick, I'm a bitch! I'm a bitch! Oh, big black Riddick, I'm a bitch in heat."

"You're a frantic slut," Professor Samuels screamed.

Naturally Reverend Riddick resented Professor Samuels addressing such a fine white woman in that manner, even though she was his wife. So he caught Professor Samuels' head in a nelson. Professor Samuels was not one to be nelsoned without retaliating, so he gripped Reverend Riddick's most vulnerable limb. The only thing was he was too weak to take a good hold and his hand kept slipping up and down.

And when Kit Samuels noticed this she entered into the spirit of the match with greater abandon.

"Oh, big black Riddick, I'm a frantic slut. Oh, I'm a frantic slut. Oh, big black Riddick, I'm a frantic slut."

Such behavior on the part of his wife so intensified Professor Samuels' agitation that he wrapped his legs about one of Reverend Riddick's big black legs and began to wrestle in earnest.

"Oh, you whore!" he reviled his wanton wife.

"Oh, I'm a whore, I'm a whore," Kit Samuels cried, dancing in even greater frenzy.

"I'll divorce you, you whore!" Professor Samuels cried. "I'll throw you out!"

"Oh, I'm a whore and I'll give you cause to throw me out," Kit Samuels said and immediately launched into such frenzied cause that Professor Samuels cried out.

"I'll kill myself! I'll jump into the river!"

Which, for some inexplicable reason caused Kit Samuels to cry joyously, "Go kill yourself! Go jump into the river! Or I'll give more cause!"

Professor Samuels broke from Reverend Riddick's hold and ran, still dripping, out of the door.

"Jesus save us!" Reverend Riddick bellowed, and ran, still dripping, to bring him back.

Just as day was breaking, Professor Samuels came running down the stairs from Lucy Pitt's fourth-floor flat beside the railroad tracks on West 10th Street, in the Village, white-baby naked. Reverend Riddick came running down behind him, black-baby naked.

Early Village risers looked up and saw a naked white man highballing down the street with a naked black man chasing him and hastened back inside their homes and locked their doors, thinking the Africans were invading.

The naked white man ran underneath the elevated railroad tracks and headed toward the Hudson River. The naked black man ran after him. The naked men ran past one big trailer truck after another big trailer truck. They ran past one freighter dock after another freighter dock. The naked white man couldn't find any way to get close enough to the river to jump in and drown. The naked black man couldn't run fast enough to catch him and stop him in case he got to the riverbank.

One of the Bowery bums who had strayed over on that side during the night, a former professor of Greek mythology at an Ivy League university, dozing fitfully on the sidewalk, looked up in time to see the fleet-footed naked runners rounding the walls of Troy, and exclaimed weakly, "History repeats itself!"

Shortly afterwards two truck drivers came out of an all-night greasy spoon and caught the runners and held them for the police.

Which just goes to show that the phallus complex is the aphrodisiac of the Negro Problem.

Summer Madness

Nan Saville

Tonight
there is nothing
between us
but a bottle
of dry wine.
Your skin is smooth
Your eyes probe me
where your fingers
have not
I cannot smoke
another of these cigarettes
Inside your eyes,
all else disappears.
From your tongue
I sip the taste
of my body and
what is left of
your wine
You are warm
and you love me

into the darkness
of the evening.
It is midnight
you have vanished
and with you my sense of reason
I can think
of nothing else.

From *Platitudes*

Trey Ellis

They swallow, and neither coughs. They drink, and drink some more.

Monk still zigzags around the walls, different piano notes peeping out from different corners of the room.

I need to hold somebody, says Janey, laying her arm over his shoulder. Her nose strokes his neck, her lips smear his jugular, her eyelashes brush his jaw. A tear from her touches hot, lengthens quickly to his collarbone, stops, wells again, lengthens quickly under his shirt, over his breast to ball over his nipple. He hugs her, he sweeps his hands over the back of her silk blouse *(sheepsheepsheep)*. She kisses his jaw, his chin, his lips; the tip of the tongues lightly touch, lightly touch, swirl over each other. Janey squeezes Earle's chest, then pulls away.

Come on, she says, rising, raising his hand, pulling him up.

She opens the door, and her father's wide bedroom again vibrates brown: mahogany and tortoiseshell and smoked glass. Inside she carefully presses closed the door, she pulls loose the bow around her blouse's neck, she unbuttons it, then dips each shoulder, pulling her arms from the soft holes of silk. She pushes the plaid kilt off her hips, pushes the white slip off her hips, steps from her brown loafers. She reaches behind herself with both hands, unlatches the bra clasp, squeezes her shoulders forward; the bra falls to her elbows, then to the rug. She pushes her white panties off her hips, off her knees; they drop to her toes, she steps free.

She steps toward Earle carefully; his blazer and tie already cover the brown couch. Then he too is nude and she hugs him again, they kiss again. I'm on the pill now. She kisses his dark ear. Both his brown hands replace the white bra, her red nipples grow to warmly stigmatize his palms. He flushes. The sable penis has now risen higher, taps her lily hip. They slow-dance to the bed, kneel together, then lower themselves to the wide support. Rolling on top of him, she rises, her white knees at his colored waist, the vagina at the penis. Earle looks at them, at her creamy breasts, at her face. She smiles. He smiles too. She holds his raven penis, insinuates it into her snowy self. They smile again. Hers is hot and soft; his warm and hard. Her pearl hands pad his inky shoulders; she raises, lowers herself onto, off of him. Her mouth is soon big, her eyes very closed. As her rhythm increases, her thighs flex, relax around him, her white stomach flexes, relaxes too, her wine nipples *are* warm erasers, she *does* moan as he presses her breasts. Cries rise from her mouth but start somewhere much deeper. She now curves back, her fingers squeeze her hair, her elbows high, riding no-handed, cries now short and quick. Then slow.

MmmmmmmmmmMmmmmm. She rises from him, kisses hard his face, her breasts smear on his chest, her hips and thighs jam the penis, so she lies over him crossways, kisses down the curve of his chin and neck to his clavicle, to each breast; kisses down his stomach, kisses through his pubic hair, returns to kiss his navel. She tilts her head, licks at the penis, at the scrotum, especially the intertesticular area, then licks the underside of the darker ring high on the penis's neck, then the cap itself. She breathes full, eclipses his penis with her mouth. She raises and lowers her face over it, now steadying it with the lips while the tongue presses that darker ring. Earle watches the ceiling as he tugs a bit at her arm, her side, her leg, until she has rotated over him, kneeling. His hands braid over the two small dimples low on her back, then he pulls up to the vagina to press with his pink tongue her pink clitoris, which shines.

Straining between licks, each lap makes the other tighten or curve. Then Janey breathes a long and high cry, twitches quickly. Now Earle breathes long and high, he freezes, then twitches and pumps. Eventually she raises her mouth from his penis—a moist and even gasket.

Interpenetration Side Two

Akua Lezli Hope

For Thrill

This crispy critter walks in demi plié
stands in nether time
mule slung even when slack, jack
every girl's dream strung
from beebee dripping chords
strung through sanity's diatonic scheme

I like it raw, boy wonder
lick sweat from your vertebrae
jam from your size 12

you tentacled child's play
brazen breakthrough braintrust
novitiate in nexusrealms of fructuous funk
acolyte of afroclassic thrust

plucking seconds toward heart's harmolodic dream
ascendence of new energy's parabolic twang
twitch me twat, doc.

The Hog Caller's Party

M. J. Morgan

Looking thru the rearview mirror, Naomi put on her cherry-red lipstick with great care, and fluffed up her hair. She was on her way to one of the "Hog Caller's" parties. She knew he would be especially good today because they hadn't seen each other for a few weeks.

He was a sexy-looking blue-black man. He stood about six-three and had a body that looked like he spent hours each day sculpting his physique. He was known for his parties that turned into orgies. He had a three-bedroom home that he designed to put you in the mood. Two of his three bedrooms had king-size water beds, wall-to-wall mirrors, piped-in music, TV monitors that played porno movies all the time, and subtle colored lighting. By day he was Mr. Brown, a bus driver; by night he was the "Hog Caller," always ready to do it.

As Naomi rang the bell to his home, she began to wonder what surprises he had in store for his guests. She also hoped he had a special surprise for her. He opened the door nude, with a buzzing dildo in his hand.

"Oh, I must be at the wrong house," Naomi kidded as she turned to walk down the stairs.

"You betta get your fine ass in here. I've been waiting for you," he said.

Those were the words she wanted to hear. She threw herself into his arms and kissed him.

As they walked into the living room, he started peeling her clothes off as he licked, kissed and sucked her lips, neck and shoulder. Sensuous melodies played softly in the background as they began to dip and sway in each other's arms. She could see their silhouette in the mirror, and his massiveness made her juices flow. He pulled her bra off with the flick of his wrist, and began sucking and licking her nipples. Naomi's golden-brown nipples stood up on her full round breasts in response to his tongue. She cupped her breasts in her hands and put both her nipples in his mouth, and watched him suckle. The "Hog Caller" slid his hand down, down into the depths of her pussy, and buzzed her with the vibrator. She let out a moan, as she remembered how good this man was the last time they fucked. He laid her down on the living-room floor and began licking her pussy in feather-like strokes. He moved the dildo in and out of her pussy as he talked to her and told how he intended to fuck her. The "Hog Caller" always told her it was his job to satisfy his women, and that he wouldn't come until she had. Impulsively she guided his movements as she arched her back and rubbed her pussy in his face. The "Hog Caller" opened her legs wider and she gasped with pleasure. He licked and sucked her cunt until he felt her warm wetness come down, and then he licked her like a cat licks a dish of milk.

As she lay on the floor trying to catch her breath, he told her there were two couples due to arrive at any minute. Just as soon as he uttered those words, the doorbell rang. Naomi ran around the living room grabbing her clothes and dashed into the bathroom to freshen up.

She could only hear female voices outside the bathroom door, and she was really curious to see who was there. In her eagerness to return to the party, she forgot to put her panties on; in fact, she didn't realize she never picked them up off the living-room floor.

When Naomi came out of the bathroom she met Kim and Carol. Kim was a top-notch photographer for a major magazine. She was petite and attractive. She had something about her that made her seem shy, but in fact she was the aggressive one of the two women. The "Hog Caller" had met Kim and Carol, a tall brown-skinned sister with an Angela Davis Afro and beautiful long legs, at the club the last time they were there.

The "Hog Caller" passed out a few joints while Naomi got a bottle of wine and some glasses from the kitchen. After everyone had a couple of hits off the joint, Kim said, "I have heard about the 'Hog Caller.' The ladies in the hair salon were talking one day and said he's got the best cock on the South Side of Chicago."

"What do you think about that, Naomi?" Kim asked as she picked up Naomi's panties and put them to her face.

Naomi simply smiled and said, "You'll see." Then she looked at the "Hog Caller" and said, "Take it out and show it to them, baby."

The "Hog Caller" unwrapped his robe and took his cock in his hand. Kim and Carol's eyes grew bigger as they stared at his beautiful long cock. As if drawn to a magnet, they went down on him. They both licked and sucked his cock while they played with each other. Naomi lay on the floor beside them and played with her pussy as she watched Kim open her mouth wide and take in all of the "Hog Caller's" cock. Naomi was overcome with lust, and she started kissing and rubbing first Kim's ass, then Carol's. She thrust her tongue in Carol's ass so deep that it made Carol let out a holler. The sight of all this was enough to take the "Hog Caller" over the edge. He shot his come all over Kim's and Carol's faces as he now started his famous holler. His holler sounded like the sound made when you are calling hogs, and that is how he got his name. Hearing him come aroused Naomi even more, and she came again while she continued to milk his cock until he was limp.

The "Hog Caller" lay there in the midst of three beautiful women, and smiled. We smoked a few more joints and drank a little more while he gained his composure.

Pretty soon, he got up and led us into his special water-bed room. Once in the room, he began to meticulously set the stage for our next encounter. He put a plastic mat over the bed and dimmed the lights. He turned on the TV monitor, and instructed us to get in the bed and play with ourselves. He left the room for a moment, and when he returned he had a gallon of oil. He poured the oil all over us, and rubbed us, as he described how good we looked. He said that the different colors of our skin lying side by side in his bed, glistening, were beautiful. He stroked Naomi's body so good that she felt she left the planet. Faintly in the background she could hear the doorbell ring.

"That must be my reinforcements. Y'all 'bout to really get fucked now," he said. He came back moments later with two men, twins. Ron and Don were identical in every way . . . even down to their cocks.

The twins undressed, while the girls watched and gave them encouragement. Everyone jumped in bed and formed a circle of bodies, each one going down on someone. This is wild, thought Naomi, as she gently parted the lips of Carol's pussy. Carol responded to her by opening the lips wider to allow Naomi free access to her clit. She removed every thought from her mind, except that of taking Carol to the top of ecstasy. Naomi tongue-fucked Carol until Carol tightened her long legs around her neck and dripped come all over her. Naomi had hardly noticed that Ron—or maybe Don—had been playing with her ass with his cock. She now directed her attention to fucking him. She guided his dick inside her ass and began rolling her ass all over the bed. Don could hardly hold on, her passion was so intense. After a few minutes of a slow rhythmic rock, the pace intensified. She could feel him inside her swelling, as she undulated with all her might. The "Hog Caller" stood in front of her and she sucked his cock as the three of them reached a climax. Exhausted, Naomi lay beside them remembering how often she had fantasized about a night like this. And now the fantasy was this night.

PART TEN

Exotic Landscapes/Erotic Mindsets

Untitled by Eddie Jones

Is the erotic just a landscape, waiting for us as nonexploitative explorers to gaze at its beauty and turn away, unchanged forever, or is it a topography that begs our touch to make it realize more fully all that it can be? Can we leave the landscape of *Erotique Noire*—now initially surveyed and marked—unchanged as when we first came to it? I think not, but then, even if we could, who would want to? In this last section the past calls to us, will not let us forget its touch, what it looked and felt like, will not let our old lovers be sealed in the tomb of forgetfulness. Barbara Chase-Riboud's "Cleopatra" entwines us in history's most foolish and erotic embrace, as her harem scene moves our minds toward the pleasures of multiplicity in the erotic. Naomi Nelson's "Poetica Erotica" takes us back still farther—and deeper—to the banks of the Nile where the initial thrusts of the erotic were so forcefully made, and Claire Harris's "The Joy of Sex" brings us back toward the future again, still leaving us sweating in the past, Rameses "squeezing a little too hard." As we reflect, is anything ever as bittersweet as the erotic contact that was so good but is now gone, leaving its fragrance now and then to waft up from the past and entice us when we least expect it in the present? If we doubted this truth, Jewelle Gomez's "Piece of Time" reconfirms our sweetest remembrances. Letitia and Michael's "Hot Missives" and R. Bruce Nugent's "Smoke, Lilies and Jade" take us deeply, intimately, into the ways that the erotic makes connections in the minds of its adherents. Finally, the ontological thing that these writers feel as "erotic blackness" is made corporeal in Nan Saville's "Venus Rising," as it ejaculates us forcefully into the present with its "waves of electric heat." But the past—the past still lingers, like a last bead of moisture at the end of our fingers. We put it into our mouths, taste it, and it stays with us forever.

And, dear reader, we go now, but we shall come again. We promise.

WON'T YOU COME WITH US?

The Joy of Sex

Claire Harris

He was a darker Rameses
an older Tutankhamen
he was cool
     crazee
polished ebony
still even with him
it was a much overrated activity
he had flair
his hands
     lilting
his tongue
     intelligent
on curves and creases
     no need of manuals
     or comfort
but she had honed
her expertise in groups
had read and listened to travelers' reports
     so she dreamt
when he moaned

squeezed a little too hard
began his dark thrust
and press she
flooded with images
lifted in a ravished
        approbation
of cannonballs of liquid fire . . .

        it wasn't bad

Piece of Time

Jewelle Gomez

Ella kneeled down to reach behind the toilet. Her pink cotton skirt pulled tight around her brown thighs. Her skin already glistened with sweat from the morning sun and her labor. She moved quickly thru the hotel rooms sanitizing tropical mildew and banishing sand.

Each morning our eyes met in the mirror just as she wiped down the tiles and I raised my arms in a last wake-up stretch. I always imagined that her gaze flickered over my body; enjoying my broad, brown shoulders or catching a glance of my plum brown nipples as the African cloth I wrapped myself in dropped away to the floor. For a moment I imagined the pristine hardness of the bathroom tiles at my back and her damp skin pressed against mine.

"OK, it's finished here," Ella said as she folded the cleaning rag and hung it under the sink. She turned around and, as always, seemed surprised that I was still watching her. Her eyes were light brown and didn't quite hide their smile; her hair was dark and pulled back, tied in a ribbon. It hung lightly on her neck the way that straightened hair does. My own was in short tight braids that brushed my shoulders; a colored bead at the end of each. It was a trendy affectation I'd indulged in for my vacation. I smiled. She smiled back. On a trip filled with so much music, laughter and smiles, hers was the one that my eyes looked for each morning. She gathered the towels from the floor and in the same motion opened the hotel-room door.

"Goodbye."

"See ya," I said feeling about twelve years old instead of thirty. She shut the door softly behind her and I listened to the click of her silver bangle bracelets as she walked around the veranda toward the stairs. My room was the last one on the second level facing the beach. Her bangles brushed the painted wood railing as she went down, then thru the tiny courtyard and into the front office.

I dropped my cloth to the floor and stepped into my bathing suit. I planned to swim for hours and lie in the sun reading and sip margaritas until I could do nothing but sleep and maybe dream of Ella.

One day turned into another. Each was closer to my return to work and the city. I did not miss the city nor did I dread returning. But here, it was as if time did not move. I could prolong any pleasure until I had my fill. The luxury of it was something from a fantasy in my childhood. The island was a tiny neighborhood gone to sea. The music of the language, the fresh smells and deep colors all enveloped me. I clung to the bosom of this place. All else disappeared.

In the morning, too early for her to begin work in the rooms, Ella passed below in the courtyard carrying a bag of laundry. She deposited the bundle in a bin, then returned. I called down to her, my voice whispering in the cool private morning air. She looked up and I raised my cup of tea in invitation. As she turned in from the beach end of the courtyard I prepared another cup.

We stood together at the door, she more out than in. We talked about the fishing and the rainstorm of two days ago and how we'd spent Christmas.

Soon she said, "I better be getting to my rooms."

"I'm going to swim this morning," I said.

"Then I'll be coming in now, alright? I'll do the linen," she said, and began to strip the bed. I went into the bathroom and turned on the shower.

When I stepped out, the bed was fresh and the covers snapped firmly around the corners. The sand was swept from the floor tiles back outside and our teacups put away. I knelt to rinse the tub.

"No, I can do that. I'll do it, please."

She came toward me, a look of alarm on her face. I laughed. She reached for the cleaning rag in my hand as I bent over the suds, then she laughed too. As I kneeled on the edge of the tub, my cloth came unwrapped and fell in. We both tried to retrieve it from the draining. My feet slid on the wet tile and I sat down on the floor with a thud.

"Are you hurt?" she said, holding my cloth in one hand, reaching out to me with the other. She looked only into my eyes. Her hand was soft and firm on my shoulder as she knelt down. I watched the line of the muscles in her forearm, then traced the soft inside with my hand. She exhaled slowly. I felt her warm breath as she bent closer to me. I pulled her down and pressed my mouth to hers. My tongue pushed between her teeth as fiercely as my hand on her skin was gentle.

Her arms encircled my shoulders. We lay back on the tile, her body atop mine, then she removed her cotton T-shirt. Her brown breasts were nestled insistently against me. I raised my leg between hers. The moistness that matted the hair there dampened my leg. Her body moved in a brisk and demanding rhythm.

I wondered quickly if the door was locked. Then was sure it was. I heard Ella call my name for the first time. I stopped her with my lips. Her lips were searching, pushing toward their goal. Ella's mouth on mine was sweet and full with hungers of its own. Her right hand held the back of my neck and her left hand found its way between my thighs, brushing the hair and flesh softly at first, then playing over the outer edges. She found my clit and began moving back and forth. A gasp escaped my mouth and I opened my legs wider. Her middle finger slipped past the soft outer lips and entered me so gently at first I didn't feel it. Then she pushed inside and I felt the dams burst. I opened my mouth and tried to swallow my scream of pleasure. Ella's tongue filled me and sucked up my joy. We lay still for a moment, our breathing and the sea gulls the only sounds. Then she pulled herself up.

"Miss . . . ," she started.

I cut her off again, this time my fingers to her lips. "I think it's OK if you stop calling me miss!"

"Carolyn," she said softly, then covered my mouth with hers again. We kissed for moments that wrapped around us, making time have no meaning. Then she rose. "It gets late, you know," she said with a giggle. Then pulled away, her determination not yielding to my need. "I have my work, girl. Not tonight, I see my boyfriend on Wednesdays. I better go. I'll see you later."

And she was out the door. I lay still on the tile floor and listened to her bangles as she ran down the stairs.

Later on the beach my skin still tingled and the sun pushed my temperature higher. I stretched out on the deck chair with my eyes closed. I felt her mouth, her hands and the sun on me and came again.

Ella arrived each morning. There were only five left. She tapped lightly, then entered. I would look up from the small table where I'd prepared tea. She sat and we sipped slowly, then slipped into the bed. We made love, sometimes gently, other times with a roughness resembling the waves that crashed into the seawall below.

We talked of her boyfriend, who was married and saw her only once or twice a week. She worked at two jobs, saving money to buy land, maybe on this island or her home island. We were the same age, and although my life seemed to already contain the material things she was still striving for, it was I who felt rootless and undirected.

We talked of our families, hers so dependent on her help, mine so estranged from me; of growing up, the path that led us to the same but different place. She loved this island. I did too. She could stay. I could not.

On the third night of the five I said, "You could visit me, come to the city for a vacation or . . ."

"And what I'm goin' to do there?"

I was angry but not sure at whom: at her for refusing to drop everything and take a chance; at myself for not accepting the sea that existed between us, or just at the blindness of the circumstance.

I felt narrow and self-indulgent in my desire for her. An ugly Black American, everything I'd always despised. Yet I wanted her, somehow, somewhere it was right that we should be together.

On the last night after packing I sat up with a bottle of wine listening to the waves beneath my window and the tourist voices from the courtyard. Ella tapped at my door as I was thinking of going to bed. When I opened it she came inside quickly and thrust an envelope and a small gift-wrapped box into my hand.

"Can't stay, you know. He waiting down there. I'll be back in the morning." Then she ran out and down the stairs before I could respond.

Early in the morning she entered with her key. I was awake but lying still. She was out of her clothes and beside me in moments. Our lovemaking began abruptly but built slowly. We touched each part of our bodies, imprinting memories on our fingertips.

"I don't want to leave you," I whispered.

"You not leaving me. My heart go with you, just I must stay here." Then . . . "Maybe you'll write to me. Maybe you'll come back too."

I started to speak but she quieted me.

"Don't make promises now, girl. We make love."

Her hands on me and inside me pushed the city away. My mouth eagerly drew in the flavors of her body. Under my touch the sounds she made were of ocean waves, rhythmic and wild. We slept for only a few moments before it was time for her to dress and go on with her chores.

"I'll come back to ride with you to the airport?" she said with a small question mark at the end.

"Yes," I said, pleased.

In the waiting room she talked lightly as we sat: stories of her mother and sisters; questions about mine. We never mentioned the city or tomorrow morning.

When she kissed my cheek she whispered "sister-love" in my ear, so softly I wasn't sure I'd heard it until I looked in her eyes. I held her close for only a minute, wanting more, knowing this would be enough for the moment. I boarded the plane and time began to move again.

Cleopatra

Barbara Chase-Riboud

O friendly enemy, we have loved,
Loin and haunch, limb and flank, truth and lies,
Tressed like a pair of ancient Armenian vines
Grown together root and branch in stunted
Commingling without End or Beginning.
If we part, you will leave with half of me,
Or I with half of you, and nothing will kill
The pain of dismembering.
That ache like some rare jewel
Will hang round our necks to touch,
In tender tremulance, an old wound of amputation
That burns and groans in limbs no longer existent
But splintered and crushed
In some long-forgotten and useless War.

Antony

Barbara Chase-Riboud

One who has loved remembers that he has loved.
This is Recollection, invented
By those who know that love is hardest to recall
The morning after or the morning after that,
When we find ourselves curled up in canonized squares
Of cracked light like stunned pink-lit snails,
Remembering only the slap of *Eros* on mortal flesh,
A blow that leaves us amnesiac and running naked
In the melancholy aftermath of disaster,
 A regiment of Love lost, sequestered, or destroyed,
pursuing Memory into the distraught cosmos,
Leaving only Cleopatra's drunken fleet
Ransacking pastel waters, heading for
The marriage feast of Time and her bridegroom Revenge.

On a Night of the Full Moon

Audre Lorde

Out of my flesh that hungers
and my mouth that knows
comes the shape I am seeking
for reason.
The curve of your waiting body
fits my waiting hand
your breasts warm as sunlight
your lips quick as your birds
between your thighs the sweet
sharp taste of limes

Thus I hold you
frank in my heart's eye
in my skin's knowing
as my fingers conceive your flesh
I feel your stomach
moving against me.
Before the moon wanes again
we shall come together.

II

And I would be the moon
spoken over your beckoning flesh
breaking against reservations
beaching thought
my hands at your high tide
over and under inside you
and the passing of hunger
attended, forgotten.

Darkly risen
the moon speaks
my eyes
judging your roundness
delightful.

Venus Rising

Nan Saville

Dark man
whose quiet eyes
and fingers lightly
trace the nylon
pattern of my leg
pulls me close
to his vast world
reaching deeper than
we have ever
before tonight
waves of electric heat
fasten our bodies
his breath
on my face
sounds of pain
a past outrun
forceful hands
push through softness
tapping an emptiness
fiercely

does he fill me
we are many
we are one
in a glory
of panting sweat

An Utrillo, Possibly

Dennis Brutus

Mounted
this thing became another thing—
this thing of browns and pinks and creams
of bulk and shapes
of passages and shadows—
masses acquired substance,
grew vibrant, set up subtle tensions
solids yearned towards solids;
one penetrated endlessly
to suspended horizons,
thrust at bulk
rubbed against masses
suspired in a timeless atmosphere
and in a great ocean of delicious pressures
swooned mind heart and flesh in a blissful surcease.

Hot Missives

Letitia and Michael

SCENE: *Letitia and Michael; yin and yang; lust and indirection; but eventually meeting, joining, in a circle because there can be no love in a square; senior investment banker by day, but she has never been done right at night; beginning assistant d.a. by day, he thinks he knows how to do her right—with all his might; but first, they write.*

Cut to: October 4

October 4

Honey,

   Did you need me tonight? In my sleep you came to me so sweet and warm, and we talked and touched for what seemed to be days. Then, finally we woke together, but when I opened my eyes, there was only me and the remembrance of you in my room. I thought you may have been calling me.

   You know that I am always less than a phone call away from you *whenever* (day or night) you need me.

MIKE

October 9

Michael,

Your letter made me blush!

You believe in getting right to the point, don't you?

Saturday I wrote you a long letter, which I tore up because some things are better left unsaid.

Michael, I hardly know you, and you don't know me at all. Beyond this flirtatious game of the past few months, we have scarcely even communicated.

What you suggest is impossible for so many reasons.

LETITIA

October 18

Letitia Love,

If I made you blush, I'm not ashamed of that (proud even?), but to provoke that response, or any, was not why I wrote so early that morning. I wrote what I did because I couldn't help myself. I wrote those things because I felt those ways, and *you had* been floating around my bed-room all night. You just came to me that night, and I had to write what I did.

I knew when I first met you that I was drawn to you, and I tried to figure out polite and discreet, yet clear and inoffensive ways of letting you know, but none of that stuff worked. And so finally, I got you out to lunch. And I told you. And you told me. And that was that for about five minutes, but after being so close to you, all my little fantasies in the flesh as it were, I knew that I had to express myself more fully at least one more time . . . but I said nothing for months after our July lunch.

Then . . . something happened. Isn't it Anaïs Nin who writes, "All unfulfilled desires are imprisoned children"? Well, my sublimated longing evidently was a bit too much for my resistance factors those last few days of September, and so you got a note full of sensual explosions and interstices of my willingness to be available to you concerning anything at any time.

But you must know that I am a book you can open at any time. I am in fact longing to be read by you. The little I have been allowed to read in your pages has intrigued me so that I want to read your entire collection from cover to cover.

I realize that when the night whispers you, I cannot continue answering if you do not want to hear my reply . . .

Love,
MICHAEL

October 22

Dear Michael,

Hardly an hour passes, day or night, that I don't think of you and want you and need you. Your last letter has broken down all my carefully contrived defenses. Really, I knew that I was lost when I read, "I thought you may have been calling me," and I blushed because that night you caught me in the midst of a wonderful erotic fantasy of you. I did call you that night and it unsettled me that you heard that call, because it means that we were connected in ways which I had not perceived.

At first, I thought that it was a harmless pleasure to conjure up these thoughts of you, these delicious fantasies that helped me get through the hours of the night when I lay awake watching the shadows on my bedroom wall and listening to the sounds of breathing next to me. The fantasies were safe, I thought, because you were just a creature of my wild imagination. Before I knew it, however, I was trapped by your determined persistence and the intensity of my feelings for you, which my voice and looks must have betrayed.

I often swim against the current, but when, finally, it's to no avail, I turn downstream and go with the flow . . .

I want you.

Shall I promise you a rose garden?

All my love,
LETITIA

October 23

Pretty L.,

Now I'm the one blushing! Whew! I now have so much I want to say, so you'll have to give *me* time to respond.

Right now, I need to be alone in the dark for a while.

M.

October 25

Dear Miss L.,

Well, I've gotten myself *somewhat* more together, and I think I can respond now.

Your letter is so much like you: hot, warm, cool, cool, warm, hot. You're serious, girl! I feel the circle forming, and I want it to join.

Honey, you already know that I want *you seriously,* but when you come to me—and I do so want you to come—I want you to feel completely real, in sync about us. I hate this serious-relationship shit. The technicalities.

I wanna get back to fantasy . . . you've got your nerve, you know

Hot Missives 401

that? Over there thinking about my dark body, and here I was thinking you liked me for my inner self. Ha! We're not locked in *come-bat,* but I think my erotic thrusts are better than yours, and I didn't get *any* of your daytime dreams with me as their object of affection, but as usual, you get all I have. Here's one I had the night after you left my party.

You sat alone on my sofa, looking out over my moonlit yard, listening to the Najee tape I'd put on for you, and sipping on the glass of wine I'd poured for you before I left the room. You still had on the satiny purple dress you'd worn to the party, high heels, everywhere, everywhere, the glint of your brown body and the smell of your scent . . . I won't tell a soul if you want to be *totally* discreet . . . Let me hold you near till the morning light . . . Najee plays, reverberating my own thoughts as I stand over you now in my black velour robe; you don't hear me come back, you're lost somewhere in the music of the tenor saxophone; you don't see me come back, your eyes closed, your head tilted back, letting the whole ambient scene wash over you. So I must let you know that I am near . . . that I want only one heartbeat tonight in my den, that I want only one body there where there are now two. I bend toward you, and let my right hand cup your head and face. You don't move, don't make a sound, as I roll my tongue lightly and moistly over your slightly parted lips. As I bend, my untied robe falls open, and you see that sensuousness has undone all of my composure; my composure stands in front of us, a steel cable to be secured to you, in you.

I slide my tongue down your chin, your neck, to your breasts, where your dress stops me, and I rest my head on your hard nipples. As I fall to my knees, between your open legs, I raise your legs, first one, then the other, and place them on my shoulders. As I push that purple satin back with my forehead, I almost lose control when I see and touch and smell that you're wearing nothing under your dress. My groans of pleasure become audible, and I give myself away; I can't wait to have you. I cross your legs firmly behind my back, sweating now and trembling. You open those beautiful eyes and they gaze first into mine, and then at the entire scene, me, on the floor between your legs, my chest heaving and sweating, my hands and forearms now completely under you and cradling your ass, pulling your sex toward me. As you say "yes," I bend my head down as you hold it, and I brush the wet flat of my tongue over the little flesh that obscures your clitoris from me. I let all of my wetness flow down and mingle with yours. And as I feel you start to move in my hands, I push my tongue all the way inside where it has wanted to be for years. I feel you climbing as my tongue and lips languish in your juices, reveling in your taste, your smell, your feel.

I feel you press my head tightly between your soft thighs, as I hear you say "now." I pick you up in my arms, stand you up, turn you around, and bend you over my monitor; you stare out at the moonlit yard as I raise your dress again, revealing your beautiful caramel-colored ass. I part your high-heeled legs, cup both your breasts in my hands, and whisper "now" to you, as I enter softly, but firmly, your pussy so hot and wet. I start to pump you slowly, rhythmically.

"Let me keep you warm till the early dawn warms up to the sky" . . . And as I feel you start to suck harder on the finger I've put between your lips, as I see your legs quiver and your ass begin to spasm, I hold you as close to me as possible, making two into one, as my screams drown out your own, and we explode together, now, yes, now. If only for one night. As I fall to the floor shaking, sweating, completely spent, a heap of muscle and flesh that your love has undone, you let your dress fall slowly over your wetness, and you sit beside me, us holding each other, only our breathing to give us away to the night; only our heartbeats to show that we are more alive than we have ever been before.

MIKE

November 1

Sweet Mike,

You make love with beautiful words, words that tantalize and titillate, erotic images that evoke deep pleasure. ME starring in your little mini-drama, all decked out in purple satin and high heels . . . I like that.

Two reflections, though.

You missed some of my erogenous zones . . . my whole body, down to the tips of my fingers and the ends of my toes, is made for love, so that, when I am overcome by passion, joy ripples out from my center through every part of my body like concentric circles in a pond. I shall have to teach you how to make love to me.

In your fantasy I am so passive: "You sat alone . . . looking out over my moonlit yard . . . You don't move [hell, that's no fun!], don't make a sound [but I love to moan, whisper, scream]." All those first-person pronouns and verbs: I bend, I slide, I raise, I cross . . . All that one-sided activity! What's for me to do? You should know by now that nothing about me is passive. I have been known to get up from a long night of serious lovemaking and run ten miles just to stretch out my muscles.

(Hold on. I have to stop and get some chocolate cake; all these erotic thoughts are making me hungry.)

You'll have to wait for my variation on your fantasy. Like Salome, I shall drop my veils slowly, one by one. I think I'm down to veil four now with three more to go . . .

Yours,
TISH

Tish Baby,

No, you don't have to promise me a rose garden, but *do* save that body for me. Honey, you couldn't treasure it more than I do. Stay in *close* touch, and I'll tell you what I do with your picture every night.

Love,
M.

November 8

Michael Mine,

I spent the afternoon shopping—for a few *little black lacy things.* I bought a sexy low-cut bra, and I thought to myself how I would love for you to slip it off me and run your fingers over my breasts. (Did you get the black lace bikini panties that I sent you yesterday—the ones with the thin straps and the little red roses? How'd you like the taste and fragrance of my body?) Pretty soon I'll have a complete wardrobe in black. Instead of my etchings, would you like to come up and see my undies?

By the way, I didn't get a chance to tell you that you have the most gorgeous legs. I saw them as I spied on you running in the park yesterday. (You have made me so wicked.) Yum-yum. That is my *second* favorite part of the male anatomy. I had said to myself, "I bet Mike has skinny legs. Fine legs would be almost too good to be true." I'm just going to love running my hands up and down your thighs, around your calves, down to your ankles—and back up.

I'm going to have to get in the bed tonight and do some serious fantasizing. But I promise to stop "messing" with you—tiptoeing into your room (in my dreams) unannounced and upsetting your equilibrium. (Witch that I am, I'm trying to keep you from fucking *her!*) I guess it's all right, though, if I think of you over there, and you think of me over here, and we "connect."

When I ran into you at the Safeway yesterday, I wondered if I should feel guilty for lusting in my heart, silently. I thought about how wonderful it would have been to spend the day with you. We could have had lunch in some quiet, out-of-the-way restaurant, and then gone to a motel, where we would have talked for hours while sipping wine, and then made love—breathtakingly fast the first time, and then slowly, languidly, patiently, each giving pleasure to the other the second time.

From that point on my erotic meanderings got *deep!*

And then I received your last opus . . .

What're you going to do with this shameless hussy?

Love,
LETITIA

November 11

Dear Shameless Hussy,

I am staring at your picture as I try very hard *not* to get hard, and instead concentrate on the writing. But you make it hard.

So, your favorite fantasy of me starts in the lake, huh?—"two nude bodies surfacing in the moonlight" . . . and then? And then? You're not going to treat me in real life like you treat me in your fantasies, are you? I mean, you are going to let me finish them, aren't you?

In my trance state I move between wet thoughts of you, thoughts of what I have to do that day, and back to thoughts of you. You're deep in me; be gentle.

You're so nasty, and yes, please do *train me,* you bully! For my part, I promise not to leave *one* part of your body untouched or unlicked, especially your toes and your lower back. I promise to electrify you with hot cum and clean us both up afterwards. What more do you want, a lover and a butler in one body. And after I've said, "Pull over to the dirt road," are you still gonna give me some? God, I hope so.

You lusted for me in your heart in the Safeway? I lusted for you in the same store, but slightly lower. "Breathtakingly fast" you said our first would be, then "slow and languid the second time." Yes, that's about right, because I intend to completely ravish you the first time, completely devastate *both* our bodies, and we'll be so much better the many times to follow, but nothing will be like that first time, I PROMISE. And by the way, please *do* scream all you want. I *may* even hear you over my own screams. You will *not* be running ten miles when I'm done with you.

But . . . it's not the '90 sexual Olympics; I simply intend to fuse our two souls and bodies with all the force of my being.

When I meet you at Mr. Henry's Tuesday at 1:30, you *will* have on a dress, the black bra you mention, a garter belt with stockings, but you will *not* have on panties. That's a loving order. I will save a quiet table for just us two. I can't wait.

Love

MICHAEL, your empty-headed, pretty sex slave

November 15

My sweet "empty-headed, pretty sex slave,"
   (I like the ring of that!)
   I want to check out the moonlight on your roses and the candlelight on your black satin sheets. I just want to look . . . not touch. My sweet love, I am getting so horny.

I hope I am getting *inside* of you, *deep* inside of you where the soft tender core of your being lies. I want you to get inside me too, literally and figuratively. Oh, God, how I want you in me.

It feels so good to snuggle up against the thought of you each day, to hold you in my heart, to smile at your image in my mind's eye, to carry on these lengthy conversations in my head, to wait for your letters, and to listen for your voice at night.

But what are you doing to my picture over there? At that rate, you're going to wear me out!

Sweet dreams,
TISH

November 19

Sexy L.,

I'm starting everything over since our "talk" last night (you with your red negligee on and me wearing my very sleek birthday suit).

About last night . . . I confess, thinking of you in that red gown, heels up on the bookcase, wet pussy open, "thinking of my dick in you" as you lay, I smeared your picture . . . but it was *so* good, and I wiped it off right away. The only harm done was to my sheets.

Love you and miss you
tremendously,
MIKE

November 25

Darling Michael,

I know very well what I want you for. I want you to be my *lover* and my *friend.* I want to have fun. I want to turn you on, and I want you to turn me on. I want to bring you joy, and I want you to give me pleasure. I want to climb some walls with you; I want to scale the mountaintops with you. Can you handle it? I didn't ask you to come into my life, and I tried damned hard to get you out. But since you're determined to stay (you Capricorns are *so* damned stubborn!), then let's get on with it.

You asked me which position I like best. Most of the 69! The real question is: how do I like to make love? I like it fast and hard and frenzied. But my very favorite is slow, slow, slow and long, long, long. I want you to tease me, to build me up to a frenzy and then stop, so that I am wild with desire, just hungry and thirsty for more. I want you to open me—slowly and gently—like a day lily in the morning sun. I like *all* of my senses aroused. I want to *feel* the rippling muscles in your calves, the sharp angles of your pelvis, and the smooth skin inside your thigh. I want to *taste* the sweet elixir of your mouth, the salt flavor of your sweat, the rich honey of your come. I want to smell the *musk* of your body. I want to *hear* the sounds of your pleasure: the moans, the screams, the giggles. I want to *see* your body in the light of candles and look deep into your eyes when our bodies melt into one.

I want to be caressed and fondled, stroked and petted until I can't stand it anymore and I cry for mercy. I want to explore every little nook and cranny of your body with my fingers and my tongue. I want to run feathery little kisses and tiny little bites all up and down your body until I hear you holler. (Can I be any clearer?) I want to feel your tongue on mine, sending sharp pinpricks of desire up and down my spine. I want to feel your hands cupping my breasts, and your mouth encircling my nipples, coaxing them into hardness. (Do you get the picture?) And then I want you to mount me, impale me on your burning spear. And then I want to mount you, and ride the crest of the wave until the sea foam bursts against the breakers. Such exquisite pleasure!

I have waited a long time for you, and now I'm ready.

Love,
Letitia

November 28

Sweet Thing,

I'm writing this after our lunch, and so I'm very hard and very horny, so, like, I'm not responsible, O.K.?

Now here's the plan. We'll meet at the Sheraton near the expressway about 7:00. You'll park in the back lot and come in through the rear entrance that faces north. You can take the elevator from that level right up to the top floor, where I'll be waiting for you with dinner (though we'll probably be too hungry for each other to eat—food, any way) and a bottle of champagne.

As you enter the room—the bridal suite—to your left will be the entertainment center with the VCR on which we can watch our "art movies." Ha! To your right is the bathroom and, beyond that, our sitting room. Immediately in front of you is the king-size bed with black satin sheets.

If a person were to lie on this black-satined bed and turn on her right side, she could look out the picture window at the mountains in the distance. Next to the window is an extraordinarily comfortable lounge chair, which I could sit in and in which you could sit on top of me and put your legs around my neck, and we could discuss . . . oh, I don't know, music or something. Behind that chair is an enormous Danish dresser with an equally enormous mirror resting on it, and I could pick you up out of that chair and turn your face to the mirror so that you could see my ass and back discussing music with your stomach and pussy. I love music!

When we're ready to *cum* out of that discussion, I could turn you around to the southwest wall, where we could cum and see the beautiful Odalisque by Matisse.

I want you to know that I appreciate certain moments of existence, because they outweigh others because of what happens in those captured moments. Today at lunch you were the most beautiful, most sexy, most fascinating woman in the world; ha! and I had you all to myself.

Love,
MIKE

December 1

Sweetie,

I'm feeling sooooo good, and very much in the mood, thinking of you, remembering the other night . . . so I thought I'd send you this hot little epistle that I wrote (but never mailed).

I'll be alone Wednesday night, so come early and I'll fix a casserole with a salad. Bring the wine you like, one of your "art movies," and your appetites (*both* of them—tee-hee). After dinner, we'll watch the movie, take a long, hot bath (with candlelight, soft music, and lots of bubbles), and then . . . well, oh then.

Sweet dreams!
LETITIA

December 19

Bewitching One,

Whew! Your erotica certainly seems to have been . . . inflected by something or someone since first we mailed hot missives, lo, those many months ago. How am I to take all this now: do you want to make love in our old way, with your caramel legs stretched in a 90° angle on the edge of your silken bed, my tongue deep in your crevice and my nose against your clit, my right thumb and forefinger squeezing your left nipple and my left finger in your mouth? Or do you want me to come to your office pretending to be the deliveryman, but the second I see you, locking your office door, throwing you on the floor, plunging into you after making you an ocean, doing it from behind slow, hard, and time-consuming?

MIKE

December 26

My wild sweet love,

Last night was exquisite, richly textured with sensual pleasures: the feel of your body against mine, the taste of your lips, the sweet fragrance of your after-shave, and the sound of your words in my ear. I awoke at 1:30, and images of the night kept racing through my mind, and I couldn't go back to sleep.

Now, about New Year's Eve. We'll dine at Chez Moi on broiled cornish hens seasoned with a dash of wine, some sort of pasta, Récamier peas with baby carrots, and spinach salad with sliced pecans and a walnut-raspberry dressing. You can bring a bottle of champagne.

I shall greet you at the door in my new red velvet strapless dress, elegant but sassy with a tight skirt (under which I shall be wearing a black garter belt, sheer black hose, and no panties). After dinner, I shall undress you: first, the jacket and a big hug; then I'll loosen your tie and run my lips, soft and wet, over your mouth; next, I'll unbutton your shirt, slipping it off your arm, and planting little kisses along the way; and then I'll slide your pants down to your black bikini underpants and I'll encircle your waist and run my arms up and down the curve of your back. CENSORED! Tune in tomorrow for the next installment!

Oh well, if you insist . . . and then I'll let you undress me, slowly, piece by piece, climbing higher and higher as we move into a sensuous, undulating dance, our bodies moist in the heat of our love. By then, it will be time for candles, soft music, another glass of champagne, and that certain ambience, as our bodies melt into one long, sustained embrace. Then we shall let our imaginations run wild and dark with the night. You can make all my fantasies come true, and I shall play out all your fondest dreams, like the one of the Lady in Purple. Remember?

And we'll have a new year to remember . . .

Always,
LETITIA

From *The Tomb of Sorrow*

Movement III

Essex Hemphill

You stood beneath a tree
guarding moonlight,
clothed in military fatigues,
black boots, shadows,
winter rain, midnight,
jerking your dick slowly,
deliberately calling attention
to its proud length
and swollen head,
a warrior dick,
a dick of consequences
nodded knowingly at me.

You were stirring it
when I approached,
making it swell more,
allowing raindrops
escaping through
leaves and branches

to bounce off of it
and shatter like doubt.

Among the strangest gifts
I received from you
(and I returned them all)—
a chest of dark, ancient wood,
inside: red velvet cushions,
coins, paper money
from around the world.
A red book of hand drawn runes,
a kufi, prayer beads,
a broken timepiece—
the stench of dry manure.

And there were other things
never to be forgotten—
a silver horse head
to hold my chain of keys,
A Christian sword,
black candles,
black dolls
with big dicks
and blue dreads
that you nailed
above my bed
to ensure fidelity.
A beer bottle filled
with hand drawn soap,
a specificity—
a description of your life,
beliefs, present work,
weight and height;
declarations of love
which I accepted,
overlooking how I disguised
my real motivations—
a desire to keep
some dick at home
and love it as best I can.

I was on duty to your madness
like a night nurse
in a cancer ward.

Not one alarm went off
as I laid with you, Succubus.
I've dreamed of you
standing outside my soul
beneath a freakish tree,
stroking your dick
which is longer
in the dream, but I,
unable to be moved
and enchanted,
rebuke you.
I vomit up your snake
and hack it to pieces,
laughing as I strike.

No, I was not
your pussy,
she would be
your dead wife.
I believe you
dispatched her soul
or turned her into a cat.
I was your man lover,
gambling dangerously
with my soul.
I was determined to love you
but you were haunted
by Vietnam,
taunted by demons.
In my arms you dreamed
of tropical jungles,
of young village girls
with razors embedded
in their pussies,
lethal chopsticks
hidden in their hair,
and their nipples clenched
like grenade pins
between your grinding teeth.

You rocked and kicked
in your troubled sleep,
as though you were fucking
one of those dangerous cunts,

and I was by your side,
unable to hex it away,
or accept that peace
means nothing to you,
and the dreams you suffer
may be my only revenge.

I Have a Memory

Juanita Mitil

Last night I was with my black man
and I have a memory.
I have a memory of his brown skin
I have a memory of himself
in my self . . .
Yes, I have a memory.

I have a memory of his strong body
his lean body, yes
of the feeling of my hands on him
his broad shoulders
his clean back . . .
I have a memory.

But I have a memory of his self
soul, spirit, flesh and all
coming and going like some kind of god.
I have a memory a very rich memory
of this man's love.

And I will always have a memory
of his sweet charm
his warm kisses
his wet body next to mine.
I'll have a memory of this man's manness
all my life.

From *Smoke, Lilies and Jade*

R. Bruce Nugent

Alex could feel Beauty's hair on his forehead . . . breathe normally
. . . breathe normally . . . could feel Beauty's breath on his nostrils
and lips . . . and it was clean and faintly colored with tobacco . . .
breathe normally Alex . . . Beauty's lips were nearer . . . Alex closed
his eyes . . . how did one act . . . his pulse was hammering . . .
from wrists to finger tip . . . wrist to finger tip . . . Beauty's lips
touched his . . . his temples throbbed . . . throbbed . . . his pulse
hammered from wrist to finger tip . . . Beauty's breath came short now
. . . softly staccato . . . breathe normally Alex . . . you are asleep
. . . Beauty's lips touched his . . . breathe normally . . . and pressed
. . . pressed hard . . . cool . . . his body trembled . . . breathe
normally Alex . . . Beauty's lips pressed cool . . . cool and hard . . .
how much pressure does it take to waken one . . . Alex sighed . . .
moved softly . . . how does one act . . . Beauty's hair barely touched
him now . . . his breath was faint on . . . Alex's nostrils . . . and
lips . . . Alex stretched and opened his eyes . . . Beauty was looking
at him . . . propped on one elbow . . . cheek in his palm . . .
Beauty spoke . . . scratch my head please Dulce . . . Alex was breathing normally now . . . propped against the bed head . . . Beauty's

head in his lap . . . Beauty spoke . . . I wonder why I like to look at some things Dulce . . . things like smoke and cats . . . and you . . . Alex's pulse no longer hammered from . . . wrist to finger tip . . . wrist to finger tip . . . the rose dusk had become blue night . . . and soon . . . soon they would go out into the blue . . . .

the little church was crowded . . . warm . . . the rows of benches were brown and sticky . . . Harold was there . . . and Constance and Langston and Bruce and John . . . there was Mr. Robeson . . . how are you Paul . . . a young man was singing . . . Caver . . . Caver was a very self assured young man . . . such a dream . . . poppies . . . black poppies . . . they were applauding . . . Constance and John were exchanging notes . . . the benches were sticky . . . a young lady was playing the piano . . . fair . . . and red calla lilies . . . who had ever heard of red calla lilies . . . such a dream . . . red calla lilies . . . Alex left . . . down the narrow streets . . . fy-ah . . . up the long noisy stairs . . . fy-ahs gonna bu'n ma soul . . . his head felt swollen . . . expanding . . . contracting . . . expanding . . . contracting . . . he had never been like this before . . . expanding . . . contracting . . . it was that . . . fy-ah . . . fy-ah Lawd . . . and the cocktails . . . and Beauty . . . he felt two cool strong hands on his shoulders . . . it was Beauty . . . lie down Dulce . . . Alex lay down . . . Beauty . . . Alex stopped . . . no no . . . don't say it . . . Beauty mustn't know . . . Beauty couldn't understand . . . are you going to lie down too Beauty . . . the light went out expanding . . . contracting . . . he felt the bed sink as Beauty lay beside him . . . his lips were dry . . . hot . . . the palms of his hands so moist and cool . . . Alex partly closed his eyes . . . from beneath his lashes he could see Beauty's face over his . . . nearer . . . nearer . . . Beauty's hair touched his forehead now . . . he could feel his breath on his nostrils and lips . . . Beauty's breath came short . . . breathe normally Beauty . . . breathe normally . . . Beauty's lips touched his . . . pressed hard . . . cool . . . opened slightly . . . Alex opened his eyes . . . into Beauty's . . . parted his lips . . . Dulce . . . Beauty's breath was hot and short . . . Alex ran his hand through Beauty's hair . . . Beauty's lips pressed hard against his teeth . . . Alex trembled . . . could feel Beauty's body . . . close against his . . . hot . . . tense . . . white . . . and soft . . . soft . . . soft . . . .

up . . . up . . . slow . . . jerk up . . . up . . . not fast . . . not glorious . . . but slow . . . up . . . up into the sun . . . slow

. . . sure like fate . . . poise on the brim . . . the brim of life . . .
two shining rails straight down . . . Melva's head was on his shoulder
. . . his arm was around her . . . poise . . . the down . . . gasping
. . . straight down . . . straight like sin . . . down . . . the curving
shiny rail rushed up to meet them . . . hit the bottom then . . . shoot
up . . . fast . . . glorious . . . up into the sun . . . Melva gasped
. . . Alex's arm tightened . . . all goes up . . . then down . . .
straight like hell . . . all breath squeezed out of them . . . Melva's
head on his shoulder . . . up . . . up . . . Alex kissed her . . .
down . . . they stepped out of the car . . . walking music . . . now
over to the Ferris Wheel . . . out and up . . . Melva's hand was soft in
his . . . out and up . . . over mortals . . . mortals drinking nectar
. . . five cents a glass . . . her cheek was soft on his . . . up . . . up
. . . till the world seemed small . . . tiny . . . the ocean seemed tiny
and blue . . . up . . . up and out . . . over the sun . . . the tiny
red sun . . . Alex kissed her . . . up . . . up . . . their tongues
touched . . . up . . . seventh heaven . . . the sea had swallowed the
sun . . . up and out . . . her breath was perfumed . . . Alex kissed
her . . . drift down . . . soft . . . soft . . . the sun had left the sky
flushed . . . drift down . . . soft down . . . back to earth . . . visit
the mortals sipping nectar at five cents a glass . . . Melva's lips brushed
his . . . then out among the mortals . . . and the sun had left a flush
on Melva's cheeks . . . they walked hand in hand . . . and the moon
came out . . . they walked in silence on the silver strip . . . and the
sea sang for them . . . they walked toward the moon . . . we'll hang
our hats on the crook of the moon Melva . . . softly on the silver strip
. . . his hands molded her features and her cheeks were soft and warm to
his touch . . . where is Adrian . . . Alex . . . Melva trod silver . . .
Alex trod sand . . . Alex trod sand . . . the sea *sang* for her . . .
Beauty . . . her hand felt cold in his . . . Beauty . . . the sea *dinned*
. . . Beauty . . . he led the way to the train . . . and the train dinned
. . . Beauty . . . dinned . . . dinned . . . her cheek *had* been soft
. . . Beauty . . . Beauty . . . her breath *had* been perfumed . . .
Beauty . . . Beauty . . . the sands *had* been silver . . . Beauty . . .
Beauty . . . they left the train . . . Melva walked music . . . Melva
said . . . don't make me blush again . . . and kissed him . . . Alex
stood on the steps after she left him and the night was black . . . down
long streets to . . . Alex lit a cigarette . . . and his heels clicked . . .
Beauty . . . Melva . . . Beauty . . . Melva . . . and the smoke
made the night blue . . .

    Melva had said . . . don't make me blush again . . . and kissed him
. . . and the street had been blue . . . one *can* love two at the same

time . . . Melva had kissed him . . . one *can* . . . and the street had been blue . . . one *can* . . . and the room was clouded with blue smoke . . . drifting vapors of smoke and thoughts . . . Beauty's hair was so black . . . and soft . . . blue smoke from an ivory holder . . . was that why he loved Beauty . . . one *can* . . . or because his body was beautiful . . . and white and warm . . . or because his eyes . . . one *can* love . . . . . .

Tell Me You Love Me

Gloria Wade-Gayles

Tell me you love me
NOW
not tomorrow
NOW

Tell me in this place
I have entered naked
to embrace you
to be clothed
by your passion
NOW.

Tell me you love me
with words that speak my name
with eyes that cameo
my passion-flushed face

with strokes
and caresses
and oils

and wet kisses
and moving hands
that journey
from the North
to the South of me
without missing
pleasure poles
that run from the East
to the West of me
to my center.

Tell me you love me
NOW
and I will hold my breath
until
you tell me again
tomorrow
and tomorrow
and . . .

Poetica Erotica

Naomi Nelson

Patiently
she waited . . .
longing,
throbbing
she waited.

Thought
of masturbation,
considered a lover,
dreamed of another.

Felt the thrust
of drumrolls.
Still she waited.

Hot summer nights
lulled by cricket cries
carry the weight of
eons past.

Break the night.
She stretched.
Magenta skies
irradiate pulsating
scarlet inclinations.

She bathed in the
sparkling light,
bedazzled by the
brilliance of celestial
horizons, she danced.

Danced naked.
She twirled under
the light of a
poet's moon.

Forgetting all passion.
Forfeiting old lovers.
Denying masturbation.
Voiding all dreams
that came too quickly.
She slid into a magenta
space, tumbled into caverns
of Deir el-Bahri.

Escorted by Amon Ra
she came quickly. She
who once embraced the Gods.
Daughter of Ahmose.

Drunk from the currents
of the Nile, she swam
swiftly.
At the first cataract
she rested.
Remembering the salty
taste of his sweat,
their bodies clutched,
deeply rooted, forever
tied, like the trunk
of a tree . . . a baobab
with roots sinking deep
into the black earth.

Sunrise, Africa.
Crack the dawn.

She danced at Thebes
til the Gods deserted
her amidst the false
doors and inner chambers.

She ran. Frantically
searching for the grand
court, the sacred court,
where all love was nurtured.
where all eyes stretched for
the Sirius Star . . .
She searched the Valley
of the Kings where now
only dust remained, where
once there had been a vision.

She longed for blue turquoise
walls and incrustated hieroglyphs.
She desired pyramidal protection
and the wing spread of Isis.

No blue Nile waters this morn.
No blue Nile waters inundate
this violet season.

Parched, she searched
for a sacred reef raft.
Where were the sacred halls?
Where was the Nile?
She lay on the hot sands
amidst the jackal cries
in a space that once graced
the head of a sphinx . . .
and waited.

Patiently, she waited.
Total devastation and
annihilation is the end
result of a world that
forgets what it is to live,
she thought . . .
as she waited.

From *Valide*

Godze 1783

Barbara Chase-Riboud

PALMIRE: How can I be yours?
I am not even mine!
—VOLTAIRE, *Mahomet*, 1714

Naksh-i-dil opened her eyes one moment before the harem bell, a wooden machine fixed with iron hammers, rang the hour. It was five ante meridien. The wooden bell announced sunrise and sunset, mealtime and prayertime, reverie and curfew, each day at the same hours. Topkapi was regulated with a precision that only the Black Eunuch, who held supreme but invisible power, could modify. It was now more than eighteen months since she had stood before Sultan Abdulhamid in the harem gardens, and it had been the last time she had seen him or Kizlar Aga. Had she been abandoned forever in this godforsaken cell to die of boredom, isolated and solitary for the rest of her life? Naksh-i-dil's green eyes moved like those of a small trapped animal. She was fifteen years three months old, and she wanted to live!

· ·

"Mistress is ready for her bath?" asked Issit.
"Your Mistress is going to the baths with me," came a lovely voice from the doorway.

Naksh-i-dil looked up in surprise and real pleasure. It was not Hadidge, but her beloved Fatima.

The baths were the harem's theater. Kadines, Ikbals, Odalisques and Gedicli went, as did Fatima and Naksh-i-dil, in groups of two or three or in veritable troops of ten or fifteen, carrying cushions, rugs, toilet articles, sweets and sometimes their dinners. There in the innumerable cells and dimly lit great hall, long bars of light fell on a hundred women and their slaves, nude, or wearing silken gauze shirts. They carried perfumed towels, lotions and henna as if to a sacred place. "The most sacred element, according to our Prophet Mohammed, is water," Fatima said.

There were Odalisques as white as snow side by side with Gedicli as black as ebony; the Sultan's powerful Kadines and Ikbals who represented the panorama of ideal Turkish beauty. They had heavy hips and thighs, small waists and torsos, high bosoms, minuscule feet and hands, endless black silken hair in thousands of tiny plaits, invisible mouths and overwhelming black eyes. Others, younger, were more lithe, long, and with hair so short they resembled young boys. There were Circassians with hair of gold falling to their knees; Armenians with a hundred black tresses spread out over breasts and shoulders; Greeks with hair divided into a thousand separate, disordered coils that gave the effect of enormous wigs. One had an amulet around her neck, another a string of garlic around her head to combat an eye infection. Some had tattoos on the palms of their hand, their arms, their backs and buttocks. Naksh-i-dil and Fatima took in the gracious and bizarre groups without joining any. There were women smoking stretched out on Oriental carpets, others having their hair brushed by slaves. There were women embroidering, women singing, laughing, rinsing their bodies with enormous sponges. Some moaned under the hands of massaging slaves, others screamed under the cold showers, or perspired beneath woolen towels. Arranged in circles or grouped in corners, they gossiped about their neighbors. And in unveiling their bodies, they unveiled their souls. Scattered phrases reached Naksh-i-dil's ears: "I am so beautiful," or "Do you realize you are more beautiful than I?" Another said, "I'm passable," or "I cannot deny that I am upset about this blemish." Someone would reproach a friend or another Gozde with "But look at Farahshah, how fat she's gotten eating all those dolmas . . ." "Rice balls are better," another would reply complacently. And when there was a Kadine or an Ikbal present, she would be surrounded and asked a thousand questions or offered courtesies, for she represented power.

Souls shriveled in the endless steam and running fountains without any of the restraints that education could give. They dissolved into excessive and brutal passion and never evolved into anything but an instinctive desire for youth and beauty. All these provocative curves hid the infantile characters, the most shameless caprices, pursued with fury which had to be satisfied at any price.

She had noticed, especially in the baths, that here the women, inferior by birth and education and far from men who would by nature restrain them, fell into the habit of using the most crude and incredible language. They knew no nuance of expression. They spoke in a language as nude as their bodies. They loved obscenity, dirty words, filthy jokes, which now made her blush in comprehension. From those lovely, languorous and perfectly formed mouths came the most obscene, impertinent and gross language imaginable, mordant and insolent. All the frustrations and helplessness found expression in the language of the gutter; curses, insults, inexpressible lewdness were propounded in Greek, Russian, Persian, Arabic, Turkish, Polish, Lithuanian, Bosnian, Rumanian, Albanian, Egyptian and Hebrew. The walls of the harem were covered with crude graffiti.

And the tyranny the inmates had endured was transferred to their peers or their inferiors. It was a tyranny more capricious than that of the most ruthless despot since it was administered by the powerless. Fatima had seen riots break out in the baths, mêlées of incredible violence and beauty, as raw and nude flesh massed into one sensuous animal of twenty arms, legs, breasts, heads, shoulders, hips, knees. She watched now the curve of an arm draped almost in an attitude of flight; a flexed knee, open thighs, bent backs, heads thrown back in attitudes that could be ecstasy or the last throes of death; hands pressed on every part of the body absently. As if in desire to touch oneself or stem an open wound. The heavy mist and the slow movements seemed more a vision than reality. Heads, arms, shoulders appeared and disappeared in waves of steam that supplemented one another. Barely discernible features would suddenly become as sharp as a painted porcelain tile, a disembodied hand would reach out, a voice from nowhere would suddenly ring out in laughter, the heavy swish of water on tile and marble, the tap of wooden patterns, sighs and whispers unneedful of a national language to be understood rose on the hot air. Long tresses of wet hair gleamed on white shoulders. Rosy nipples and white turbans shot with gold thread, the splash of cold water on warm skin, dark hands handling the heavy hair of an Odalisque, raised arms arranging a chignon of red-blond tresses, the flash of a ruby earring in a pierced ear, the slap of flesh against flesh . . . all this was the baths where Fatima and Naksh-i-dil were washed, shaved, steamed, perfumed and purified every single afternoon. Fatima and Naksh-i-dil sat side by side in silence. Fatima glanced at the Gozde, but she seemed lost in thoughts of her own. The baths were not only a stretching out of endless time, Fatima knew, but a savoring of forgetfulness, a detachment comparable to that of a narcotic. Naksh-i-dil's eyes had glazed over, but she was not, as Fatima imagined, in a state of detachment or forgetful-ness. Naksh-i-dil was remembering her first true lesson of slavery. . . .

The Kiaya had led her into a small cabinet in the baths, and Naksh-i-dil had trembled instinctively, as if she realized some ritual was about to take place. She had made no protest as her transparent shirt was lifted by the Kiaya and pulled over her head, leaving her totally nude. The Kiaya had then sat down heavily on the stone bench lining the tiny cubicle.

Wordlessly the Kiaya had reached over and pulled her over her knees so that her torso rested on the Kiaya's outspread thighs. Naksh-i-dil's head was thrown back, her neck arched and exposed, her legs stretched open and bent with the heels flat on the warm tiled floor. She had cried out, but was too afraid to move. She had never felt so open, so exposed, so vulnerable. With all the expertise and tenderness at her disposal, the Kiaya began to explore her body with her hands, testing her reactions. She had realized that the Kiaya was required to gauge to the narrowest guess the erotic and sensual possibilities of her new charge. She had gone about her job coldly but not sadistically. It was part of her responsibili-ties. Her huge hands had caressed her innocent flesh, pressing and pulling the nipples, which had become erect at the first touch of the Kiaya's hands, testing for firmness, texture, the rising of the blood to the surface skin, the odor, the beauty and color of its complexion, its softness. The Gozde's navel was perfectly placed, said the Kiaya, her neck was an opu-lent, round column with the required three rings of beauty.

Suddenly Naksh-i-dil had begun involuntary movements in response to the insistent hands of the Kiaya. A moan had escaped her lips. The Kiaya's hand had ridden down the lifted rib cage, waist and flanks of the childish body laid across her knees. Naksh-i-dil had opened her legs wider, and the Kiaya's fingers had entered the soft tiny slit between her legs; she had opened the lips and inspected her *kouss*. "It is royal," the Kiaya had said, "a fit throne for a Sultan." The Kiaya's hand softly ca-ressed the wide-spaced, hard, round breast of her prisoner. With a soft downward thrust of her fingers, the Kiaya had moved her hand on her, careful not to bring about full climax, until the Gozde had been bathed in perspiration and writhing with unknown and unrealized pleasure. Her back had arched as tightly as a bow. The Kiaya had bent over her flexed body and kissed her on the mouth. She had opened her lips and allowed the Kiaya's tongue to enter and explore at will. Violently she had clung to the Kiaya's mouth; her arms, which had been dangling, had come up around the Kiaya's neck. But Kurrum Kadine had pushed them back brusquely.

"You are to make no move, Naksh-i-dil. You are only to submit. You have no right to take the liberty to return my kisses . . ."

As if to underscore the breach in decorum, the Kiaya had lifted Naksh-i-dil's legs onto her own stomach with the crook of her arm and had thrust the fingers of her left hand rhythmically into her widened kouss, careful not to harm the precious hymen. Methodically the Kiaya had continued until Naksh-i-dil had swooned with pleasure, crying out as the other woman brought her to her first climax. The Kiaya had watched her open-eyed reaction coldly. Naksh-i-dil found herself in the throes of a muscular spasm which she hadn't known she possessed, but which had pleased the Kiaya. In the months that followed, she had learned all the techniques of lovemaking in the Kiaya's repertoire, but her own sensuality frightened her. Naksh-i-dil had wept from the prolonged pleasure the Kiaya had given her, which had also pleased the other woman.

Kurrum Kadine had allowed her to touch with her small hands the pendulous amplitude of her breasts and place her hands between her thighs. Next time, she would show her how to bring pleasure to another woman, she had said. For the moment, the Kiaya had taught her to bring pleasure to herself. She was to try it alone in her rooms . . . every night.

"You are to allow no one to touch you as I have, Naksh-i-dil. Do you understand? If you do, *everyone* will know it. I will know it and you will be spoiled forever for the Sultan. He will never touch you. . . . You believe me?"

"Yes," she had whispered, still lying supine on the outstretched knees of her mentor.

The Kiaya had slipped her hands under Naksh-i-dil's hips and cupped her buttocks, opening and closing them in rhythm to Naksh-i-dil's moans. The Kiaya had continued to do so, faster and faster until, without touching her, she forced Naksh-i-dil to experience those strange spasms again and again as the Kiaya bore down on a new place. "A good sign . . . perfect for the two doors of love," the Kadine had said.

"Now, Naksh-i-dil, touch yourself like this. Yes. Now. See if you can make your own pleasure, but think of the Sultan . . . think only of him . . . not so fast . . . no. Harder . . . now softer . . . now downward . . ." The Kiaya had watched, noting how she did so, and what movements brought her pleasure. There were women who could satisfy themselves without touching themselves at all, Kurrum had told her, by merely closing their thighs. The Kiaya had said that the next time she would paint the nipples and the nether lips of Naksh-i-dil with hashish . . . it evoked a most enduring effect. Kurrum Kadine had then bent down toward Naksh-i-dil and with surprising strength had picked her up in her arms and laid her face up on the marble slab, her legs apart hanging over the edge, not touching the floor. Then she had taken Naksh-i-dil's small narrow foot in her hands and covered it with kisses. The Kiaya had moved upon the tiny inert foot with more and more pressure and force until the narrowest part was inside her. Then she had flung herself upon the outstretched Godze, clasping the edge of the marble couch, forcing more and more of the flesh inside her with violent turbaned head flung back, her eyes closed. Finally she had shrieked with pleasure. It had been a strange animal sound, half bird, half beast. A sound that Naksh-i-dil had never heard before . . . it revolted her as nothing ever had. . . .

Naksh-i-dil told Fatima of her humiliation at the hands of the Kiaya. "It is nothing," sighed Fatima, and she put her arms around Naksh-i-dil's neck and held her while her friend sobbed with shame and incomprehension.

"Desire," explained Fatima, "should not lead only to procreation. It is a reality of life. . . . The pleasure that accompanies its satisfaction is comparable to none other. It should make us dream of the sumptuousness promised us in paradise. . . ." Fatima looked away. The Kiaya had only been doing her duty . . . testing Naksh-i-dil's reaction to a real phallus —that of the Sultan.

Naksh-i-dil and Fatima left the baths. They returned through the odors of perfumes, the murmur of water, the shadow of slaves; and the mountains of Asia, remote, cold, silent, pierced through the black steel of the grilled windows with a rustling branch of honeysuckle, evoking an inexpressible melancholy: fragile impressions that expressed themselves in time, trailing, inconclusive gestures, unfinished sentences, unstructured thoughts and a kind of blindness of the mind.

Tears were not tolerated in the harem.

405 Scott Street

Reginald Lockett

pushin a hard forty, ten years away
from a half century of livin,
he down shifts from third into second
and hooks a right off fulton onto scott
down the hill, towards mcallister,
where the apartment buildin
now conjures up enough strength
to withstand the bombardment
of another quick decade
comin at it like an angry, irrational mob
bent on its total destruction.
he knows it well
because in that same building, on the same floor,
right across the hall from each other,
seven years apart, he'd loved two women.
yes, as a grad student at twenty-two,
when the only thing he was drivin
was that pair of adidas, or them frye boots
when the weather was bad, it was vera.
long, tall, fine high yella drink of water

vera with the flamin red, sky high 'fro
vera, four or five years older,
who was gettin down with a movement
for a people oppressed and hungry for change.
and oh! the motion that vast ocean
when them ripe lean, creamy banana legs
were spread out beneath him,
thrustin upwards so hard it, it damn near
knocked him clean on out that fourth floor
bedroom window one wintry night
two weeks before finals.
vera. cool drink of lemonade vera,
gettin down with the people, the movement
and him
then at thirty, when that buildin
had begun deterioratin so suddenly,
connye was there in the apartment across the hall,
where a daughter's curses and disrespect
for her mother had flowed so profusely
seven years before.
all one-hundred and eighty pounds of sweet,
delectable chocolate goodness there to listen,
comfort and drive him into uncharted realms
of ecstasy with gargantuous number fifty
double d's good, skilled head
and tons and tons of iowa farm girl passion
every wednesday or thursday night
on schedule
when all that desperate desire, that just couldn't wait,
came tumblin down out of both of them.
no matter the time, he'd
somehow get there from way out in the mission
for just one more taste of that chocolate
that melted into his heart
as well as in his mouth.

Eroticism in Sub-Saharan African Films

Françoise Pfaff

Since the advent of film, eroticism (which appeals to the viewer's voyeurism and provides vicarious sensuous gratification) has been an essential and often very profitable component of numerous Western motion pictures. Under such circumstances is eroticism the necessary, even indispensible, illustration of love within the story that unfolds on the screen? Does it match a new social permissiveness? Is eroticism in film a way to confront visual taboos and fulfill, without punishment, sexual fantasies or drives? Does eroticism lend itself to cinema because of its aesthetic qualities? Should eroticism be analyzed in a realistic context or in a metaphoric, even subversive, perspective? These questions should be considered when attempting to delineate the nature and function of eroticism in sub-Saharan African films.

The most common types of sexually suggestive poses in sub-Saharan African cinema are shots of heterosexual couples walking hand in hand, as seen in Kramo Lacine's *Djeli* (Ivory Coast, 1981) or Ababacar Samb's *Et la neige n'était plus* (Senegal, 1965); and/or of couples kissing while standing and embracing, as filmed in Timité Bassori's *Sur la dune de la solitude* (Ivory Coast, 1964), Jean-Pierre Dikongue Pipa's *Le Prix de la liberté* (Cameroon, 1978), Ola Balogun's *Black Goddess* (Nigeria, 1978), and Kwaw Ansah's *Love Brewed in the African Pot* (Ghana, 1980). Scenes in bed appear in films such as Bassori's *La Femme au couteau* (Ivory Coast, 1968), where actress Danielle Alloh sits on a bed fully dressed, and leans toward actor/director Timité Bassori, who is in pajamas under a sheet; or Souleymane Cissé's *Baara* (Mali, 1978), in which a woman and her lover lie naked in bed under sheets after their adulterous sexual encounter. In *Baara,* there are few signs of passion or affection between the two: the woman's companion holds her briefly before pouring himself a glass of whiskey. This scene underscores their middle-class status, as well as the sexual independence of a married female shop manager.

In *L'Herbe sauvage* (Ivory Coast, 1977), an Henri Duparc love story, the man shows more interest in his partner. Although naked in bed, the couple is covered by a sheet, but the filmmaker emphasizes the contrast between actress Vivian Touré's dark-skinned breasts and the light-colored sheet. Later, in a shower scene, the shiny, plastic beauty of her bronze body is underscored by her slow movements and the flow of running water. In the frame, however, her naked body appears only from the waist up.

Most sex scenes in sub-Saharan African films are rather static and emotionless. Exceptions include such films as *Sur la dune de la solitude* and Dikongue Pipa's *Muna Moto* (Cameroon, 1974). *Sur la dune de la solitude* is a modernized version of the legend of Mamy Watta, the seductive, mermaid-like temptress who lures men into her deep-water realm. In this early work, Timité Bassori offers several lyrical and poetic shots of a Westernized couple's amorous games. Walking at night on an Abidjan beach, Elia attempts to embrace Enje, the beautiful woman he has just met, but she playfully escapes. After he catches up with her, the two finally disrobe and enter the sea, where they kiss. They have on bathing suits, but the camera lingers lasciviously on their slender, well-shaped bodies. Then Elia picks Enje up, carries her out of the water, and lays her down on the white sand. Afterwards, Enje confesses that she is a reincarnation of the legendary West African mermaid. They then embrace, and the director cuts the shot by fading in on their half-naked bodies.

Another technique used by African filmmakers is the exchange of languorous, love-filled gazes as a part of the seductive process. Such erotic gazes occur in Ousmane Sembene's *Black Girl* (Senegal, 1966) and *Ceddo* (1976); in Med Hondo's *Soleil O* (Mauritania, 1969) and Cissé's *Finyé* (Mali, 1982), a film about the forbidden love between two adolescents. Since interracial relationships are rarely depicted in African cinema, of particular interest is a scene in *Soleil O* portraying the casual affair between an African accountant and a Parisian woman. The woman takes the initiative while they are waiting for a bus. At one point, a close-up shows the woman with a slightly open mouth and twitching lips, images of sexual desire in Western films. Such representations of sexually aggressive females are more frequent in Western than in African films. One has to remember, however, that *Soleil O* was shot entirely in France by an expatriate filmmaker whose aim was probably to reach non-African as well as African audiences.

African directors, most of whom are male, depict the naked female body as the primary object of desire. They portray the female body in an incidental, even utilitarian fashion, making it a part of the narrative. Examples include the opening shot of *Ceddo,* where a bare-breasted woman goes to fetch water, or Henri Duparc's *Bal poussière* (Ivory Coast, 1988), in which topless women bathe in the sea. In a bathing scene in *Yeelen* (Mali, 1987), Cissé shows the male protagonist's nude body and his mate's naked breasts; but their gestures are commonplace rather than erotic. These filmmakers use nude female bodies in a static fashion, underscoring their symbolic significance rather than their seductive qualities. In *Xala* (Senegal, 1974), a film which describes the sexual and economic impotence of a middle-aged, polygamous businessman, Sembene offers a back shot of the man's third wife, who lies motionless and indifferent on the nuptial bed. The middle third of the wife's naked back also appears in the foreground of *Xala*'s poster. In both the poster and the film the erotic connotation of the female body is suppressed, while the body's symbolic significance is highlighted.

Désiré Ecaré uses a different approach in depicting a woman's body in his 1970 film *A nous deux, France* (Ivory Coast), which satirically portrays the life of Ivorians in Paris. The acculturated African protagonist is married to France, a French woman by whom he has a child. One scene shows France's husband, Tarzan, strumming her undressed body. In spite of France's passivity, Tarzan's rhythmic hand movements and the color contrast of the couple's skins evoke erotic reactions in both African and non-African audiences, especially since Ecaré visually transgresses the taboos against interracial love.

Since most West African filmmakers have lived or studied in Europe, they are aware that prolonged shots of a naked body in motion have highly erotic connotations. In *Black Girl,* Sembene filmed Diouana from the back, in the process of undressing. Later, in *Ceddo,* a stylized and otherwise stern epic, the Senegalese filmmaker portrays a sensuous princess, letting his camera linger on the princess's half-naked body as she walks toward the sea. As she steps into the water, she removes the short piece of cloth around her waist. At this moment, Sembene opts for erotic suggestion—a shot of the cloth falling to the princess's feet—rather than direct visualization. Then the director offers a full shot of the princess's partially covered body as she slowly and provocatively returns to her hammock under the watchful eyes of the ceddo and of Fara, the male griot. Shortly thereafter, the princess goes to get a phallus-shaped gourd of fresh water, which she offers to her captor. In *Finyé,* Cissé also handles nudity with subtlety and restraint. Batrou, a Westernized high-school student, invites her boyfriend to join her bath. The filmmaker emphasizes the purity and beauty of the young couple's amorous adventures, but his close-up of Batrou's breasts dripping with water—a close-up which isolates and emphasizes the breasts—seems to be an erotic celebration of her beauty.

In African motion pictures, sexual desire is often expressed verbally. In *Ajani-Ogun* (1975), *Muzik Man* (1976), and *Black Goddess* (1978), the Nigerian filmmaker Ola Balogun uses songs and serenades to express the love of his male characters for the women of their dreams. *Xala* includes sexually explicit dialogue in which older men joke about the deflowering of a virgin; in Hondo's *Sarraounia* (Mauritania, Burkina Faso, 1986) African women discuss the intimate attributes and sexual preferences of 19th-century French soldiers; and in *Yeelen,* the young protagonist denies seducing the wife of the village chief by emphasizing the autonomy of his penis, which triggers laughter in African and non-African audiences.

Although sexual images appear in a number of sub-Saharan African films, *Touki Bouki* (Senegal, 1973) by Djibril Diop Mambety and *Visages de femmes* (Ivory Coast, 1985) by Ecaré are the motion pictures most often cited by critics for their eroticism. Mambety presents an intellectualized, ritualistic, and metaphoric depiction of intercourse, while Ecaré offers a naturalistic rendition of it. *Touki Bouki* reflects the rules of conventional narrative and decries the sociocultural alienation of young Africans. The film portrays Mory, a former shepherd, who lives in Dakar, where he meets Anta, a young university student. The love scene between Mory and Anta is thematically and stylistically erotic because it prolongs and defers, through cuts and repetitions, the viewer's vicarious release: Anta undresses on the beach, revealing only the upper part of her body, but the scene shifts unexpectedly as she prepares to lie down. (Mory's body is not shown in the entire sequence.) The next scene depicts the slaughter of sheep, which metaphorically suggests, perhaps, sexual violence or the rupture of the hymen, and a full shot of foaming waves hitting shiny black rocks, a symbol of the couple's passion. A subsequent close-up of Anta's fingers clenching a Dogon cross, a Malian fertility symbol, on the rear of Mory's motorbike, accompanied by off-screen orgasmic sounds, finally confirms that Anta has actually made love with Mory. Ironically, this scene is one of the most innovative and puritanical love encounters of African cinema.

Visages de femmes humorously depicts the changing condition of women in the Ivory Coast. It also includes the most explicit act of intercourse in the history of African cinema: shots of a licentious Eden in which bronze bodies dive into a river and copulate in the water, surrounded by thick, erect trees. Lovemaking is initiated by a young African village woman (a rare occurrence in African motion pictures), who seduces her Westernized lover. Furthermore, *Visages de femmes* offers the only shot of both partners' genitals, as well as shots of various sexual postures. Although some critics considered the scene a pantheistic representation of love in its primeval beauty, *Visages de femmes* was banned in the Ivory Coast for eight months, probably because of its sexual audacity. The film also triggered a controversy between the filmmaker and festival participants in the 1987 Pan-African Film Festival of Ouagadougou (FESPACO). Probably because of its eight-minute love scene, *Visages de femmes* was very successful in Paris, where it played simultaneously in eight movie theaters. Ecaré's film drew large audiences, whose interest might have been fueled by the stereotypical myth of uninhibited African sexuality.

Eroticism is still incidental and scarce in sub-Saharan African films, perhaps because of the puritanism of traditional African cultures or because filmmakers consciously or unconsciously want to destroy the stereotype of the sexually potent African. The fact is that African films and literature are generally characterized by a rather pious chastity, which is especially surprising given the fact that many initiatory erotic tales are contained in African oral literatures. Can one, therefore, attribute such puritanism in Africa to the influence of Islam and Christianity, two religions which have linked sex to procreation rather than to erotic pleasure? For Abiyi Ford, a film theorist and practitioner at Howard University, erotica is not often found in these motion pictures because they derive from an environment in which

> sex is not the mysterious taboo it is in the West, where showing publicly something that should be hidden and done in the dark is a prime force and device to sell anything from cars to movies. In other cultures sex is a natural thing, nothing to be frowned upon, and it does not have the same voyeuristic impact it has on Judeo-Christian Westerners.

Because sub-Saharan filmmakers are to a large extent still influenced by traditional values and because many have a profound sociopolitical commitment, eroticism is rather limited in their works. Nevertheless, as these film practitioners and their audiences become increasingly Westernized and urbanized, it is to be expected that their motion pictures will give a larger place to the kinds of commercially beneficial, sexually suggestive scenes which are rather frequently found in present-day Western cinema. Let us hope that such works will not achieve a cultural bastardization which may prove highly detrimental to their societies and to their cinematic art.

After/Play

John A. Williams

In 1965 French editor Maurice Girodias compiled *The Olympia Reader,* made up of selections from *The Traveller's Companion* series. There were forty-one pieces, including works by some of the well-known eroticists, like Jean Genet, Henry Miller, the Marquis de Sade, Frank Harris, and John Cleland. Only two of the writers were women, Pauline Relage and Harriet Daimler. Two men used women's names. One Black writer was represented, Chester Himes with an excerpt from *Pinktoes.*

Given the importance Black people seem to have in the sexual fantasies of Whites in the United States and Europe (an impression that is often reflected in the way many Blacks see themselves), it is a wonder that only just now are we presented with an *Erotique Noire.*

But here it is, a lush potpourri of poetry, fiction, essay, and narrative, a sensual journey through the Black eroticism of four continents (as well as the Caribbean). If women were almost nonexistent in *The Olympia Reader,* here they are a multitude and, like the men, released from the conventions of the past, a situation some called "the sexual revolution." I think, however, Whites *always* believed Black people were sexually revolutionized. (A quarter of a century ago Black and White readers wondered why Max Red-dick, the protagonist in "The Man Who Cried I Am," seemed to be "doing it" all the time. I didn't think he was. A former professor of mine concluded that Max's last name was really two words symbolizing an overworked male organ.)

Sex, it seems to me, has always figured unselfconsciously in the everyday lives of Black Americans. (Drag out the best of the Richard Pryor albums.) Not that it wasn't special. It most certainly was (is). But it was taken for granted—like breathing. That it was in many ways not so considered by other, mainly White cultures may be seen in their religions and literatures. There would have been no need for biblical laws against adultery if there hadn't already been a considerable amount of it taking place.

The explorer/adventurer/writer Sir Richard Burton (1821–90) discovered extensive exoticism among the peoples he visited in Africa and the Middle East, which titillated the Victorians and gave rise to a genre of exotic, underground writing. Six years after Burton's death, *National Geographic* magazine published its first photograph of a bare-breasted woman. She was a Zulu bride (with her husband). Thirty years ago the French documentary *The Sky Above, The Mud Below* indulged in the same kind of "revelation" when it screened "a variety of primitive life" in New Guinea. One can cite endless examples of how extensively Whites view Black people as exotic and erotic.

Erotique Noire is, in fact, a righteous reaffirmation that sex beats just about everything, including greed, which is only worth celebrating if you avoid jail; and greed certainly isn't ever magical, while eroticism is. This collection continues the exploration into Black American eroticism first published in works like Linda Brent's *Incidents in the Life of a Slave Girl* (1861) and William Wells Brown's *Clotel* (1867 version) and *My Southern Home* (1880) and elsewhere, as noted by Sandra Y. Govan. The Black writers of the Harlem Renaissance and "The Jazz Age" were heirs to a perpetually renewing sexual freedom, as were later writers such as Ann Petry *(The Street)*, Margaret Walker ("Poppa Chicken"), and Gwen Brooks ("The Sundays of Satin-Legs Smith"). Their male counterparts were, to again name but a few, Ataway, Ellison, Hayden, Himes . . .

In short, the literature since then continues to work toward an erotic liberation that had always been found in the literatures of the ancient Egyptians and the Indians of Asia, as well as in their sculptures and ideograms.

Erotique Noire is a turning to the distant past in the language of the present with new sculptors and word-workers, some familiar, some not, but the mix is like sipping ambrosia. Only now and again does a shadow fall across the pages, driven by mention of condoms or, as R. Pope puts it, "Satan-Is-a-Bitch diseases," the darker reality of our times. But no plague, no disaster, nothing, has ever stopped Eros, who, after all, was born in Chaos. It is devoutly to be wished that this collection is only the first of several more to come.

NOTES ON CONTRIBUTORS

OPAL PALMER ADISA, Jamaica-born writer and storyteller of Caribbean and African tales, has lived in California since 1979. Her published works include *Traveling Women,* a poetry collection with Deborah Major; *Bake-Face and Other Guava Stories* and *Pina, the Many-Eyed Fruit.* Her plays have been produced in the Bay Area, where she teaches and is currently pursuing a doctorate in English and drama.

AHMASI became interested in poetry when he worked as the first cultural coordinator at the Langston Hughes Community Library and Cultural Center. His articles and poetry have been published in *Essence, Encore, Black Enterprise,* and the *Black Collegian.*

S. D. ALLEN is Assistant Professor and Coordinator of Cataloging Services at Kutztown University in Pennsylvania. Her current study centers around Jung's Great Mother archetype.

LUZ ARGENTINA CHIRIBOGA, a graduate of the Universidad Central of Ecuador, has written *La noche está llegando* (a collection of short stories), and *Bajo la piel de los tambores,* which was recently published by the Casa de la Cultura in Ecuador. She has published many articles and short stories, and, in 1986, she won the José de San Martín Fiction Award in Buenos Aires.

THELMA BALFOUR is a native of Memphis, Tennessee, where she is a full-time freelance writer for the Memphis in May International Festival, and a stringer for *USA Today* and *Newsweek*. She has studied astrology for twelve years and hosted an astrology program on a radio station. A Cancerian, she was born on June 30 with Gemini rising.

ROMARE BEARDEN, 1912–88, gained worldwide acclaim for his collages, which capture the myths, rituals, and rhythms of Black life in Harlem, Pittsburgh, and Mecklenburg County, North Carolina. Educated in New York and Paris, he is represented in every major exhibition of Afro-American artists, and his work has appeared on the covers of *Time, Fortune,* and the *New York Times Magazine*. He produced a series of richly textured erotic works, such as *Dream Images* and *Hidden Valley,* which depict nude figures in shadowed rooms and lush gardens.

ROSEANN P. BELL was a southern/world woman who began reading and writing erotica in the seventies. She produced a seven-year radio show, and edited or wrote newspaper articles, scholarly essays, and three books, among them *Sturdy Black Bridges: Visions of Black Women in Literature*. A former Associate Professor of English and African American Studies at the University of Mississippi, she was writing *Tales Black Sistren Tell* before her death in 1992.

LEE BEN is a poet, singer, songwriter, playwright, actor, martial artist, and filmmaker. He has participated in productions of the Neighborhood Gallery and the Alliance for Community Theater, as well as the Chakula Cha Iua Theater Company, both located in New Orleans. His performance credits include Tom Dent's *Ritual Murder,* Jeff Stetson's *The Meeting,* and Monroe Bean's *Eyes of the Devil.*

CHARLES L. BLOCKSON, curator of the Afro-American Collection at Temple University, is a bibliophile who has collected Black erotica for over twenty years. His seminal works include *Pennsylvania's Black History, Black Genealogy, The Underground Railroad in Pennsylvania, The Underground Railroad First Person Narrative,* and *One Hundred and One Influential Books By and About People of African Descent (1556–1982).*

SDIANE BOGUS is based in Turlock, California, where she teaches and writes energetically. Two of her publications are *Dykehands in Common Lives/Lesbian Lives,* and *Dykehands and Sutras, Erotic and Lyric.*

DENNIS BRUTUS was born in Salisbury, Southern Rhodesia (now Zimbabwe) and came to the United States in 1971. Chair of the Department of Black Community Education at the University of Pittsburgh and a prolific poet, his works include *Sirens, Knuckles, Boots, Letters to Martha, Poems From Algeria, A Simple Lust, China Poems, Stubborn Hope,* and *Salutes & Censures.*

JAN CAREW was born in Guyana (then British Guiana), and has lived in Jamaica, Ghana, Canada, and the United States. His works include *Black Midas, The Wild Coast, The Last Barbarian, Moscow Is Not My Mecca, Save the Last Dance For Me, The Twins of Llora,* and *Greneda: The*

Hour Will Strike Again. Although primarily a novelist, he has also written poetry, plays, and children's books.

SHIRLEY CARTER is a freelance artist, who lives and works in the Bay Area. Born in Des Moines, she grew up in California and Indiana. After obtaining a Bachelor of Fine Arts degree from the Herron School of Art, she won a Graduate Minority Fellowship to the University of California Berkeley, from which she received a Master of Fine Arts in 1992.

BARBARA CHASE-RIBOUD is a novelist, poet, and sculptor, whose first novel, *Sally Hemings* won the Janet Heidinger Kafka Prize for the best novel written by an American woman. She has also published two other novels, *Valide* and *Echo of Lions,* as well as two collections of poetry, *From Memphis to Peking* and *Portrait of a Nude Woman as Cleopatra.*

CHERI is a graduate of LeMoyne-Owen College in Memphis, Tennessee, where she majored in art. She presently works as a real estate affiliate broker. A divorcée and the mother of a fourteen-year-old daughter and of a four-year-old son, she describes herself as "pulsating, daring, sensitive and assertive."

ESPERANZA MALAVÉ CINTRÓN, who is of Puerto Rican descent, was born in Detroit and currently resides in upstate New York. She has received a Michigan Council for the Arts individual artist grant, the Judith Siegel Pearson Poetry Award, and a New York State Museum Award. Her first novella, *Shades,* is nearing completion.

WANDA COLEMAN recently completed a residency at the Djerassi Foundation. Her published books include *Heavy Daughter Blues (Poems and Stories), A War of Eyes,* and *Dicksboro Hotel.* Her new collection, *African Sleeping Sickness (New and Selected Writings),* will soon appear, and the first critical review of her work was published in the Fall 1989 *Black American Literature Forum.*

AFUA COOPER is a Jamaican-born poet living in Toronto, where she combines reggae and other Black musical forms with the written word. She has completed two books of poetry—*Breaking Chains* (1983) and *The Red Caterpillar on College Street* (1989)—and has recorded *Sunshine,* a collection of children's poetry. She has collaborated on two other record anthologies with Caribbean artists Louise Bennett and Jean Breeze.

STANLEY CYRUS, a professor of Spanish language and literature, was born in Grenada and has lived in the United States, where he taught at Howard University. A founding editor of the *Afro-Hispanic Review,* he has published extensively on the literature of Blacks in Ecuador, and his works include *El cuento negrista sudamericano: antología.*

DOLORES DA COSTA is the *nom de plume* of Miriam DeCosta-Willis.

DARYL DANCE, a Professor of English at Virginia Commonwealth University, has published *Shuckin' and Jivin': Folklore From Contemporary Black Americans, Folklore from Contemporary Jamaicans,* and *Long Gone: The*

Mecklenburg Six and the Theme of Escape in Black Folklore. She has also edited *Fifty Caribbean Writers: A Bio-Bibliographical and Critical Sourcebook.*

O. R. DATHORNE, born in Georgetown, British Guiana (now Guyana), received his M.A. and Ph.D. degrees from the University of London. A professor of English and Afro-American Studies, he has edited and written many works, including *Dumplings in the Soup, The Scholar-Man, Africa in Prose, Afro-World: Adventures in Ideas,* and *Caribbean Verse.*

MIRIAM DeCOSTA-WILLIS, Professor and Director of Graduate Studies in the African American Studies Department at the University of Maryland Baltimore County, edited *Blacks in Hispanic Literature,* and co-edited *Homespun Images: An Anthology of Black Memphis Writers and Artists* and *Double Stitch: Black Women Write About Mothers and Daughters.* Her work has appeared in *Libido: The Journal of Sex and Sensibility, Memphis* magazine, *Callaloo,* and other journals.

RENÉ DEPESTRE was born in Haiti and presently lives in southern France. His novels and works of poetry, and nonfiction include *Etincelles, Gerbe de sang, Le mât de cocagne, Pour la révolution, pour la poésie, Bonjour et adieu a la négritude, Alléluia pour une femme jardin,* and *Hadriana dans tous mes rêves.*

TOI DERRICOTTE, an award-winning poet, teaches creative writing at the University of Pittsburgh and lives with her husband and son in Potomac, Maryland. Her collections of poetry include *Natural Birth, Empress of the Death House,* and *Captivity.*

R. H. DOUGLAS, who has recently moved to Poughkeepsie, New York with her family, is the past Vice President of the Writers Union of Trinidad and Tobago. Her work has appeared in Trinidad's *The New Voices,* which published her short story, "Uncle Willie," in the March 1990 issue.

RITA DOVE has published *The Yellow House on the Corner,* and *Thomas and Beulah* (1986), which garnered the 1987 Pulitzer Prize in poetry. She has received numerous awards and honors from the National Endowment for the Arts, Ohio Arts Council, John Simon Guggenheim Fellowship, Rockefeller Foundation, and others. Her work, which includes poems, short stories, and essays, is well represented in anthologies.

TREY ELLIS is a young writer whose first novel, *Platitudes,* was recently published.

NELSON ESTUPIÑÁN BASS, one of Ecuador's most distinguished poets and novelists, has written many works, including *Canto negro por la luz: poemas para negros y blancos, El paraíso, El último río, Senderos brillantes, Toque de queda,* and *Cuando los guayacanes florecían,* recently translated into English by Henry J. Richards.

CHARLES FRYE is director of The Center for African and African-American Studies at Southern University, New Orleans. He has published seven books, including *The Peter Pan Chronicles,* published in 1989 in the *Callaloo* Fiction Series, and his most recent novel, *A Good Knight's Leap.*

CONSTANCE GARCÍA-BARRIO is a Philadelphia-based freelance writer, whose stories have appeared in *Antietam Review* and *Talk That Talk: An Anthology of African-American Storytelling.* She occasionally tells the truth, and has done so in more than 100 articles in publications like the *Philadelphia Inquirer* and *Essence.* She has a doctorate in Romance languages and is writing an historical novel.

P. J. GIBSON has written twenty-six plays, and her published works include *Long Time Since Yesterday, Brown Silk and Magenta Sunsets,* and *Konvergence.* She is currently working on a novel entitled *Neidyana,* as well as a collection of erotic short stories. Her many honors include a Shubert Fellowship for the study of dramatic writing, a grant from the National Endowment for the Arts, and two prestigious Audelco Awards.

BERYL GILROY was born in Guyana, and received a B.A. from the University College in London, an M.A. from Sussex University, and a Ph.D. from Century University. The author of *Black Teacher* (1976), *Frangipanni House* (1986), and a collection of poetry, she is a psychologist who runs a private clinic in England, working primarily with women of color.

MARITA GOLDEN's early works include an autobiographical narrative, *Migrations of the Heart,* and her first novel, *A Woman's Place.* Her second novel, *Long Distance Life,* published in 1989, was a bestseller, and deals, according to one reviewer, with "staying the course, living as fully and as well as one can, [and] cherishing whatever happiness and love one can find." Her latest novel, *And Do Remember Me,* will be published in 1992.

JEWELLE GOMEZ is the author of *Flamingoes and Bears,* a collection of poetry. Her essays and short stories have been widely anthologized in works like *The Black Women's Health Book* and *Serious Pleasure,* a collection of lesbian erotica. Her reviews have appeared in the *New York Times, The Village Voice, Gay Community News, Belles Lettres,* and *The Black Scholar.* She is completing a novel to be published by Firebrand Books.

SANDRA Y. GOVAN is Associate Professor of English at the University of North Carolina–Charlotte. She has published widely in the fields of African-American literature, popular culture, particularly science fiction, and women's literature. Although she has read her poetry in the Charlotte area, she has only recently come out of the closet with her creative writing.

ANN T. GREENE is a short story writer and librettist. Her work *The Mother of Three Sons* premiered at the 1990 Munich Biennale, and her fiction has appeared in *Callaloo.*

Lois Griffith is proud of her Barbadian roots. Her plays, *Cocoanut Lounge* and *Dance Hall Snapshots* were produced by the Nuyorican Theatre Festival; *Hoodlum Hearts* and *White Sirens* were also produced in New York. Her stories have appeared in *The Iowa Review, Ikon Magazine, Confirmations, Heresies,* and *Between C & D Magazine. Set in Our Ways* is a collection of stories in progress.

L. Edward Hardin works in two categories: children's art with text and mixed media with portraits. His drawing for *Erotique Noire* is his first effort at erotica, but he promises that it will not be his last. A native of Memphis, Tennessee, his drawings have been exhibited at the National Bank of Commerce and Memphis State University.

Claire Harris, born in Trinidad, writes and teaches in Canada. Her poetry has been anthologized in collections of Canadian and Caribbean writing. In 1985, *Fables From the Women's Quarters* won a Commonwealth First Book Poetry Prize, and *Traveling to Find a Remedy* won the Alberta Culture Poetry Prize in 1987. Her latest book is *Gathering to Parturition.*

Essex Hemphill is a poet, writer, performance artist, and editor of *Brother to Brother: New Writings by Black Gay Men* (1991). His poetry was featured in two critically-acclaimed, award-winning Black gay films: *Looking for Langston* and *Tongues Untied.* He is the author of two chapbooks, *Earth Life* (1985) and *Conditions* (1986), as well as *Ceremonies,* a collection of poetry to be published by Penguin/Plume.

Calvin Hernton, a professor of creative writing and of Black literature at Oberlin College, is the author of *The Sexual Mountain and Black Women Writers: Adventures in Sex, Literature, and Real Life* and of seven other books, including *Sex and Racism in America,* which has been translated into six languages. He recently served as technical consultant for the ABC television series "A Man Called Hawk."

Chester B. Himes was a prolific novelist and autobiographer, who lived for many years in France. His works include *If He Hollers, Let Him Go, The Big Gold Dream, The Real Cool Killers, The Heat's On, The Crazy Kill, Lonely Crusade, A Case of Rape, Blind Man With a Pistol, The Autobiography of Chester Himes, Black on Black, For Love of Imabelle, All Shot Up,* and *Cotton Comes to Harlem.*

Akua Lezli Hope has published works in *Contact II, Obsidian II, Confirmation, Extended Outlooks, The Iowa Review Anthology of American Women Writers,* and Isaac Asimov's *Science Fiction Magazine.* The recipient of several important awards, she is currently editing and publishing *New Heat,* a new world literary magazine. She says that she writes to record the urban, Black, émigré, techno-peasant mythos.

Gloria T. Hull, Director of the Women's Program at the University of California, Santa Cruz, has published *All the Women are White, All the Blacks are Men, But Some of Us Are Brave; Give Us This Day: The Diary* of Alice Dunbar-Nelson; *Color, Sex and Poetry: Three Women Writers of the Harlem Renaissance,* and a first collection of poetry, *Healing Heart.*

KRISTIN HUNTER has published many works of fiction, including *The Soul Brothers and Sister Lou, Boss Cat, Guests in the Promised Land, The Survivors, The Lakestown Rebellion, Lou in the Limelight,* and *God Bless the Child.* "Cabin Fever" is taken from the thirteenth chapter of *The Lakestown Rebellion.*

TED JOANS is a poet whose work gained prominence during the Black Arts Movement. His collections of poetry include *Black Pow-Pow, Afrodisia, A Black Manifesto in Jazz Poetry and Prose, A Black Pow-Pow of Jazz Poems,* and *Flying Piranha.*

LEMUEL JOHNSON of Sierra Leone is Professor of English at the University of Michigan, Ann Arbor and at the Centro de Estudios de Asia y Africa in the Colegio de México. His collections of poetry include *Highlife for Caliban, Hand on the Navel,* and *Carnival of the Old Coast.* He has also published *The Devil, the Gargoyle, and the Buffoon: The Negro as Metaphor in Western Literature,* and is completing *The Utopian Bent in African, Caribbean and Latin American Literatures.*

BEN JONES received an M.A. degree from New York University and an M.F.A. from Pratt Institute. The winner of numerous awards and fellowships, he has had solo exhibitions at the Studio Museum of Harlem, New Jersey State Museum, and Howard University. His paintings are included in the collections of the Museo Nacional in Cuba, DuSable Museum in Chicago, and Terada Gallery in Tokyo. Concerned about empowerment, he produces socially significant art, which deals with such themes as sexual rights and apartheid.

JOHN EDDIE JONES received a Bachelor of Professional Studies from Memphis State University with a concentration in photography and television film production, and a Master of Fine Arts from the Memphis College of Art. His photographs have been exhibited at the Festival de Las Artes in Venezuela, the Conference of Black South Literature and Art at Emory University, and the Mississippi Museum of Art's "Dimensions and Directions: Black Artists of the South."

HILLERY JACQUE KNIGHT, III studied biology at Tougaloo College, where he won an NEA award for a collection of thirty-nine poems written between the ages of nineteen and twenty. After obtaining an M.A. at Chicago's Illinois Institute of Technology and writing short stories in California, he returned to Mississippi to teach at Tougaloo. His current project is a three-volume biography of Muhammed Ali, for whom he worked between 1979 and 1982.

LETITIA is a systems-analyst for a major corporation in New York and has published erotica in *Yellow Silk.*

REGINALD LOCKETT lives in Oakland with his daughter, Maya, where he is writing a first novel. His second book of poetry, *Where the Birds Sing*

Bass, was published in 1990 by Blue Light Press. He performs with the Wordwind Chorus, an ensemble of three poets and a musician. His poems, reviews, short stories and articles have appeared in many magazines and anthologies, and he has published a collection of poetry, *Good Times & No Bread.*

AUDRE LORDE, a poet and essayist of Grenadian ancestry, has written fourteen books, including *Coal, The Black Unicorn, Our Dead Behind Us, A Burst of Light,* and the highly acclaimed *Sister Outsider.* She won the American Library Association Gay Caucus Book Award for her first book of prose, *The Cancer Journals,* and was nominated for a National Book Award. She is a founder of Kitchen Table: Women of Color Press and of Sisterhood in Support of Sisters in South Africa (SISA).

TERRY L. MCMILLAN has written two widely-acclaimed novels, *Mama* (1987) and *Disappearing Acts* (1989), and has sold film rights to *Acts* to Tri-Star Pictures. Her third novel, *Waiting to Exhale,* will be published in 1992. Presently teaching at the University of Arizona, she has also written articles and reviews for the *Atlanta Constitution,* the *New York Times Book Review,* and the *Philadelphia Inquirer.* She has been a three-time fellow at Yaddo Artist Colony and The Macdowell Colony.

REGINALD MARTIN has published poetry and fiction in the *Xavier Review, Yellow Silk,* the *Ball State University Forum* and *Callaloo,* and his unpublished novel, *Everybody Knows What Time It Is,* won best novel in the 1988 Deep South Writers competition. He is past Director of Professional Writing Programs and Professor of English at Memphis State University. He has edited several journals and books, and his scholarly work, *Ishmael Reed and the New Black Aesthetic Critics,* was nominated for the Clarence L. Holte Award from the Schomburg Center. His most recent scholarly works are *A Primary and Secondary Bibliography of New Black Aesthetic Criticism* (Garland Press), and *Recent African-American Literary Theory* (University of Alabama Press).

MICHAEL is a real estate attorney in Washington, D.C., who writes film scripts and screen plays for a hobby. He notes that he and Letitia have exchanged a "trunk full" of erotic letters.

E. ETHELBERT MILLER is the author of *The Land of Smiles/Land of No Smiles, Andromeda, Synergy: An Anthology of D. C. Black Poetry,* and *Women Surviving Massacres and Men,* among others. He directs the Howard University Afro-American Resource Center, hosts a weekly radio program "Maiden Voyage" on WOCU-FM in Washington, and directs the Ascension Poetry Reading Series.

JUANITA MITIL was born in the Republic of Panama, and writes in both Spanish and English. A freelance writer, she has published articles on gourmet cooking and national politics. Her interests include African religion, history, ritual, and mythology, as well as Afro-Cuban (salsa) music.

NANCY MOREJÓN, a Cuban poet of African descent, has published ten collections of verse, including *Richard trajo su flauta, Octubre imprescindible,* and *Piedra pulida,* as well as works of literary criticism. A graduate of the University of Havana, where she received degrees in French language and literature, she presently heads the Caribbean section of the Casa de las Américas in Havana.

M. J. MORGAN is the pseudonym of a technical and creative writer, who travels extensively. When not writing or traveling, she serves as an educational consultant in Chicago.

GLORIA NAYLOR is a native New Yorker, whose first novel, *The Women of Brewster Place,* won the American Book Award in 1983, and was later developed into a television movie. She has published two other novels: *Linden Hills* and *Mama Day.*

NAOMI NELSON, a jazz poet and arts administrator, says, "My erotic poetry is an attempt to merge my interest in the universe, my womanhood, and jazz and history into a whole form." An art history graduate of Rutgers, she has studied at the Sorbonne and attended the graduate school of Egyptian Archeology at Bryn Mawr. She travels extensively with her jazz musician husband.

R. BRUCE NUGENT was an artist, writer, and actor, who wrote under the pseudonym Richard Bruce. His work gained prominence during the Harlem Renaissance, and he has been described as the ultimate bohemian in works such as *Lightning Fire!! Fire!!* (1982).

FRANÇOISE PFAFF is Professor of French at Howard University, where she also teaches courses in African film. She has published *The Cinema of Ousmane Sembene, A Pioneer of African Film* and *Twenty-Five Black African Filmmakers.* Her articles have appeared in *Africa Quarterly, Black Art, CLA Journal, Commonwealth, Jump-Cut, Black Film Review, Positif, Cinemaction* and other publications.

M. NOURBESE PHILIP, a Canadian, received a Guggenheim Fellowship in poetry in 1990. She has published three works of poetry, including *Thorns, Salmon Courage,* and *She Tries Her Tongue: Her Silence Softly Breaks,* which won the 1989 Casa de las Américas Award in Cuba. Her first novel, *Harriet's Daughter,* was short listed for the Toronto Book Awards in 1988.

FRANK LAMONT PHILLIPS was an early winner of poetry competitions in the classic *Black World Magazine* of the sixties and seventies. He was born in Eloy, Arizona, and now lives in Memphis. His poetry and fiction have been widely anthologized, and his scintillating "Wet Kisses" is part of a forthcoming novel.

MICHELLE RENÉE PICHON is a graduate of Xavier University, and plans to teach African and African-American literature. She was active in Xavier's Writers' Group and edited the college's first creative writing magazine, *The Bard.*

TED PONTIFLET is a graduate of the California College of Arts and Crafts with a B.F.A. in sculpture, and of Yale University's School of Art and Architecture with an M.F.A. in painting and honors in creative writing. His work is a part of the permanent collections of the Bronx Museum of New York, Smithsonian Institute, Studio Museum of Harlem, and New York State. Collectors of his art include Bill Cosby, Roberta Flack, and Tom Feelings.

R. POPE is the *nom de plume* of Roseann P. Bell.

BESSIE N. PRICE is the pseudonym of an award-winning poet, who wrote "Pin-Up Poems," one poem a month for a year, as a gift to a friend.

REVONNE L. ROMNEY's "life in creation took firm root" at New York's celebrated High School of Music and Art. She studied silversmithing, jewelry and art history in Guadalajara, and painting with expressionist Trauta Ishida. She graduated from the Maryland Institute College of Art in Baltimore.

KALAMU YA SALAAM is a professional writer/editor and producer/arts administrator. For thirteen years, he edited *Black Collegian,* and now he organizes Black arts festivals. He has recently completed two anthologies: *Word Up/Black Poetry of the 80s From the Deep South* and *Black New Orleans.*

NAN SAVILLE lives and writes in New York City, where she is the Assistant Director of New York University's Higher Education Opportunity Program and Director of the Science Technology Entry Program.

NTOZAKE SHANGE, one of the country's most creative and prolific poets and novelists, wrote the highly acclaimed *for colored girls who have considered suicide when the rainbow is enuf, Nappy Edges, Three Pieces, Sassafrass, Cypress & Indigo, A Daughter's Geography, From Okra to Greens,* and *Betsey Brown.*

SAUNDRA SHARP writes that she "keeps a polished toe in the creative soup." She is most proud of her third collection of poetry, *Soft Sound,* and her stage play *The Sistuhs.* She starred in the television movie "Minstrel Man," and published the first directory of Black Hollywood technicians. An independent filmmaker, she has produced and directed "Life is a Saxophone" and "Picking Tribes."

ANN ALLEN SHOCKLEY, Associate Librarian for Special Collections and University Archivist at Fisk University, has written two novels, *Loving Her* and *Say Jesus and Come to Me,* and a collection of short stories, *The Black and White Of It.* She also edited *Afro-American Women Writers,* and co-edited *Living Black American Authors* and *Handbook of Black Librarianship.*

IAN SMART was born in Trinidad, and is Professor of Spanish at Howard University. A founding editor of the *Afro-Hispanic Review,* he has published widely in the fields of Afro-Hispanic and Caribbean literatures. His third and most recent book is *Guillén, Popular Poet of the Caribbean.*

Jessie Carney Smith is Director of the Fisk University Library. Her published works include *Black Academic Libraries and Research Collections, Ethnic Genealogy, Images of Blacks in American Culture,* and *Notable Black Women.*

Jo Smith is the pseudonym of a poet who lives and writes in Chicago. Her poem "Victory" was written specifically for *Erotique Noire/Black Erotica.*

Thomas Stanley is a graduate of Brown University, and writes from a large farm near the Washington metropolitan area. He hosts a weekend radio program, "Textured Expressions," that airs on WPFW. He has written numerous music and film reviews, and is currently writing a book on the musical contributions of George Clinton. During his four-year tenure as Minister of Information for the Republic of New Afrika, he traveled to Libya, Cuba, and Jamaica.

Lorenzo Thomas, who lives in Houston, Texas, is the author of several collections of poetry, including *Chances Are Few* and *The Bathers.*

Piri Thomas is a New York writer of Puerto Rican ancestry. His works include the highly-acclaimed *Down These Mean Streets, Savior, Savior, Hold My Hand,* and *Seven Long Times.*

John Turpin was born and raised in rural Virginia, and attended private schools in the Midwest. He studied and worked in Nigeria, and is currently translating Yoruba religious texts from the Ifa language.

James Van Der Zee, 1886–1983, was a master photographer who documented the cultural and social history of Harlem in the first half of the twentieth century. One of the first Black photographers to portray the Afro-American female nude, he photographed the celebrated *Nude by the Fireplace* in 1923. His work was exhibited at the Studio Museum of Harlem and at the Metropolitan Museum of Art's "Harlem on My Mind" exhibition. He is also the subject of numerous books, monograms, and television documentaries.

Gloria Wade-Gayles is a poet, novelist, literary critic, and Professor of English at Spelman College. Her poetry has been anthologized in journals and books such as *Black World, Sturdy Black Bridges* and *Homespun Images,* while her scholarly essays have appeared in *Sage, Catalyst,* and *Callaloo.* She is the author of *No Crystal Stair: Visions of Race and Sex in Black Women's Fiction* and of a collection of poetry, *Anointed to Fly.*

Alice Walker captivated the country with her 1982 novel, *The Color Purple,* which has been translated into over twenty-five languages. Her works of poetry, fiction, and criticism include *Once, Revolutionary Petunias, The Third Life of Grange Copeland, You Can't Keep a Good Woman Down, Meridian, In Search of Our Mother's Gardens: Womanist Prose, Living By the Word: Selected Writing 1973–1987,* and most recently *The Temple of My Familiar.* Her latest novel, *Possessing the Secret of Joy,* will be published in 1992.

Jerry W. Ward, Jr., is the undisputed mentor of many fine writers. The

Lawrence Durgin Professor of Literature at Tougaloo College, he is a poet and critic whose work has appeared in numerous scholarly and literary magazines.

KEITH WARNER, poet, novelist, literary critic, and college professor, was born and educated at Trinidad. He taught French and Francophone literature at Howard University before returning home to teach at the University of the West Indies. His poetry, fiction, and critical essays have appeared in numerous journals. He is chair of the Department of Foreign Languages at George Mason University.

YANA WEST is an administrator with a Ph.D. degree. She has worked for several years in journalism, has traveled extensively, and has brought these experiences to bear on her writing.

JOHN A. WILLIAMS is one of America's most distinguished novelists with more than fifteen books to his credit, including *The Man Who Cried I Am, This is My Country Too, Sons of Darkness, Mothersill and the Foxes, The Most Native of Sons, !Click Song, Sissie, The Berhama Account,* and *Jacob's Ladder.*

KIMMIKA WILLIAMS is an actress, freelance journalist, poet and arts host/producer for WXPN-FM in Philadelphia. She teaches creative writing and has written several books of poetry: *God Made Men Brown; Halley's Comet;* and *It Ain't Easy To Be Different.*

MANUEL ZAPATA OLIVELLA, a physician, folklorist and anthropologist, is one of Colombia's most distinguished novelists. His works include *En chimá nace un santo, El hombre colombiano, Chambacú, Las claves mágicas de Américas, Nuestra voz,* and the highly acclaimed *Shangó, el gran putas.*

ACKNOWLEDGMENTS

This collaborative project owes its existence to many gifted and generous people: writers who shared their most intimate thoughts and feelings, translators who spun gold from the words of others, and artists who framed desire in black and white or rainbow-hued images.

A special thanks to Charles Radford, a friend and former colleague at LeMoyne-Owen College, who produced the first draft of the manuscript. A computer expert with a penchant for word processing, Charles spent long hours, after work and on weekends, to meet our pressing deadlines. We are also grateful to Deborah Morgan, a former student, presently on the staff of Memphis State University, who labored for months, typing, correcting, and copying, to prepare the final copy for the publisher.

Several other friends and colleagues helped in significant ways. Charles L. Blockson, to whom the book is dedicated, was a cherished collaborator. E. Ethelbert Miller of Howard University's Afro-American Studies Department—poet, talk show host, and cultural entrepreneur—put us in touch with writers throughout the country, while James Davis of Howard's Romance Languages Department provided lists of writers from the Caribbean and Latin America. The editor of Calaloux Publications, Selwyn Cudjoe of Wellesley College, offered advice, contacted writers, and provided an extensive list of Caribbean women writers.

Also helpful were Keith Warner of George Mason University and Françoise Pfaff of Howard University, longtime friends and esteemed associates, who assisted with correspondence to Francophone writers. We also appreciate the wise counsel of William S. Mayo of Howard University Press, whose experience in publishing was invaluable to us in the final stages of our work. Countless other friends and family members offered their love and support: Odessa Martin, Monique Sugarmon, Erika Echols, Elena Williamson, Tarik Sugarmon, Sandra Vaughn, Phillip Dotson, Gloria Wade-Gayles, Frank Phillips . . . and, in spirit, A. W. Willis, always cherished, forever remembered. This collection of things sensual and erotic is offered in tribute to our friend Roseann Pope Bell, gifted writer, righteous sister, who crossed over the bridge to the other shore in the spring of 1992.

We are particularly indebted to Sallye Leventhal, our editor at Doubleday, for her enthusiastic support of this project. Her unfailing patience, persistence, and professionalism guided us smoothly from book proposal to printed page.

Finally, we acknowledge below the individuals and publishers who permitted us to reproduce their works.

OPAL PALMER ADISA: "There" and "Insatiable" copyright © by Opal Palmer Adisa. AHMASI: "Baby" and "Erector Set" copyright © by Ahmasi. S. D. ALLEN: "A Single Rose" copyright © by Sandra D. Allen. LUZ ARGENTINA CHIRIBOGA: Excerpt from *Bajo la piel de los tambores (Under the Skin of the Drums)* (Editorial Casa de la Cultura Ecuatoriana), copyright © 1991 by Luz Argentina Chiriboga. Reprinted by permission of the author. THELMA BALFOUR: "Sexy Signs" copyright © by Thelma L. Balfour. LEE BEN, JR.: "Double Congas" copyright © by Leroy K. Ben, Jr. CHARLES L. BLOCKSON: "African American Erotica and Other Curiosities: "The Blacker the Berry, the Sweeter the Juice . . ." copyright © by Charles L. Blockson. SDIANE BOGUS: "The Joys and Power in Celibacy" and excerpts from "Dyke Hands" and "Making Whoopee" were published in *Dyke Hands and Sutras Erotic and Lyric* (W.I.M. Publications), copyright © 1988 by SDiane A. Bogus. "P.G." copyright © by SDiane Bogus. Reprinted by permission of the author. DENNIS BRUTUS: "Untitled" (Gaily teetering) was published in *Sirens, Knuckles, Boots* (Mbari Publications) copyright © 1963 by Dennis Brutus; "Untitled" (I will not agonize over you) in *South Africa Voices* (University of Texas Press), copyright © 1975 by Dennis Brutus; "An Utrillo, Possibly" in *Stubborn Hope: Selected Poems of South Africa & a Wider World* (Heinemann), copyright © 1978 by Dennis Brutus; "At Sixty," and excerpt from *GAR,* in *A Simple Lust* (Heinemann), copyright © 1973 by Dennis Brutus. Reprinted by permission of the author. JAN CAREW: "The Initiation of Belfon" was excerpted from a story published in the *Journal of the Association of Caribbean Studies,* October 1987. Copyright © by Jan Carew. Reprinted by permission of the author. BARBARA CHASE-RIBOUD: "The Seal" was published in *From Memphis & Peking, Poems* (Random House), copyright © 1974 by B. Chase-Riboud. Excerpts from *Valide, A Novel of the Harem* (William Morrow and Company, Inc.), copyright © 1986, and *Echo of Lions* (Morrow), copyright © 1989 by Barbara Chase-Riboud. "Antony" and "Cleopatra" were published in *Portrait of a Nude Woman as Cleopatra* (Morrow), copyright © 1987 by Barbara Chase-Riboud. Reprinted by permission of the author and International Creative Management, Inc. CHERI: "Erotic Note #4" copyright © by Cheri Akins. ESPERANZA MALAVÉ CINTRÓN: "Stray Thoughts" and "Temple Oranges" copyright © 1990 by Esperanza Malavé Cintrón. WANDA COLEMAN: "Lonnie's Cousin," copyright © 1988 by Wanda Coleman. Reprinted from *A War of Eyes and Other Stories* by permission of the author and Black Sparrow Press. AFUA COOPER: "Untitled 2" was published in *Breaking Chains* (Weelahs Publications), copyright © 1983 by Afua Cooper. "Faded Roses" copyright © by Afua Cooper. Reprinted by permission of the author. STANLEY CYRUS: Translation of "Under the Skin of the Drums" by Luz Argentina Chiriboga copyright © 1991 by Stanley Cyrus. DOLORES DA COSTA: "Black Male/Tales" copyright © by Miriam DeCosta-Willis; "I Wanna Be Wild and Wonderful" copyright © by Miriam DeCosta-Willis and Gloria Wade-Gayles. DARYL DANCE: "Teasing Tales and Tit(Bits)s," including "Just in Case," "Let Me Be Frank," "Not Even for a White Woman," "Pass the Pussy, Please," "Peter Revere," "Pretty Like a Peacock," and "Yo' Mama," were published in *Shuckin' and Jivin': Folklore for Contemporary Black Americans* (Indiana University Press), copyright © 1978 by Daryl Cumber Dance. Reprinted by permission of the author and Indiana University Press. O. R. DATHORNE: *Woman Story* copyright © by O. R. Dathorne. RENÉ DEPESTRE: Excerpt from *Hadriana dans tous mes rêves* (Editions Gallimard), copyright © 1988 by René Depestre. Reprinted by permission of the author and Editions Gallimard. TOI DERRICOTTE: "Dildo" copyright © by Toi Derricotte. R. H. DOUGLAS: "Dear Diary" copyright © by Rodlyn H. Douglas. RITA DOVE: "For Kazuko" was published in *The Yellow House on the Corner*, copyright © 1980 by Carnegie Mellon University Press. Reprinted by permission of the author and Carnegie Mellon University Press. TREY ELLIS: Excerpt from *Platitudes* (Vintage Books), copyright © 1988 by Trey Ellis. Reprinted by permission of the author and Random House. NELSON ESTUPIÑÁN BASS: "All in Good Taste," "Sunburst from the Earth," and "You Knew . . ." copyright © by Nelson Estupiñán Bass. CHARLES A. FRYE: "A Good Knight's Leap" (excerpt from the forthcoming novel), copyright © 1991 by Charles A. Frye. Published by permission of the author. CONSTANCE GARCÍA-BARRIO: "Plain Wrappers" copyright © by Constance García-Barrio. P. J. GIBSON: "Teaching the Sweet Thing," "Midnight Licorice Nights," and "We'll Be Real Good Together," are excerpts from her story, "Honey Black Sweetness," copyright © by P. J. Gibson. BERYL GILROY: "Man to Man" and "The Fight" copyright © by B. A. Gilroy, Ph.D. MARITA GOLDEN: Excerpt from *Long Distance Life* (Doubleday), copyright © 1989 by Marita Golden. Reprinted by permission of the author and Doubleday. JEWELLE GOMEZ: "Piece of Time" was published in *On Our Backs*, 1984. Copyright © 1984 by Jewelle Gomez. Reprinted by permission of the author. SANDRA Y. GOVAN: "Forbidden Fruits and Unholy Lusts: Illicit Sex in Black American Literature" and "Channeling" copyright © by Sandra Y. Govan. ANN T. GREENE: "Gorgeous Puddin' " copyright © by Ann T. Greene. LOIS GRIFFITH: *First Person Singular* copyright © by Lois Griffith. CLAIRE HARRIS: "The Joy of Sex" was published in *Nebula* 7. Copyright © by Claire Harris. Reprinted by permission of the author. ESSEX HEMPHILL: Excerpt from *The Tomb of Sorrow*, copyright © 1990 by Essex Hemphill, was published in *Bastard Review*, 1990; *Tribe*, Winter 1990; Hemphill, ed., *Brother to Brother: New Writings by Black Gay Men* (Alyson Publications), 1991; and Hemphill, *Ceremonies* (Penguin/Plume), 1992. Reprinted by permission of the author. CALVIN HERNTON: "Dew's Song," copyright © 1990 by Calvin Hernton. CHESTER B. HIMES: Excerpt from Chapter "Wrestling and Pole Vaulting," from *Pinktoes* reprinted by permission of Roslyn Targ Literary Agency, Inc., New York. Copyright © 1961, 1965, 1989 by Chester Himes. AKUA LEZLI HOPE: "when the horn fits, blow it" was published in *Contact* II, No. 53/54/55, copyright © 1955 by Akua Lezli Hope; and "Interpenetration Side Two" in *Obsidian II*,

454   *Acknowledgments*

Winter 1988, copyright © 1988 by Akua Lezli Hope. "Songs They Could Sing #789" and "Telegram from Topeka" copyright © by Akua Lezli Hope. Reprinted by permission of the author. GLORIA T. HULL: "Saint Chant" and "From Running Come Touch" were published in Hull's *Healing Heart: Poems 1973–1988* (Kitchen Table Press), copyright © 1989 by Gloria T. Hull. Reprinted by permission of the author. KRISTIN HUNTER: "Cabin Fever" was excerpted from *The Lakestown Rebellion* (Charles Scribner's Sons), copyright © 1978 by Kristin Hunter. Reprinted by permission of the author. HILLERY JACQUE KNIGHT, III: "Black Borealis" copyright © 1992 by Hillery Jacque Knight, III. TED JOANS: "Cuntinent" was published in Joans's *Afrodisia* (Hill & Wang), copyright © 1970 by Ted Joans. Reprinted by permission of the author. LEMUEL JOHNSON: "sudden ecstasies in lefthanded places (whatever the traffic will bear)" and "bangarang mestiçagem" were published in *A Carnival of the Old Coast*, copyright © by Lemuel Johnson. Reprinted by permission of the author. LETITIA AND MICHAEL: "Hot Missives" copyright © by Letitia Williams and Michael D. REGINALD LOCKETT: "The X-Lovers" was published in *Good Times & No Bread* (Jukebox Press), copyright © 1978 by Reginald Lockett; and "405 Scott Street" in *Yellow Silk: Journal of the Erotic Arts*, 1989. Copyright © 1989 by Reginald Lockett. Reprinted by permission of the author. AUDRE LORDE: "On a Night of the Full Moon" was published in *Coal* (W. W. Norton & Co.), copyright © 1968 by Audre Lorde; "Love Poem" in *New York Head Shop and Museum* (Broadside Press), copyright © 1974 by Audre Lorde Rollins; "Meet" is reprinted from *The Black Unicorn*, Poems by Audre Lorde, by permission of the author and W. W. Norton & Company, Inc. Copyright © 1978 by Audre Lorde; and "Uses of the Erotic: The Erotic as Power" from *Sister Outsider* reprinted by permission of the Charlotte Sheedy Agency and Regula Noetzli. Copyright © 1984 by Audre Lorde. TERRY L. MCMILLAN: "Touching" was published in *Coydog Review*, 1985, and in *Touching Fire: Erotic Writings by Women* (Carroll & Graf Publishers), 1989. Copyright © 1985 by Terry L. McMillan. Reprinted by permission of the author. REGINALD MARTIN: "The 1st 3 Daze" was published in *Yellow Silk: Journal of the Erotic Arts*, July 1989. Copyright © by Reginald Martin. "What Makes Siedah Zip" from *Everybody Knows What Time It Is* copyright © by Reginald Martin. Reprinted by permission of the author. E. ETHELBERT MILLER: "Birds" and "Summer" copyright © by E. Ethelbert Miller. JUANITA MITIL: "I Have a Memory" copyright © by Juanita Mitil. NANCY MOREJÓN: "A un muchacho," "To a Boy" from *Piedra pulida*, Havana: Editorial Letras Cubanas, 1986. Copyright © 1986 by Nancy Morejón. M. J. MORGAN: "My All Day Sucker" and "The Hog Caller's Party" copyright © by M. J. Morgan. GLORIA NAYLOR: "Mattie Michael," from *The Women of Brewster Place* by Gloria Naylor. Copyright © 1980, 1982 by Gloria Naylor. Used by permission of Viking Penguin, a division of Penguin Books USA, Inc. NAOMI NELSON: "Poetica Erotica" copyright © 1992 by Naomi Nelson. FRANÇOISE PFAFF: "Eroticism in Sub-Saharan African Films" copyright © 1991 by Françoise Pfaff. A longer version of "Eroticism in Sub-Saharan African Films" appeared in *Zast: Zeitschrift fur Afrikastudien.* 9–10 (1991), pp. 5–16. M. NOURBESE PHILIP: "Commitment to Hardness" copyright © by M. Nourbese Philip. FRANK LAMONT PHILLIPS: "Stolen," "Wet Kisses," "Café Noir," and "Love Poem" copyright © by Frank Lamont Phillips; "Sexionnaire" (with R. Pope) copyright © by Frank Lamont Phillips and Roseann P. Bell. MICHELLE RENÉE PICHON: *Teach Me* copyright © by Michelle Renée Pichon. R. POPE: "The Three-Token Stradivarius" copyright © by Roseann P. Bell; "Sexionnaire" (with Frank Lamont Phillips) copyright © by Frank Lamont Phillips and Roseann P. Bell. BESSIE N. PRICE: "Pin-up Poems" copyright © by Bessie N. Price. REVONNE L. ROMNEY: "Beached" copyright © 1990 by ReVonne L. Romney. KALAMU YA SALAAM: "Haiku #9," "Haiku #25," "Haiku #28," "Haiku #29," "Haiku #52," "Haiku

#79," "Haiku #102," "Haiku #107," "Tasty Knees," and "The Sweetest Sound" copyright © by Kalamu Ya Salaam. NAN SAVILLE: "Venus Rising" and "Summer Madness" copyright © by Nan Saville. NTOZAKE SHANGE: "Comin to Terms" was published in *Deep Down: The New Sensual Writing by Women* (Faber and Faber), copyright © 1988 by Ntozake Shange. "Tócame" copyright © by Ntozake Shange. Reprinted by permission of the author. SAUNDRA SHARP: "Fresh" and "(hug)" were published in *Typing in the Dark* (Harlem River Press), copyright © 1991 by Saundra Sharp; and "Warning" in *Soft Song*, copyright © 1978 and 1990 by Saundra Sharp. Reprinted by permission of the author. ANN ALLEN SHOCKLEY: Excerpt from *Say Jesus, and Come to Me* (Naiad Press), copyright © 1982 by Ann Allen Shockley. Reprinted with the kind permission of the author and the publisher, Naiad Press. IAN SMART: Translation of "Afro-Hispanic Triptych: Three Women" by Manuel Zapata Olivella, copyright © by Ian Smart. JESSIE CARNEY SMITH: "Edible or Incredible: Black Erotic Collectibles" copyright © by Jessie Carney Smith. JO SMITH: "Victory" copyright © by Jo Smith. THOMAS STANLEY: "Put Your Tongue in It" copyright © by Thomas Stanley. LORENZO THOMAS: Excerpt from "Sounds of Joy," published in *Jambalaya: Four Poets* (Reed, Cannon, and Johnson), copyright © 1975 and 1992 by Lorenzo Thomas. Reprinted by permission of the author. PIRI THOMAS: "Nasty Delightful Things" as excerpted from *Down These Mean Streets* (Alfred A. Knopf, Inc.), copyright © 1967 by Piri Thomas. Reprinted by permission of Alfred A. Knopf, Inc. JOHN TURPIN: "Trotting Through the Park," "Fuck," and "All Wet in Green" copyright © by John Turpin. GLORIA WADE-GAYLES: "Discoveries" and "Tell Me You Love Me" copyright © by Gloria Wade-Gayles; "I Wanna Be Wild and Wonderful" (with Dolores Da Costa) copyright by Miriam DeCosta-Willis and Gloria Wade-Gayles. ALICE WALKER: "Olive Oil" was published in *Ms.*, August 1985, copyright © 1985 by Alice Walker. Reprinted by permission of the author and the Wendy Weil Agency, Inc. JERRY W. WARD, JR.: "Opening Night" copyright © 1992 by Jerry W. Ward, Jr. Reprinted by permission of the author. KEITH WARNER: "Taking Six for a Nine: Sexual Imagery in the Trinidad Calypso" copyright © by Keith Warner. YANA WEST: "A Dinner Invitation" and "A New Year's Eve Celebration" copyright © by Yana West. JOHN A. WILLIAMS: "After/Play" copyright © John A. Williams. Reprinted by permission of the author. KIMMIKA WILLIAMS: "Lust" was published in *It Ain't Easy to Be Different* (In The Tradition Press), copyright © 1986 by Kimmika L. Williams. Reprinted by permission of the author. MANUEL ZAPATA OLIVELLA: "Afro-Hispanic Triptych: Three Women" includes excerpts from the novels *El fusilamiento del diablo* (Plaza & Janes), copyright © 1986 by Manuel Zapata Olivella and *Shangó el gran putas* (Editorial Oveja Negra), copyright © 1983 by Manuel Zapata Olivella. Reprinted by permission of the author.